a decade of i-Deas

the encyclopaedia of the '80s

In September 1980 i-D magazine was launched and the fashion world has never been the same since. The first 'manual of style' to feature real fashion from the streets in its pages, it became the major document of new talent in the '80s.

Over the past decade, as i-D's reputation as the 'style bible' to the creative global community has grown, so it has also become the most copied magazine in the world – its graphics, photography and information surfacing in advertising, TV and other magazines.

Responding to ideas rather than press releases, i-D has consistently encouraged innovation in fashion, music, clubs, film, books, art; in any field, in fact, where convention is being challenged. This book is i-D's version of the '80s, an encyclopaedia of a decade when ideas were up for grabs.

a decade of i-Deas

the encyclopaedia of the '80s

compiled and produced by i-D magazine

EDITED BY JOHN GODFREY

PENGUIN BOOKS

a decade of i-Deas

the encyclopaedia of the '80s

PENGUIN BOOKS

Published by the Penguin Group
27 Wrights Lane, London W8 5TZ, England
Viking Penguin Inc., 40 West 23rd Street, New York,
New York 10010, USA
Penguin Books Australia Ltd, Ringwood, Victoria,
Australia
Penguin Books Canada Ltd, 2801 John Street,
Markham, Ontario, Canada L3R 1B4
Penguin Books (NZ) Ltd, 182-190 Wairau Road,
Auckland 10, New Zealand

Penguin Books Ltd, Registered Offices:
Harmondsworth, Middlesex, England

First published 1990
10 9 8 7 6 5 4 3 2 1

Copyright © i-D magazine 1990
All rights reserved

Colour origination by Latent Image Ltd, 6 Balmoral
Grove, London N7
Typesetting by Wordsmiths, 55 East Rd, London N1

Made and printed in Great Britain by William
Clowes Ltd, Beccles and London

Except in the United States of America, this book is
sold subject to the condition that it shall not, by
way of trade or otherwise, be lent, re-sold, hired
out, or otherwise circulated without the publisher's
prior consent in any form of binding or cover than
that in which it is published and without a similar
condition including this condition being imposed on
the subsequent purchaser

CONTENTS

There was a streetcar from San Diego by
then, but the town was still quiet — too
quiet. Not hardly anybody got born here.
Child—bearing was thought kind of too
sexy. But the war changed all that. Now we
got guys that sweat, and tough school kids
in Levi's and dirty shirts ...

Raymond Chandler.
Playback.

Editor
John Godfrey

Deputy Editor
Beth Summers

Art Editors
Corinna Farrow and Stephen Male

Assistant Editor
Matthew Collin

Production Editor
Lucy Olivier

Contributing Editors
Caryn Franklin, Andy Darling, Oscar Moore, Steve Beard and Jim McClellan

Design
Corinna Farrow
Stephen Male
Paul Baptiste
Neil Edwards

Advertising
Jo Peters
Marc Picken

Publishers
Terry Jones and Tony Elliott

Publishing Director
Adele Carmichael

Contributing Writers
Jane Alexander, Bruce Dessau, Mark Heley, Steve Dixon, Glyn Brown, Stuart Cosgrove, Francis Cottam, Lucy O'Brien, Jay Strongman, Kathryn Flett, Iain R Webb, John McCready, Rick Glanvill, Sheryl Garratt, Georgina Goodman, Haoui Montaug, Sean O'Neill, Julie Pritchard, Jonathan Romney, Mike Von Joel, Dave Swindells, Vaughn Toulouse, Simon Witter, Sean O'Hagan, Candida Clark, Ann Hogan, William Leith, Owney Lepke, Laurence Earle, Dave Dorrell, Abigail Frost, Allan Campbell, Robert Yates, Catherine McDermott, Annie Bennett, George Barber.

Cover photograph of Sarah Stockbridge by Nick Knight

i-D magazine, 134-146 Curtain Rd, London EC2A 3AR
The editors would like to thank Trish Jones for her support, James Burchell and Omaid Hiwaizi for their eleventh hour help, the photographers, stylists, writers, and army of people who have ever been associated with **i-D** over the decade. This book would not have been possible without them and the blood, sweat and tears of those who put the book together. We would also like to thank whoever invented vodka.

cade of i-Deas

the encyclopaedia of the '80s

The '80s was the decade when everybody dealt in ideas. From the pages of magazines, the catwalks, art galleries, music to nightclubs, the energy that punk unleashed at the end of the '70s became the rationale of a decade. Broken glass stuck on canvas became art, records were made in bedrooms, magazines bred like rabbits, anything and everything became fashion, and *the* publishing success story was a comic with a character called Johnny Fartpants. Ideas were reworked with such speed that nothing ever stood still, and the information technology that evolved made sure that everybody knew what was happening *then*, even if it couldn't predict what was going to happen next. Popular culture became a game in which anybody could join in, and everybody broke the rules. Soap stars became pop stars, pop stars became politicians, comics became graphic novels, Wimbledon FC reached the First Division, a Soviet leader became a hero, and everybody turned into hippies. When i-D magazine started in September 1980, it was responding to the creative energy of London – by 1989 it was reacting to events all over the globe. The '80s may have started in London but the '90s will belong to the world...

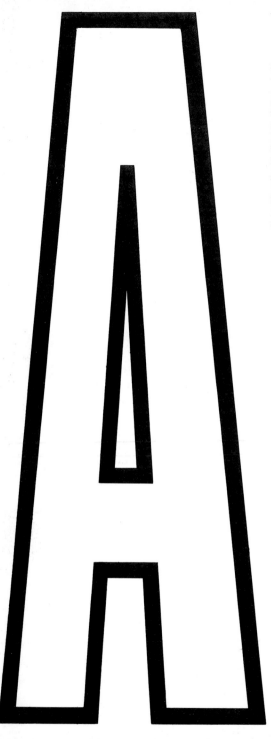

ABC From gold lamé suits and NEW POP with an entryist smile ('Lexicon Of Love' in '82) right up to optimistic HOUSE ('Up' in '89), ABC have attempted to purvey stylish dance music that knows where it's coming from. Most of the press interest, however, has revolved around their failure to consolidate the massive success of 'Lexicon Of Love'. The perennial runners-up of British pop.

Abortion "It was the busiest, the dirtiest and the most bizarre ever," was how Diane Munday from the British Pregnancy Advisory Service described the Alton anti-abortion campaign in '88. Liberal MP David Alton's Private Member's bill was the 14th attempt to scupper the '67 Abortion Act since it was passed. If the bill had become law this meant that doctors, allowing for a margin of error, would not carry out abortions after the 14th or 15th week. In response to this massive restriction on women's rights, the National Abortion Campaign moved into action. In March '88 over 20,000 people joined a national demonstration against the bill. The bill fell at report stage. However, a new Government

L to R ABC (photo: Paul Cox).
Acid House T-shirt (photo: Dave Swindells).
Danny Rampling at Spectrum '88 (photo: Dave Swindells) **See Acid House**.

Bill being prepared in '89 will ensure that abortion will remain on the political agenda in the '90s. In America, it already is. A Supreme Court ruling in '89 set women's rights back 22 years – in some states abortion could soon be illegal.

Acid House What initially started in two clubs (Future and THE SHOOM) in late '87, became the biggest youth phenomenon since punk and the most misunderstood. A group of south Londoners who spent every summer in IBIZA started to hold reunion parties at the Project Club in Streatham until DJ Paul Oakenfold realised that the beach bum ethic was starting to catch on. Danny and Jenny Rampling's SHOOM club opened in November and then Paul opened Future behind HEAVEN. The music varied from The Woodentops

to acid house, everybody dressed in their summer wardrobes, and screamed 'aceeed!' surrounded by a heaving mass of sweaty bodies and artificial smoke. Not since TABOO had such an atmosphere of euphoria and dance abandon occurred, and not since the '60s had hippy ideals begun to permeate youth culture. Talk was of 'love and peace', DRESSING DOWN and people apologised for standing on your toe. When THE TRIP opened in June '88, the scene went overground and was given a name.

Although it's been labelled 'acid house' ever since, the truth is that acid house was only ever one part of it. The music encompassed everything from Spanish disco to PUBLIC ENEMY and the most important thing

Aerobics

Although actress Jane Fonda has made her name synonymous with this faddy form of keep-fit, the term is merely a generic to describe any system of sustained exercise designed to increase the amount of oxygen in the blood and so strengthen heart and lungs. Fonda swamped the VIDEO market with her military-style self-improvement tech-

nique, exhorting us to "go for the burn". This effect of muscle overwork proved subsequently to be more detrimental (unless mixed with a more general toning programme) than not having exercised at all. Fonda will, however, remain responsible for making the work-out a fashion accessory See Health Clubs and Health Farms

place all over the country. By June the tabloid press had discovered 'acid house' again and ran front page scare stories that even exceeded their previous 'exposés' in inaccuracies and untruths. The irony is that by this time, 'acid house' as a term had become defunct and the scene had turned into something else. Quite what though, will only become apparent in the '90s. *See Boy's Own and Nightclubbing*

Acid Jazz Acid Jazz sounds like the scam it initially was. Dreamt up by JAZZ DJs Gilles Peterson and Chris Bangs during '88's SUMMER OF LOVE, the term was inevitably inspired by the spread of all things hippy and was intended to provoke a

TATTOOS, shaved skull, and pierced attitude. But plagiarism, cut-up cliché and all the avant-garde techniques this side of Bill Buroughs still can't stop Acker's books from reading like post-Sher Hite boddice-rippers. But then that is not the point. Like numerous '80s luminaries, her real artistic vehicle is the interview.

Adult Oriented Rock Having emasculated Elvis, Woodstock, and punk, the music industry relaxed in the '80s, the decade in which it turned 30, and released records that its managing directors liked. Now dubbed 'adult oriented rock', Eric Clapton, The Who, Yes, Pink Floyd, Steve Winwood, The Rolling Stones and Fleetwood Mac all enjoyed

was that nobody cared. More accurately described as BALEARIC BEATS, the music was almost secondary to the uninhibited freedom that was unleashed. The fashion victim voyeurism that had dominated clubs for so long was suddenly turned on its head as clubbers swapped their designer labels for T-SHIRTS and shorts and started dancing. As the High Street erupted in a sea of SMILEYs and acid house paraphernalia, the tabloid press latched onto it with fabricated stories about 'drug-crazed orgies' and the police reacted with predictable zeal. Warehouse parties and clubs were raided, acid house was dubbed 'an evil cult', and the scene went underground. It also went suburban. As warehouse parties like SUNRISE got bigger and better organised, the impetus moved outside London, and by '89 large scale parties were taking

reaction. After the initial howls of derision, cynics had to swallow their purist prejudices when Urban Records released the compilation LPs 'Acid Jazz & Other Illicit Grooves' and 'The Freedom Principle'. Rather than the collection of re-releases that had dominated the JAZZ scene for so long, the albums featured young bands who had grown out of the RARE GROOVE and JAZZ club scenes, and had found a common interest in the new freedom and enthusiasm acid jazz had introduced. Possibly the most contrived yet innovative musical invention of the decade.

Acker, Kathy When this ex-42nd Street porn star was washed up on our shores in '84 with her avant-feminist novel *Blood And Guts In High School*, she was marketed as the Original Literary Punk – sporting

career resurgences, amply covered by *Q* magazine, and London's Capital Radio devoted its FM space to Capital Gold for non-stop 'proper' music. *See Rock Dinosaurs* for the fruits of their labour.

Advertising If you wanted to know what was really happening in the '80s, you watched the ads. Paranoia about hidden persuaders took a back seat as ads were celebrated as a non-stop carnival of images which didn't just sell, but also crystallised contemporary aspirations, fantasies, moods and fears. Ads captured the real entrepreneurial spirit in the 'people as bastards' ads (Midland Vector, BA's Red Eye) and showed you YUPPIE cynicisms in the smirk on the face of JONATHAN ROSS as he smarmed his way through another endorsement. They revealed the real purpose of the YTS – one early ad depicted a trainee being processed into propaganda image, and caught the vacant melancholia at the heart of the MATT BLACK dream home in adverts for the Woolwich. With so much marketable meaning in there, it was little wonder that media culture arose to trade off advertising. Adwatching analysis clogged up the qualities, glossies and airwaves. Tabloids gossiped about Gold Blenders, young ad types got pop star profiles on 'NETWORK 7' and adland got its own soap ('Campaign').

Movie memories were revived endlessly, alongside old TV, sports footage and golden oldie pop as ad agencies discovered nostalgic pas-

tiche and showed that to them the stylistic jamboree of POST-MODERNISM was an open (cheque) book. Ads parodied their own conventions as pop ART, as in the BRYLCREEM scratch VIDEO. Mass avant-gardism? All in a day's work for ad agencies who reworked surrealism and performance art, eventually creating conceptual ads which didn't look like ads. It's not easy being a dolphin – can you make sense of it?

Things got so clever that critics made a cult out of the Shake and Vac ads, and some ad men longed for a return to the hard sell, where you could at least draw the line between advertising and 'real life'. But the distinction became blurred in the '80s with everything – ART, ARCHITECTURE, newspapers, magazines, design, film – beginning to look like an advert. We all trade in images

African Colours Black consciousness in rap inspired by PUBLIC ENEMY, Stetsasonic and KRS-ONE led to a renewed interest in Malcolm X, the Nation Of Islam and all things Muslim. By '89 though, the fashion aspect of black pride had caught on as rappers rushed to trade in their gold chains and KANGOLS for African pendants and Muslim prayer hats. On the streets, the sporting of African colours became so popular that every new dance act who wanted to court credibility appeared with leather medallions in red, gold and green, and shops like World, Four Star General and MASH started stocking entire ranges of African accessories. *See The Daisy Age and The Jungle Brothers*

L to R Andy i-D straight up '82.
Adrian Thrills and Andy i-D straight ups '81.
Acid Jazz emblem (photo: Dave Swindells).
Amazulu
Andy and Shirley i-D straight ups '81.
Adeva.
All About Eve.
Andi from Sex Gang Children.

now, and everyone's in advertising – politicians, corporate moguls and bank managers. The hard sell belongs back in the '60s world of fast-moving consumer goods and 2p off at the Co-op. The archetypal ads of this decade? Financial services spots pushing THE CREDIT ECONOMY's funny money (Nat West's 'Pinball Wizard' cashpoint ad), government ADVERTOCRACY, the global marketing media events organised by Pepsi and the pop culture industries, or the multi-purpose cross-branding of the LEVI'S ads.

The most influential ad of the '80s, Bartle Bogle Hegarty's LEVI'S launderette, scrambled history into a sexy nostalgia mode pop VIDEO, shifted product and sold the con-

sumer choices of STYLE culture - soul, classic teen, 501s and NEW MAN models to the mainstream. It also symbolised the way, by mid-decade, the ad agencies had bought up the notion of 'STYLE' and reworked it into a new pop psycho-sociology, 'LIFESTYLE'. Redrawing the marketing map, LIFESTYLE defined identity not in old terms like class and profession, but in people-watching stereotypes, determined mainly by consumption – Strivers, Stay-At-Homers, YUPPIES, you are what you buy. It may not hold up to rational analysis, but it meshes perfectly with Mrs Thatcher's owner-occupier popular capitalism. No wonder she gets on so well with ad men. *See Soap Ads*

Advertocracy A term coined to describe the rise of government

ADVERTISING in '80s Britain and something quite different to the straight political sell associated with America. However, as Labour found out, winning the political ad campaign isn't really enough, now that the government advertises all year round, and has turned the old public information film into glossily packaged propaganda. Increasingly the Tories' solution to a difficult problem is to advertise their way out of any potential credibility crisis, and forget about anything practical (as in the AIDS and HEROIN campaigns). With privatisation ads, and ET, DTI and YTS adverts in '87, the government spent £88 million, and representative democracy began to be replaced by PR advertocracy, which redefines

politics as marketing and seeks to replace allegiance based on principle with a kind of political brand loyalty. Don't buy it.

African Music Europe's love affair with its former colonies' culture blossomed as early as '82, when Nigeria's King Sunny Ade's multi-layered album 'Synchro System' reached Island Records boss Chris Blackwell's ears, but Ade spent two decreasingly successful years with Island and his juju rival Chief Ebenezer Obey had even less luck at the then hapless Virgin. In Paris though, throughout the decade, musicians from Francophone Africa found the runnings easier than their English-speaking rivals, stranded in a London which had next to no appreciation of their ART. By mid-'80s, the French capital had

a-ha Voted the best band of '86 by *SMASH HITS* and *No. 1* readers and with a lead singer voted the Most Fanciable Male and Sex God Of The Year, a-ha were regarded as one of the most shallow pop bands of the '80s by the British MUSIC PRESS. But then they would think that, because a-ha were Norwegian. Facing a decade of musical prejudice that stretched back to Abba and beyond, European pop was always regarded as fit only for the Eurovision Song Contest. What a-ha proved was that good pop music was not the sole prerogative of the British and that three Norwegian Jimi Hendrix fans could succeed too. Unfortunately, as their music grew up their audience didn't and they were left with three platinum discs and an uncertain future.

become a mecca for performers and fans alike, with Alpha Blondy, Youssou N'Dour, Kassav and Salif Keita regularly commanding huge crowds, and studios like Harry Son breaking new ground with their polished, hi-tech product. But with the emergence of London as a point on the touring map of African bands from '84 onwards, the musicians' attitude changed. The *'capitale de la rock musique'* was an increasingly inviting prospect for those with international ambitions. Singers like Papa Wemba and Mory Kante (whose crossover Afro-house 'Ye Ke Ye Ke' reached the UK top 20 in spring '88) were willing to accept fees much smaller than those available in France for a pitch at the world market.

Instrumental in preparing the ground for this shift were indepen-

dent record labels like Earthworks, who almost broke Thomas Mapfumo in the UK before going broke themselves and becoming part of Virgin; Stern's influential African HQ and record centre; and Covent Garden's Africa Centre. As the decade closed, the polar opposite sounds of rough house Zimbabwean jive (popularised by the Bhundu Boys) and hi-tech West African sounds of Keita, N'Dour and others dominated the live arena and CD land, while clubs like Dave Hucker's Tango Upstairs and Bass Clef buzzed to the sophisticated soukous sound of Wemba, Pepe Kalle and Mbilia Bel. Yet with typical English reserve, the public still baulked at pronouncing the song titles. *See World Music and Zouk*

Alice In Wonderland Opened in '83 by Christian Paris, this Monday night club anticipated the boom in hippy culture by nearly five years. Until '86, when he forsook the world of music to breed snails in Wales, the DJ was the Doctor from Dr & The Medics, who played old Jimi Hendrix and Love records to psychedelic GOTHS and '80s flower children. Their infamous Magical Mystery Trips attracted 4,500 people at their peak in '86, travelling to such alluring localities as Lowestoft and Clacton. The weekly club is now held in collaboration with The Sugar Lump and the music now includes inevitably, ACID HOUSE. But some things never change – after six years the club still has toilet paper hanging from the ceiling. *See Planet Alice and New Psychedelia*

*L to R Morten Harket from a-Ha in '83, when he went round London nightclubs telling everyone he was going to be a star (photo: Sebastian Sharkles).
Rik Mayall and Ben Elton See Alternative Comedy. Alice In Wonderland '88.*

Age Of Aquarius When is the Age Of Aquarius? It all depends on who you ask. Some say vaguely that it's happening 'around now', others reckon it's not due for a hundred years or more. A period of 'expanded consciousness' when people start to get more spiritual, the theory that the Age Of Aquarius started in the mid-'60s and continued through the '70s and '80s would at least account for hippies (both times round), Pink Floyd, ACID HOUSE and flares (both times round). But ultimately, the only certain thing about this New Age concept is its very uncertainty.

Alcohol Alcohol is the world's oldest, most popular and most destructive drug. Consumed in concoctions of flavoured water (varying in strength from three to 40%), it is responsible for more death, disease and distress than all the more infamous drugs put together. But because it's the establishment's drug (and a major source of government revenue), alcohol enjoys both legal immunity and an exalted social standing.

A government report suppressed by the incoming Tories in '79 (and later uncovered by journalists), revealed that the alcohol sales that were providing the exchequer with about £5,000 million in VAT a year were contributing enormously to illness, road accidents and acts of violence, resulting in visible costs of £51 million in health care, £648 million in policing and punishing offenders and a loss to industry of as

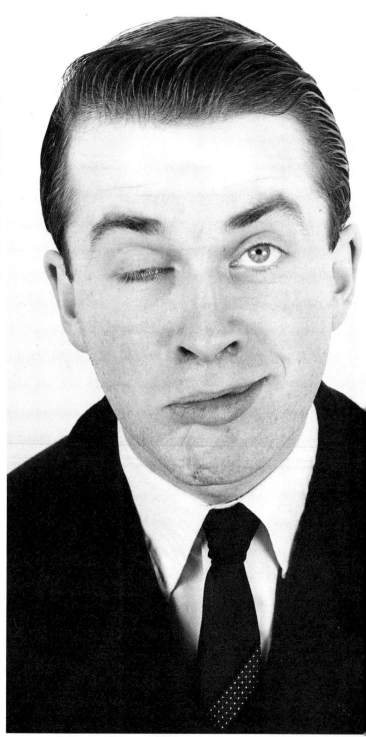

much as £500 million through lost time. Britain's 15-18 year olds, who shouldn't legally be drinking, spend £250-300 million a year on alcohol, and heavy drinking leads to deterioration of every apsect of human performance, and can lead to death in a variety of ways. It's now thought that by drinking no more than a certain amount of units of alcohol per week – 21 for men, 14 for women – drinkers will be safe from any physical damage (one unit = one glass of wine, one measure of spirits or half a pint of beer). Interestingly though, in the health conscious late '80s, it was alcohol's high calorie count that resulted in consumption dropping for the first time. *See Ecstasy and Heroin*

Allen, Keith Forget his fine performance in 'The Yob' and his Comic Strip background, Keith Allen's place in history was assured after his walking out of a fledgling CHANNEL 4' 'open access' youth programme, 'Whatever You Want'. Having its liberal pretensions pushed a little with his film of trade unions, the tenuous thread snapped and the threat of a genuinely daring TV programme vanished. Facing a principled stand from someone not prepared to back down was more than they could take from the man who should have been Britain's Morton Downey Junior. *See Alternative Comedy*

Alternative Comedy An '80s term for comedy which, through its subject matter or its unconventional approach, sits outside the mainstream. Each decade has had a crop of alternative humourists, all of them sailing too close to the wind in their raw early days. One glance at any old Monty Python tape reveals that Ben Elton is just another student obsessed with dead parrots and funny walks. Alternative comedy is nothing new. In the '50s Harry 'Highway' Seacombe was considered an alternative comedian. In the '80s, however, the number of women writers and performers attempting to provide

Almond, Marc

The original poison dwarf of pop, emerged out of the Leeds club scene with Soft Cell, pop's ultimate purveyors of bedsit angst and tribal alienation. His finest hour, '81's 'Tainted Love', took a NORTHERN SOUL classic and put it through a mincing synthesizer riff (to date still the longest resident of the Billboard Hot 100). After toing and froing in the wilderness with nothing but his pet snake for companionship, Marc reclaimed his rightful place on 'Top Of The Pops' in '89 in the unlikely company of Gene Pitney, dueting on 'Something's Gotten Hold Of My Heart'. Legend has it that after passing out in a nightclub, the diminutive debaucher had his stomach pumped and out gushed copious quantities of semen.

L to R Harry Enfield (photo: Peter MacCarthur) **See Alternative Comedy/Loadsamoney.** *American Football. The American Classics look '85 (photo: Eamonn McCabe).*

AIDS The mystery illness of the decade. Over ten years after the first reported cases, the scientific jury on AIDS still isn't in yet and it's become a vehicle for the transmission of prejudice, superstition and paranoia as well as being an infectious disease. The medical establishment don't know how it originated, but there's speculation about African swine fever and green monkeys – just the sort of coagulation of images (blacks, animality, degeneracy) to revive all kinds of eugenic myths. Conspiracy theories have also surfaced and done their worst to promote a kind of resentful defeatism – like the one about AIDS being the result of a CIA chemical warfare experiment gone wrong (let *them* clean it up). There's confusion too about how far AIDS is likely to spread.

It was initially tagged as the '4H killer' because it seemed that there were certain 'risk groups' particularly susceptible – homosexuals, haemophiliacs, HEROIN addicts and (bizarrely) Haitians. The figures from July '89 appeared to support this categorization – out of a total 2,296 recorded cases over 95% belong to the risk groups. But the government spent over £15 million in ADVERTISING on a campaign backed by the British Medical Association whose subliminal message was that AIDS was out to get *everyone*. The laudable aim was to avoid minority stigmatisation, but where does that leave all the health warnings about the dangers of screwing around? For the bald fact is that heterosexual promiscuity – at the moment – is much less dangerous than gay promiscuity when it comes to the probability of contracting AIDS. It would have been more useful if the government had selectively targetted its ads instead of doing its best to promote generalised sexual paranoia.

There's a danger of scientific examination of the clinical evidence being overtaken by a plague mentality whose final result is the revival of primitive anti-pollution rituals – no fucking, no kissing, no touching. Then again maybe mass hysteria is preferable to YUPPIE indifference (the flipside to 'compassion fatigue') – the assumption that AIDS is a disease confined to the urban underclass. On top of all this is the fact that AIDS isn't properly speaking a disease at all but a clinical construct. People don't die of AIDS but of infections like pneumonia or Kaposi's sarcoma which attack the body once its immunity has been severely depressed. But depressed by what exactly?

The HIV virus has been the generally accepted culprit, but in the late '80s an American doctor called Peter Duesberg started a massive controversy over whether HIV was in fact completely unrelated to AIDS. It's no wonder some people have given up hope of a scientific cure and are instead retreating to holistic therapy, MACROBIOTICS and multigym work-outs. There may be something to it, but as Susan Sontag pointed out in her '89 polemic *AIDS And Its Metaphors* the final stage of this particular attitude is the psychologization of the disease – beating AIDS as the art of positive thinking. Don't die of ignorance? If only it were possible. *See Condoms and Safe Sex*

a humorous alternative to Benny Hill and the Two Ronnies has increased. In this sense alternative comedy really is something new – even those free-thinking Python chaps resorted to cheap and nasty bikini gags on more than one occasion. As the '80s come to a close, Mayall, Elton and co, show few signs that they might consider 'doing a Harry'. The continuing popularity of Little And Large will ensure that their alternative status remains intact. *See The Young Ones and Keith Allen*

Alternative Miss World

Less a parody of the annual non-event than an opportunity for some serious cross-dressing. Organised by sculptor Andrew Logan the first one started as a private party in '72, the last one was in '87 and there is one planned for '92. The beauty pageant with the biggest fashion queens in the business.

American Classics

What's got 200 legs, an IQ of 16 and no pubic hair? Answer – American

Classics on a Saturday afternoon. Although, since 1980, it has been one of the best places to get secondhand 501s, it was really only in '87 that American Classics reached a peak when an army of BROSettes discovered that Matt and Luke bought their RIPPED JEANS there on a Saturday. Despite the distraction of prepubescent girls stuffing messages for BROS in racks of jeans, they are still building on their original reputation to supply the best in US retro gear as well as urban SURFWEAR like Mambo and Stussy, and could claim to be one of the first shops to legitimately sell the b-boy label Troop. *See Sportswear*

American Football Along with the four-letter words on 'Brook-

side', the main talking point of the newly launched CHANNEL 4 in '82 was its coverage of American football, which, with basketball, took up 40% of its sports coverage time. It might have been a minority sport, but its cast of improbable characters like 'The Fridge' attracted nigh on three million viewers. The Super Bowl, the FA Cup Final of American football, incited pub owners throughout the UK to extend their licenses (it's a long game), splash out on a few rosettes, buy a fridgeload of Budweiser and act as if they knew the rules which no-one, not even those who've read Nicky Horne's explanatory book, understands. The sport attracted more than just COUCH POTATOES, though, with heavily padded gladiatorial combat taking place in parks everywhere as well as the more established USAF bases (in

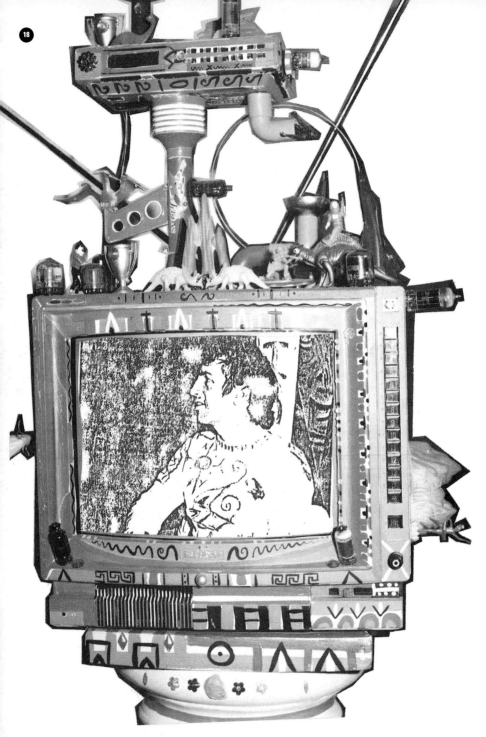

L to R Kenny Scharf's Art '85. Norman Foster's Hong Kong & Shanghai Bank **See Architecture**.

'86 there were 237 UK teams). By the end of the decade, though, the backlash that had always threatened got into gear with a LAGER advert contrasting the helmets, pads and excess bulk of American football with the minimal requirements of rugby. 'Less Is More', announced the slogan. Whatever it may be (Rollerball goes ballet?), American football will simply never be cricket.

Amis, Martin English literature's poison pen dwarf wrote one of the decade's funniest books, '84's *Money*, a speedy, slangy tour through the kitsch'n stink of materialistic modernity in the company of ad man anti-hero, John Self. It didn't get the prizes it deserved – instead Amis got

the Bomb (an attack of nuclear panic; the modern version of an old-style conversion to Christianity), published the anti-nuke collection, *Einstein's Monsters* in '87 and went on to show, with his '89 effort, *London Fields*, that nuclear angst hasn't lessened his singular ability to keep tabs on modern male yobbery. *See Booker Prize*

Amnesty International
The '80s were a particularly bleak period for human rights issues, with over half the member states of the UN holding their own citizens in jail in violation of the 1948 Universal Declaration. After increasing public awareness with a series of star-studded charity events, the Secret Policeman's Balls, in '88 Amnesty went into overdrive with their 'Human Rights Now!' campaign and

Anderson, Laurie The first New York performance artist to have a worldwide chart hit, the first lady of Mass Avant Gardism followed up '81's eight and a half minute long 'O Superman' (which reached number one in the UK charts – the surprise hit of the decade) with three albums of anecdotal collage, pop allegory and that irritating tone of voice. But her finest hour (six hours actually) came with the multi-media extravaganza 'United States Parts 1-4' in '84, a schizoid State of the Union address which mixed shaggy dog stories, shadowplay and an all-American Ultrabrite smile.

L to R Anthrax (photo: Chris Clunn).
Sophie Hicks, editor of Tatler '84, See Androgyny. male or female?
Adil and Fay i-D straight ups '83 (photo: Steve Johnston)
Ron Arad's Concrete Music.
Adam Ant (photo: Simon Brown).

the British government finally ratified the United Nations' Convention Against Torture. At the end of the decade though, half the countries of the world still imprisoned people for speaking their minds. Amnesty's work is far from over.

Androgyny Look up 'androgyny' in the dictionary and you'll find the definition of 'hermaphrodite': a person having the body characteristics of both male and females. It's a definition that, in the '80s at least, was considered a little heavy-handed. An early to mid-decade buzzword, androgynous was applied to virtually any girl with short hair to whom stilettos were considered sartorial anathema and any boy with

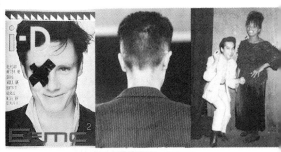

hair longer than his collar who understood the meaning of 'T-Zone'. It was also used, inaccurately, to describe BOY GEORGE at the height of the 'Is it a her, a him, or neither?' tabloid hysteria. To the majority of sane, well-balanced people under 40, however, George made an unconvincing woman. At over six feet, solidly built with hands like bunches of bananas and a throaty growl to boot, it was hard to see what all the fuss was about. Still, George played at gender gamesmanship with considerable skill.

In fact it all looked like so much wacky pop fun that Annie Lennox decided to join in with The Eurythmics' '84 VIDEO for 'Who's That Girl?', in which she played both male and female romantic leads and climaxing with a steamy kiss. 'Gender Bender Annie' screamed the tabloids.

Annie, who was nothing of the sort but knew she looked pretty damn good in a suit, promptly went off and got married. But long before either Annie or George there was GRACE JONES. The supermodel turned disco diva had laid claim to the androgyny tag in the late '70s and turned it into something of an ART form. The sleeve for the '81 LP 'Nightclubbing' still remains one of the most arresting pop images of the decade, a look so successful that BOBBY BROWN (no gender bender he) appears to have laid claim to it nearly ten years on. But that's fashion for you.

Animal Liberation Front
The organisation that turned animal rights into one of *the* issues of the '80s started life in '76 as a bunch of former Hunt Saboteurs calling themselves the Band Of Mary. Adopting 'criminal' means to draw attention to the plight of non-human creatures, they carried out raids against animal laboratories. Initially portrayed as romantic idealists by a sympathetic media, it wasn't until the Life Science Research Lab raid of '82, when £76,000 worth of damage was caused and 60 people were arrested, that their relationship with the press started to turn sour. By '84 tabloid coverage of the ALF concentrated on their balaclavas and 'terrorist' methods and the police had started to take them seriously. In '86 a series of police raids resulted in ALF leaders ending up in prison and the organisation became increasingly isolated from its mainstream supporters. The

British Union For The Abolition Of Vivisection withdrew their support as stores were fire-bombed and the ALF's methods became more violent. Today many animal rights campaigners believe that the ALF has gone down the wrong path – aiming to put companies out of business rather than focusing on the abuse of animals in industry, but everyone agrees on one point. Without the ALF, the general public would probably still think that battery hens are sold in Hamley's. *See Beauty Without Cruelty and Lynx*

Arad, Ron *See Creative Salvage*

Area The original New York concept club with constantly chang-

ing themes and decor. Opening on September 15 '83 its theme nights became a model for clubs around the world – natural history, suburbia, fashion, ART and sex were among the explorative environments that featured innovative performance artists. The mélange of fashion, film personalities and neophytes from the established uptown celebrities to the emerging downtown creative forces who, by the decade's end would become the leaders in their respective fields, gave this club a special flair and energy. The club closed in spring '87 but a coffee table book reliving the golden years of Area is nearly completed.

The Arielette The only significant corporate development in domestic washing was the Arielette, a small ball into which you poured

Ant, Adam In the late '70s Adam Ant was the darling of the hardcore London punk crowd, but come 1980 he ditched his bondage gear, donned warpaint and a swashbuckling pirate costume to become the first of the '80s teenybop idols. He produced a string of swaggering energetic hit singles that included the tribal drums of 'Kings Of The Wild Frontier', the anthemic 'Ant Music' and the tongue-in-cheek 'Goody Two Shoes'. The theatricality of his costumes, records and VIDEOs gave pop music an almost music hall vitality that all but disappeared with the bland pop-funk of later teenage idols. After '83 though, Adam's dominance of the charts declined and he turned his attention to movies. Arguably the last showman rocker of the '80s.

Architecture The '80s was the decade when architecture hit the headlines as London's built environment – or rather the unbuilt plans for the environment – became a battleground for a host of vested interests struggling to establish a national cultural agenda. The conservationists skilfully rode the popular backlash against the wrecking crew mentality associated with '60s concrete brutalism, and attempted to list every crumbling gothic pile in sight as an example of Our Glorious Heritage. They were successful first time round in their defence of the Mansion House site against Peter Falumbo's '85 plans for a heroically austere tower by one of the original 'white gods of modernism' Miles van der Rohe, but were forced to give up the fight when he returned four years later with a less dramatic design courtesy of Sir James Stirling. In the interim Prince Charles had wandered into the fray. Combining aristocratic disdain for progress with the stupid bloody-mindedness of the layman (this building's like a word-processor, that one's like an old wireless), he articulated wide public resentment with a profession perceived to be high-handed and out of touch and managed to nix arch-modernist RICHARD ROGERS' hi-tech proposal for the National Gallery extension.

In place of the ruined modernist utopia of the planned city Prince Charles promoted an architectural vision that was folksy, vernacular, and decidedly anti-urban, but it was ironic that in the end he was unwittingly doing a lot of publicity work for the deregulated architectural scramble of somewhere like DOCKLANDS. Here popular disaffection with tower block modernism was used as the excuse to throw up a pile of disposable, gimmicky buildings which rifled through architectural history, although an honourable exception was Nicholas Grimshaw's functional *Daily Telegraph* building.

DOCKLANDS was where the postmodern STYLE hit home almost a decade after it was first launched in the States. But it's a long way from Philip Johnson's imposing Chippendale-topped AT+T building in New York to Piers Gough's kitschy apartment block, 'Cascades', in the Isle Of Dogs. In DOCKLANDS architecture became a form of packaging, the architect a designer label. This was no longer the modernist dream of the city as urbane public meeting place but the postmodernist nightmare of the city as phantasmic urban scene, a collage of images where form disguises function. But it was good for business. As a result every time a plot of London real estate was up for redevelopment the new unholy alliance of developers and postmodern architects quickly moved in to grab a piece of the action.

But from London Wall to Charing Cross to the South Bank the architect has usually been Terry Farrell, the figure responsible for the toytown TV-AM building, with Britain's internationally acclaimed triumvirate of hi-tech modernists – RICHARD ROGERS, NORMAN FOSTER and James Stirling – all relegated to the status of prophets without honour in their native land. Foster has picked up the plaudits for his Hong Kong and Shanghai Bank skyscraper and Stirling for his elegant Stuttgart gallery, while Rogers is in demand in Japan. The nearest they got to redesigning London was in their 'New Architecture' exhibition at the Royal Academy in '86. But the clientele may be changing. Not only is Stirling working on the Mansion House site but Foster has recently been appointed to develop King's Cross, while Rogers is putting up a building for Reuters in DOCKLANDS. Maybe in the '90s it'll be time to go back to the future rather than forwards into the past.

liquid washing powder and then placed into a washing machine. Considered to be a dangerously innovative concept for Britain's clothes washers, it was launched on the Continent long before Britain's

markets were tested. A suitably incredulous ad campaign followed ("She's washing my son's clothes with a ball! Now I know she's mad!"). Fortunately the biodegradable ARK and Ecover washing powders arrived in '89 to provide the terminally backward Washing Giants with some *real* innovation.

Armani, Giorgio

Giorgio Armani ended the decade as he began it – in considerable STYLE. 1980 was the year in which Armani dressed Richard Gere's 'American Gigolo', bringing Italian sophistication to a generation of American men seeking a way to combine fashion with formality. In February '89 Armani opened the London based Emporio Armani in Brompton Road, his flagship European store for a multi-million dollar spinning DIFFUSION RANGE (which started in '82), as well as launching his Armani Jeans collection. Subtlety and tastefulness are the hardly revolutionary

Arena They said it could never be done, that the British male just wasn't ready for his own fashion magazine, that the only way to sell a magazine for men was to call it *Trout News, Brake Pad Monthly* or to combine, as it were, Big Ends with, uh, big ends. Fortunately for the much-touted NEW MAN with an unashamedly dandyish streak, *THE FACE* pub-

and JULIAN SCHNABEL became a millionaire from gluing crockery to canvas, was mirrored in Britain. For the first time in art history large numbers of young artists were making money on the open market and a bewildering infrastructure of NEW DEALERS, critics and labels evolved to make sure they continued to do it. A new art buying public was spawned from television, ADVERTISING, pop music and the other *nouveau riche* culture ghettos. YUPPIES started buying art, not for its aesthetic value, but because it had become *fashionable*. 'Movements' like Bad Painting, GRAFFITI, Neo-Geos, and Pittura Colta; art stars like Basquiat, GILBERT AND GEORGE, Baselitz, Koons, and SCHNABEL – all made art an *issue* and identified new

Modern British revival. And it was a conservative backlash that was mirrored by the collectors, not renowned for putting artists' interests before their own. Make no mistake, in the '90s the crash will come. *See Glasgow Pups, The New Artists, The New Dealers and Sculpture*

Art Of Noise

A trio of middle-aged mixing boffins who never showed their faces and were one of the first groups to base all their music on SAMPLING techniques. Originally signed to ZTT they later recorded a typically kitsch version of PRINCE's classic 'Kiss' with TOM JONES on lead vocals. To this day nobody knows, or cares, what they look like.

adjectives that come to mind when you focus on what Armani does: but his success is testimony to the fact that *what* he does, nobody does better. *See Fashion Designers*

Art

It was an important factor in the profile of British art in the '80s that the prime movers were the children of the '60s, people who were treated like pop stars (Hockney, Peter Blake) and ended up teaching in ART SCHOOLS. Their students emerged as the leaders of the '80s: brash, confident, completely *au fait* with media manipulation and image building. They weren't content to serve their time and graciously accept the muted accolades of the older generation – they wanted it *now*. The early '80s boom in Greenwich Village and SoHo in New York, when art became a hot commercial commodity

lisher and editor Nick Logan ignored the dissenting voices and at the end of '86 launched Arena – a bi-monthly that combined glossiness with guts, and STYLE with substance, finally tapping into the elusive men's magazine market. *See Music Press*

L to R Andy at The Hacienda '86 (photo: Dave Swindells). Leslie Ash. Simon Forbes from Antenna **See Hair Extensions**. The Alternative St Martin's Show '84 **See Art Schools**. Annie from Ar K ent '80. Rachel Auburn's collection Spring/Summer '86 (photo: David Zanes).

and ever-rarified markets and made sure that *anything went*.

All added up to an art sensibility that threw off the structured concerns of '70s MINIMALISM, and certain artists became embroiled in what some observers saw only as out and out gimmickry. Artists aimed their works at the market, as new 'movements' became used as a marketing device, and if by the end of the decade it was becoming clear that too much, too often was being shown by those of too little talent, in the UK SCULPTURE emerged as a major creative force.

By '89 though, there was evidence that a 'young fogey' attitude was emerging from the neon enthusiasm, demanding a return to traditional values and concerns and referring nostalgically to a heritage symbolised by the artists of the

Art Schools

ART schools, in particular fine art departments, were squeezed in the '80s, as the government moved to replace public funding with private SPONSORSHIP, and all-round EDUCATION with vocational training. The cuts don't just mean Britain won't produce anymore Hockneys; in future, new MCLARENs may also be hard to find. In the post-war period, fine ART departments have functioned as unofficial Research & Development departments for the music industry, and ART schools in general have been like intellectual clearing houses where avant-garde ideas get reworked for fashion and mass media. In other words, they've been informal business schools, responsible for everything from psychedelia and SCRATCH VIDEO to '80s street fashion. However, literally trying to turn them into business

Ark Baby of the environmental groups, Ark was launched at the end of '88 with a superstar line-up which included Chrissie Hynde, Kevin Godley, David Bowie, Sting, Peter Gabriel and Dave Stewart. Although their emotive manifesto pinpointed global issues, Ark took the pragmatic step of entering the marketplace as a manufacturer. Within six months of their inception they had a range of brightly packaged bio-degradable household products on the super-market shelves. Mean-while, they are developing a range of frozen meals (vegetarian and organic) plus there are now plans for an 'alternative' fast food chain – selling tasty nutritious burgers, chips and shakes which *don't* involve the destruction of the rain forest or the depletion of the ozone layer. The environmental body who have thrown off the old image of be-san-dalled and bearded ecolo-gists and given the Green world a new image for the '90s. *See Green Aware-ness*

Auburn, Rachel Clothes designer and DJ at TABOO amongst other places, Rachel's highly theatrical and surreal designs were based at her shop in HYPER HYPER called Spend Spend Spend which she shared with fellow cohort LEIGH BOWERY. Between them their des-igns summed up THE NEW GLAM period of fashion so closely linked to the rev-ellers at TABOO, which included a mix of glam rock, SEVENTIES FASH-ION, tacky sex and a pantomime aspect. Often merged with Rachel and Leigh's unique styling and make-up it became a look which many at the doors of TABOO tried to ape but somehow never quite got right. The fact that 50% of TABOO's queue was turned away demonstrated that it wasn't *what* you wore but *how* you wore it. *See Fashion Designers*

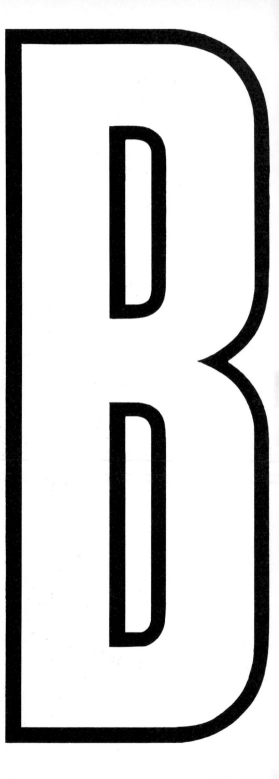

Asian Rap
Asian rap grew up alongside the British hip hop scene in the '80s. Although it co-existed with the more mainstream BHANGRA scene, Asian rap was dominated by young rappers, DJs and PIRATE RADIO broadcasters rather than the middle-aged men in sequinned suits who controlled BHANGRA. Asian hip hop represented a new gener-

ation who preferred to create their own music rather than adopting the Punjabi lyrics of BHAN-GRA and the musical trad-itions of their parents.

L to R: Asian Rappers
(photo: Simon Fleury).
Baldricks (photo: Ian Tilton).
Jeff Banks.
Bandana as headscarf
(photo: Eamonn McCabe).
Baggies (photo: Keith Seume).
Baggies (photo: Eddie Monsoon, styling: Nikos)

schools will only threaten this promiscuously productive intellectual trading, and may have dire con-sequences for the fashion and music industries in the '90s. *See St Martin's School Of Art*

Artists Against Apartheid
Launched on 15 April '86 by former Specials member Jerry Dam-mers, AAA was the spiritual heir of the late '70s Rock Against Racism organisation and one of only two pressure groups (the other being RED WEDGE) that involved pop musicians in politics outside the pop philan-thropy of LIVE AID. Aiming to increase awareness of apartheid it monitored and promoted the cultural boycott of South Africa, urging pop artists to withdraw their records and stop performing at Sun City (a huge white-only entertainment complex). On June 28 '86 it staged an open-air concert in Clapham Common that drew a quarter of a million people, but its greatest success was the Nelson Mandela Concert in June '88. Initiated by AAA the event was watched by a worldwide audience of 600 million and turned Nelson into the most famous prisoner since Patrick McGoohan and Tracy Chap-man into a star. Under-manned, under-funded and overworked, AAA is one of the success stories of pop activism in the '80s – a massive feat of overpowering righteousness over a prevailing apathy.

Automatic Toilets
Like underground ticket barriers and PHONECARDS, automatic toilets were technology that no-one asked for but got anyway. Their major contribution to society was to create not one, but two new toilet traumas. Firstly, there's the fear that the automatic doors will swing open in mid ablution, which happens rarely but is enough to put most people off using the one in Leicester Square. Secondly, there is the fear that you'll be drowned, trapped in the machine when it goes into its automatic cleaning cycle. As yet there have been no reported fatalities.

Baker, Arthur When the seminal ELECTRO record 'Planet Rock' threw Afrika Bambaataa & The Soul Sonic Force onto the global dancefloor in '81, it highlighted its producer Arthur Baker, a man who was to go on to produce an incredibly diverse range of music – Freeez, New Edition, 'Walking On Sunshine' by Rocker's Revenge, collaborate with NEW ORDER, work on songs for BRUCE SPRINGSTEEN and Cyndi Lauper, and co-ordinate the 'Sun City' all-star anti-apartheid record. One of the original stars of the mixing desk.

Baldricks Named after the character in the TV comedy 'Black Adder', they are Manchester's surreal scallies. First spotted roaming round

earic Islands. In fact, the criteria is best defined as anything played on the Balearic Islands. Confused? You should be. Probably the loosest musical category ever to be coined, it has confused DJs, clubbers, record companies and magazines alike. Initially used to describe the musical policy of early ACID HOUSE clubs, it was pioneered by Paul Oakenfold in his club Future and was forgotten in the hysteria over ACID HOUSE. Marketed by London Records on a compilation album it remains every DJ's best friend – anything he/she wants to play.

Bambaataa, Afrika See Zulu Nation

Bananarama The most success-

Baggies Bigger and more versatile than BOXER SHORTS, baggies originated from California in the '60s as SURFWEAR. Predating the boom in SURFWEAR as street fashion they first emerged as summerwear for ROCKABILLIES/ PSYCHOBILLIES and were adopted as an alternative to CYCLING SHORTS in '87. MEMPHIS designs were a strong influence, and early

skitted the group during Comic Relief '89 and even cut a record with them, a cover of 'Help!'. Anyone who still believed Bananarama were just in search of the crack was rudely awakened when, during a live performance with French & Saunders on BBC1, custard pies were thrown with more than mere gusto. Chroniclers of girl groups might perhaps see a connection between this and the onstage bust-up between Diana Ross and Mary Wilson of The Supremes at the Motown Birthday Tribute performance in '83.

Bandanas A predominant feature of gay fashion in the late '70s, the bandana entered the '80s round the necks of bikers, ROCKABILLIES,

THE HACIENDA in packs circa '86, their hands buried in pockets and eyes hiding behind mop fringes, what made them different was their flared trousers. A love of psychedelia instinctively drew them to ACID HOUSE nearly two years before anybody else, and they spent 18 months waiting for the rest of the country to catch up with them. Responsible for spawning The Happy Mondays, The Stone Roses, Inspiral Carpets and the 18 inch flare.

Balearic Beats The Balearic Islands are a group of half a dozen Spanish Mediterranean islands which include Ibiza and Majorca. Until the beginning of '88 not a lot of people knew that. Balearic Beats, on the other hand, is a diverse range of dance music that can, although not necessarily, originate from the Bal-

ful application ever of the 'just having a laugh' principle, Bananarama, with more hit singles than any other girl group in history (they overtook the Supremes in '89), still frequent London clubs, get pissed, fall over, etc. Theirs is a classic '80s provenance: living in a post-punk squat in '81, going to the BLITZ, doing an impromptu performance at THE WAG CLUB and getting a record deal. In '86 they enlisted the aid of fledgling production team STOCK, AITKEN & WATERMAN, who turned the weak voiced trio into a corporate sound. Original member Siobhan Fahey left in '88 to collaborate nuptially and musically with Dave Stewart in the preposterously named Shakespear's Sister. Her replacement, Jacquie O'Sullivan, was perfect: an inveterate clubber, reportedly able to sing in tune. Comedy duo French & Saunders

brands like Off Shore, Catchit and Stubbies became popular. As shops like M-Zone in Carnaby Street and the Quaterback chain in the north sprung up, baggies found their way onto the legs of everyone from THE SUNBED KIDS to YUPPIES, and by the end of the '80s, along with a sunburn and Jackie Collins novel, were part of every British holiday abroad.

HILLBILLIES and Kevin Rowland. A part of the pseudo-cowboy look popularised by JOHNSONS, it wasn't until the DRESSING DOWN phenomenon of the summer of '88 that the bandana became used as anything other than a neckerchief. Tied round the forehead and worn 'til the stains showed, it became available in a range of garish dayglo colours from shops like AMERICAN CLASSICS. A possible challenger to the football scarf on Britain's terraces in the '90s.

Banks, Iain His '84 debut, *The Wasp Factory*, suggested that he was another literary nasty boy, like '70s man Ian McEwan. But as his output increased to take in Kafkaesque fantasy, a rock novel, action adventure, and space opera, it became clear that Banks was actually a have-a-go pulp hero, prepared to ▶

Baier, Fred

RCA-trained furnituremaker whose work embodied the best of '80s craft, combining innovative construction and traditional standards of finish with a completely personal delight in colour, humour and eclectic imagery. At his best, Baier is one of Britain's most gifted furnituremakers, and his aeroplane jokes, sweeping curves and witty veneered

patterns are always perfectly integrated with a practical function. Like the short stubby ties he used to wear, Fred Baier's designs are masterworks of unorthodoxy.

L to R: Fred Baier.
Fred Baier's furniture.
Slim Barret (photo: John Hicks)

Barrett, Slim

Originally a sculptor Slim Barrett pioneered a completely new sculptural approach to fashion accessories. Since '84 he has used chain mail, metal, crystal, wire, brass, glass and a plethora of ur orthodox materials that made him instantly in demand from FASHION DESIGNERS such as Bruce Oldfield, RICHMOND/CORNEJO and NICK COLEMAN. His most memorable creations have included his entire surreal collection of faces and finger rings, chain mail dresses and skull caps. In '87 Slim, along with his partner Jules, opened Danlann De Bairead in Camden Town which became not only a gallery for the jewellery and larger sculpted pieces he'd created, but also a showcase for the work of other artists. A sure sign of popular approval came when BROS employed him to design their DM accessories for their 'Push' tour.

See Fashion Designers

◄ pursue his favoured themes of violence, obsession, dreams and games into areas of generic trash where other authors fear to tread. Sometimes it's worth following him.

Barcelona In the mid-'80s, Britain discovered Barcelona. The capital of Catalonia, the city where ART permeates the cafes and bars, and where nightclub ARCHITECTURE reached new heights of imagination, became feted by British magazines, journalists and SADE. Regarded as the 'Mediterranean Manhattan', its reputation as a centre of cultural hedonism leapt into overdrive with the news that it was going to be the host of the 1992 Olympics. Even the local Catalans started to believe it – 'Barcelona Better Than Ever' declared posters. If, and many people have their doubts, they manage to build the necessary facilities for the Olympic Games in time, it shouldn't eclipse Barcelona's vital contribution to the '80s – a city that turned places where people go to dance and drink into ART galleries.

Barker, Clive A homegrown Steven King (in best-seller/box office terms) and the original splatter punk. In '84 Barker sliced and diced his way through the bloated body of horror fiction and served up the meaty bite-sized chunks of *The Books Of Blood* – six volumes of short stories which spliced together ancient sacrificial terrors and modern fears. A powerful novel, *The Damnation Game*, followed in '85, before Barker's horror fantasy hit the wide screen. 'Underworld' and the 'Hellraiser' series were unabashed B-movies, briefly propping up the ailing fortunes of US backers New World Pictures and topping VIDEO charts worldwide, but diehard fans suspect Barker has swapped the pulp meatwagon for the Hollywood gravy train.

Barnes, John John Barnes is a black footballer. Sadly, in the '80s, his real significance is not often his breathtaking skill but the fact that he is black. Barnes has run the gauntlet

of banana throwing racists at various FOOTBALL grounds across the country. A calm individual, he appears to be able to deal with this. Despite Italian transfer ambitions he is currently an erratic star at LIVERPOOL FC. It's not his taste for Funkadelic and JAMES BROWN but an explosive and often brilliant footballing skill which makes him a giant of '80s sport. The fact that he is black should be between him and his mirror.

Bartsch, Susanne Susanne Bartsch reenergised New York nightlife at a time when many clubbers were tolling its death bell. Originally a fashion retailer who had been waving the flag for British designers, she put on shows for BODYMAP and

SUE CLOWES in the early '80s. Starting with weekly events in '87 at Savage and Bentley's, with the emphasis on dressing up in colourful outrageous costumes, she brought NY a taste of TABOO and inspired a whole new generation of clubgoers. In '89 she ran the once monthly events at the Copa and organised the highly successful Love Ball. The undisputed NY Queen Of The Night.

Baseball Caps First surfaced in the UK in the early '80s as b-boys and skateboarders popularised the caps and retro Americana started to fill the streets. By '84 BIG APPLE, a Brixton based hat shop, was selling more than they could supply, and FLIP's collegiate secondhand styles, along with their baseball jackets, were worn by all and sundry. As high street stores mass-produced brightly

Batman Messages of congratulations were scarce for the 50th Anniversary of Superman, but with Batman it was a whole different story. GRAPHIC NOVELS like Frank Miller's *THE DARK KNIGHT RETURNS* and ALAN MOORE's *The Killing Joke* made sure of that, exploding the camp crusader reputation inherited from the '60s TV series and retooling the original Batman myth from the '30s to define a new crime-buster for a cynical new decade – violent, repressed, driven. The image overhaul spelled a grisly end for the Boy Wonder, who was voted out of the regular monthly title in a reader's poll, and an increased profit margin for Warners, who made $300 million in merchandising on the back of Tim Burton's 'Batman' movie. Who says crime doesn't pay?

L to R: Batman jacket '88. Mastermind DJ '85 wearing Baseball Cap. Three Baseball Caps (photos: John Hicks). MCM Baseball Cap (photo: John Dawson). Baseball Cap (photo: John Hicks). i-D straight ups Steven and David '86 See Baseball Caps.

coloured copies, people started devising new ways to wear the caps – on the side of the head, on the back of the head, perched on top of the head, two together or with the brim folded back. Designer versions inevitably appeared, taking the humble baseball cap into fashion orbit with exaggerated brims, leather caps, fake fur numbers, and eventually the BOY version. Modelled by BOY GEORGE and THE PET SHOP BOYS, the BOY baseball cap became part of London's club uniform, so much so that no teenage tourist was seen without one. With the emergence of DESIGNER BOOTLEGGING in '87, baseball cap variations from Louis Vuitton to MCM became part of the extended b-boy uniform, and no budding DJ

was complete without a box of 12 inch singles and plastic brown MCM baseball cap.

The Batcave Next door to the Golden Girl bar above Gossips was the Gargoyle Club. It was a strange mix. A mini-cinema (showing old Boris Karloff flicks and porn videos), a dancefloor and a bar area – every Wednesday a crowd of black-clad GOTHS, stinking of cigarettes and bleach, gathered on the corner of Meard and Dean St waiting to board the lift, four at a time, to be admitted to The Batcave. Girls wore fishnet stockings and little else, boys were thin and spotty, and every ex-punk celeb from Pauline Murray to SIOUXSIE could be found lurking in the corners. After a few months it moved to Fouberts, but at its height in '83, it caught the post-punk mood perfectly. Dark, morbid, sulphate-fuelled and completely humourless.

Baudrillard, Jean The postmodern guru who made a career confusing the hell out of his disciples (eg. New York's Neo-Geo artists). The piecemeal translations of his texts mid-decade didn't help, with cannibalized chapters from different books indifferently repackaged as MATT BLACK, slimline paperbacks by the New York publishers SEMIOTEXTE. Then there was the arcane vocabulary: 'implosion', 'seduction', 'deterrence', 'simulation'. Baudrillard was a writer who had 'cult' scribbled all over him. But what was his message? Well... 1) Capitalism will not be

Dead', later used in the Bowie/ Catherine Deneuve movie 'The Hunger'. The Bowie connection continued in '82 with their biggest hit, a straight cover of 'Ziggy Stardust' which, strangely, used the later 'Aladdin Sane' make-up stripe on the label. Like most of the POSITIVE PUNK/ GOTH bands, Bauhaus were ridiculed by the MUSIC PRESS for their overstated sinister image and overdetermined 'weird' lyrics. The band were so riled that they invited journalists to interview them onstage before gigs. Few accepted the offer, and the band split in '83, despite a massive cult following, particularly in the north.

The Beastie Boys An inspired

Bazooka Simon Foxton graduated from ST MARTIN'S in '83 and launched design team Bazooka with Cheryl Eastap and Angela Aurora. Way ahead of its time, the Bazooka manifesto mixed SPORTSWEAR with tailoring to create the hooded jacket and fitted jacket STYLE. But it was their Bazooka blazer, a classic jacket woven into college stripes of orange and

PSYCHEDELIA, the teenagers who had discovered the '60s through their brothers and sisters' record collections, were forced to become part of Britain's tapestry of youth culture, just another anonymous colour on an overcrowded canvas. Overlooked by youth chroniclers, who dismissed their pebble glasses, corduroy regency jackets and collar length hair as 'students' (which many of them were), they smoked dope in their bedsits, bought records at Plastic Passion and Vinyl Experience, listened to contemporary bands on the Bam Caruso label (and subscribed to its magazine *Strange Things*), and wondered where all the other hippies were. It wasn't until the SUMMER OF LOVE '88 that they found out, when

defeated by its contradictions so long as it can make a media spectacle out of them, ie. forget socialism. 2) The society of the spectacle will not be undermined by scandal so long as it can make it an incentive to consume, ie. forget SITUATIONISM. 3) The consumer economy will not be subverted by irony so long as it can make a fashion out of it, ie. forget STRUCTURALISM. 4) If you think you can escape the judgement of fashion – forget it. According to Baudrillard, the only retaliatory gambit left is 'hyperconformism' or homoeopathic idiocy, ie. it's hip to be square. *See Postmodernism*

Bauhaus Formed in '78 in Northampton, and featuring the lemon suck cheekboned Pete Murphy, Bauhaus presaged the GOTH movement with their '79 debut single 'Bela Lugosi's

mixture of rock, rap and crass Americanisms, The Beastie Boys were a trio of spoilt white brats who namechecked brands of beer and hamburgers in their raps, wrecked hotel rooms, humiliated female go-go dancers onstage, did everything in the worst possible taste, and sold millions of copies of their first LP 'Licensed To Ill'. Their '87 UK tour caused riots and group member Adam Horowitz ended up in court in Liverpool for throwing a can of Budweiser into the audience, hitting a fan. Although disliked by the rest of the hip hop community, black rap DJ Eric B praised The Beastie Boys for doing what we'd all like to do – giving free rein to our most childish feelings and not giving a damn. *See Volkswagens*

Beatniks Left over from NEW

black or maroon and white, which made the biggest mark on London's streets. In '84, at a time when people were buying blazers from jumble sales, Bazooka's stood out like a frigate on the Serpentine. *See Fashion Designers*

they set up their own club, Happenings at Violets (replete with poetry readings, musical bumps and action painting), and discovered that they weren't the only ones wearing lovebeads, paisley smocks and sandals.

Beauty Without Cruelty Established in '83 by vegetarians, BWC was the first make-up house in the UK to produce and promote products not tested on animals. Despite being the laughing stock of the cosmetics industry, by the late '80s it was seen as a trendsetter in tune with popular concern for animal rights. The news in July '89 that leading companies Revlon and Avon were no longer going to test their products on animals signalled a major victory for activists everywhere. *See Animal Liberation Front,*

The Body Shop and Lynx

Becker, Boris When Boris 'Boom Boom' Becker won Wimbledon at the age of 17 in '85 he gave the term 'wunderkind' fresh meaning, removing with one stroke of his heavily endorsed racket the myth that only a player with championship pedigree could win the world's most prestigious tennis tournament. And now? Boris is hardly a has-been at 21, but he will never again be as good as when he didn't know how good you had to be – because thought has replaced instinct and taken the edge off the confident spontaneity that once baffled his rivals. When Becker told the tabloid press, "Bonking isn't in my diction-

ary", losing wasn't either. It is now.

Beineix, Jean-Jacques The front runner in the new generation of French CINÉ BRATS, Beineix's work is more nouvelle vogue than *nouvelle vague* ('new wave'), with its penchant for lush photography and limp plots. 'Diva' – his first and best – was the archetypal director's debut; a virtuoso showing of all the colours in his ciné-palette. But his work since, 'The Moon In The Gutter' and 'Betty Blue', succumbed to the worst indulgences of French cinematic posing: beautiful women talking in non-sequiturs to fashionable drunks and idolising that infuriating French species, the sex kitten. A question mark still remains – are the new boys on the block (add Besson, Carax, MONDINO and GOUDE) more cute than clever?

Bell, Steve Arguably *the* political cartoonist of the '80s. In his blackly humorous, acidic and extremely left-wing strips for *The Guardian*, Steve Bell was one of the few people who could make politics truly funny.

Benn, Nigel Founding member of the 'Black Pack' of high-earning black British sportsmen, middleweight puncher Nigel Benn was the perfect subject for the hype that has come to surround professional BOXING. He was heavily muscled, flamboyant and he talked a great fight. Many in the trade believed there were not only better fighters but better *British* fighters than Nigel Benn before he got pasted in a

Finsbury Park tent by Michael Watson in May '89 – but neither press nor the promoters told the punters. Benn entered the tent to a fanfare that would have done Zsa Zsa Gabor proud and was knocked out in the sixth.

Berkoff, Steven The angry genius of fringe theatre, Berkoff was feared as much as admired, his irascible eloquence venting scorn and fury on those who dared to dislike his apocalyptic visions. Stabbing the establishment in the neck with his vitriolic pen, his work ('East', 'Greek', 'Decadence') was an inspiration to actor-writer-managers across the theatrical hinterland of pub venues and subsidised arthouses. Then Berkoff traded his cult for cash and became baddy of the year in a string of Hollywood blockbusters, from

Belgian Fashion Walter Van Beirendonck, Dirk Bikkembergs, Dries Van Noten, Ann Demeulemeester, Dirk Van Saene and Marina Yee took the British Designer Collections by storm in '86 with their refreshing creative air. Collectively known as The Antwerp Six, their designs (which were as disparate as any of the British contingent) were seen as one, united by their enthusiasm and elaborate imagery which was carried through into lavish booklets and an ear-piercing, mind-blowing show in '87. They laid down a trail for more design talent to emerge from the same fashion college they attended, namely The Antwerp Academy Of Fine Art which briefly began to look like it was taking over the mantle held by ST MARTIN'S. For a moment there, the British fashion industry looked worried.

See Fashion Designers

L to R: Mick Jones from Big Audio Dynamite (photo: John Stoddart). Patrick De Muynck's collection '88 – the second wave of Belgian Fashion (photos: Phil Inkelberghe).

'Octopussy' to 'Beverly Hills Cop'. Fame led to fortune and Berkoff's oeuvre now plays West End dates to first night crowds, but if the political bent of his audience is less sympathetic, the quality of his rage is undiminished. Before he played to the converted, now he harangues the guilty.

The Berlin Club Seminal Manchester nightclub, small and dark, where DJ Colin Curtis pioneered the sort of jazz/funk/soul mix that would later storm London clubland and where an employee would occasionally cruise the crowd with a notebook asking them what records they'd like to hear played.

Bhangra The strongest statement of young Anglo-Asian identity in the '80s. The bhangra disco was a daytime session where British-born Asian kids, skiving off school and dodging their parents, went to dance to a mixture of traditional Punjabi wedding music and electric beats. Bhangra bands like Heera and Alaap were unknown outside the Asian community until '87, largely due to their Punjabi lyrics and the fact that the Asian all-dayer crowd at London venues like THE CAMDEN PALACE, Hippodrome and Busby's never intermingled with the nocturnal club set. The bhangra scene generated its own newspaper, *Ghazal And Beat*, bhangra fashion, a hybrid of British casual and Asian STYLE, plus bhangra posses, 18-25 year olds whose allegiance was to their territory, be it Wembley, Croydon or Birmingham. Later on it also helped instigate the more Westernised crossover music, house bhangra, and ASIAN RAP, which grew out of many younger Asians' frustration with the bhangra scene's domination by middle-aged men in sequinned suits.

Big Audio Dynamite In '84, the day after he left The Clash, Mick Jones started looking for like minds and a sympathetic beatbox. It took

DESIGN: GET SMART! ASSOCIATES

BAZAAR

1 & 4 SOUTH MOLTON ST, LONDON, W1. TEL 629·1708/499·3127

him 18 months, and he found a bloke who couldn't play a musical note (Don Letts), three soul/funk/punk veterans and a brilliant idea. Integrating the punk and hip hop DIY ethic and turning it into a mini spaghetti Western, BAD concentrated on the rogue cowboy imagery and sellotaped the names on the notes of Don Letts' keyboards so he could play. After two albums and five singles they still haven't managed to get beyond first base – how to convince the public that they're not joking.

The Big Bang October 27 '86 was The Big Bang for the expanded universe of the London stock exchange. It was the day of financial

wasn't the point. Surrounded by a bevy of fashion talent, they became (for better or for worse) Birmingham's most famous early '80s export, the tip of a creative iceberg if you like. Their clothes were designed by Kahn And Bell, aka Jane Kahn (who now owns Kahniverous) and Patti Bell, who were the social focal points of the NEW ROMANTIC scene in Birmingham. The Rum Runner and The Holy City Zoo clubs were their playground, where others like Martin Degville (*See Degvilles*) and Jane Farrimond gathered with their exaggerated cheekbones, studs, frilly shirts and leather. Degville and Farrimond opened a clothes shop called Ya Ya, Dave Edmonds (who now runs Pure Sex) ran a chain of shops called

Memphis, Tennessee, and originally only found in this country in Afro-Caribbean chemists in Brixton and Dalston, B&W was soon found on sale in almost every trendy hairdresser and '50s clothing store around.

Black Leggings The most universal and versatile fashion garment of the late '80s was the black legging. The boom in LYCRA and body conscious trend in fashion in the mid-'80s resulted in many bemused looks in dance shops as people with no interest in dancing other than the fashion flocked to shops like Pineapple and The Dance Centre. For better or for worse, the streets became full of contour hugging black

Bernstock Speirs Paul Bernstock and Thelma Speirs met at Middlesex Polytechnic and decided to form a company creating accessories which made statements by themselves. They created hats which were themselves a fashion trend, not merely an afterthought to it, and made designer hats fun and affordable. Their designer clients include Jacques Azagury, Bruce Oldfield, Monica Chong, and WORKERS FOR FREEDOM, but more recently they have become heavily involved with the music world, designing hats for THE PET SHOP BOYS and U2, as well as releasing their own pop record 'Act Sexy' in late '89. Probably the most multi-faceted partnership around, they have designed hats (their most memorable being the topless brim hat in '82 - copied by many high street stores), several collections of clothes, run a club (White Trash), made a record, and even, started their own fan club/magazine. There is no telling what they will do next. *Fashion Designers*

creation when share-trading was computerised, deregulated and internationalised – or in other words sent into electronic orbit. For as data slammed round the globe on a green screen rollercoaster of reflex buying and selling it soon became clear that this had nothing to do with the national economy on the ground. The October Crash of '87 came and went and the only ones to panic outside the City were the media. For everyone else Black Monday was another working day – or No Big Deal.

The Birmingham Contingent Outside London, in the wake of the BLITZ club and during the heyday of the NEW ROMANTICS, DURAN DURAN were playing at the Rum Runner club in Birmingham. Nobody was in the audience, but that

Dimentia, stocking early London fashion as well as his own label. The Oasis Market became Birmingham's answer to KENSINGTON MARKET and the Hosteria Bar the equivalent to The Chelsea Potter. Eventually, most of the Birmingham Contingent found their way to London, where they found fame and mixed fortunes. *See Sigue Sigue Sputnik*

Black And White Hair Grease Virtually unknown in this country before 1980, Black And White became the favourite hair grease of the up-and-coming rockabilly fraternity and ended up being *the* hairdressing accessory of the decade. Much imitated but never bettered, B&W was perfect for quiffs, FLAT-TOPS and DAs, and its appeal also lay in its packaging which hadn't changed since the '50s. Made in

leggings that left nothing to the imagination.

Black Polo Necks Traditionally evoking scenes of smoky jazz clubs and beatnik STYLE, the black polo neck almost became a cliché. By '85 pop groups like Swing Out Sister and Curiosity Killed The Cat were flirting with the look, and the film 'Absolute Beginners' ensured its place in STYLE mythology. The most enduring and unusual example though, was designed by painter Peter Doig, and featured a print based on human sperm.

Black Rock Coalition The support group for black rockers founded in '85 by Vernon Reid, guitarist with black hard rock quartet Living Colour, it aimed to emphasize rock's roots in black R&B and ease

Big Apple Deny White set up Big Apple in Brixton in the early '80s stocking the most exciting hats this side of New York. All the stock came from New York, Jamaica or Italy and included anything from beavers, fur-lined cossack hats, Greek fishermen models, leather flat caps and weatherman skank caps. A melting pot of youth culture, the shop was frequented by ragamuffins, b-boys, The Fun Boy Three and even STEVE STRANGE. Now named Private Stock it is still one of the few places to get a skin print BOWLER HAT.

L to R: Beastie Boys. i-D straight up Birgit '83. Black Polo Neck Bernstock/Speirs '86. Big Apple '82. Hats by Bernstock/Speirs '88 (photo: Jacqueline L Palmer, styling: Daryl Black). Black leather '84 (photo: Monica Curtin) **See Vintage Leather.**

the rock'n'roll stereotype away from the blond, blue-eyed all-American boy image. Organizing Black Rock Coalition tours and taking up the cause on FM radio, Reid soon found that his own group Living Colour, like fellow black rockers Roachford, were getting taken very seriously indeed, ending '89 on a US tour with The Rolling Stones.

Black Uniformity It's March '85 or October '87 or July '89 in Paris, Florence or London. The world's fashion press are waiting to see the latest offerings from any of the top European designers. For a hundred metres the uniform is black. Black uniformity dominated the catwalks and queues from Tokyo to Milan in

the late '80s and individualists stuck out like a light in a coal mine. The conservatism of fashion journalists and buyers has lasted more than ten designer seasons from '85-'89, as the Japanese minimalist rule 'any colour as long as it's black' lost its status power and became a high street convention. Black silk bomber jackets from KATHARINE HAMNETT, black denim jackets from DEMOB, black LYCRA CYCLING SHORTS from JEAN PAUL GAULTIER and black latex rubber dresses from Aquagirl all had their high street imitators. There was a brief departure in '84 when club fashion went dayglo and again after the summer of '88 with ACID HOUSE inspired graphics and SURFWEAR, but from the post-punk Carnaby St bondage trousers of 1980, to the high street ski suits of '88, black was the most popular fashion colour of the

decade. *See Matt Black*

Bladerunner The movie from '82 which called time on all the old myths of progress and defined a new mood for a post-affluent society: nostalgia for the future. Here was an underpopulated 21st Century LA which was already past it – the VIDEO phones were scrawled with GRAFFITI, the jet cars were old and dirty, the ARCHITECTURE was a scratched collage of crumbling stone and wall-curtain neon. Adapted by Ridley Scott from Philip K Dick's science fiction novel *Do Androids Dream of Electric Sheep?* the film abandoned the paranoid energy of its model and wrapped itself up in a melancholic languor which stretched to include Harrison Ford's rain-washed detective hero. It also abandoned along the way any pretence at narrative coherence and was entirely defined by its effects – the venetian-blind chiaroscuro, the blue-filter haze, the swooping Vangelis score. The STYLE was immediately ripped off by a pile of ads – not least Ridley Scott's own for Barclays Bank.

Blame, Judy More a fashion creator than straight jewellery designer, Judy Blame (aka stylist Fred Poodle, aka Chris Barnes from Leatherhead) transformed the idea of accessories as minor details into creations in their own right. Judy cornered the market in salvage with

Bikers Boots Lewis Leathers in Great Portland St has always been the place to get the real McCoy, but by the beginning of the decade JOHNSONS had adapted the classic biker boot adding straps, zips, buckles and fabric, and a STYLE that ADAM ANT quickly picked up on. Ever since, the biker boot has become a street fashion accessory worn by both

is not only innovative but commercially successful too.

Bleasdale, Alan After Stratford's Shakin' Will and Liverpool's other major pen-pusher Willy Russell, Alan Bleasdale is Britain's most read and performed playwright. Bleasdale began writing to amuse and appease rough and ready teenage schoolkids in his early days as a teacher, but through his epic dole culture series 'Boys From The Blackstuff' and later film 'No Surrender' he established himself as a working-class writer whose true grit realism enjoyed mass appeal.

Blitz Blitz has become the yardstick by which all other clubs have been

L to R: Customised JPG jacket by Judy Blame (photo: Marc Lebon). Judy Blame in Chemical Warfare Collection (photo: Monica Curtin). Judy Blame. Early Blitz clubbers. The Blitz Club (photo: Virginia Turbett).

his magnificent handiwork using beads, dyed rope, wrapped chains, buttons, badges, cigarette packs, drink labels, coat hangers, string, RUBBER, leather and anything else that wasn't nailed down. In the early '80s his designs, in particular in conjunction with CHRISTOPHER NEMETH, became a constant feature of the fashion-pages of *i-D* and *THE FACE*, and he evolved into a fashion personality not unlike LEIGH BOWERY, becoming a walking advert for his creations and feted by fashion designers from Anthony Price to JOHN GALLIANO. The Judy Blame touch soon became a common sight in videos, catwalks and glossy magazines, whether it was in his work with BOY GEORGE, styling the pages of *Vogue*, or at Olympia. Responsible for NENEH CHERRY's image in '89, he has proved that he

sexes and an essential part of the GREBO/Zodiac Mindwarp appropriation of biker STYLE. Recently, the Engineer Boot with its rubber commando sole (biker boots have flat soles), has become a popular alternative, although both boots are not as tough as they look. If threatened by a drunken GREBO, stamp on their toe.

measured. Like seeing the Sex Pistols live, it has become one of those things that young London lies about 'being there'. David Bowie was let in. Mick Jagger wasn't. Steve Strange was the notorious doorman who said 'no', Rusty Egan was the DJ and BOY GEORGE was the cloakroom attendant. SPANDAU BALLET wore their KILTS and got very drunk. It was a poser's paradise – a ST MARTIN'S meeting place where the young designers awarded themselves with a Wednesday morning hangover. To a soundtrack of T Rex and the smell of hairspray, this was the first club where the boys used the 'ladies' and pretended they were Marilyn. Marilyn, of course was there. When it closed in '81 it signalled the end of the beginning and the birth of something new. From JOHN GALLIANO, BODYMAP to STEPHEN LIN-

Bimbos A term thought to have been coined by 'Doonesbury' in *The Guardian* circa '85 to describe women who took part in wet T-shirt contests. It soon gained tabloid credence, referring to pouting young women (preferably blonde) who became famous for doing absolutely nothing – whether it was hanging on Bill Wyman's arm at 13 (Mandy Smith) or singing very badly in a put-up pop group called Eighth Wonder (Patsy Kensit). The ideal bimbo finds an influential man to drape herself over, failing that, a stab at the charts with STOCK, AITKEN & WATERMAN will do. *See Wannabees*

ARD; BOY GEORGE, Marilyn to SPANDAU BALLET, the Blitz Kids stumbled into Great Queen St and discovered that everybody was waiting to see what they'd do next. *See New Romantics*

Blitz Magazine Launched in September 1980 by two Oxford University undergraduates Carey Labovitch and Simon Tesler and named after the club, *Blitz* aimed to balance THE FACE's initial musical bias. Covering a diverse spread of topics it acted as a springboard for young talent (including fashion writer Iain R Webb) and achieved its greatest success with the denim Levis jacket exhibition in '85, when 22 top UK designers customised jackets that spawned a book and ended up in the V&A Museum. Now concerned with ever more general topics, it has

concentrated on becoming a feature-heavy magazine aimed at a more mature readership than when it started.

Blue Rondo A La Turk
Formed by several stalwarts of LE BEAT ROUTE underground scene (including Mark Reilly who went on to form Matt Bianco, and Chris Sullivan who runs THE WAG CLUB), Blue Rondo gained a brief reputation as the most stylish group in the country. Dressed like '40s bebop fashion plates the band played a wild mixture of funk and salsa rhythms that gained them enthusiastic followers among soulboys and trendies alike. Although their debut single 'Klactoveesedstein' was a huge hit on the underground circuit in '82 it didn't get the crossover success it deserved and the band's

fortunes never quite recovered. Their biggest success was probably sartorial – along with Kid Creole, they were responsible for popularising the ZOOT SUIT and pencil moustaches.

Blueprint The bigger than life ARCHITECTURE and design magazine has been an essential guide for the club-class traveller in hyperreality ever since it was founded by critic Deyan Sudjic, publisher Peter Murray and Richard Leeks in '83. Informed, spiky and passionate, it has rinsed the halo from the cult objects of the designer decade and picked a wary path through a minefield of styles – MATT BLACK, retro-tech, soft-tech, hi-touch, industrial baroque. In fact it's only got one drawback: an unimaginative design.

The Body Shop It started as a

BMX Bikes

BMX stands for Bicycle Motor Cross and it was the only bike to be seen on if you were prepubescent in the mid-'80s. BMX riding became a big time sport, spawned national championships and commercial SPONSORSHIP, plus a series of 'BMX Bandits' movies. But in the end the only BMX riding that really counted was done in the concrete walkways of suburban shopping centres, where Saturday shoppers still have to dodge the spins and wheelies of rampant BMX bandits. *See Skateboarding*

L to R: BMX Bikes (photo: Nick Knight).
Betty Boop (photo: Robert Erdmann).
Bodypoppers at The Wag Club (photo: Sebastian Sharkles).
Bodybuilder Sonia Newsam (photo: Normski)
See Bodybuilding.

small shop on a Brighton side street in the hot summer of '76. With an overdraft of £4,000 and a big idea, Body Shop managing director Anita Roddick decided to take on the cosmetics industry on her own terms. With skin and haircare products originating wholly from natural materials, traditional ingredients from all over the globe, and no testing on animals, Roddick welded '60s idealism with '80s entrepreneurial flair. A gifted communicator and '85's Business Woman Of The Year, she's hardly had to spend a penny on ADVERTISING. Her personality is the Body Shop's selling point (in '89 the company was worth £200 million and had 366 shops worldwide), a symbol of commitment and inspiration and a business iconoclast. Every time you buy a Peppermint Foot Lotion, it's 'up yours' to Elizabeth Arden and one more point for the Amazonian rain forest. A sound philosophy indeed. *See Animal Liberation Front and Beauty Without Cruelty*

Bodybuilding The avant-garde obsession of health and efficiency culture started to seem less like a freak show as pumping iron crossed over to the mainstream in the '80s. Suburban health addicts turned to the modern equivalents of medieval instruments of torture, the multi-gym, targetted those pecs, delts, traps, abs, glutes and lats and went for a new mechanised high. Following ARNOLD SCHWARZENEGGER's success, the modern male's ideal body

has become a toned-down version of the body builder's toned-up, hairless, fatless, anatomy chart physique. Whether modern women will swap shoulder pads for the real broad shoulders of female bodybuilders is another matter. These bona-fide strong women are now the last word in useless muscle and artificial physiques. After literally training their tits off, some now have COSMETIC SURGERY to put 'feminine' curves back onto their bulked-up frames. For them, the body isn't something you're lumbered with at birth. Instead it's a plaything, a biological kit of parts waiting to be technologically transformed and aesthetically reshaped. *See Health Clubs and Health Farms*

BodyMap In '83 BodyMap won 'The Most Innovative Designer Of The Year' award for their 'Olive Oyl Meets Querelle' collection of black and white towelling and cotton jersey separates. The work of BodyMap designers David Holah and Stevie Stewart was indeed innovative – with swirling ruffles on swirling skirts, tighter than tight LYCRA casuals, skinny rib tops and loose baggy bottoms, their designs were new and exciting, like nothing ever seen before. Contradictions in colour and shape made them the stars of the international catwalks, and they spearheaded the new wave of mid-'80s UK designers bringing the fashion spotlight back to London. Young London hadn't been as hip since the '60s, and BodyMap's CATWALK SHOWS became even wilder with grandmothers, babies,

L to R: Five of the many faces of Leigh Bowery (photos: Nick Knight). BodyMap's Spring/Summer '84 collection (photo: Marc Lebon).

bald heads and ballet dancers all sharing the spotlight until the bubble eventually burst in the mid-'80s when the trend in fashion about-turned towards tradition and conservative elegance. Still finding outlets for their creative flamboyance via costumes for MICHAEL CLARK, they have managed to stay successful during the era of DRESSING DOWN, and their name will be forever associated with the golden era of British fashion. *See Fashion Designers*

Bomb The Bass Tim Simenon – slight, shamefully modest and then 20 years old – took everybody by surprise with the success of his debut single 'Beat Dis' on Rhythm King in

'88. A DJ who had maintained a low profile up 'til then, he drew on his hip hop roots and fascination for comics and released the first British DJ album 'Enter The Dragon', a cut-up mix of rap beats and celluloid imagery. The only DJ act to attempt a proper live tour, just like SOUL II SOUL, COLDCUT and S'XPRESS, he nurtured a loose group of club-based musicians/artists whose talent he consistently showcased. *See Neneh Cherry*

Bonfire Of The Vanities The publishing hype of the decade, Tom Wolfe's blockbuster aimed to close the book on the '80s Big Apple and top the New York Babylon novels written by JANOWITZ and McInerney. Appropriately for someone whose New Journalism borrowed fictional techniques, Wolfe

Bowery, Leigh Arriving from Australia in 1980, Leigh Bowery wandered into Club For Heroes and never looked back. He opened a stall in KENSINGTON MARKET selling his own designs – glamorous concoctions made from loud fabrics and draped in glitzy accessories – and opened the legendary TABOO club in '85 with Tony Gordon. Bored with the fashion design world he started making costumes for MICHAEL CLARK, joining his dance company in '87 (most famously appearing as a teapot in 'Because We Must'), and appeared in promo videos for THE FALL. He also played Cardinal Marcinkus as half-priest, half-pantomime horse in Fall singer Mark E Smith's play 'Hey Luciani', and his apotheosis came in '88 with a series of performances at the Anthony d'Offay Gallery, in which he posed for two hours at a time behind a two way mirror. When he entered mainstream consciousness in '89's series of Pepe jean ads, it was a fitting exit from a decade which Leigh made into his own playground. *See Rachel Auburn*

produced a readable journalistic fiction – 15 *Vanity Fair* articles in search of a plot, not the modern version of Thackeray's 'Vanity Fair' he promised.

The Booker Prize In the decade that publishing had its own BIG BANG, The Booker turned into the book trade's Oscars. It had the embarrassing acceptance speeches, the safe winners (Anita Brookner's *Hotel du Lac* in '84), even its own Meryl Streep ("RUSHDIE on the shortlist *again!*"), and it put bums on seats, or books on shelves – a shortlist place increased sales tenfold and can bring a six figure advance for the next book. Serious Money, but does it encourage

Serious ART?

Botham, Ian After the dull domination of English cricket in the '70s by Yorkshireman Geoff 'Stonewall' Boycott, Somerset (and later Worcestershire)'s Ian Botham emerged as a Roy Of The Rovers type hero, with sun-in streaks in his hair and a swashbuckling approach to batting and bowling. After single-handedly winning the Second Test against Australia in '81 it became apparent that 'The Gorilla' was England's only true world class character cricketer. But Botham got too big for his boots as far as the establishment was concerned. The stiff upper lip heroes of the past hated his flashness, and when he admitted to having smoked cannabis in his youth he was carpeted by the blazered committee. Unwilling to defer to such "gin swilling dodderers", he rode out his various periods of suspension by playing FOOTBALL for Scunthorpe United, endorsing Nike products, and, losing many of his sympathizers in the process, ghosting a column for *The Sun*.

Bovine Spongiform Encephalitus

The animal disease of the '80s could turn out to be the human disease of the '90s. The first case of BSE was recorded in April '85, although not publicly broadcast. Some scientists claim it originated as scrapie, a sheep brain disease, but others disagree, suggesting that it is an attempt to cover-up the seriousness of the disease. Fatal, causing

madness and death, the virus is not destroyed by heat and is particularly hardy. Any infected animals are destroyed and used in cattle feed, causing the disease to be transferred to cattle with the same deadly effect. Each time a case of BSE is found, the cow is slaughtered (although not the entire herd) and as the government pay out only a percentage of the livestock's value, farmers who detect early signs of BSE often take their whole herd to market. Beef and milk are already infected, and government research into BSE won't bear fruit until the mid-'90s. As yet, no-one knows if humans can contract the disease (or whether we could contract it through BSE-infected meat), and the incubation period is up to five years, so it could be a while before we find out. But if it does affect humans, the repurcussions for both

Bowler Hats

Despite their City gent stigma, the '80s was the decade when the bowler went AWOL. Appropriated by everyone from ragamuffins, CLOCKWORK ORANGE SKINS, Mica Paris to BOYS WONDER, the hat gave an immediate look of austerity to the wearer and was soon taken up by FASHION DESIGNERS. BERNSTOCK SPEIRS' series of bowlers

including the 'inside-out' design of '86, JEAN PAUL GAULTIER's bowlers with cod piece accessories in '87, Atelier's bowlers with gold crown pieces in '88, and a diverse range of customised alternatives ensured that nobody would look at the bowler hat in the same light again.

L to R: The play 'Bouncers' '86 **See John Godber**. *Bowler Hat (photo: Andy Lane). Boy T-shirt '84 (photo: James Palmer). Boy George '80 (photo: Simon Brown). Boy George '87*

Boy Originally involved in Acme on KING'S ROAD, which along with WESTWOOD and MCLAREN's shop, Sex, clothed most of the early punks, John Krevine went on to open Boy in '77 with its bondage gear and T-SHIRTS, gaining immediate notoriety with his shock value window displays and inevitable prosecutions. Despite its punk roots the shop-cum-label soon became a mainstay of the high street boom with the BOY logo becoming the most bootlegged name of the decade. Their clothes were always diluted versions of street trends from the LYCRA skirts and vests to the ACID HOUSE uniform of T-SHIRTS and shorts, and pop stars like BOY GEORGE, THE PET SHOP BOYS and YAZZ, ensured that their name appeared on 'Top Of The Pops' more often than any other fashion label. Today Boy has become synonymous with London street fashion and they have opened up shops all over the world, in places as far afield as Philadelphia, Hong Kong and Saudi Arabia.

farmers and meat-eaters will be extremely serious. *See Food Scares*

Boxer Shorts It took the LEVI'S launderette ad on Boxing Day '85 with Nick Kamen stripping down to his boxer shorts to bring them out of the history book and back into vogue, and fashion designers and high street stores wasted no time in meeting the new demand. Designers like Scott CROLLA and PAUL SMITH started paying serious attention to the boxer – but by the middle of the decade even the most riotous designs were staple fare at branches of M&S and British Home Stores. Traditional Y-FRONTS have since made a comeback via Calvin Klein but for men keen to avoid the visible pantie line (VPL), boxers remain the most confident bet. The disadvantage? Boxers can't combat bag-sag.

Boxing Charismatic Olympic champion Sugar Ray Leonard launched the present boxing boom when he beat Thomas 'Hit Man' Hearns in '81, unifying the world welterweight title with ring skills unseen since the tragic decline of Mohammed Ali. In the last couple of years the rise of 'Iron' MIKE TYSON has restored credibility to the heavyweight division, seeing off the belly-and-butt contenders used to hitting the larder rather harder than the punchbag. Promoters like ex-con and Shakespeare scholar Don King keep the hype high on the safe side of the ropes – and names like Hagler, McGuigan, Curry, Sanchez, Mugabi and latterly Michael 'Second To' Nunn, made the decade a great one for the hardest game. *See Nigel Benn*

Boy George From 'London's top nandbag thief', squatting in Warren Street to reformed HEROIN addict in Hampstead, Boy George lived the '80s like they were the final decade, which, for him, they nearly were. After debuting with Bow Wow Wow as backing singer Lieutenant Lush in late '80, he formed Culture Club (originally called In Praise Of Lemmings) in '81 with Mikey Craig. Adding

Jon Moss (later George's lover and then bitter ex-lover) and Roy Hay and dressing in clothes emblazoned with Stars of David and Ethiopian flags, the band made it big at the end of '82 with the number one 'Do You Really Want To Hurt Me' and numerous 'Top Of The Pops' appearances flabbergasting the nation and its tabloids which promptly came up with the expression 'gender bender'. 1983 was the band's peak, with the 'Colour By Numbers' LP and George's quip that he would rather have a cup of tea than sex. At this stage the papers loved George, who seemed to have taken over wrestler Big Daddy's mantle as 'The Mums and Dad's favourite'.

In '85, in Paris, George was introduced to HEROIN and by his July '86 appearance at an anti-apartheid concert on Clapham Common was heavily addicted. The press was unrelenting in their pursuit of George, Marilyn and associates. New York keyboard player Michael Rudetski died of an overdose in George's flat and the singer was even apprehended for cannabis possession. In '87 Culture Club finally dissolved. Declaring himself cured on 'Wogan' and thus redeeming himself with the mums and dads, George began his solo career in STYLE with an instant number one, 'Everything I Own'. That single, at the time, was the lowest selling number one single in the UK, and its successors bombed, with the album 'Sold' peaking at number 29. It was significant that the best song on 'Sold' was 'Little Ghost', a tribute to a fellow sybarite Trojan who died

Breakdancing

Back-spins, head-spins, one-hand gliders, smurfing – breakdancing and bodypopping evolved from the 'robotic dancing' that Jeffrey Daniels displayed to the world on his 1980 'Top Of The Pops' appearances with Shalamar. Developed by the fledgling hip hop (or ELECTRO as it was then known) movement, bodypopping (violent, highly controlled muscle spasms) and breakdancing (acrobatic flailing on the floor) American and British crews, practising on street corners to the boom of massive ghetto-blasters, developing their moves to such an extent that tourists would pay busking breakdancers big money to strut their stuff in Covent Garden. By '84 breakdancers were competing for prizes of £2,500 in top-level UK competitions, and even Prince Charles pretended to breakdance on TV. But as hip hop crossed over into the commercial charts, by '86 breakdancing and bodypopping, like GRAFFITI art, had become outmoded, the subject only of hip hop historians and Russ Abbot sketches. *See British Rap*

L to R: Gary Haisman of D-Mob at Spectrum in Boy's Own T-shirt (photo: Dave Swindells).
Breakdancer (photo: Nick Knight).
Boys Wonder.
Broken Glass Street Crew from Manchester (photo: Kevin Cummins) **See Breakdancing.**

of a HEROIN OD. George's voice seemed shot and the lyrics, like the interviews, were obsessive rants aimed at Jon Moss. 1989 saw his second solo LP re-recorded and then shelved. It also saw him apparently enjoying himself at various London ACID HOUSE shindigs, though not, he was quick to point out, with any nefarious stimulants. George's '80s have been a far cry from the sentiments of the Blue Mink song 'Melting Pot' that Culture Club covered in their early days and which stressed the need for homogeneity. The boy's difference will, it seems, constantly undo and redeem him. A fine singing voice too...

Boy's Own The title is a clue to this fanzine's major concerns, a lively if provocative mixture of football news and club views. *Boy's Own*

represented the suburban hordes that West End clubs had successfully kept from their doors for years, until ACID HOUSE. Its humour came from the soccer fan's LIFESTYLE and their music stemmed from the clubs they frequented *après* the big match. The brainchild of Terry Farley and Steve Maze, their six issues have been sporadic to say the least, but with an ever-growing circulation and interest from advertisers, they are now planning regular appearances – with FOOTBALL, ironically enough, receiving less and less coverage.

Boys Wonder Formed in '85 out of the remnants of POSITIVE PUNKers Brigandage, Scott and Ben Addison have taken their vision of British music hall pop culture through half a dozen band members, three singles and 400 gigs. Currently at a cross-

roads, somewhere between Carnaby St and GUNS'N'ROSES, they are wondering why the public never understood. The best British pop band that never was.

Bragg, Billy From Barking, via the British Army, pop's most persuasive leftie has cajoled the jaded conscience of this nation's youth for most of the Thatcher years. In the age of the consumer durable, Billy Braggs' East End vowels and battered electric guitar set permanently on total treble, have been constants, defying the vagaries of fashion and ideology. His '84 debut mini-album, 'Life's A Riot' set the tone with songs of love and leftie sentiment dragged under the banner of cheap and cheerful lo-fi. In many ways, Bragg remains the lone flame of socialist functionalism in a music business whose corporate capitalism he despises. Ironically, it was the charity ethic that brought him his only number one, a reading of 'She's Leaving Home' for Esther Rantzen's Help A London Child. Now a huge cult in the USA, Russia and Europe, his British profile is forever tied to the political pulse where, as one of his recent songs attests, he and his audience are 'Waiting For The Great Leap Forward'.

Branson, Richard Hairy hippy capitalist who tamed the Sex Pistols, BOY GEORGE and wild man of rock Phil Collins, flew the Atlantic (nearly) in a balloon and launched his own range of 'Mates' CONDOMS. Might have made it if he'd tried to fly the

illusion of a local boulevard watering hole. The stunningly revamped Criterion Brasserie also attracted some attention, yet suffered from being on the wrong side of Piccadilly Circus, but it was the SOHO Brazz, as it was affectionately known, that spearheaded the regeneration of SOHO and spawned a thousand imitations in High Streets the length and breadth of the land.

The Brat Pack As Hollywood got hip to the youth audience and MTV, a new star system was born, and Emilio Estevez, Charlie Sheen, Molly Ringwald, Demi Moore, Rob Lowe, Patrick Swayze, Matt Dillon, Tom Cruise, Kiefer Sutherland and others became The Brat Pack.

British Rap

Starting life as a poor relation of its American cousin in the early '80s, by the end of the decade nobody was laughing at British rap anymore. Early UK outfits like Family Qwest and Faze One made little impact beyond Streetsounds ELECTRO compilation LPs and it wasn't until Derek B's funky rap 'Get Down' was picked up by the US label

step closer with the arrival of Breakfast TV in '82. Countering fears about the imminent Americanisation of the airwaves, the Famous Five (Peter Jay, Angela Rippon, Anna Ford, David Frost and Michael Parkinson) announced a Reithian 'mission to explain', but lost out to the Beeb's sofa and sweaters, clearing the way for the ersatz Americana of the new TV-AM, and eggcup full of Anne Diamond, deep trivia and depthless celebrities. CHANNEL 4's early morning yuppievision didn't really improve things. If you actually wanted to wake up to a high fibre high information diet, you still read the paper or listened to the radio. If you wanted to go back to sleep, you watched Breakfast TV.

Atlantic in a condom. His airline Virgin Atlantic was more successful, founded in June '84 with a brief to offer quality flights at cheaper prices – by '87/'88 its profits were £10 million, making Branson Airways the third most profitable airline in the world, and the only airline in the world to use biodegradable carrier bags.

Brasseries Not so very long ago in a bustling SOHO thoroughfare there was a pub very much like any other pub. Until, that is, it became a Brasserie: a vague Gallic interpretation of the traditional combined bar and restaurant. The SOHO Brasserie boasted doors that opened onto the street and close to authentic lopsided tables just large enough to balance four glasses, a packet of Gauloise and a FILOFAX, creating the

Famous parents were optional, photogenic pouts essential as the young guns and teen queens did adolescent angst for their Big Daddy, JOHN HUGHES and others. If the movies didn't always have legs, the phrase itself ran and ran. With everyone wanting the youth market, young talent was found to fit the label and we had the Literary Brat Pack, and the Media Brats. With the necessity of finding a headline pun to hold onto the casually cruising reader, The Brat Pack became The Hack Pack's last resort. Hence, The Brit Pack, The Rap Pack, The Frat Pack, The Comics Rat Pack, The Splat Pack, The Snap Pack, The MATT BLACK Pack, The Chat Pack, The Bat Pack... Time to pack it in – *please*.

Breakfast TV The eventual demise of dead air time came one

Profile Records in '87 that people started to take notice of the new British wave that was getting ready to explode. The Cookie Crew, Overlord X, She Rockers, MC Duke, Monie Love... almost overnight, British rap got its beats and rhymes in place and The Cookie Crew's album, recorded in New York with hip hop heroes Stetsasonic, proved that British rappers had at last achieved global impact.

British Film Year When Colin Welland picked up his '82 Oscar and told a smug Hollywood audience the British were coming, was this a threat or a promise? Hard on the heels of 'Chariots Of Fire' came a whole pile of Empire Daze Classics like 'Another Country', 'Ghandi', and 'A Passage To India', all labouring mightily under Waugh-time illusion and all benefiting greatly from the '85 exercise in silver screen nostalgia that was British Film Year. The publicity campaign even included a special postage stamp issue featuring a Heritage Pantheon of stars like Vivien Leigh and David Niven. It was left to state of the nation diatribes like 'My Beautiful Laundrette', 'Empire State' and 'The Last Of England' to lob into cinemas a more incendiary English Romanticism – contemporary, urban and violent.

Little chance of the Royal Mail approving that.

British Gospel When Madness released 'Wings Of A Dove' in the summer of '83, for once the attention centred not on the nutty boys themselves, but on their backing singers: the snappily-titled Inspirational Choir Of The Pentacostal First Born Church Of The Living God from north London. Suddenly British gospel – a vital force in the black community here since the '50s and before – had gone overground, and everyone wanted a piece. Choirs like the Inspirational or the Rev Basil Meade's innovative, cross-denominational London Community Gospel

Bros The most precocious pop brats in the business were convinced from their early teens that they would become pop stars. Originally called Gloss, Matt, Luke and Craig left school in '84 and immediately started gigging round working men's clubs and south London pubs. Teaming up with their svengali, producer and publisher Nicky Graham, they became transformed from a long-haired pub act into the ultimate '80s teen pop dream. Immaculately styled, clean living and perfectly attuned to the demands of a new teen generation, the three schoolfriends literally became overnight sensations, invoking memories of Osmond mania and declaring their 'love' for their fans. With a stringently researched look of

Bruno, Frank

Frank Bruno was British boxing's great heavy-weight delusion. They said he could take TYSON. He couldn't. The only thing Frank's title fight evoked was the memory of the late great Joe Louis. Each month Joe would fight a new contender, in his own inimitable STYLE he called them The Bum Of The Month Club. Only Britain thought Bruno was great,

heavy funk, he spent most of the '80s being recycled by rappers, record producers and two-bit rogues. At the height of his renewed popularity he did the ungentlemanly thing and tried to shoot his wife, the local law man and anyone else who got in the way. The Godfather has returned to his own poor and semi-criminal roots and now resides in the state penitentiary where the only sex machines on hand are hard bitten southern guards. Suddenly, neither foot's the good foot.

Buffalo Buffalo, in the words of the song, is a stance, an attitude – dare I say it – evolving from and pertaining to, The Street, and thankfully nowhere near as pompous as it

Choir were in demand for concerts in secular venues, to add spark to anything from TV variety programmes to 'Songs Of Praise'. But of the vocal talent that emerged, few have successfully crossed over to pop careers. Paul Johnson, a former member of the influential funk/gospel group Paradise, has released two sophisticated solo albums on CBS without yet producing a hit single, while Sister Lavine Hudson, despite sensitive marketing from Virgin, has yet to make a real impact. Ironically, 18 year old Mica Paris has made most inroads into the charts, but dressed in minis that would make even the most progressive pastors frown, she has kept few of her gospel roots. Proving perhaps, that though the pop public may be ready for the voices, they are not yet willing to accept the beliefs that inspired them.

RIPPED JEANS and customised DMs, they borrowed every street fashion cliché and filled the streets with a million lookalike Brosettes. But it took their second single 'When Will I Be Famous' (their first one flopped) to do it – an insight into the aspirations of their generation and the most fitting eulogy to the decade. *See American Classics*

Brown, Bobby The soul sex symbol of '89, 19 year old Bobby sang 'My Prerogative', swivelled his hips to producer Teddy Riley's syncopated swingbeats, and the whole of black America went weak at the knees. It was the first time a black soul sex symbol was aged under 35.

Brown, James James Brown is more sinned against than sinning, but only just. Always the Godfather of

to the rest of the world he was a bum of the month.

L to R: Brasserie See **Brasseries**. *Billy Bragg (photo: Jayne). Bass Weejun loafers (photo: Nick Knight). Dianne Brill. Joseph Beuys. i-D straight up Belinda '82. Frank Bruno. James Brown.*

sounds. The godfather of Buffalo – a loose knit clique that includes lensman MARC LEBON and i-D contributing fashion editor JUDY BLAME – is the late menswear STYLIST supremo Ray Petri (died August '89), whose work with photographer Jamie Morgan – most memorably in *THE FACE*, but also within the pages of i-D and *ARENA* – defined the predominant STYLE of the decade. 'Tougher Than The Rest' is Petri's Buffalo definition. It's a tag he first used to describe the attitude and dress code of a bunch of his Parisian friends in the early part of the decade, before redefining and exporting it back across the Channel and into the pages of the new breed of simpatico magazines. It was Petri who dressed the world in the black MA-1 FLIGHT JACKET, and gave the young urban male a strong, sartorial voice, even flaunting convention and putting them in skirts. His influence on the look of the decade, from the streets of London to SYDNEY, via Milan, New York, Paris, Tokyo and all points between cannot be over-estimated. From ADVERTISING to cinema, from catwalks to dance-floors, Petri's children will continue to stake out their territory with a Buffalo Stance well into the '90s and beyond. *See Neneh Cherry*

Burchill, Julie The most re-viled journalist of her age, Burchill is the ultimate punk apostate. Born of working class stock in Bristol, she started life as a speed-toting *NME* hack, moved onto *THE FACE* where her opinionated column found her

wooed by the grown-up press. *TIME OUT*, the *Mail On Sunday* and Murdoch have all employed her but her financial future seems assured with her second marriage to pub-lisher Cosmo Landesman. Her first, to punk contemporary Tony Parsons is the subject of much bitter, public dirty washing. After three pretty sharp critical face-offs against society *The Boy Looked At Johnny*, *Damaged Gods* and *Girls On Film* she succumbed to the lucrative lure of the shopping and fucking genre with *Ambition*, a steamy (but not as steamy as the hype suggested) tale of Fleet Street backstabbing that made her pots of loot and a lot more enemies. Julie Burchill hates every-thing except for Jewish left-wing American men with big penises.

Brylcreem

Times have changed since sleekly groomed cricketer Dennis Compton was pic-tured brushing a brillian-tine called Brylcreem into his carefully parted hair back in the '50s. The name has remained the same but since a carefully marketed revamp in '85, the Brylcreem product range has broadened to include gel, deodorant, aftershave – the cosmetic

arsenal modern , man needs to face the world beyond his bathroom with confidence. In Dennis' day Brylcreem came in a glass jar with a red lid. Now the range comes fashionably packaged in black.

L to R: Buffalo styling by Ray Petri.
Buffalo styling by Ray Petri (photo: Robert Erdmann).
Buffalo styling by Ray Petri (photo: Marc Lebon).
Buffalo styling by Ray Petri (photo: Jamie Morgan/Ray Petri).

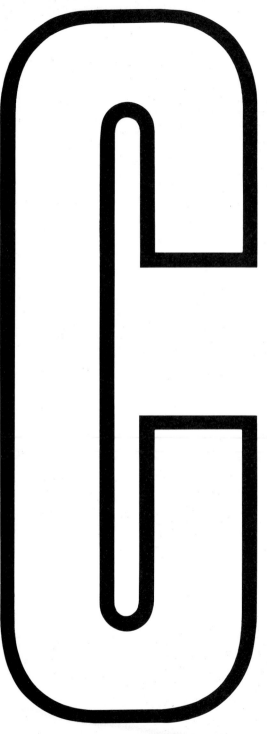

Cafe de Paris A joint venture for photographer/host Nick Fry and Parisian DJ Albert, the Cafe de Paris opened on April 16 '86 at just the right time. THE MUD CLUB, Black Market and even TABOO were all over-familiar and London's nightlife needed the perfect posing and cruising venue that the '20s ballroom provided. It only took a month for the Gallic charm of Albert's *chansons* and Latin rhymes to catch on, then *everybody* came and they all had to pay admission, regardless of their fame – a real shock to Tina Turner, who wasn't pleased, and to the London clubland's ligger circuit. At its peak, Sloanes, buppies, fashion victims, dancefloor ravers and Evita-clone Euroclubbers in mini-skirts

would all party together, squeezing past one of the toughest door policies in town. Although it was no longer *essential* by late '87 and was almost dragged into the ACID HOUSE explosion in '88, it has remained *the* midweek club classic despite being open to the charge of letting too many Top Shop trendies in.

Camden Market Camden as marketland began in the '70s around the canal at Camden Lock. By the '80s the weekend stalls had spread like wildfire with two main sites – the original Lock and an area just north of the tube station. In the early part of the decade it was still the preserve of Londoners alone who appreciated the good mix of bargain records, bootleg tapes, retro clothing, innovative jewellery and street fashion by young designers. BODYMAP

Camden Palace From the ashes of the Music Machine, the Camden Palace became the first purpose-built club of the '80s that wasn't owned by Mecca. Co-designed by Steve Strange, it opened in April '82, and waved a fond farewell to the NEW ROMANTICS. With BLITZ still fresh in the minds of London clubbers, Steve Strange could do no wrong and for about a year 'Slum It In Style' on Tuesdays was the only place to be. It signalled a move away from the one-nighter ethos of taking over anything with four walls, but after STEVE STRANGE left, by the end of the '80s the venue was a shadow of its former self. Today, the only excitement is in the photographs of the early '80s hanging on the walls.

L to R: Cafe De Paris (photo: Dave Swindells). Craig Charles.

started here, MARK & SYRIE touted their wares and Red Or Dead launched their DMs from a small stall at the lower market. But rumours of cut-price HAMNETT and dirt cheap Eccentrics quickly spread and before long Camden was firmly on the tourist trail. Prices and originality inevitably suffered and by '88 the whole of Camden Town became one big market with stalls crammed into every available nook, and even the Electric Ballroom became a makeshift market on Sundays. Even as we speak, the face of Camden is changing yet again with the original Lock complex undergoing a complete revamp, and some people fear that it could end up looking like Covent Garden. *See King's Road and Kensington Market*

Cameo Double-taking '70s giants like Earth Wind & Fire through a melodic sensibility as weird as the Gang Of Four, Larry Blackmon's group Cameo presented a fusion of acid funk and cartoon rock with a repertoire of dance routines and costumes that were the epitome of stupid fresh. Thanks partly to his depiction of the black man as overlord in control (as opposed to the prevalent Trenchtown outlaw fantasy), and his productions' use of subtlety as an offensive weapon, Blackmon had to wait seven years and ten albums to taste international success with 'She's Strange' in '84. After that the hits flowed like wine – 'Attack Me With Your Love', 'Single Life', 'Word Up', 'Candy' – but, symptomatically for the '80s, Larry became more famous for his image than his music. In America he can boast the most influential haircut in black music history, whilst in Britain (where people still remember GRACE JONES and the Mac Curtis) the name Cameo has become synonymous with gleaming red codpieces.

Caplan, Melissa In the early '80s Melissa Caplan's fashion design company Palium Products created bizarre combinations of clothing. Tabards, multi-pleat trousers,

dresses, aprons and shirts with cutaway sleeves were worn layer upon layer, held together with tie belts. These odd looking garments featured hand drawn prints and were modelled by a trendy London set including Toyah Wilcox, STEVE STRANGE and John Maybury. Part of the first wave of young '80s UK designers, Palium Products shone bright but faded fast. *See Fashion Designers*

Car Boot Sales The jumble sales of the '80s, these alfresco SHOPPING MALLS are ideal if you have £5 to spend and want to buy platform sole boots, Osmond '70s annuals, GARY NUMAN albums, cheap trinkets, high camp light shades and Star Wars toys. They can supply you with everything you never needed the first time round but are prepared to purchase now they cost only pennies. Anyone who has a highly developed sense of instant nostalgia should try wasting a couple of hours picking up on our immediate past. This is recycling suburban '80s STYLE.

Cartoon Movies An '80s phenomenon, toon films are films made to look like cartoons whilst not actually sporting a single animated frame. Whether they're based on a real cartoon strip (*Superman, BATMAN, Swamp Thing, THE WATCHMEN*), or just filmed to look like one ('Robocop'), all good toon films are distinguished by their appropriation of the visual tricks cartoonists use to bring drama to the frozen page. The subtle lighting, gracious sweeps and static camera angles of traditional cinema are replaced by primal colours and OTT special effects, violent editing and crooked close-ups to appeal to a generation that has fallen in love with comics afresh.

Casuals Perhaps no so-called STYLE cult of the '80s has been so obviously anti-fashion as the Casual. Predominantly urban and working-class the Casual first reared its head at the tail-end of the '70s. Spawned

Casely-Hayford, Joe

Part of the second wave of young UK fashion talent that included NICK COLEMAN, RICHMOND/ CORNEJO and JOHN GALLIANO, Joe Casely-Hayford always paid acute attention to detail. Although he left ST MARTIN'S in the late '70s it wasn't until '86 that he produced his first full collection. Well-tailored and wide-ranging, his clothes are exceptionally well-made with intricate and idiosyncratic detail and high quality fabrics.

See Fashion Designers

Carphones

When the boys' toys and fad gadgets of executive chic returned with a vengeance, transforming your motor into a mobile office with a carphone was less about making a commitment to efficiency and more about making a status gesture. Being seen doing deals was the thing. With some execs claiming to prefer work to sex, carphone users were like exhibitionist braggarts. Even stuck in a jam on the M25, they made sure everyone knew they were still on the job.

by the football terraces and suburban discotheques, its original colours were those of the prematurely middle-aged. Dressed in Farah 'slacks', Pringle 'meres' (Cashmere sweaters), silk shirts and Burberry macs the Casual (boy or girl) cherished a passion for the expensive side of fashion that was ruled by the tenet 'beg, borrow or steal'; if you couldn't beg your mum to buy it, borrow it from your Dad, and if you couldn't borrow it from your Dad...

Outfitted like young Gary Players (and often armed with an outsize golfing umbrella – or worse, the eventually ubiquitous STANLEY KNIFE) these arch-conservatives would spend their time fly-pitching, shop-lifting, gambling or just drifting (favoured haunts: the nascent pub-discos of the Hackney Road, Bethnal Green and Old Kent Road). Perms, 'tom' (tomfoolery – jewellery, gold and lots of it) and Gabbiccis (leather edged Italian cardigans) were favoured by both male and female Casuals and this trend remained as the '80s developed and the look softened. By '84 the Casual had moved wholesale into a brave new world of leisure wear; Lacoste and Fila polo shirts had replaced the silks, tight Italian jeans had replaced the more formal slacks and Diadora trainers had replaced the expensive crocodile slip-ons (which fortunately put an end to the danger of accidentally scuffing a Casual's shoe). Grooming however, remained paramount and rivalry on the terraces increased as fans battled to outdress each other (fever pitch was reached when opposing fans started to throw paint on each other's clothes – far more damaging to the individual than six stitches).

Sports stores were frequent targets for burglary and shops started to sport bouncers in attempts at thwarting rising thefts; shoplifting plumbed new depths as youngsters, desperate to increase their own status, took to carving off Lacoste crocodiles instore, re-applying the legendary marque to their own inferior brand shirt at home. As we

L to R: The Christians. Fashion designer Alice Rycroft in one of her own Catsuits '84 (photo: Monica Curtin). Lynne Franks modelling at The Parachute Show See Catwalk Shows. Model Naomi Campbell (photo: Marc Lebon). Michael Clark wearing BodyMap '84 (photo: Richard Houghton).

enter the '90s the Casual is, to a certain extent dead. Having never been anything really other than an easy tag and a loose uniform they have been superseded by the far happier children of the revolution (circa '88 SUMMER OF LOVE) – the so-called Acid Teds. Gone but not forgotten the Casual will be remembered rather ironically as the ushers of leisure wear and the late '80s fashion of non-fashion. *See Dressing Down, Eurostyle and Paninari*

Catsuits The catsuit, pioneered by The Avengers' Emma Peel in the '60s and glammed up in the '70s by David Bowie and Gary Glitter, made a re-appearance in '85 when designer Alice Rycroft under the label Atom

re-introduced the body conscious catsuit. Overnight the body became (some) girls' best friend, as the layers and folds of the predominant fashion trends of the early '80s gave way to an emphasis on the contours of the female frame. When PAM HOGG, Emilio Cavallini, BODYMAP, Alaia and a host of other designers updated this silhouette in '88, everybody from Mandy Smith to Naomi Campbell ensured that women's bodies stayed under the spotlight. The growth in fetish fashion also contributed to the trend, with She An Me, Zeitgeist, Pure Sex and SKIN TWO offering RUBBER, PVC and leather catsuits with zips and stud details in intimate places. KATHARINE HAMNETT put the icing on the cake with her luxurious velour version for winter '89 and brought new meaning to slinky simplicity. *See*

Bodybuilding, Health Clubs and Health Farms

Catwalk Shows The catwalk formula of six foot waifs in formation sweeping down a runway suddenly became a thing of the past in '84 when BODYMAP staged their first catwalk show. It grabbed the fashion headlines worldwide as organised chaos reigned supreme. Pop stars, performers, dancers, and assorted friends mingled freely with various members of Stevie Stewart and David Holah's families, to a party atmosphere provided by Jeffrey Hinton's manic soundtrack. Suddenly it was more a question of how the clothes were shown rather than what, as ever stranger gimmicks were thought up. The Parachute show in the same year caused a riot when the models, already planted in the audience, got up on stage, stripped and dressed in front of everyone and then proceeded to trash the show. MOSCHINO, RICHMOND/CORNEJO and MARK & SYRIE amongst others, all applied their own individual ideas for catwalk extravaganzas, and by '89 it became a matter of course for designers like VIVIENNE WESTWOOD or KATHARINE HAMNETT to have their starlets strip off or come on accompanied by half empty bottles of drink. *See Fashion Designers*

Cazals Square-framed specs so popular in Manhattan circa '84 that people would literally kill for them.

Censorship In the '80s censor-

ship cut deeper and deeper into our lives, and it wasn't just a question of removing the designer violence from 'MIAMI VICE'. Behind the scenes the government has massaged figures and abolished unflattering statistics, and in public it has been to court and changed laws – all to control the free flow of information. The key events – the VIDEO NASTIES scare, the Ponting and Tisdall trials, the Zircon affair, and the Spycatcher fiasco. The key piece of legislation – the '84 Video Recordings Act, CLAUSE 28, the '88 ban on broadcast interviews with 'terrorists and their supporters' in Northern Ireland, and the new Official Secrets Act which radically curtails press and broadcast freedoms. In the '90s when you want to know what's really happening here, you'll have to read the *New York Times*, *Liberation* or even *Pravda*.

Champagne Socialism One of the decade's big dilemmas – whether it was possible to own a JPG suit and a Labour Party membership card without experiencing a political identity crisis – seemed to be solved by Champagne Socialism, an attempt to mix the pleasure principle with political principles. The key moment came in '86 when Neville Brody redesigned the *New Socialist*, while inside Robert Elms suggested that worrying about what LOAFERS to wear didn't preclude worrying about the government. The new equation – socialism minus guilt plus STYLE – was meant to add up to an increase in the Left's political potency. But after DESIGNER MARXISM, the red rose replacing ideology, Champagne Socialism now just seems like the first step in the rightward drift towards the new Policy Reviewed Labour Party – an SDP for the '90s.

Channel 4 While deregulation brought scores of new channels to America, in Britain we got just one more button on the remote control, when Channel 4 came on-screen in '82. Although the tabloids screamed 'Channel Bore' and other critics

Cha Cha's A young model/hairdresser turned club hostess, Scarlett hit upon the idea of turning the seedy, gay Cellar Bar behind HEAVEN into Cha Cha's. The opening in summer '81 heralded the start of a non-serious, easy-going relationship between the club and its patrons. The door policy was so relaxed that the odd Arab and American tourist leaked past the

door and musically, anything went. Film soundtracks, glam rock, Hi-NRG and hit parade pop – a pot pourri of anti-fashion sounds – attracted gays and straights in equal numbers, a first for London clubland.

Clark, Michael As at home on a catwalk as he is at the barre or on stage at Sadler's Wells, Michael Clark is the man who, with the help of his company, dragged contemporary dance kicking and screaming out of a fusty, closet full of legwarmers and crumpled photos of Nureyev and into the '80s. Trained at The Royal School, Michael was the prodigiously gifted pupil who opted out of the dance mainstream and sought sanctuary amongst FASHION DESIGNERS, pop stars and nightclubbers. Drawing inspiration from his nights spent tripping the light fantastic in clubs like TABOO, his company's performance eschewed Tchaikovsky in favour of THE FALL and T Rex, danced in dildoes and platforms and included guest performers like the graceful LEIGH BOWERY. As well as a penchant for BODYMAP, whose electrifying early CATWALK SHOWS he choreographed, he looks great in a tu-tu, too.

labelled it ITV 2, C4 has made and continues to make a difference. It may sometimes resemble a clearing house for televisual imports (AMERICAN FOOTBALL, SUMO WRESTLING, Brazilian SOAPS, 'HILL STREET BLUES') but it has also produced 'Brookside', 'The Last Resort', C4 News, 'THE TUBE' and 'NETWORK 7' (first series). It stimulated the British film industry with Film On Four and its multi-coloured tumbling bricks in space logo turned TV graphics upside down. On the downside however, C4 was responsible for the most over-rated invention of the decade, the Video Box (and Access TV) – enough to make anyone wish there was a good tele-evangelist to channel hop to instead. *See Short Films*

Chaps Outside Clint Eastwood movies, chaps started the '80s as part of the gay and fetish club uniform in PVC and leather, and ended up as designer fashion. First utilised by Helen Robinson of PX in '83, it wasn't until '88 when PAM HOGG and JP GAULTIER took the basic idea of the cowboy chap and swapped the usual fabric for fake fur, gold and silver leather, and pinstripe, silk and lace respectively. With PAM HOGG especially, the chap became seen as part of a cowboy revival that never really happened. The COUNTRYBILLY scene in the mid-'80s was the closest, and even in clubs like Son Of Redneck in '88, the predominant look was still checked shirts and boot lace ties. With the demise of the clone gay scene (*See AIDS*) and so long as the only cowboys remain the fly-pitchers on Oxford St, it's unlikely that chaps will ever cross back over to the streets.

Chat Shows TV's chattering classes held forth and held sway like never before in the '80s. There was mainstream blarney from 'Wogan', silvery smoothness from 'Aspel', highbrow waffle from 'The Late Clive James' and ironic patter from the 'Last Resort' and the Youth TV Chat Pack (JONATHAN ROSS, Ruby Wax, Rowland Rivron). Although, like the

Prime Minister, TV talk threatens to go on and on and on, there have been changes. Recently real people have replaced so-so celebs as the human cannon fodder in the TV war of words. TV chat now comes from ordinary Joes and Josephines, who chew the fat on 'Kilroy' about SALMAN RUSHDIE or why the trains don't run on time, or talk through their problems on 'Family Affairs'. But though TV talk now wants to get real, the decade's best chat was the most unreal. Glitzy, glamorous and tightly scripted, 'The Dame Edna Experience' left the rest looking tongue-tied.

Chernobyl The effects of the Soviet nuclear reactor explosion at Chernobyl are still being felt. The explosion, caused by a series of human errors, occurred at 1.23 am on April 26 '86 and was first detected in Sweden on April 28. Two people were killed outright, plus a further 28 from acute radiation sickness and within a week, much of Europe had been covered by radioactive fallout. Although less severely affected than Italy, West Germany or Greece, the UK did not escape contamination, despite MARGARET THATCHER's immediate claim to the contrary in the House Of Commons on April 29. In fact, the British government adopted the same policy of secrecy as the GLASNOST-era GORBECHEV regime, not warning citizens about radioactive fallout and never acting until the last possible moment. Milk was contaminated by Iodine-131 and Caesium, as was lamb. On 20 June, the slaughter of sheep was banned in certain areas, and although the government stated that the bans would last three weeks, 21 months later they were still in operation. The long term effects of the radioactive fallout from Chernobyl are not calculable; estimates of the numbers of cancers caused by the fallout range from 25,000 to 500,000, and the disinformation issued by both British and Soviet governments in the wake of the accident make it clear that if it happened again, they still wouldn't tell us the truth.

Clause 28 Already hemmed in by tabloid AIDS paranoia and hysteria over the children's book, *Jenny Lives With Eric And Martin*, gays began to feel positively claustrophobic when in '88 the government moved to stop local authorities 'promoting' homosexuality with the infamous Clause 28. Worded vaguely enough to allow for the suppression of gay film,

Cherry, Neneh She smiled out from the cover of *THE FACE* in November '88, and within weeks Neneh Cherry had conquered the British charts with her tough pop/rap 'BUFFALO Stance' (number three UK and USA). Originally recorded by STOCK, AITKEN & WATERMAN in '86 as the b-side to the Morgan/McVey single 'Looking Good Diving', the song had been revamped by DJ Tim Simenon and was promoted by a heavily pregnant Neneh. By the time of the next single, 'Manchild', baby Tyson had been born but still featured in the act by appearing in the VIDEO. Smart, sexy and with all the right connections, Neneh is a face perfectly suited to the '90s.

arts and literature, its basic intent is unmistakable – to turn the clocks back to pre-'60s days of prejudice, censorship, discrimination and intolerance.

L to R: Jasper Conran (photo: Steve Dixon). Neneh Cherry '85 (photo: Marc Lebon). Sue Clowes '82 (photo: Steve Johnston). Glasgow designers The Cloth '86.

Chinos Attempting to further cash in on the universal craving for all things rugged, authentic and American, after the success of 'TOP GUN' and their own jeans advertising campaigns, LEVI'S pushed their Chinos trousers onto the late '80s market. Originally worn in the Spanish-American war in the Phillipines in the early years of the 20th Century, these cotton twill khaki peg tops (with full button fly) worked their way into the collective psyche during the 2nd World War when worn by American aviators and GIs who 'pitched their courage against machine and elements'. By '88 they had become a part of the AMERICAN CLASSICS uniform of LEVI'S 501s, Bass Weejun LOAFERS and John Smedley shirts, and the only fighting they experienced was over their creases – they are a bastard to iron.

Clogs Traditionally a northern factory workwear shoe, it was adopted by New Model Army and their fans, commonly known as 'The Followers', in the mid '80s, who bought their clogs from the Walkley Mill 'clog clinic' in Bradford. GAULTIER used them in his show in '86 but it was S-Tek who introduced them to the fashion market with their dayglo, studded varieties and their high heeled versions for RICHMOND/CORNEJO.

Red Or Dead, ever tuned to a nascent street trend, came up with the high street answer and made a killing. A word of warning: even though they were designed to let you spend eight hours on your feet, this does not include dancing.

Clowes, Sue Sue Clowes saw herself essentially as a TEXTILE DESIGNER, but was fortunate enough to parade her first collection across our TV screens in '81 when BOY GEORGE and Culture Club wore her designs printed with iconoclastic images of Judaism and Catholicism. Her designs became an instant hit with teenyboppers and fashion editors and were copied worldwide. A later collection, 'Flesh & Steel', in '84 pre-empted the move towards SPORTSWEAR as a fashionable concern, with its 'MPH' print vests and jersey leggings. Later still, prompted by the OLYMPIC MANIA overkill, she created a collection of pyjama suits and smoking jackets, 'In The Arms Of Morpheus', which were intended for daywear. "They are for passive people who sleep during the day in front of the TV," she remarked. *See Fashion Designers*

Ciné Brats With JEAN-JACQUES BEINEIX the new enfants chics of the French cinema, Luc Besson and Leos Carax, looked briefly like a return to the heady iconoclasm of the '60s, when Truffaut, Godard et al stormed the establishment at Cannes. But the promise of Besson's captivating 'La Dernier Bataille', a black and white, near silent, post-holocaust vision of quirky beauty and eccentric imagination, was unfulfilled by the trendy vapidity of 'Subway' in which Christopher Lambert and Isabelle Adjani posed against metropolitan backgrounds. The New Age mysticism of 'The Big Blue', the dolphin movie to end them all, won huge audiences in France but barely sold a ticket abroad. Carax is the most inventive

of the group. His 'Boy Meets Girl' and 'The Night Is Young' are strongly influenced by comic books, but unfortunately, his metaphysical longeurs make for barely watchable movies.

The Circus Along with THE DIRTBOX, The Circus was one of the seminal warehouse parties of the decade. From the first Haysi Fantayzee Party (of whom Jeremy Healy helped run The Circus) in September '82 at Cleveland St, to the eighth and final one at Bagley's Warehouse in King's Cross in '84, The Circus was a mixed media event in every sense of the word. Celebrities, ragamuffins, models and media brats all rubbed shoulders listening to Healy's pre-recorded cut-up tapes, surrounded by John Maybury's paintings, early SCRATCH VIDEOS, drapes and trans-

L to R: Caffe Bongo in Tokyo by Nigel Coates (photo: Stephen Male). Nick Coleman '87 (photo: Kevin Davies). Carwash See Westworld (photo: Dave Swindells). Condoms (photo: Roberto Carra)

Condoms

The '80s was the decade when condoms shed their toilet vending-machine image and became one of the major topics of dinnertable discussion. As the first ever Durex TV advertisements cajoled us to find a place in our hearts (and underpants) for these pale pink, rolled-up balloons, the growing concern about AIDS caused RICHARD BRANSON to launch

parent plastic, as everybody wallowed in a sense of occasion. The precursor, however modest, to WESTWORLD.

City Limits

Formed from the *TIME OUT* strike of '81 over pay parity, the London listings magazine *City Limits* was set up as a workers' collective (not co-operative – there is a difference, although nobody was quite sure what). All staff from editors to receptionist were paid the same and it catered to a perceived 'alternative' readership whose interests weren't served by *TIME OUT*. That was the theory anyhow. The most successful worker's collective in publishing, it managed to pay off a GLC loan by '84, but never really happily resolved one fundamental problem – how do you run a weekly magazine where every

Coleman, Nick

Although Nick Coleman's '84 ST MARTIN'S graduation collection leaned more to fetish fashion, with his studded and nailed leather garments, it was his innovative yet classic tailoring that made his name. Beautiful fabrics, old fashioned cutting and his use of a multitude of buttons, hooks, pleats and folds incorporated S&M influences that accentuated body shape and possessed a sexual elegance that was always wearable. Immediately snapped up by the Italians, who now handle all his headaches, Nick has earned himself a reputation as the young businessman of British fashion.

See Fashion Designers.

decision, in theory, is made by 40 people? Testament to the fact that democracy breeds debate.

Clarke, Frank

A vituperative tornado of camp rage and acerbic wit, Frank Clarke and sister Margi (self-styled Queen of the Scallies) bounced into national colour supplements when 'Letter To Brezhnev' joined 'My Beautiful Launderette' as the most quoted low-budget hit of the year (the two ended up playing in West End double bills). This Liverpudlian love story, penned by Frank and starring Margi with 'Brookside' refugee Alexandra Pigg, was a shot in the arm for a depressed industry, demonstrating that with a bit of initiative, a lot of balls, and a good script, anything can happen. Successor to (Willy) Russell and (ALAN) BLEASDALE, Clarke's follow up 'The Fruit Machine' proved a disappointing allegory, but one minute in his high-octane company and you know this man is destined to hotwire his way into the fast lane.

Cleese, John

"The funniest man in England" (Rowan Atkinson) surfaced from silence and soul-searching (and a book about families) to take the Hollywood hot one hundred by storm with 'A Fish Called Wanda'.

his Mates (cut-price condoms sold in a variety of shops, relieving male embarrassment at the chemists), and KATHARINE HAMNETT to add condom pockets to her BOXER SHORTS in '87. The standard rubber johnny now appears in a variety of shapes, sizes, colours and flavours, and even the Pope's most recent decree on birth control accepted their use – provided they had a hole in the end. *See AIDS and Safe Sex*

The first non-Bond British film to reach the US number one slot since the War, this superthin comedy had Cleese hamming only inches away from the Fawlty persona that has dogged him to the point of near breakdown. While some of Cleese's previous films like 'Clockwise' succumbed to Basil-dom, 'Wanda' escaped however, and septuagenarian director Charles Crichton delivered a lightfingered slapstick charmer akin to his early work at Ealing. Cleese may have made millions from 'Wanda', but Basil remains his classic invention. One of the first TV programmes to become a VIDEO hit, every 'Fawlty Towers' repeat is a sure ratings grabber, and "Don't mention the war!" has entered into the vernacular.

Clinton, George One of the most imaginative manipulators of sounds and word ever to have graced any musical genre, George Clinton matched his ambition with success in the '70s, and though he was at the forefront of the ELECTRO boom in '82 with his 'Atomic Dog' hit, a legion of problems have kept Clinton's profile fairly low this decade. Nevertheless the influence of his legacy is visible in every facet of current black music – sampled by hip hop acts, plagiarised lock, stock and barrel by GO GO bands, and cited as an inspiration by everyone else. Meanwhile, Bootsy Collins – the yin to George's yang within P-funk – has been working with everyone from Ryuichi Sakamoto to MALCOLM MCLAREN, and a P-funk relaunch now seems imminent.

The Clothes Show 'The Clothes Show' first appeared on TV screens in '86 presented by Jeff Banks, Selina Scott and then later *i-D*'s fashion editor Caryn Franklin. Preceded by CHANNEL 4's tongue in cheek but short-lived fashion series 'SWANK', 'The Clothes Show' was the first ever BBC programme dedicated totally to fashion, and was closely followed by the not so successful ITV answer 'Frocks On The

Couch Potatoes

Mid-'80s America, with its 40 plus channels, spawned the couch potato phenomenon, the most sedentary movement in history, comprising of telly addicts proud of their inactivity. As Bob Armstrong, Sacramento-based 'father' of the movement attests, "In half an hour of television you can experience more than most people do in a whole month." Watch 'Dallas' and 'Dynasty' and you'll be served a LIFESTYLE that you could never attain anyway." Britain, with its paltry number of channels was slower to take up the cause, but VIDEO rental sales boomed and the imminent deregulation of TV caused apoplexy in moral guardians throughout the land. Membership of this 10,000 strong body is easy - anybody who can watch 'Bull's Eye' for the full 30 minutes can join.

Box'. A reflection of fashion's increased mainstream profile in the '80s, 'The Clothes Show' became an important platform for ideas, designers and shops – even student awards such as The Smirnoff fashion show and The Courtelle Awards were given national airtime.

CND

"When things go bad for the world, they go well for CND," remarked a spokesperson at the end of the '80s. By that logic, the '80s have been the perfect decade for the Campaign For Nuclear Disarmament. After the fallow period of the mid-'60s to mid-'70s when Vietnam dominated all right-thinking persons' thoughts, nuclear weapons were back on the agenda as, with the aid of the newly elected Tories, America decided to plant Trident, Cruise and Pershing 2 in Europe. As sites were discussed, CND's membership boomed: in October '81 a Hyde Park Rally attracted 250,000 sympathisers, and KATHARINE HAMNETT's '58% Don't Want Pershing' T-SHIRTS provided ample photo opportunities. As the GREENHAM COMMON women dug in at the proposed Cruise missile base, the government set up, with a million pounds, a special propaganda unit to put the nation right.

In mid-'83, however, another Hyde Park rally attracted a record 400,000, as well as the debut performance by Paul Weller's STYLE COUNCIL, and by '84 CND had 200,000 paid-up members and manifold offshoot groups like Christian CND and Youth CND. CHERNOBYL reactivated concern in the now Cruise filled UK, but optimism rose with December '87's REAGAN/GORBACHEV INF treaty. Although in favour of any scheme that could reduce the arms arsenal, CND were branded unilateral loonies and Stalinist Fifth Columnists by the dominant press throughout the '80s, and were frequently cited as a prime reason for the Labour Party's ailing fortunes. In return, the 'peace' (always in inverted commas) movement accused the government of various dirty tricks,

from phone tapping to the suspicious death of veteran campaigner Hilda Murrell. By the late '80s though, the entrance of GLASNOST into the media vernacular and the relaxing of 'nuclear panic', the newspapers and general public lost interest in CND resulting in a fall in membership and speculation of its continuing relevance. CND's very success has contributed to the current state of almost media indifference, but so long as the world has an arsenal of 46,000 nuclear warheads (the equivalent to 100 million Hiroshimas) and the potential scenarios (Korea/Middle East/Pakistan/South Africa, etc) that could result in someone pressing the nuclear button, CND's work will never be over.

Coates, Nigel

The man who put the street back into ARCHITECTURE. Chief guru at the Architectural Association in the early '80s, Coates looked like staying a paper architect until in '85 Tokyo gave him the chance to make concrete his ecstatic visions of an eclectic, carnivalesque "narrative architecture". Raiding imagery from film, music, fashion and the decaying inner city to construct a series of Garbage Baroque bars and restaurants, he transformed the art of building into a form of urban landscape design and made his reputation as Britain's most exciting new architect.

Coca Cola

Running scared in the Cola Wars, Coke met the Pepsi Challenge in '85 by changing the recipe of its all-American tooth solvent. Launched in April, the slightly sweeter new Coke didn't wash with the Great American Public who staged a consumer revolt. By July, heralded as a DESIGN CLASSIC, as Coke's sales figures regained their fizz, the world was left wondering – an example of consumer power or the cleverest marketing scam of the decade?

Cocktail Pubs

SPANDAU BALLET have got a lot to answer for.▶

Cox, Patrick

Six months into his first year at Cordwainer's College, Patrick Cox was already designing shoes for VIVIENNE WESTWOOD. By his second year he was designing for BODYMAP, and after graduating he worked on collections for GALLIANO, Alistair Blair and John Flett. His most prominent shoe design was the extended tongue, black and

white lace up, that was copied by every high street store two years after Patrick designed it in '86. Pioneer of the chain mail heel and RUBBER wedge sole, Patrick secured a licensing deal with the Italian market in '89

L to R: Jack Mingo author of **The Couch Potato Guide To Life***(photo: Bob Wagner).*
Patrick Cox's '88 collection (photo: Andrew MacPherson).
Tom Dixon in his studio '86.
Ron Arad's 'Rover Chair' '85 See Creative Salvage.

Creative Salvage When Tom Dixon coined a phrase to characterise the baroque MAD MAX furniture he had constructed from old engine parts and plumbing pipes he demonstrated one way to screw cash from post-industrial chaos and ensured that 'Steptoe And Son' would never seem quite so funny again. Ron Arad was another figure who rag-picked his way through the scrapyard and into the converted warehouse interior, stripping down old cars and recycling the parts into cult objects with names like the Rover Chair and the Aerial Light. In each case it was hard to spot the ART from the design, the theory from the hype, and rather easier to figure the use-value from the image-value. *See Customising, Funkapolitan and Drive-In Demolition Disco Derby*

LOW TO MIDDLE
Warning: SMOKING CAN
Health Departments'

AR As defined by H.M. Government
CAUSE FATAL DISEASES
ief Medical Officers

◄ Steering clear of sawdusty pub rock, the pansticked posers conducted interviews and generally 'hung out' in cocktail bars, swigging back pina coladas and generally being hedonistic and sporting cardboard umbrellas behind their ears. Kid Creole consequently made a career out of cocktail chic, and the whole caboodle was feebly lampooned by bandwagon-jumping epicurians Wham! on 'Club Tropicana', which only succeeded in persuading landlords up and down the land, to serve slow screwdrivers instead of pints and turn their pubs into garish altars to pseudo-sophistication. *See Fun Pubs*

Coldcut At the beginning of '87 a white label 12" called 'Say Kids What Time Is It?' was released by Coldcut – the first British DJ record of any note, ever. Jonathon More and Matt Black, two KISS FM DJs with strong roots in the London club scene, recorded it in their bedrooms on a four track cassette player, two turntables and with the copious use of the pause button, pressed 2,000 copies and waited to see what would happen. Everybody assumed it was American, five month's later it turned up as a sample on M/A/R/R/S' 'Pump Up The Volume', and by February '88 they had a number six hit with 'Doctorin' The House' with YAZZ on lead vocals. Probably the most diverse of the British DJs they have since collaborated with everybody from Lisa Stansfield, Junior Reid to Mark E Smith, and are threatening to make a HEAVY METAL album.

Compact Discs More than just a techno-fetishist's wet dream, the hiss free CD held up a mirror to the changing pop marketplace when it was launched in '83 (although it was invented by Philips in '76). A silver symbol of the revenge of golden oldie ADULT ORIENTED ROCK, and yet another emblem of the death of the Teen-age, the CD's shiny surface reflected the rise of a NEW POP consumer, the Q-reading, Dire Straits-listening COUCH POTATO who

preferred to buy all his old records again rather than listen to something new.

Computer Games The home computer has evolved from a bulky box that you needed a diploma to operate into a sleek, well designed home entertainment system. But the games which can be played on them have gone even further, blurring the boundaries between computer animation and VIDEO. The emergence of 16-bit home computers like the Amiga and Atari ST around '87, with their high powered chips and fast speeds made it possible for games designers to be freed from the tedium of learning difficult programming languages, into an area in which they could experiment with narrative, animated effects and slick graphics. The result was the growth of the interactive VIDEO game as pioneered by the American company, Cinemaware. With writers, musicians and filmmakers, including BOMB THE BASS, Stakker Productions and Snapper Films, now exploring the medium, the computer game could shed its adolescent bedroom image in favour of a sleek CYBERPUNK one. People may well even start using the computer in the same way they use the VCR now. Why watch the same old film when it can be different every time?

Computer Games Crackers With the growth of COMPUTER GAMES making it *the* biggest male pastime between the ages of 10-16, it naturally fostered its own subculture, the computer crackers. Completely at ease with the inner workings of even the most sophisticated home computer, crackers could rip into the machine code of a game bypassing any protection a softwear company might put in their way. Since '86 computer games crackers have not only grown into the best software pirates, but also often the most creative users of what the machine has to offer. Crackers seem unconcerned with the prospect of writing games commercially, often

The Credit Economy The credit card economy comes from the simple Thatcherite concept that you don't have to be rich to spend money. Ideologically, it's a very meritocratic idea on the surface - it favours clever poor people over stupid rich ones. In the end, though, it's like all Thatcherite ideas - those who are neither clever nor rich end up in a lot of trouble. Look at what happened to the deregulated credit card stock market. Brokers were suddenly allowed to take your money *and* to play around with it instead of being legally obliged to accept a fixed rate from a jobber. Suddenly they were playing around with money that wasn't their own. The whole thing came tumbling down after two years. Early on in a credit card economy - just like a stock market boom - it's very easy to buy things. This creates demand. Prices go up. Interest rates go up. Life in the end is more expensive.

L to R: i-D straight ups Claire and Jackie '83 *(photo: Steve Johnston)*. Cameo's Larry Blackmon. The Cult. Converse Sneakers *(photo: Dave Swindells)*

preferring to work on 'demos' which perform technical wizardry, but earn them no money. They have developed an underground network which communicates through modem to form a vast string of pirates, artists and programmers who make up clubs with tag names that parallel the world of GRAFFITI. 1% of the active population of computer users are thought to be crackers or affiliated to cracking clubs, and in the '90s, it'll be the crackers, not the software companies who define the nature of COMPUTER GAMES.

Computer Hackers New technologies always bring possibilites and pleasures they don't tell you about in the instruction manual. The mass marketing of the Personal Computer gave punters a passport to a new multinational landscape of data banks, classified files and confidential information, and when people went networking round this new realm, the modern crime of computer hacking went mainstream. If it is a crime. The legal status is unclear, and after headline hacks like the Friday 13th virus, and the German break-in into NASA's computers, hackers themselves remain hard to pin down. Are they in it for personal gain, or are they just access freaks? Are they cybernetic wrecking crews, desperate to drop their logic bombs and set virus programmes loose, or are they the freedom fighters of the information age? The files are still open.

Converse When Converse All Stars baseball boots became the essential ACID HOUSE footwear in '88, the 300% rise in sales took the company completely by surprise. Other manufacturers, able to produce similar flimsy canvas boots in an even wider range of primary colours, took up the initiative and by the time Converse responded with a series of advertisements in the surf/skate press in '89, not only had the ACID HOUSE scene started wearing KICKERS, but the manufacturers' supply of Converse had been almost completely exhausted. *See Skate/ Surfwear*

Corporate Fashion There is a beautifully circular logic behind the phenomenon of coporate fashion. If you spend millions of pounds promoting your brand, you make the brand as desirable as the product. So it follows that the brand name will sell, say, a line of clothing, which in turn will sell the product. It's a logic that many cigarette companies tried in the '70s and record companies have always adopted, but it took the '80s to turn it into fashion. Coca Cola, Marlboro and Harley Davidson produced a collection of DENIM, cotton and leather merchandise that became adopted as street fashion. The Coca Cola long-sleeved tops in particular defied initial howls of derision from fashion pundits to become a status symbol of casual fashion. Whether or not Harley Davidson can repeat their success with their HD lager though, is another question.

Cosmetic Surgery In the decade of the designer body, cosmetic surgery involved more than just face-lifts, nose jobs and collagen-inflated pouts. If you couldn't hack it in HEALTH CLUBS, the short cut to that dream physique was to go under the knife, for tummy-tucks, silicon breast implants and all-over fat-busting liposuction sessions. By '86 Americans were spending over half a billion dollars a year on bodywork – spurred on by surgically altered stellar bodies like Brigitte Nielsen and Cher.

Countrybilly Short-lived subculture plugging the gap between the NEW ROMANTICS and GOTHS. The '50s garb of checked shirts and LEVI'S spilled over from HARD TIMES chic and the music was the unwitting spawning ground for the British roots scene. The Shilleleagh Sisters were briefly hailed as Cowpunk's answer to The Supremes but fizzled out, only for lead singer Jacquie O'Sullivan to find herself seconded into BANANA-RAMA by the late '80s. Karma or

what? *See Gaz's Rockin' Blues*

Cox, Alex Working class Liverpudlian Cox went from Oxford to UCLA and exploded onto the scene with the utterly bizarre 'Repo Man' in '84. Since then he has never quite matched the blend of anarchy and surrealism; too often politics and his predilection for casting muso friends instead of actors got in the way.

Crap Drinks As ALCOHOL came into disrepute in the '80s, its negative effects on health and bodyweight loudly publicised and socially-lubricating party-time role usurped by other drugs – the breweries fought back with an ever-expanding arsenal of idiotic ideas. One involved dressing varying concoctions of the same old tosh up in new packaging, and giving it new names – Bezique, Taboo, Mirage, et al. Whilst the public mysteriously failed to go bananas over drinks describing themselves as 'a mixture of white wine and lemonade with a hint of orange brandy', the crap drink did score a victory in cocktail circles. Suddenly they were invaded by lowlife whose only aim was to invent the most embarrassing and unappetising cocktail names. Slow Comfortable Screw? Navel Fuzz? No thanks mate. I'll have a Toe Cheese and Tibetan Monkey's Gonad for the lady. Crap drinks are the last resort of a desperate industry.

Crass The ultimate anarchist punk band, Crass took the Sex Pistols' 'Anarchy In The UK' to heart and tried

Crack If ECSTASY was the upside of so-called 'designer drugs' crack was the downside, a cocaine derivative causing instant high followed by crashing low and rapid addiction. Crack gang wars and crack-inspired crime devastated inner city America, leading to deep concern when the drug started to emerge on run-down council estates in places like Liverpool

and Wolverhampton in '89, and the announcement that a special national UK police task force was being created to tackle the drug. The pitiful crying of crack-addicted babies on US TV, their dependence inherited from their mothers, did nothing to halt the drug's spread. Crack is Britain's drug problem for the '90s, waiting to explode.

to make it a reality. Their stark graphics and collage shaped punk's GRAPHIC DESIGN for the '80s, their anti-FALKLANDS WAR single 'Sheep-Shagging In The Falklands' caused a Parliamentary furore in '82, their organisation fuelled the Stop The City anti-materialist protests of '84 and their book *A Series Of Shock Slogans And Mindless Token Tantrums* was an unusually poignant and thoughtful contrast to their raucous thrash music, and one of the best adverts for anarchism yet. Crass split in '86 and were last seen raising goats in Epping Forest.

Cronenberg, David The film industry's top 'body horror' director literally started the decade with a

bang when he released the oedipal conspiracy thriller 'Scanners' in '81. Sure the movie may have been a clinical examination of body politics both corporate and carnal, but what everyone remembers is the exploding head sequence – the special effect that wore out a thousand pause buttons. Exotic mutilation was to be Cronenberg's continuing obsession thereafter, from the veined TV sets and VIDEO slot stomachs of 'Videodrome' to the metastatic mutations of 'The Fly' and the weird gynaecological science of 'Dead Ringers'.

The Crypto Amnesia Club You shouldn't really judge a book by its cover, or its press coverage, but when Michael Bracewell's *The Crypto Amnesia Club* appeared in '88, a lot of people decided to make an exception. Checking the cover's

*L to R: 'The Mad Cad',
Larry Fuente's customised
car '86 (photo: Louie
Psihoyos).
Wigan's flight jacket '87
(photo: Nigel Law).
Customised shoes '87
(photo: Sandro Hyams)*
See Customising

promise of nightclub melancholia in West Wonderland, the name-dropping interviews, the moody author photos, they figured that the British answer to the Literary Brats had finally arrived – at last, '80s swinging London and the Media Generation captured on paper in a STYLE novel. If they bothered to read *The Crypto Amnesia Club*, they soon found that Bracewell's overheated purple prose exceeded the STYLE novel's limited brief. However, Robert Elms was just around the corner with STYLE novel number two, the more straightforward *In Search Of The Crack*. But by then the STYLE novelist's role had

changed. No longer the spokesman for a generation, he'd become an all-purpose scapegoat, forced to carry the can as pundits queued up to kill off STYLE culture.

The Cult Formed in '82 by Ian Astbury, they were originally known as Southern Death Cult and sported chicken bones and Red Indian tribal gear with, they claimed, rather more sympathy for the sources than ADAM ANT had. SDC evolved into Death Cult and then lopped off the 'Death', got into The Stones and Led Zeppelin, moved to LA and became one of the late '80s most succesful hard rock

and eventually HEAVY METAL band with LP titles evoking the 'classi era': 'Dreamtime', 'Sonic Temple 'Electric'. Duffy and Astbury wear a the signifiers of outlaw chic, from long hair to Iron Crosses and take a the posturing and 'hard lovin' woman lyrics absolutely seriously. Despit international success they remaine throughout the '80s with UK semi independent label Beggars Banquet.

Cultural Cross-Dressing Although ethnic references hav always occured on a cyclical basis i fashion, during late '88/early '89 th catwalks became swamped by Afro

Eastern designs. Echoing street trends in hippy chic it almost seemed as though the SUMMER OF LOVE had permeated the designer collections and it was only a matter of time before saris were being worn in clubs. However, in true '80s STYLE, the street had moved on. Adapting the emerging trend in SPORTSWEAR, Troop tracksuits were being crossed with Afghan tops, and CYCLING SHORTS under 'Love' emblazoned T-SHIRTS. As ever, VIVIENNE WEST-WOOD proved the most attuned with her African print wraps and swim-suits, and as b-boys entered THE DAISY AGE and SKATEWEAR pilfered

reggae and rap imagery, all roads seemed to lead to a sportswear/cultural crossroads. Specialist shops opened to cater for this trend like World, Off-Beat and Bond which offered UK made and imported ethnic clothes and jewellery alongside b-boy paraphernalia and surf/skate shorts and accessories. Probably one of the most diverse yet universal fashion trends of '89, its global perspective could bode well for the '90s.

Customising What had always been an inherent part of postwar youth culture, from the bikers' studded leather jackets to the

L to R: Early Crolla brocade collection '84 (photo: Marc Lebon). David Claridge from Skin Two and friend at The Great Wall club '8[ ]
Cycle Couriers '88 (photo: Nigel Law).

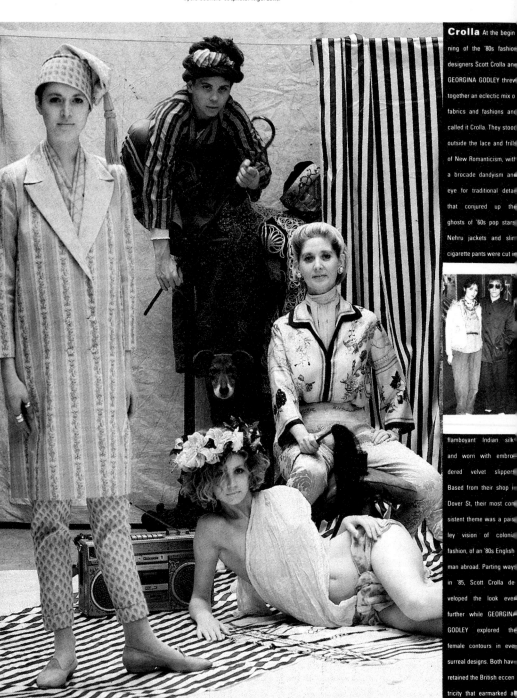

Crolla At the begin
ning of the '80s fashion
designers Scott Crolla and
GEORGINA GODLEY threw
together an eclectic mix of
fabrics and fashions and
called it Crolla. They stood
outside the lace and frills
of New Romanticism, with
a brocade dandyism and
eye for traditional detail
that conjured up the
ghosts of '60s pop stars.
Nehru jackets and slim
cigarette pants were cut in

flamboyant Indian silk
and worn with embroi
dered velvet slippers.
Based from their shop in
Dover St, their most con
sistent theme was a pais
ley vision of colonial
fashion, of an '80s English
man abroad. Parting ways
in '85, Scott Crolla de
veloped the look even
further while GEORGINA
GODLEY explored the
female contours in eve
surreal designs. Both have
retained the British eccen
tricity that earmarked a[ ]

the early '80s designers.
See Fashion Designers

Cycle Couriers

Emerging in a fluorescent LYCRA blur in the latter half of the '80s, cycle couriers became the bane of bus conductors whose vehicles they clung to on tough uphill hauls, and the darlings of the media, whose rough artwork and typeset copy they slipped into their orange *Guardian* bags, formerly used solely by paper boys. The streets became a sartorial battlefield as smog-masked warriors, able, unlike the increasingly redundant motorbike DESPATCH RIDERS, to let their locks flow free, raced to the photolab on their Muddy Fox chargers. The proliferation of FAX machines didn't deter the influx of new companies, and as motorised London traffic ground to a halt, it truly seemed the only way to despatch, never mind the only eco-conscious way. By the end of the decade it even had its own magazine; *Moving Target*, a courier 'zine full of inspeak and demands for self-regulation of the business before the inevitable government intervention. *See Mountain Bikes*

furniture upholstery waistcoats of hippy Woodstock, became the modus operandi of the '80s. Punk unleashed a DIY ethic that plundered tribal uniforms and reconstructed history, and by the early '80s, anything was up for grabs. Badges, buttons, bottle tops, beer mats and bus tickets all helped define an emerging street fashion that was as amorphous as it was all-pervasive, as young people attached ever expanding armouries of consumer detritus to their wardrobes. Fashion designers were quick to apply the customising ethic to their designs and by the end of the decade there wasn't an accessory, look, fabric or household utensil that hadn't been employed. *See Blitz, Designer Bootlegging, Judy Blame,*

Leigh Bowery, Bowler Hats, Creative Salvage, Doctor Martens, MA-1 Flight Jackets, Mark & Syrie, Mutoid Waste Company, Christopher Nemeth, New Ecologists, New Romantics, Salvage Fashion, Volkswagens

Cuts Occasional model James Lebon was one of *the* name hairdressers of the '80s. Beginning with a small salon, Cuts, in KENSINGTON MARKET he soon moved to his own salon/ART gallery in Kensington Church Street, then to SOHO. He was a dynamic haircutter, creating images for magazines and pop stars alike. He also recorded the ultimate homage to hairdressing, 'Sexify You' – 'Cuts – I'm debonair/Cuts – I'll do your hair'. Lebon has since moved into VIDEO, producing images for BOMB THE BASS and Alyson Williams, but

Cycling Shorts As CYCLE COURIERS proliferated it was inevitable that some of their fashion would rub off on London's streets. Removing the padded crotch that protected against chaffing on the saddle, people were wearing them as early as '84. But it took BODYMAP's show in the same year which put LYCRA shorts on the catwalk, to launch the cycling short as a fully-fledged fashion trend. Since then cycling shorts have been included in countless designer collections including JP GAULTIER in '86 and KATHARINE HAMNETT who adapted the cycling short to hipsters, and eventually became *de rigeur* wear for pop groups from THE STYLE COUNCIL to YAZZ. Along with the MA1 FLIGHT JACKETS and LEVI'S 501s they have now become a street fashion cliché that high street stores regurgitate every summer. *See Sportswear*

L to R: Comagne Chopin Ballet Le Defile wearing costumes by Jean Paul Gaultier '87. Quentin Crisp '85 (photo: Discipline). DJ Elayne (photo: Kevin Davies). Danceteria's third birthday party '83.

further recording success has so far eluded him.

Cyberpunk In the early '80s science fiction's outdated machinery was checked in for an overhaul and the result was cyberpunk. The new improved model of future schlock mixed cybernetic input with punk attitude, noir-ish nihilism with pulpy techno-slang, and had its first outing in '84 with William Gibson's *Neuromancer*. Replacing outer space and inner space with cyberspace, a computer generated datascape, Gibson's enthralling vision of a brand name future got the cyberpunk bandwagon rolling. Fellow travellers included Bruce Sterling, John Shirley, Michael Swanwick and Pat Cadigan. Others, like hard SF author Greg Bear and anti-science SF man Lucius Shepard, resented being caught up in the slipstream and slammed the 'Cyberpunk Hype'. But it wasn't just hype. Although Gibson and Sterling have abandoned it for a new STYLE, 'steampunk', cyberpunk continues to influence films, comics, COMPUTER GAMES and even hackers. It may even last into the '90s – after all, the Great British Cyberpunk novel is yet to be written.

Cycling A boom activity of the '80s, with Green interest, high profile logo wear and ultra-fitness combined. Irish and Scottish interests were well served by the international successes of Sean Kelly, Steven Roche and Robert Millar, and CHANNEL 4's Tour De France commentator Phil Liggett became a cult figure with his rapturous descriptions of the whole *maillot jaune* scenario. The best dressed competitors in the '84 and '88 Olympics were the cyclists, with their streamlined, ergonomically designed headwear and upright handlebars, though many still fell off when negotiating the acute transitions of the velodrome. The late '80s saw interest increase still further with the emergence of the Triathlon, combining long distance cycling, swimming and RUNNING.

The Daisy Age

When DE LA SOUL emerged in '88 with peace symbols shaved in their hair, throwing flowers into the audience and hailing the dawn of 'The Daisy Age' nobody expected b-boys raised on the braggadocio beats of LL Cool J and RUN DMC to take any notice. But the influence of groups like PUBLIC ENEMY and THE JUNGLE BROTHERS had begun to make itself seen and heard – gold chains were already being swapped for AFRICAN COLOURS and talk was of unity rather than whose dick was the biggest (*See Stop The Violence*). DE LA SOUL simply took it, almost literally, into orbit. Tapping in to the hippy chic of the SUMMER OF LOVE, they wore Jesus sandals, psychedelic prints,

and baggy SURFWEAR, and broadened the b-boy's perspective both fashionwise and musically. As CULTURAL CROSS-DRESSING becomes universal and HIP HOUSE hybrids unite previously separate scenes, it may only be a matter of time before club dancefloors of every description enter The Daisy Age. *See Sportswear*

The Dark Knight Returns

Frank Miller's savage '86 reworking of the BATMAN myth transformed Gotham City into a skyscraping future-noir slum and BATMAN himself into an ageing and ambiguously psychotic vigilante, seized by guilt and fury and provoked by an incessant TV screen chorus of talking heads. Cleverly combining claustrophobic boxed-in panels and iconic full page spreads, Miller pushed his story

of revenge and absolution all the way to its killing conclusion but then inexplicably faltered and retracted everything on the last page. Nearly a masterpiece.

Day-Lewis, Daniel

Son of Poet Laureate Cecil Day-Lewis, Daniel has the lanky, brooding presence, both on stage and screen, that makes him a heartthrob of the first rank. He compounds his cover boy sins by being extraordinarily gifted, displaying a rare versatility in diverse roles. His role as the gay National Front punk in HANIF KUREISHI's 'My Beautiful Laundrette' brought him to international notice, and he went on to star as Lothario Thomas in Milan Kundera's 'The Unbearable Lightness Of Being'. Day-Lewis has turned out to be a vital injection of new blood in the ranks of young Brit actors, both able *and* rebellious.

De Niro, Robert

Critic's darling but never a crowd-puller, De Niro is the thinking person's actor; a man whose method never obscures his mission to *inhabit* the part. Imitators from ROURKE to Penn ape without finesse the technique of a man whose personality remains an enigma but whose impersonations are precision.

Deadline

In September '88 *2000AD* regulars Steve Dillon and Brett Ewins hurriedly put together their own "cult comic and media magazine" to coincide with the staging of the UK Comic Art Convention. The result was a stinging combination of original strips, rants, interviews and music reviews which had such an impact that what was intended as a one-off quickly became a monthly.

Deep House

Deep house is a marriage of hi-tech HOUSE beat to gospel-tinged soul vocals, often with an uplifting message. Ever since HOUSE emerged from Chicago in '85, deep house tracks were popular worldwide, but it was only after acid

The Danceteria

Launched in the summer of 1980 by Jim Fouratt and Rudolf, The Danceteria became a legend in New York clubland. The authorities closed it down after an incredibly successful six month stint, but the club reopened in February '82 on West 21 St. Danceteria served as the base for a whole generation of club-

bers until it finally closed in '86.

De La Soul

They called themselves the 'hippies of hip hop', they rapped about dandruff and yoghurt, they wore peace signs and brightly customized clothes and declared the start of a new 'DAISY AGE'. The influence of their dayglo image ensured that the b-boy would never look the same again.

Demob Run by Chris and Sue Brick, Demob opened in '81 in a former fishmongers in Beak Street, and was one of many fashion stalls that ended up in permanent premises. Originally a stall in the Great Gear Market in 1980 the shop became a home for young design talent like Willie Brown, Elaine Oxford, Richard Ostell, Robin Archer, Chris Sullivan and also sold its own designs. One of its most enduring and successful looks was the NORTHERN SOUL baggy uniform, complete with black DENIM workwear jeans and check anoraks, but it also offered tailored suits, dungarees, checkerboard shirts and jackets with print dresses. The shop also ran warehouse parties, a milk bar and hairdressers called Demop (moving over the road in '86), which soon attracted a following of its own. Unfortunately, Demob burnt down in March '87, leaving Demop and a thousand copies of their check hooded jacket in CAMDEN MARKET.

*L to R: Demob '84.
Denim customised by
Stephen Linard '84 (photo:
Phil Ward).*

PUT YOUR FOOT DOWN.

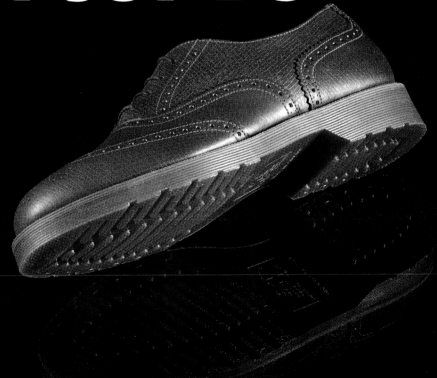

Insist on GENUINE

Dr. *AirWair*
Martens
WITH BOUNCING SOLES

FROM ALL GOOD SHOE SHOPS

went mainstream in late '88 that London's clubs began to pick up on it. Producer Marshall Jefferson earned the title of deep house genius, while his protegés Ten City went on to achieve chart success worldwide. Classic deep house songs are Ce Ce Rogers' 'Someday' and Joe Smooth's 'Promised Land' – the message is pure peace and love.

Def Jam Rap record label formed by a real life odd couple. College student Rick Rubin and rap promoter Russell Simmons built Def Jam around Simmons' brother's group RUN DMC. Like the group themselves the recent Def Jam declined in the late '80s despite hits from artists like LL Cool J, as new school rappers like

DE LA SOUL and THE JUNGLE BROTHERS threw the hard and unsubtle brag STYLE of Def Jam into the shadow. In the mid-'80s though, Def Jam was the finest and most successful exponent of loud mouthed me rap, as RUN DMC, THE BEASTIE BOYS and LL Cool J took their rhymes to American stadium crowds opening many white doors for subsequent artists. *See Public Enemy*

Delirium Opening in November '86 and originally run by Nick Trulocke, Delirium was the first big West End club to concentrate on hip hop and attract a racially mixed crowd. It was also the first major London club to play HOUSE MUSIC and to add all sorts of live action into the club mix. BMX riders and skateboarders performed freestyle on stage on the opening night. Later,

mudwrestlers, tight-rope walkers and even a helter skelter were squeezed into the Astoria. Noel and Maurice Watson played the latest dance tunes, including HOUSE MUSIC that fell on deaf ears: they even had to build a cage around the DJ box to protect them from beer cans and other flying missiles thrown at them by b-boys who would only listen to hip hop. The massive dancefloor was usually packed with teenage trendies wearing what became the clubland uniform of '86/'87: MA-1 FLIGHT JACKETS weighed down with (Russian enamel) badges, BMW or VW motifs and any hip hop regalia worn over torn 501s and black DOCTOR MARTENS. In '87 the club moved to HEAVEN bringing a new direction as Noel and Maurice dropped hip hop altogether in favour of a HOUSE-only dance policy. The BMX bikers were gone and the dance mix of GARAGE, DEEP and even ACID HOUSE attracted a small but intensely enthusiastic crowd. It set the scene for the HOUSE explosions in the spring of '88, but its contribution wasn't appreciated at first. After closing at HEAVEN in December the club moved to THE CAMDEN PALACE in the summer of '88, but it rarely caught the intensity it had before, and later changed its name to Freestyle.

Denim In an era when denim became street fashion's lowest common denominator, the price of new denims hardly altered, but by the end of the '80s 30 year old LEVI'S jackets were fetching up to £200. Shops like FLIP and AMERICAN CLASSICS built their names around the boom in vintage denim, specialising in US imported secondhand jeans and jackets that to some looked more at home in a jumble sale. Of course, to the real aficionado, who could date a pair of jeans by the stitching (yellow='50s/'60s, red selvedge='60s/'70s, orange='80s) it was the minor details that mattered. Lee stormrider jackets with corduroy collars and blanket lining, the extra rivets on early LEVI'S jeans, the ▶

Depeche Mode The suburban FUTURISTS who became stadium rockers. Depeche Mode grew from the naive electro-pop of their first hit single 'New Life' in '81 to become the world's leading electronic group, playing to capacity stadium crowds in the US and making a film of their life on the road, '101' to prove it. Although every one of their immaculately tuneful singles was a hit, they never had a number one. Through ten years of global success, they never left the independent record label, Mute, and they always – always – wore black.

Designer Bootlegging Copy it and sell it cheap. That was the ethic of designer bootlegging and by the end of the '80s, everyone was doing it. From DEF JAM and Chanel T-shirt copies in '86 to fake Louis Vuitton luggage and cheap Korean Gucci prints from New York's Canal Street, if it was expensive 'and good-looking, someone was faking it by the thousand.

*L to R: Divine **See John Waters.** Dandy fashion '89 (photo: Terry Jones). Designer Bootleg fashion '87 (photo: Monica Curtin).*

TONI & GUY.
HAIRDRESSING

Lifestyle

Davies Street, Mayfair, London W1 Tel 01-629 8348/499 2249

Sloane Square, Chelsea, London Tel 01-730 8113/730 4313

St. Christopher's Place, London Tel 01-486 0733

London Road, Twickenham, Middx. Tel 01-891 0047

Southampton St, Covent Gdn, London Tel 01-240 7342

Fife Road, Kingston, Surrey Tel 01-549 0477

North Park, Dallas, Texas, USA Tel 214-750-0067

Key Biscane, Miami, Florida, USA Tel 305-361-6886

Sherry Lane, Dallas, Texas, USA Tel 214-696-3825

The Galleria, Dallas, Texas, USA Tel 214-991-7992

Sakurai Bldg, Tokyo, Japan Tel 03-797-5790

Arlington, Texas, USA Tel 817-784-0922

Valleyview, Dallas, Texas Tel 214-960-6896

Prestonwood, Dallas, USA Tel 214-980-1988

Using Tigi Linea products

◄ smaller top pockets on LEVI'S yellow-stitched jackets – these were crucial sartorial decisions for any self-respecting denim devotee.

The major denim companies, realising the market had shifted, attempted to give new denim the look of old denim, and developed 101 washing techniques from stonewash, snow wash, bleached, marbled, stretch to dyed. Their success led to a maze of cuts and labels that produced its own hierarchies. FIORUCCI's Classic Nouveau and Liberto, Chipie, and a host of European labels proliferated as everybody from THE SUNBED KIDS to the PANINARI adopted denim as part of their uniform. The new fabric treatments liberated this previously stiff material for designers who explored the use of denim and confirmed its new exalted status. Led by the likes of Calvin Klein in the late '70s, everybody from MOSCHINO, JP GAULTIER, BODYMAP, RICHMOND/CORNEJO, GIORGIO ARMANI to KATHARINE HAMNETT utilised a fabric that began life in 1850 on the legs of gold prospectors. *See Eurostyle, Hard Times and Ripped Jeans*

Design Consultancies Just what is it that makes today's designs so different, so appealing? British consultancies like Wolff Olins, Fitch & Co and Pentagram reckon they know the answer. Although established back in the '60s and '70s they didn't come into their own until the '80s when the design business was transformed. No longer the window-dressing of industry it was now a major industry in its own right, contracted to service everything from book jackets to airports. Over half the consultancies now trading were set up in the last ten years – most conspicuously David Davies, who started off designing the interiors of the Next retail chain and went on to open his own string of menswear shops. Together they have installed themselves as the high priests of the new marketing shibboleth which in '85 was worth a combined turnover of £990 million. Sounds less like design for living and more like living

Diamante Not since the WOMEN'S TOILETS at BLITZ had so many boys wanted to look like girls. In '84, as designers and clubbers erupted in a kaleidoscopic display of FLUORESCENT FASHION, the only distraction was diamante. Huge chunky necklaces, dangling bracelets, earrings that touched your shoulders and obtrusive brooches – the bigger and

cheaper the better. The likes of BOY GEORGE and DJ Tasty Tim rummaged through costume jewellers and designer Monty Don produced coloured paste jewellery. Even KATHARINE HAMNETT adopted the look, utilising diamante accessories and ripped jeans on the catwalk.

for design. *See Style*

Designer Emporiums In the early '80s young designers had limited options. They could either set up a stall in a market or be shoved into a corner in big department stores amongst the Burberrys or Valentinos. But the parallel growth in specialist designer shops gave young talent a showcase and custom that in some cases, eventually enabled many to open shops of their own. Shops like Jones, Bazaar and Academy in London, Equation in Bristol, Geese in Manchester, Ichi Ni San and Warehouse in Glasgow and Square and Blah Blah in Bath, became focal points of design creativity, with many employing the talents of the new

names in interior design. Ron Arad designed the interior of Bazaar and Equation, inspiring a formula look that seemed to be contagious, pretty soon every new emporium seemed to feature minimalist concrete, wrought iron fittings, sand blasted glass and salvaged mirrors.

Designer Marxism Invented when left-wing theorists convinced themselves that if you persuaded someone to buy the T-shirt, they might also buy the philosophy. What Designer Marxism really meant was that with reform in Russia and postmodern thinkers announcing the end of classical Marxism, the image was up for grabs, on everything from constructivist coffee cups, JPG leopardskin suits and *Marxism Today* teddy bears. Next stop was Glasnost Chic. *See Champagne Socialism*

Despatch Riders Despatching was one of the most dangerous growth industries of the decade. London companies like Addison Lee, Delta, and Inter City Couriers all had riders running round every major inner city, negotiating the thin gap between lanes of cars, and in effect using parts of the road that didn't exist for regular traffic. It needed balance, strong nerves and even stronger knee-caps as they tended to be on the same level as car wing mirrors. The danger of riding a big bike in heavy traffic for at least eight hours per day in all weathers is compounded by the fact that riders get paid by the job. So the more jobs, the more money, means in real terms, the faster you ride and the longer you work, the higher your pay cheque. If riders are in debt this can be a recipe for disaster – most riders have an accident every three to six months.

Diffusion Ranges Diffusion is what couture designers turn to when they want to make money without having to trade their name on high-priced scents (the traditional method). The idea was invented in Italy (predictably), by that master of marketing GIORGIO ARMANI (predictably), who launched a range of womenswear clothes christened 'Mani', and a menswear range purely entitled Giorgio Armani White Label interpreting the look of his last collection at a cheaper price. The first of the British designers were BODYMAP whose B-Basics diffusion line was launched in June 1984. Now we have GAULTIER's 'Junior' range, Ralph Lauren's 'Roughwear', Valentino's 'Oliver', Sonia Rykiel's 'Graphics', and from Jean Muir, 'Studio'. One wag suggested that KATHARINE HAMNETT should call her new diffusion range 'Kath'. She has opted to christen it 'Hamnett II'.

The Dirtbox A legend in its own chaotic lifetime, The Dirtbox was probably the most famous and influential of the early warehouse clubs. Started by Rob Milton and Phil Gray in June '82, it first opened above a chemists in Earls Court and thanks to police raids changed location every couple of months each new venue larger than the last to cope with the club's every-growing following. Cheap admission prices, a bring-your-own booze policy and the occasional punch-up all added to its anarchic reputation while The Dirtbox uniform of FLAT-TOPS, ripped LEVI'S and leather jackets ended up as the de rigeur look for the whole of the underground scene. With DJs Jay Strongman and Rob Milton spinning everything from Hank Williams and The Clash to JAMES BROWN and GRANDMASTER FLASH, almost all musical tastes were catered for, something which helped make the club a cultural melting pot that brought together ROCKABILLIES, punks, trendies and ex-soulboys, a mix that was to shape the future of London clubland.

Dirty Realism Flipside to the party-up nihilism of Urban Breakdown novels like Bret Easton Ellis' Less Than Zero and Jay McInerney's Bright Lights, Big City was the broken down populism of Hicksville Heart-ache stories by the likes of Raymond Carver, Richard Ford, Tobias Wolff and Jayne Anne Phillips. Collectively hyped as the Dirty Realists by literary editor Bill Buford, in whose magazine Granta many of them were show-cased in '83, their crafted fiction of the absurdist everyday traversed a blasted SPRINGSTEEN territory of crashed cars, failed relationships and lost jobs. Characters were typically victimized by larger social forces they couldn't understand and the prevail-ing mood was one of nagging restlessness. Usually terrific, the stories only sometimes lapsed into soft focus.

Discoteque Before ACID HOUSE, before everybody started DRESSING DOWN, Nick Trulocke's Saturday night club Discoteque was encourag-ing people to not only dress up, but to dress up in the worst possible taste. Catching the post-RARE GROOVE euphoria for SEVENTIES

FASHION, The Boilerhouse DJs Ben and Andy played a selection of '70s sounds to a strange mix of 'Shaft' lookalikes, early SHOOMers and fashion victims. Responsible for resurrecting The Gap Band's 'Rowing Dance', the much-maligned smooch hour of 'The Erection Section', and DJ dedications, Discoteque was a symp-tom of the times – tasteless, superficial and mindless fun.

Disney Studios After years of rereleasing cartoon classics and minting money at THEME PARKS Disney had all but ceased to exist as a Hollywood player, and when the studio took a raincheck on ET its credibility couldn't have sunk any lower. Then the Disney board poached Paramount highfliers Michael Eisner and Jeffrey Katzen-berg to see if they could work the same magic that had kept Paramount top studio for three years. Kicking off with 'Splash!' the turnaround has been spectacular. Disney became the front runner in Hollywood's comedy bonanza, releasing a string of pacey, if paltry, Bette Midler hits from 'Down And Out In Beverly Hills' to 'Beaches' and storming the box office mountain with the innovative 'WHO FRAMED ROGER RABBIT?'.

Dixon, Tom See Creative Salvage

Docklands Britain's disused docks became enterprise zones in the '80s, and the crumbling warehouses and left-over machinery of heavy industry were replaced by the gleaming showhouses and facades of the culture industry. It happened across Britain, in Bristol, GLASGOW, Cardiff, Liverpool, and most promin-ently in the hyperreal estate of London's Docklands. Local commun-ities were either moved out or had to put up with living on the world's biggest building site, as a new urban landscape of museums, galleries, BRASSERIES and waterfront conversions appeared. YUPPIES cashed in on unbuilt second homes, until rising interest rates burst the bubble, but the building boom

Dressing Down Clubs used to be the unofficial catwalk, an arena for self-expression and individual STYLE – essentially a time for dressing up. But ever since the SUMMER OF LOVE, T-SHIRTS and shorts have come into their own and people have started to dress down. Instigated by an influx of clubbers who, 12 months before, would never have got past THE WAG CLUB's doors, and aided by the sheer practicality of the fashion, dressing down had a levelling effect in UK clubs. The fact that every-body looked pretty much the same, shifted the emphasis away from clothes to the music, as BOY GEORGE danced next to new age Millwall sup-porters and sweating came back in STYLE. Over-night, clubs had to change their door policies and the sales of deodorant doubled. See Acid House, Dungarees, Ibiza, Sports-wear and Skate/Surfwear

L to R: Diamante '84 (photo: Eamonn McCabe). i-D straight up Debbi '82 Dancer at Delirium (photo: Oliver Maxwell).

continued.

Doctor Martens Since their adoption by SKINHEADS in the late '60s, DMs have developed into the fashion accessory of the last five years. The attraction of DM boots is steeped in their aggressive appear-ance, their resilience (oil, fat, acid, petrol alkali resistant), and their workwear origins. Standard footwear for second generation punks at the beginning of the '80s, ten eyelet black boots worn with black jeans or combat trousers, people started CUSTOMISING DMs with garish colours and eye-catching designs (including the pop group King). RICHMOND/CORNEJO played a major part in bringing the DM to the

catwalk by showing it complete with leather shoe jewellery, breaking its aggressive male image as more and more women started to wear DMs. Since then DM soles have been added to every conceivable style of shoe, reaching a zenith of popularity in '86, when the streets were awash with air-cushioned brogues, tasselled loafers, steelies, greasies and jodhpur boots and launching Red Or Dead's alternative range of DM shoes. At the same time GAULTIER made a fashion feature of the steel-toed DM (which had first appeared on London streets, natch) and high street stores copied the idea – adding a piece of flimsy metal to the top of a plain Oxford DM. Things have calmed down a bit since then, but London is still the DM capital of the world, and tourists still make special trips here to buy them.

Dodos Run by Nick Trulocke and Vaughn Toulouse, Dodos was probably the first club to use SMILEY as its logo, and anticipated the '70s revival by three years.

Drinking Clubs Perhaps the club success story of the '80s was that of The Groucho Club, which opened in '85 in Dean Street, SOHO and where the only music played is at the occasional record launch party. A gentleman's club that allows women in and has a restaurant, it swiftly became the favoured haunt of the publishing world, taking over from Zanzibar, and featured in JULIE BURCHILL's '89 novel *Ambition*. Named after the Marx brother who quipped that he wouldn't join any club that would have him as a member, Groucho's appeal, though great, appeared limited to a slightly older clientele (ex-music journalists such as Burchill, for example, as well as the occasional Bryan Ferry or Mick Jagger), and thus Fred's opened in Carlisle Street, also Soho, for the younger lush. 1989 saw Fred's expand with two floors of The Colville Rose in Portobello Road. With *The Spectator*'s "Lowlife" columnist Jeffrey Bernard fast becoming a role model for the young journalists of London, pre-club clubs, KARAOKE bars and more drinking clubs soon proliferated, keeping the media makers lubricated. And if you weren't a member you could usually get in because the doorstaff were pissed.

Drive-In Demolition Disco Derby The forerunner of the MUTOID WASTE COMANY's extravaganzas and the first visible sign of TOM DIXON's penchant for re-assembling mechanical detritus. Run by Dixon and Nick Jones, the DIDDDs were a series of four warehouse parties featuring cannibalised cars and exhaust fumes from '84, where Tom constructed junk sculpture with the aid of welding gear and beer. Probably the first time clubbers risked being blinded by standing too close to the DJ. *See Creative Salvage and*

Funkapolitan

Dungarees The dungaree did a u-turn during the decade. Although adopted by early soulboys in the late '70s, along with plastic sandals and mohair jumpers, to most it seemed fit only for diehard hippies or fine ART students. They had a brief reprieve with the rise of TEXTILE DESIGNERS during the BLITZ days, but by the summer of '88 dungarees were the height of fashion. Part of the DRESSING DOWN ethos of practicality, they were worn without a top, off the shoulder and straps tied round the waist. The most sought after label was Osh-kosh from the States, and the most common accessories were a pig-tail and a pair of KICKERS. But in '89 hip sports label Troop threatened to take the fashion one step further – leather dungarees are hardly practical but could be the last word in sweating for fashion.

Duran Duran Formed in 1980 out of Birmingham's Rum Runner club scene, with a name lifted from Roger Vadim's '60s flick, 'Barbarella', Duran Duran survived the whole decade, and whilst not exactly thriving towards the end of it, were influential nevertheless. Their significance rests mainly in their VIDEO endeavours, their 'Rio' collection of '82 being the highpoint of post New Romantic extravagance. featuring sun, sand, yachts and cocktails. The late '80s saw them attempting to 'get dirty' and assimilate newer dancefloor trends, but without much market or critical success. It was noteworthy that their final London gig of the '80s was at the newly opened London Arena, in the heart of the YUPPIE DOCKLANDS area. *See The Birmingham Contingent*

L to R: Sheena Easton '87. Eurostyle '86 (photo: Nick Knight, styling: Simon Foxton).

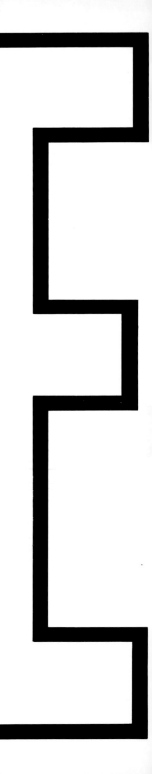

Ecclesiastic Fashion Along with the glam glitz and cross-dressing of BLITZ, a predominant look of the early '80s was the ecclesiastic fashion first sported by BOY GEORGE. Nun's habits, crosses, frock coats and Quaker shoes all contributed to a religious revival that pre-empted the BLACK UNIFORMITY of the mid-'80s. ART students and fledgling designers made their own outfits, but it wasn't until local theatrical outfitters Charles Fox had a warehouse sale of ecclesiastical extra's outfits in '82 that the fashion really caught on.

Ecstasy Originally patented in 1914 by Merck & Co. in Germany as an appetite suppressant 3,4 methyl-enedioxymethamphetamine (or

MDMA) was ear-marked for testing by the US army in the '50s as a possible drug for interrogation purposes, but was shelved because initial lab tests indicated that it harmed dogs and monkeys. Since its rediscovery in the '70s by new age chemists, it has been used in pyschotherapy, but it wasn't until the early '80s that ecstasy hit the US streets. Up until July 1 '85 ecstasy remained legal in the States, enabling a subculture to grow with impunity – in some bars you were able to buy it on your credit card (in the UK it is a Class B drug, the same as speed). Initially imported into Britain in the mid-'80s, it quickly became *the* party drug and by '86, some clubs had unofficial 'ecstasy rooms' where you could grope in peace. A drug that heightens your sense of touch, boosts confidence

and instils an inner calm, ecstasy (understandably), took off. Costing anything up to £25 the drug wasn't cheap, and until '88, was confined to a relatively small market, but by the SUMMER OF LOVE it had made phenomenal inroads into club culture.

More misinformed bullshit has been written about ecstasy than any other drug in club history. Media hysteria has resulted in people assuming that the drug is the same as LSD (two very different drugs), and the problem fast became a self-fulfilling prophecy as young kids equated ACID HOUSE with acid,

Education When the Conservative government came to power in '79, it looked upon Britain's universities with scorn. They were full of liberal academics teaching irrelevant courses in soft social sciences and ART courses, spending huge amounts of tax payers' money, not putting enough back into the economy, and showing no inclination to reform themselves. They would have to be brought into line. In '89, the traditional league tables of university performance (measured in numbers of first class degrees achieved by students and books published by academics) were officially joined by a new prestige indicator. Institutions were judged on their ability to raise money from non-governmental, private outlets – mainly industry and donations from former graduates. Throughout the decade it had become imperative for universities, ART SCHOOLS and polytechnics to find sources of finance other than the state. Public funding of universities was cut by almost 9% in April '81, setting a pattern that was steadily repeated. Government ministers spoke of 'The Switch' – a proposed move of resources and students out of arts, humanities and social sciences into sciences, technology and engineering. Morale in unfavoured departments plummeted, and as colleges imposed pay restraint and offered voluntary redundancies to save money, academic talent left the profession.

Universities also found savings in holding numbers down. Between '83 and '86, 50,000 potential university students were crammed into polytechnics. There, student-teacher ratios rose and tuition was not unaffected. In the under-resourced universities, few course options were available to students trying to build their own individual degrees. Students were being hit in other ways. In '84 their entitlement to reimbursement of travel costs was abolished, and over successive years their access to social security and welfare benefits was removed. Annual increases in the student grant consistently fell short of the inflation rate, and between '79 and '87, the National Union Of Students estimated that the value of the grant had fallen by 21%. In '89, Education Secretary Kenneth Baker, fresh from spearheading a revolution in the country's schools, was proposing to freeze the grant and introduce a system of 'top-up' loans. The government hopes that by the early 21st Century the loan element will comprise the bulk of a student's income. The '80s student was a different animal from the pre-1979 undergraduate. Students urgently pursued short-term gains in high-paid jobs (many burnt out in the financial markets) rather than long term career satisfaction. The introduction of loans will accelerate that transformation.

In the '90s students will be classed as consumers in a new marketplace, as public funding will be awarded on the basis of colleges' ability to attract students. This change in the way public money is allocated will complete the fostering of a new market culture in further education. Institutions increasingly in competition for private finance, must also compete for student numbers in order to gain public money.

There will be losers. Both government and industry have said there are limits to the amount of money available, and universities, ART SCHOOLS and polytechnics may have to curry short-term favours or pander to financiers' desires. Specialist colleges and small departments could face closure, or, at best, merger. Choice, the supposed by-word of the free market, could be severely constricted.

Electro Electro was born when New York rappers discovered computer technology, mixed it with a love of early VIDEO games and comic culture, then added a certain electronic influence from groups like KRAFTWERK and Yellow Magic Orchestra to create the first computerised strain of black music. Electro classics like 'I'm The Packman' by The Packman (a tribute to the VIDEO game of the same name) and The Soul Sonic Force's 'Planet Rock' (produced by Afrika Bambaataa and ARTHUR BAKER with a melody from KRAFTWERK's 'Trans Europe Express') started the electro boom in earnest in '82. Combined with BREAKDANCING, body-popping and GRAFFITI art, electro was exported throughout the world and formed the first wave of global hip hop culture.

made the cheaper choice and ended up in a Mickey Mouse world of full blown hallucinogenics. Undoubtedly, many clubbers take ecstasy, just as many people drink ALCOHOL and smoke cigarettes, but any moral panic over drugs should get its priorities right. Approximately 140 people die every year from HEROIN overdoses, and so far there have been no recorded deaths attributed to ecstasy abuse. Of course, anything taken in excess is not advisable, but ALCOHOL kills more people every year than any other drug. *See Lager Louts*

Electronic Bodymusic The most extreme dancefloor beat of the '80s. Electronic Bodymusic groups like Front 242, Nitzer Ebb and Skinny Puppy found most of their following in white Europe, where their mixture of rigid electronic pulses, violent vocal outbursts and totalitarian imagery nurtured a club scene who found hip hop and soul too black and HOUSE MUSIC and disco too soft. Electronic Bodymusic was roundly ignored in Britain until Nitzer Ebb's 'Join In The Chant' hit the Balearic dancefloors in summer '88.

English Menswear Designer Collections The EMDC was set up by fashion designers Roger Dack and Stephen King in '81 as a self-help body aiming to promote British menswear abroad. Originally a small group of designers who showed at UK trade shows MAB and IMBEX in London, they became frustrated by their treatment from the wider fashion trade. So they launched the British Designer Menswear Show in '86, the first organised show for new British menswear designers. Previously, if designers had wanted to show their menswear collections they had to go where the buyers went; to Paris, Milan or New York. Timed to occur between New York's Designer Collective and SEHM in Paris, the BDMS hoped to attract an international clientele of buyers and press, and establish the British menswear market as a force to be reckoned with. But the importance of the export trade in the menswear market meant that a lot of the big names in British menswear also showed in Paris, giving less of a reason for buyers to visit the BDMS. In the end the BDMS ended up with no international pulling power and wound down after four seasons. The EMDC continued until '88 but eventually folded due to a wider lack of interest. The core members, however, continue to provide a network of support and advice that is proving invaluable in an increasingly cutthroat market. *See Menswear Boom*

Enterprise Culture In practice Thatcherism meant no jobs for yobs and resulted directly in the rise of

with 1,001 Mickey Mouse services many of them funded by the £40 per week Enterprise Allowance Scheme which coincidentally deducted considerable numbers from the unemployment figures. A divided nation became even more divided as every man, woman and window cleaner scrabbled for their little piece of the cake. Enterprise Culture, with its promise of survival, self sufficiency and honorary middle class status for former dockers and steel workers effectively killed the Labour Party. Who needs socialism when you too can own a secondhand BMW? *See YTS*

Escape Magazine First published in '82 by enthusiasts Paul

ET The epitome of SPIELBERG sentimentality, ET drained millions of tear ducts world wide as it cruised to the top of the alltime box office champ league becoming the greatest tearjerker the world has ever known. The irony is that this '82 megamillion kidpic (it has taken in excess of $300 million) was turned down by the (now former) management at Disney, whose lachrymose traditions it matched perfectly. Instead Spielberg found a home at Universal and with merchandising and VIDEO (the official VIDEO release netted Stevie a neat $75 million) the dollars have never stopped rolling through their doors. Spielberg's success won him few friends in Hollywood, however. The most popular director among audiences is the least acclaimed by critics and remains unloved by the Academy who froze 'ET' out at that year's Oscars. There's no award for box office magic.

L to R: Electronic Body Music on Belgian TV (photo: Nigel Law). Echo & The Bunnymen. i-D straight ups Eden and James '83 (photo: Steve Johnston). i-D straight ups in Edinburgh '81 (photo: Chris Pring).

'82, the sweats with retro sporty graphics, pastel CHINOS and '50s print shirts became prototypes for Europe's growing influence in Britain's high streets. As labels like Radio, Best, Pepe and Mexx capitalised on the high street boom in '86 and '87, the innovators like Chipie and Chevignon in France, Boss in Germany, and Emporio Armani in Italy found and then lost favour in their own countries, but soon discovered a new market in the UK. Their universal appeal, comfortable colours and casual STYLE became, along with the CASUALS, the forerunners of the SPORTSWEAR boom in fashion.

Evangelism Evangelism was the fastest-growing sector of Christianity

Enterprise Culture. Enterprise Culture meant getting on your bike and pedalling to your own office in a revitalised dockland swarming with £20 per week units housing everything from pizza delivery services to mobile children's entertainers. Car valeting threatened to become the nation's biggest growth industry. In the New Disneyland, the new businessman was only successful if his idea was useless enough to provide a non-essential service in the leisure age. Balloon shops, KISSOGRAMS and nappy service deliveries thrived. The government saw this upsurge of surrealist initiative as a success when in reality it pointed to a complete failure to provide the employment possibilities that remains their responsibility. As vital national resources were farmed out to private enterprise, Britain was left

Gravett and Peter Standbury, the bimonthly *Escape* was the first professional comics fanzine to make it into WH Smiths. *See Deadline*

Eurostyle School trips and package holidays were two reasons for the most popular fashion boom of the decade. Coach loads of teenagers from Milan in their Chipie jeans, Best Montana sweatshirts, Charro boots and belts roamed the SHOPPING MALLS from York to Canterbury; day trippers from Calais in their Chipie shirts and labelled denims or Chevignon bombers invaded British seaside towns; Bayern Munich supporters in their Boss tracksuits and Puma trainers visited UK FOOTBALL grounds, and Eurostyle label spotting soon became the game of the decade. Pioneered by FIORUCCI's Classic Nouveau line of menswear in

in the '80s. Fifty million Americans considered themselves 'born again' fundamentalist Christians, amongst them US President RONALD REAGAN, a man who was said to believe in a Biblical Armageddon in his own lifetime. In the States, TV preachers like Jerry Falwell, Jim and Tammy Bakker and Oral Roberts built multi-million dollar empires, and a Disneyland-style Christian theme park 'Heritage USA' was even built. The evangelist movement went on building until Jim Bakker's one-night stand with secretary Jessica Hahn was revealed amidst much scandal in '86; even after that, no candidate for public office in the USA would ever dare admit they were not Christian, so strong was the fundamentalists' political clout. *See The Moral Majority and Salman Rushdie*

Paul Smith

Autumn / Winter '89

London
41, 42, 43, 44, Floral Street
Covent Garden, WC2E 9DT
Telephone 01 379 7133
23, Avery Row W1X 9HB
Telephone 01 493 1287
Harrods, Paul Smith Shop
4th Floor, Knightsbridge SW1.

Nottingham:
10, Byard Lane, NG1 2GJ
Telephone 0602 506 712

America
108, Fifth Avenue, New York
NY 10011.
Telephone 212 627 9770/1

Japan
4-19-5 Takekawa Sumida-ku
Tokyo
Telephone 03 635 1202

The Face Nick Logan had already edited the *NME* in its peak years and given the world *SMASH HITS* when, in May 1980, he launched his own, independently-published venture *The Face*. "Rock's final frontier" announced its early covers, but it soon became more than a music monthly, reflecting the mood and movements of the decade perhaps more than any other magazine. It inspired a host of new publications across Europe, and nurtured the talent of many of those who will be remembered as the stars of the '80s. STYLISTS, writers, photographers and designers found space to experiment and develop, while artists such as SADE, fashion gurus like GAULTIER, and new movements in ART, design, clubs and culture found a natural home within its pages. But times change, and in July '88 *The Face* celebrated its 100th issue by wrapping up the STYLE decade.

While other glossies and supplements continue to be obsessed by STYLE over content, in the '90s *The Face* is pushing other aspects of the magazine to the fore, looking increasingly towards Europe for inspiration, and boasting a simpler, more natural look. It will continue, though, to be irreverent and innovative as it moves into its tenth year.

The Falklands War The battle for The Falklands in '82 was a flashback to the 19th Century which resulted in pointless loss of life. In Britain, if it were ever in doubt, it showed the true and shocking extent of Fleet Street's sickness. *The Sun* in particular plumbed new depths with its infamous 'Gotcha!' headline on the sinking of the Argentinian ship Belgrano. The paper also 'sponsored' missiles inscribed with monosyllabic insults supposedly on behalf of its readership. The war was maintained at great expense over many thousands of miles and became a surreal echo of an empire spirit long gone. Despite a 'costly 'victory' and the resulting occupation, the real lesson has not been learned. If our precious nuclear arsenal is so effective as a deterrent, why did the war begin? *See CND*

The Fall Since he formed the band in Manchester in '77, The Fall's frontman Mark E Smith has proved himself to be the Sam Beckett of indie rock – a man with apparently only one (often indecipherable) thing to say, and determined to say it over and over again. After some six years as rather testy outsiders, The Fall's turning point was the recruitment in '83 of Smith's Californian wife Brix as guitarist, making the group a more marketably glamorous proposition (she eventually left them for her own extra-curricular pop project The Adult Net). Their most questionable moment as an ART Phenomenon was Smith's play 'Hey Luciani' ('86); but face was saved by the band's '88 collaboration with MICHAEL CLARK's dance company 'I Am Curious Orange'.

Fashion Compassion

In a decade when charity events became part of not just pop culture, but every facet of the entertainment industry, fashion followed LIVE AID with 'Fashion Aid' at the Royal Albert Hall in '86, the largest fashion show in the world. Punters paid £25 to see Bet Lynch in BODYMAP, GRACE JONES in Issey Miyake and various News At Ten broadcasters in Emanuel ballgowns; all the money raised going to Band Aid. In '87, the Fashion Cares T-shirt, bearing the signatures of 40 of the decade's top designers, was marketed with all profits going to the Terrence Higgins Trust. In May '89, 1,000 fashion celebrities window-shopped their way across London raising money for AIDS research, and the Newburgh Street Fashion Show in the same year helped raise £3,000 for homeless young people.

L to R: *Fashion Cares T-shirts (photo: Nick Knight).* **See Fashion Compassion**. *Ex-Frankie Goes To Hollywood member Holly Johnson (photo: Nick Knight).* *Freuds (photo: Barry Marsden)* **See Drinking Clubs**.

The Fashion Pop Syndrome Music and fashion have always been celebrity partners. Anthony Price made clothes specifically for Bryan Ferry two decades ago, but it wasn't until 1980, when VIVIENNE WESTWOOD clothed Adam & The Ants (and later Bow Wow Wow), that fashion married pop in public. It launched a relationship that strengthened over the decade as the benefits of mutual collaboration became more obvious – pop stars' wardrobes acquired 'STYLE' and the designers increased sales through higher exposure. Other memorable partnerships included KATHARINE HAMNETT and FRANKIE GOES TO HOLLYWOOD, BOY GEORGE and SUE CLOWES/BODYMAP, ABC and RICHMOND/CORNEJO, and JEAN PAUL GAULTIER and everyone. The peak of the fashion/pop marriage was the '86 Autumn/Winter London Fashion Week when there seemed to be more pop stars in the audience than journalists, and Fashion AID when everybody from GRACE JONES to Madness monopolised the catwalk. By '89 though, FASHION DESIGNERS had decided that they wanted to be pop stars themselves – PAM HOGG, JEAN PAUL GAULTIER and BERNSTOCK SPEIRS have all made records.

The Fax The long distance photocopier with instant recall began appearing in intelligent offices all round the country at the start of the decade and soon made the telex seem as archaic as the quill. Fax for the memory.

Filofaxes A real sign of the times – in the '80s the privately consulted diary was replaced by the publicly flaunted personal organiser, the filofax. As the Protestant Work Ethic turned into the YUPPIE Work Aesthetic, this pre-World War I invention came of age. Turning your life into a highly visible list of power brunches and business meetings, must-sees and must-dos, the more 'organised' you had to be, and so the streets were filled with well-dressed bag people lugging their lives around with them in FOOTBALL-sized filofaxes. As despised as chest wigs and medal-

Finley, Karen

Overly outrageous performance artist, painter and more recently rapper, who studied at the San Francisco Art Institute but is now firmly ensconced in New York. Finley has never been to the UK. Her proposed ICA performance in '87 with Haoui Montaug's 'No Entiendes!' revue was forbidden by Scotland Yard who'd been tipped off that she had live

Fashion Designers What punk initiated in '76 led to the most exciting ten years of fashion ever, releasing an energy that burst through the stagnant hierarchy of the '70s fashion world. When VIVIENNE WESTWOOD tried to show her collection to *Vogue* in '77, they didn't want to know. Fashion wasn't interested in anything outside fashion – a business that created clothes for a distinctly upmarket clientele. But a group of young designers emerged out of ART SCHOOLS and clubs, eager to assail the stiff upper lip of British fashion. They wanted to create clothes for their contemporaries, a generation who were breaking more fashion barriers than Dame Edna Everage, and who had inspired the new generation of STYLE magazines.

By '83 London Fashion Week the young designers had become the centre of attention, as the British fashion media suddenly took an interest in street fashion and a network of PRs and supportive magazines pushed the young designers into the spotlight. The European fashion industry, which had become synonymous with perfect finishing, excellent manufacturing and production techniques, did harbour doubts, however. In a society where fashion was about uniformity, the sight of models clambering over the catwalk wearing clothes that resembled a surrealist jumble sale sent buyers into spasms of mental arithmetic. Just how many of these creations could they sell?

But by '84 the scepticism had been dispelled as the British designers proved to the world that they were to be taken seriously, focusing their ideas and producing wearable collections, and the mainstream fashion press joined in the adulation encouraging hesitant buyers. The second wave of young ►

sex with turkeys. "I'm very interested in dispelling the entire notion of penis envy," she said, although whether house tracks featuring lyrics like '*I shove the yams up my granny's ass*' will contribute to this is debatable.

Pages 84, 85: Vivienne Westwood in World's End with customers '81. John Galliano's Spring/Summer '85 collection 'Afghanistan Repudiates Western' (photo: Mario Testino, styling: Caroline Baker). Jean Paul Gaultier's Spring/Summer '89 collection (photo: Sean Cunningham). See Fashion Designers.

lions by '85, the fioltad met its Waterloo, like the YUPPIE, on Black Monday – as the post-Crash anarchist broadsheet *Class War* headline put it: 'Filo-fucked!'. Despite attempts to sell an electronic version (the Psion) and expensive new alternatives (the Mulberry Organiser, the Harper House Dayrunner) the filofax, always something of a giveaway, is now something you get free from your bank manager.

Fiorucci A global magpie, Fiorucci launched the world of fun, frivolous fashion from his base in Milan, and became the catalyst for the birth of EUROSTYLE fashion. Always ahead of his time he produced VIVIENNE WESTWOOD's 'World School' collection which never left the showroom and the GAULTIER Junior line which was a great success. ►

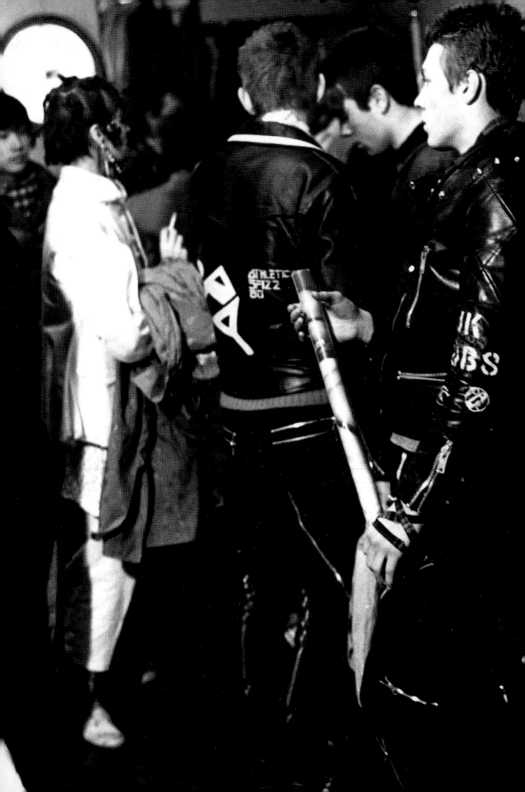

◄ Pioneering the DENIM wardrobe boom in the late '70s/early '80s he produced natural, stretch, stonewash, antique and a dozen other treatments under various labels like Appalussa, Liberto, Wrangler and Classic Nouveau, but the bubble finally burst in '89. Twenty one years after he first started, competition from global giants like Benetton and Esprit and the thousands of smaller companies that flooded the high streets, forced Fiorucci, the man, to sell the only possession he had – his name.

Flip The first of the secondhand retro fashion shops, Flip first opened in the late '70s on the KING'S ROAD and specialised in '40s, '50s and '60s US retro clothing. It was cheap and

popular because of its open 'til midnight, seven days a week policy, and for its first five years, owner Paul Wolf couldn't keep up with the demand eventually opening up two other Flip shops. Bowling shirts, lounge jackets, secondhand 501s and suede and leather jerkins were bought as rags by the container load, and it soon became a prime source for ROCKABILLIES. By the mid '80s, competition from other specialist retro shops like AMERICAN CLASSICS and American Retro hotted up, Wolf sold up, and now there is only one Flip shop in Covent Garden.

Flyers Blossoming during the early '80s warehouse club boom, flyers – printed invites for clubs distributed by hand at venues – have become the dominant language of London's nightlife grapevine. Flyers are far

Fluorescent Fashion Fluore cent colours hit club danc cefloors in '82 as a reac tion to both the battered HARD TIMES look and th emergent GOTH move ment, and gained fashio status with RAY PETRI styling and VIVIENN WESTWOOD's 'Witche collection in late '83. Hea and wrist bands, sock bobble hats and accessor ies all burst out in flashe of fluorescence, with one club even allowing any body sporting fluorescen colours in for free FIORUCCI then cornere this market with his Sprin '84 collection, which in cluded fluorescents mixe with DIAMANTE, bu fluorescent colours didn' reappear until the SUM MER OF LOVE, when club land turned dayglo e masse.

L to R: Pam Hogg's 'Warrior Queen' Autumn/Winter '89 collection (photo: Claire Pollock).
Felix, model and brief presenter of 'The Tube' (photo: Marc Lebon).
Andrew Czezowski and Susan Carrington **See The Fridge**.

◄ designers in '84/'85, spurred by the international attention and benefiting from the experience of the first wave, went for more subtle innovation rather than confrontation and became hailed as 'The YOUNG COUTURE'.

But soon the press had begun to turn on the designers. The designers' inexperience with all levels of production resulted in them selling themselves short – many failed to meet production schedules and quality expectations (but the antiquated manufacturing industry was equally to blame, unable/unprepared to deal with the small orders and innovative designs), and all were too often used as a source of ideas by buyers. At the same time, the fashion courses that had produced the glut of early '80s talent had radically changed. Students now were encouraged to aim for jobs in Next (See Retail Revolution) or serve their apprenticeships abroad, as the industry and high street saturated the market with diluted, cheaper versions. The emergent YUPPIE aesthetic of power-dressing and Preppy fashion also exerted an influence, pulling fashion back to status dressing as wealth.

Having seen some of the original innovators go under, most of the survivors chased the market, absorbing European and American catwalks and catering to a more conservative market, although a few of the more creative designers managed to survive on their own terms. Meanwhile, Paris was regaining its place in the global spotlight, as general interest shifted to Europe (See Belgian Fashion) and Christian Lacroix introduced colour and humour back to couture. Utilising flowers, tartans and gold brocades, he revitalised couture as a source of ideas, and with Karl Lagerfeld and Eric Begere, employed to relaunch Chanel and Hermés respectively, helped push couture to the fore.

Because most designer fashion had shifted towards the more sophisticated demands of the market, by '89, the young fashion consumer was looking more to street trends than the catwalk, where NIGHTCLUBBING and music were making their presence felt like never before. A new breed of fashion entrepreneur evolved – small businesses that picked up on a succession of quick-selling ideas, catering to a series of accelerating club-based 'looks'. ART SCHOOLS had started training fashion students for jobs in the high street and the maverick element that was intrinsic to the early '80s designers had almost become a thing of the past. The question is what will happen next? Without the wealth of ideas that the first wave of designers generated, and without government support of ART SCHOOLS, where will the new names in British fashion come from? Will the same few designers that dominated the '80s dominate the '90s as well? See Cultural Cross-Dressing, Customising, The Daisy Age, Dressing Down, Education, Sportswear and St Martin's School Of Art

Food Courts Just as every cheaper and more flexible than magazine ads or listings, and enable you to communicate club details only to the crowd you want – and, as most warehouse clubs are illegal, keep them away from the police (during the SUMMER OF LOVE, flyers wouldn't even give the club's address). They range from photocopies of hand-scrawled notes and maps to lavish, technicolour cards and artworked designer jobs printed on rice paper. Flyers are functional street art and London's answer to New York's GRAFFITI culture. See Nightclubbing

shopping centre built in the '70s had to have its own fountain, every SHOPPING MALL built in the '80s had to have its own food court. Five or six theme restaurants sat around a central seating area dispensing pancakes, pizza, bratwurst and pasta, all of which tasted the same. A 'revolutionary marketing concept' designed to sterilise and homogenise the foods of the world down to an instant, empty experience. This is world food through a cultural blender. Could WORLD MUSIC go the same way?

Food Scares At the beginning of the decade you could eat with

The Flat-Top The classic American haircut of the '50s re-emerged in the late-'70s amongst Britain's first ROCKABILLIES and by 1980 was the most common hairstyle for the large number of youths into the American retro look. The squared-off short back-and-sides cut, along with its variants the GI crop and the Mac Curtis, had a stylish, clean cut simplicity that soon became the ubiquitous street haircut. By '85 its popularity had spread so widely that even the male models in *Vogue* were sheepishly sporting newly cropped hair while pop stars like GRACE JONES and rappers such as Schoolly D helped make it an international look. Sported everywhere from building sites to the floor of the Stock Exchange, the flat-top is testament to the proposition that real fashion comes from below – what started as a revival by British working class youth ended up as the most fashionable male haircut of the entire decade.

blissful ignorance and relative impunity – if you caught food poisoning it was plain unlucky. By '89 Britain was reeling from a tidal wave of food scares, terrified to nibble even a lettuce leaf in fear of listeriosis. Edwina Currie set the scene in '88 with her exposure of salmonella in the egg world. Swift on its heels followed listeria in soft cheeses, BSE in meat, BST in dairy produce, aluminium in baby milk, and dioxin in food packaging. Pressure groups proliferated, demanding that the government make our food industry safe, while the beleagured consumers concluded that the only guarantee of safe food was to grow your own.

Football The Sun called it 'The Decade Of Soccer Terror', and certainly going by their headlines you could be forgiven for thinking our football grounds were populated solely by ROTTWEILER owning LAGER LOUTS. The Luton v Millwall riot of March '85, the Bradford fire (the only hooliganism here was the negligence of the board, but who remembers that now?), and then the biggie, Heysel stadium. The gross incompetence surrounding ticket sales, segregation, policing and structural safety nearly brought down the Belgian government, yet it did not merit discussion in Fortress Wapping.

Mrs THATCHER decided that Something Had To Be Done; and Luton Town showed us how to do it. Plucky little Luton Town first installed a plastic pitch (just the thing to stage those

Christian Lacroix's Autumn/Winter '88 collection (photo: Sean Cunningham) **See Fashion Designers.**

L to R: Jimmy Greaves **See Football**. *Steve Strange in Crolla and Bet Lynch in BodyMap at Fashion Aid October '86 (photo: Sean Cunningham)* **See Fashion Compassion**.

lucrative boxing matches), and then banned those drug-crazed, child-eating monsters: away fans. Families would swarm back, was the argument. Actually, the morgue-like atmosphere meant a 30% drop in attendance despite Luton having by far their most successful season ever on the pitch. "But does football really *need* spectators?" asked Mrs T, and the ID card scheme was born.

April 15th '89 – 95 die on the terraces at Hillsborough, some in glorious tabloid technicolour. Give them plush all-seater stadiums, say the same politicians who would've had us all birched a year ago. Others castigate clubs for spending cash on players, not grandstands, conveniently forgetting that while staff

are tax deductable, new stadia are not. Yes the £44 million ITV deal lined further the pockets of the big boys, but for a truer indication of financial health in the '80s think of the homeless Charlton and Bristol Rovers, those narrowly avoided mergers (Thames Valley Royals, Fulham Park Rangers), and Newport County RIP. There by the grace of God go Derby, Wolves, Swansea, Aldershot, Middlesborough, Bristol City...

All this indicated doom and despondancy, yet morale on the terraces was the highest for years – gates were up, bananas were being waved, fanzines were selling in bulk and the Football Supporters Association was gaining in membership and influence. Clubs such as MILLWALL, Preston, Halifax and Crewe learned the value of community involvement, and tolerance levels

were so high that Rangers even signed a Catholic. The '90s promise to be turbulent times, but football fans can face the future with a united front. Amongst all this, there was actually some time for a bit of football, but if one thing is certain in the '90s it's that Liverpool will ride roughshod over all opposition. Whether it's in front of 10,000 members at Wimbledon, or half of Europe via satellite from the San Siro in Milan, remains to be seen.

Football Fanzines The '80s was the age of the football fanzine. *Off The Ball* (now defunct) and *When Saturday Comes* kicked it off in '86, using the old punk fanzine format to proclaim FOOTBALL's ills. There was much to be disenchanted with – asset-strippers, squalid facilities, the complacency of the football authorities, racists, professional fouls and players with dodgy haircuts. All were targeted with intelligence and irreverence. And as these first two became typeset and tidy, so the bandwagon began to roll. By '89 there were about 200 publications, ranging from Celtic's *Not The View*, with a circulation of 12,000, to the likes of non-league *Champion Hill Street Blues* (Dulwich Hamlet), sales of which often exceed their club's attendance figures. Charlton's *Voice Of The Valley* sought (and won) a return to their hallowed ground, while Leeds' *Marching Altogether* is still seeking to eliminate racism from the Elland Road terraces. Club reaction has been varied; Bradford's *City Gent* and West Brom's *Fingerpost* were freely available on club premises, while Vauxhall Opel League Wealdstone's *Elmslie Ender* was banned by the whole non-league pyramid after some ill-advised but harmless bitching about Dagenham.

Forsyth, Bill Ironically Puttman's best collaborator was the one he left entirely to his own devices. The reclusive press-shy Scot proved a master of the quirk, a subtle smile-maker whose films left the audience with an inner glow they

could never quite place. 'Gregory's Girl' still ranks as one of the top rating films shown on TV this decade (not too far behind 'Jaws' and the Bonds) while 'Local Hero' is a peerless whimsy that won gems from its entire cast, including a positively beaming Burt Lancaster, wading into the sea after the aurora borealis. Unfortunately 'Comfort And Joy' missed its mark and 'Housekeeping' fell foul of Columbia's post-Puttman putsch, but Forsyth will be back and so will our smiles.

Foster, Jodie Unlike her child star contemporaries – Kirsty McNicol, Brooke Shields, Tatum O'Neal – Foster always had a reputation for serious talent. At 14, she co-starred with ROBERT DE NIRO in 'Taxi Driver' and thereupon became the obsession of John Hinckley who, in '82 attempted to kill President REAGAN, blaming Foster's subliminal influence. At the same time, a hardcore skate-punk band formed in California, calling itself The Jodie Foster Army. It seemed that Foster was destined, like Patty Hearst, to remain in the American psyche because of the apparent ease of her life and lack of 'real life' experience, rather than for her thespian talents. The turnaround finally came in '89 with 'The Accused', a court and bar room rape drama. Sick of the sidelines she powered her way through the part with nerve and relish to become Best Actress and the year's most popular Oscar winner.

Frankie Goes To Hollywood Although the pop public were privy to the fact that some chart-topping bands (The Monkees, The Bay City Rollers) didn't actually play on their own records, it took the case of Frankie Goes To Hollywood to finally lay bare the device. The first single, 'Relax' with its '*When you wanna come*' refrain, so outraged Radio One DJ Mike Reid that the corporation banned it, thus hastening its journey to number one in March '84. The summer of '84 was the summer of the Frankie T-shirt, the

Food Scares At the beginning of the decade you could eat with blissful ignorance and relative impunity – if you caught food poisoning it was plain unlucky. By '89 Britain was reeling from a tidal wave of food scares, terrified to nibble even a lettuce leaf in fear of listeriosis. Edwina Currie set the scene in '88 with her exposure of salmonella in the egg world. Swift on its heels followed listeria in soft cheeses, BSE in meat, BST in dairy produce, aluminium in baby milk, and dioxin in food packaging. Pressure groups proliferated, demanding that the government make our food industry safe, while the beleaguered consumers concluded that the only guarantee of safe food was to grow your own.

Foster, Norman One of Britain's architect superstars, Norman Foster went to Hong Kong in the '80s to put up what some called 'the building of the century', the £680 million high rise high tech HQ of the Hong Kong & Shanghai Bank. It was expensive, even for an 'intelligent' skyscraper, but the HKS

original being 'Frankie Say Arm The Unemployed', emasculated by ZTT distributors Island Records to 'Frankie Say Relax'. The follow up, 'Two Tribes', instantly followed to number one, as did its successor 'Power Of Love'. By now though, it was quite apparent that Frankie was not a band and that Morley and Horn were more than just mentors. The court case that followed Holly Johnson's announcement that he intended going solo revealed that Johnson was in fact the only member who'd contributed to any of the records, the three lads and Hi-NRG dancer Paul Rutherford being there just for effect. In the post-Sex Pistols decade of the music industry being wise to any attempts at subversion, perhaps an effect was all that could be hoped for from a pop group. Whatever, the Frankie singles, with their John Bonham sampled drumbeats and Morley's Sadean sleevenotes, remain valuable documents.

Franks, Lynne Having worked on teen magazine *Petticoat* in the '60s, Franks set up her own PR company in the late '70s, winning the accounts for Gloria Vanderbilt designer jeans, KATHARINE HAMNETT clothes and Raleigh bikes. The company thrived in the '80s, representing SWATCH, Next, HMV, 'NETWORK 7', BRYLCREEM and, in the '87 election, The Labour Party. By the end of the '80s the company employed 45 staff at its office off Marble Arch and was so succesful that top financial PR outfit Broad Street bought the business for £2.65 million plus a profit percentage. In true late-'80s STYLE, Franks is more famous than that which she promotes and is perhaps best known for her Nichiren Shoshu Buddhism which she and husband (and company director) Peter Howie adhere to. They chant for world peace and release their creativity in the process. Though branded 'designer buddhists', her enthusiasm has inspired many to look beyond the confines of capitalism whilst continuing to play the game, even though many of these acolytes

L to R: Simon Foxton (photo: Thomas Degen) **See Bazooka and Stylists.** *Fine Young Cannibals. i-D straight up Martin Fry '82* **See ABC**. *Brix Smith and Mark E Smith from The Fall '88.*

THE FACE – FUTURISTS **91**

appear to work for her.

Frat Pack Movies *See John Hughes*

The Fred Magazine The 'small is beautiful' creed brought to publishing, *The Fred*'s pocket-sized pontification brought magazine credibility to writers from KATHY ACKER to Marina Warner, even though the lay-out was pretty unsightly. This pint-sized publication with a name selected "because it sounded cuddly" first appeared free in shop corners and art galleries in October '83, printing everything from short stories to paintings by unknowns. Eight issues on, it now charges a pound a throw, has a print run of 20,000, but

aims for a circulation of "four and a half million". A bona fide oddity, a magazine in the land of the hard sell, *The Fred* still finds its way into the jackets of the more discerning readers.

The Fridge As an attempt to open a West End-style venue in Brixton, The Fridge was a venture that verged on madness. But if anyone could carry it off, it was Andrew Czezowski and Susan Carrington, the duo who ran the infamous punk hangout The Roxy up until its closure in April '77. The first Fridge opened in December '81 just opposite the police station at 390 Brixton Rd, featuring a cool decor based around discarded fridges, old tyres and TV sets chained to the floor. When the local council decided it should close in September '84, they

bank got their money's worth in marketable image value and even reproduced Foster's tour-de-force on their bank notes. At home he worked on a smaller scale, dabbling in shop design for KATH-ARINE HAMNETT. Expect him to put up temperatures as well as buildings in the '90s, when his plans for Stansted Airport and the King's Cross redevelopment begin to be realised.

Futurama The first alternative music festival, which brought together every independent star of the early '80s from the Young Marble Giants to Sex Gang Children. Although the first one was at the Queens Hall in Leeds in 1979, later Futuramas at Stafford proved that JOY DIVISION fans loved mud, warm beer, plastic glasses and dire toilet facilities as much as the next festival-goer.

chose the fledgling Bronski Beat to head the party and invited the 600-strong crowd to "smash up the place and take a piece home". The club reopened just over a year later in a building that had been first a cinema then a roller disco until it was destroyed by fire. It was, they admit, a shoestring operation, funded by the £600 they had in their pocket and a £5,000 loan from Joe Strummer. On the opening night, the toilets were unfinished, the sound system left much to be desired, but the crowd came nonetheless. Since then, improvements have been steady, and The Fridge now boasts three nights packed with a capacity crowd of 1,500, a huge dancefloor surrounded by banks of flickering TV screens and

decor and sound that can compete with any West End club.

Friends Of The Earth Alongside GREENPEACE, Friends Of The Earth set up in Britain in '71 as a non-political, multi-issue campaigning organisation. All the campaigns we regard as recent concerns have, in fact, been fought by FOE for years. In '83 they began complaining about acid rain, in '84 their Pesticide Campaign was launched, and it was not until '87 that Britain finally realised that their concern about the ozone layer wasn't mere scare-mongering. Generally keeping a lower profile than GREENPEACE, they shot to prominence in '88 with their CFCs boycott coupled with public support from Prince Charles. 1989 brought more prominence and their membership doubled in the first half of the

year; the organisation now receive around 300 letters a week from the public.

Fun Pubs Distinct from COCKTAIL PUBS and a peculiarly northern phenomenon that attempts to re-create the atmosphere of that wonderful week in Torremolinos. Can you drink a pint of lager from a baby's bottle? Do you want to be insulted by a screaming DJ? Fun pubs are no fun at all unless you can pass a balloon between your knees or you feel you have what it takes to win a Mr Wet Underpants competition. These palaces of low-brow entertainment sprung up as a sort of 'Hi-De-Hi' on acid, or at least Bacardi and Coke. The beginning of the end for the

traditional British pub.

Funkapolitan Straddling LINX and ABC, Funkapolitan perfected a British white funk that seemed to solve one fundamental problem of Britfunk – they dressed well. With an LP produced by Kid Creole, and ample coverage in magazines, they seemed on the poise of something. Nobody quite knew what though, and the brand broke up, leaving TOM DIXON and Nick Jones to carry their dancefloor ethos through THE LANGUAGE LAB, Titanic and DRIVE-IN DEMOLITION DISCO DERBY, and keyboard player Toby Anderson to eventually find a brief flicker of fame with Curiosity Killed The Cat.

L to R: Simon Hobart at The Flytrap '84 (photo: Sebastian Sharkels). John Galliano (photo: Eddie Monsoon). Jean Paul Gaultier (photo: Michael Momy).

The Futurists

In 1909, Italy's Filippo Tommaso Marinetti published the first Futurist Manifesto, demanding the destruction of ART's old guard and calling a younger generation to instigate a movement more in keeping with modern times. 71 years later, the baton was picked up, but rather more quickly dropped by the flotsam of the NEW ROMANTICS,

Visage and Ultravox unwisely describing their cheesy synthy pop as Futurist .music. Rather lacking the anarchic vitality of the original movement, this new wave was too concerned about smudging its eye-liner to indulge in violent struggle. Paul Morley appropriated the title of Marinetti's most famous poem 'Zang Tumb Tumb' when setting up his label in '83. *See ZTT*

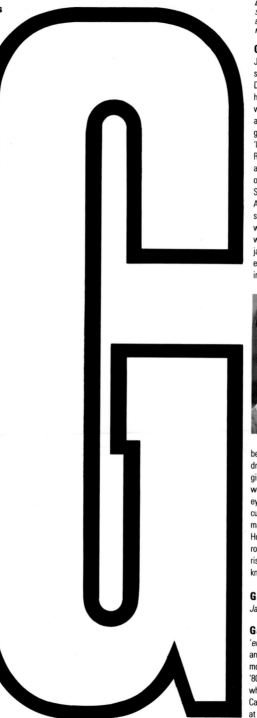

Galliano, John Even at college John Galliano was always seen as a star, and when he received the Designer Of The Year Award in '87, his star status in the fashion business was given the final stamp of approval. Within weeks of his graduation show at ST MARTIN'S in '84, his collection of stylised French Revolution costumes, 'Les Incroyables', were selling in the windows of the prestigious Brown's store in South Molton Street. Aided by stylist Amanda 'Lady Harlech' Grieve, his shows were elaborate adventures, wild mixes of clothes worn every which way – trousers worn as jackets, jackets worn as skirts, and everything worn upside down and inside out. Magpies and clocks

became head-dresses, trailing muslin dresses were soaked onto angelic girls with straw bound hair, '30s-type women paraded with heavily-kohled eyes, and always the most beautifully cut clothes. His designs were always magical – where were the seams? How did a lapel become a garden rose? Why did that hemline dip and rise so effortlessly? Only Galliano knew. *See Fashion Designers*

Garcons, Comme des *See Japanese Designers*

Gaultier, Jean Paul The 'enfant terrible' of Parisian fashion, and undoubtedly the hippest and most influential cult designer of the '80s. Gaultier's career began at 18 when he went to design for Pierre Cardin, quickly followed by positions at Jacques Esterel and Jean Patou.

In '76 aged 22 he produced his first line through neccessity (ie. poverty), and created clothes from furnishing fabrics. Although his designs were certainly unique (a biker's jacket worn with a ballerina's tutu), his first seasons were not a success. By the '80s, however, he had made his mark. And how. The favourite of fashion students and the avant garde fashion press, Gaultier produced innovation after innovation. His tapestry and tartan fabric mixes, curlicue cigarette holders, corkscrew conical bras, full length corset dresses, S&M rubber as daywear, chiffon aprons worn over pinstripe trousers suits, leather biker's jackets with no backs, tailored suits with no side panels, cowboys in lace, sailor girls in stretch stripes and knee length knickers, boys in high heels, jackets made entirely of sunglasses, and so much more.

His clothes have been worn by almost every major pop star over the past decade, and in '87 he produced the Gaultier Junior DIFFUSION LINE, a cheaper version of his main line. More affordable still was his record release in '89 called 'How To Do That', which had the designer's voice cross cut over a HOUSE beat. The VIDEO by JEAN BAPTISTE MONDINO showed his desire to be involved in other ART forms, having also worked with singer Rita Mitsouko and dancer Regine Chopinot, creating costumes for both artists. His Paris store is like no other with VIDEO screens in the floor previewing the current season's catwalk show. He is also the designer responsible for putting Hamish Bowles, fashion director of *Harpers & Queen* magazine, on the catwalk for his womenswear collection Autumn/Winter '89, when Bowles modelled identical outfits to the other 40 or so girls. More than anything else, Jean Paul Gaultier likes a good joke. *See Fashion Designers*

Gaz's Rockin' Blues On July 3 1980 Gaz Mayall opened Gaz's Rockin' Blues at Gossips on a Thursday night. Ten years later he's still there. The most important club

Garage Music A misappropriated term used to describe late '80s New York R&B, more accurately it refers to the PARADISE GARAGE, a New York gay club which entered into dance music legend due to the mixing skills of its DJ Larry Levan and his idiosyncratic choice of music which ran from The Clash, Sylvester to Gwen Guthrie. What was called Garage by a music industry running from the destructive excesses of ACID HOUSE came to the fore in '88/'89 with chart success for former underground artists like Adeva and Paul Simpson. The use of the term probably arose due to the fact that most of the musicians involved were themselves graduates of the club. At its best Garage utilises a hard house beat to transport a gospel-fired vocal message of love, peace and positivity.

L to R: Chicago's Garage club '86 (photo: Simon Witter) See House Music. Peter Mamonov from Russian rock band Zvuki Mu See Glasnost. Gaz Mayall at his Kensington Market stall '80 See Gaz's Rockin' Blues

for new young R&B-based bands in the '80s, Gaz's has presided over more youth cults than *i-D*. The club's musical manifesto of R&B/blues/ska/reggae leaned heavily towards rockabilly in its formative years (The Stray Cats played their first headlining London gigs there), but as the rockabilly scene petered away, newer bands like THE POGUES and Lash Lariat & The Long Riders started to appear. Dubbed COUNTRYBILLY, the scene monopolised the club until the first SKA band, The Potato 5, started adapting Studio One sounds to the '80s, prompting Gaz to launch a record label and inspiring a host of other SKA bands. Expect its record as the longest running one nighter in London to continue well into the '90s.

Geldof, Bob Despite a series of spectacularly bad pop songs performed with the frighteningly successful Boomtown Rats, it isn't 'I Don't Like Mondays' that Bob Geldof will be remembered for. From a minor pop star with a big mouth to a globe saving friend of Charles and Diana (becoming a Knight Of The British Empire in June '86); from Paula Yates' husband as he was described in the press at the lowest pre-LIVE AID point in his career to late night milk guzzler in TV commercials, Bob Geldof has had an eventful '80s. It was really his mouthy self belief that allowed him to press-gang the world's biggest pop names to contribute to the international LIVE AID concert. Grossing millions, this effectively fed millions ignored by the selfishness and indifference of governments. We could spend a whole

day taking the piss out of The Boomtown Rats and Geldof's god-awful voice but his achievements cancel each and every cheap gag out. His is perhaps the greatest contribution to the '80s.

Gilliam, Terry The UK-based American who came to fame as the animator of the Monty Python team, his surreal grunting creations punctuated the Flying Circus and won him cult acclaim. 'Jabberwocky', Gilliam's directorial debut, was a wonderfully grotesque medieval comedy, but it was his trilogy of '80s films – 'Time Bandits', 'Brazil' and 'The Adventures Of Baron Munchausen' – that brought Gilliam international renown as one of film's foremost fantasists. Unfortunately, after achieving effects on next to nothing for 'Time Bandits' and slightly more than nothing on 'Brazil', 'Munchausen''s budget exploded out of control running up to a total of $54 million. Was the 'Baron' Gilliam's 'Heaven's Gate' and, if so, how soon will he work again? We are impatient for more.

Glasgow Pups Hack phrase invented by ART critic Waldemar Januszczak for an innovative crew of figurative Scottish painters who only form a unified school in the sense that they all graduated from the Glasgow School Of ART (and were all feted at the Edinburgh Festival 'Vigorous Imagination' exhibition of '87). Biggest draw is Steven Campbell, with his ludic form of Bertie Wooster surrealism. Also celebrated are Adrian Wiszniewski's neo-arcadian allegories and Stephen Conroy's mysterious Edwardian epiphanies. But most impressive are Peter Howson and Ken Currie – two Heroic Social Realists who elected to stay in their native city and reconstruct in oils its vanishing tenement heritage.

Global Warming The discovery for most people that we were eating a massive hole in the ozone layer was a lot more gradual than the process itself. The explosion in publicity can be tracked to a small number of scientific papers which appeared as late as '88, although the theory was widely known years before these convinced the scientific community that the threat was worse than they had projected. Global

warming is caused by a proliferation of gases (mainly carbon dioxide and CFCs as used in aerosols and refridgerators, nitrous oxide used in fertilizers, and methane), which trap the sun's heat in the earth's atmosphere. Atmospheric change is the most intangible of ecological factors, but it's also the most deadly. An imbalance in the air effects *everything*, and the global warming caused by the destruction of the ozone layer is potentially lethal.

Estimates of the damage centre around predictions of how fast the polar ice caps will melt, and consequently how fast the oceans will rise with the predicted 2 degrees centigrade rise in temperature over the next decade. The most pessimistic would mean widespread flooding around Britain by the mid-'90s and the virtual obliteration of Holl-

Glasgow

Glasgow is the changing face of urban Britain. Never in the history of civic policy has a place pulled off a stunt quite like Glasgow. In the '60s it was the city of tenements, tough-nuts and Tongs Ya Bass. By the late '80s it had been voted European City of Culture and the centre of an aesthetic renaissance encompassing figurative painting, literature and pop music. In 1990 you will be able to visit Glasgow and be stabbed by a conceptual artist.

Glasnost A Russian word meaning 'openness' it described the policies of Mikhail GORBACHEV, the USSR's leader from '85. In theory, Glasnost meant a return to the true spirit of Lenin's socialism. In practice, it meant the booting out of corrupt officials, moves towards a better standard of living, more press freedom, the hope of new relationships between East and West, ideological thaw in the cold war and the prospect of arms reduction. He also presided over one of the greatest trade deals ever. They sold us the image of peres-

troika and when it arrived it was three dodgy rock bands who would have looked outmoded in the '70s. See CND

Godber, John
John Godber won almost every award at the National Student Drama festivals between '81 and '83, while head of drama at Minsthorpe High, the school he attended as a student. Godber switched to full-time writing in '84 when he joined the Hull Truck Theatre Company as Artistic Director, and quickly entered the big time prize league, winning the '84 Laurence Olivier 'Comedy Of The Year' award with 'Up 'n' Under' and seven Los Angeles Critics Circle Awards with 'Bouncers' in '85. But school still preys on his mind: his last West End comedy smash, 'Teechers', detailed the trials and travails of a comprehensive school drama teacher as seen through the eyes of the no-hoper bottom-graders he rescued from apathy and disillusion.

L to R: Muriel Gray. Claire Grogan. Ghettoblaster '86. Guns'N'Roses. Georgina Godley (photo: John Hicks). Georgina Godley's Summer '86 collection (photo: Cindy Palmano).

and, on the other hand, the effect could turn out to be minimal if the world drastically reduced its fossil-fuel burning and CFCs production now. This seems most unlikely, even though the West hopes to stop the production of CFCs by 1994 almost completely. China has ordered nearly 100 million fridges containing CFCs from the West maintaining that they cannot afford the alternatives.

G-Mex Or alternatively, The Festival Of The Tenth Summer. Organised by Factory Communications, this week of events in July '86 marked ten years since Manchester punk first made an impudent and refreshing nuisance of itself. G-Mex argued eloquently for the city's claim of

continued pop dominance in the '80s: the final day featured sets by THE FALL, THE SMITHS and NEW ORDER, perhaps three of the most influential English bands of the decade. Bill Grundy compered, slippery prankster Paul Morley avoided a fight with Jamie Reid, and Pete Shelley and Howard Devoto took a bow for services rendered. Northern civic rivalry was even forgotten when Liverpudlian crooner Ian McCulloch joined NEW ORDER for a closing version of 'Ceremony'.

Go Go A percussion based funk music from Washington DC, West End DJs started playing the first imports in '84. Six months later Island Records had signed a deal with the major Go Go label DETT, planned a film about it ('Good To Go' eventually released '86), and moulded leading

Godley, Georgina
Georgina Godley parted company with Scott Crolla and went solo as a designer in '85, creating ART-inspired designs that some called 'fashion surrealism'. Her show in '87 was appropriately enough staged at the V&A lecture hall (where her clothes later appeared as part of '88's Fashion & Surrealism exhibition). Her work is instantly recognisable – wired hoop hemlines, padded bums and stomachs, and an unusual choice of natural fabrics give Georgina's designs a homespun image. Queen of 'cerebral couture' and responsible for offering a new definition of the female form, she once commented: "My best friends tell me I need a lobotomy." The Earth Mother of British fashion. *See Crolla and Fashion Designers*

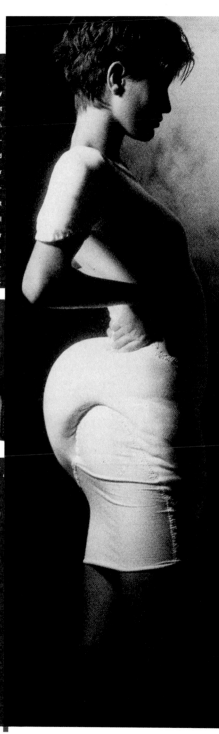

TITAN BOOKS

THE STYLE OF THE 90's

LOVE AND ROCKETS :
APE SEX
£6.50

MAI 3 :
THE PSYCHIC GIRL
£7.95

BATMAN :
THE KILLING JOKE
£2.25

AT

THE ULTIMATE COMICS, SCIENCE FICTION, FANTASY AND HORROR BOOKSHOP

FORBIDDEN
PLANET

LONDON · BRIGHTON · CAMBRIDGE · DUBLIN
GLASGOW · NEWCASTLE · NOTTINGHAM · MAIL ORDER

71 NEW OXFORD STREET, LONDON WC1A 1DG. 01-836 4179 AND 01-379 6042
29 SYDNEY STREET, BRIGHTON, SUSSEX BN1 4EP. 0273 687620
60 BURLEIGH STREET, CAMBRIDGE CB1 1DJ. 0223 66926
36 DAWSON STREET, DUBLIN 2, IRELAND. 0001 710 688
168 BUCHANAN STREET, GLASGOW G1 2LW. 041 331 1215
17 PRUDHOE PLACE, NEWCASTLE-UPON-TYNE NE1 7PE. 091 261 9173
129 MIDDLE WALK, BROADMARSH CENTRE, NOTTINGHAM NG1 7LN. 0602 584706
MAIL ORDER, C/O 71 NEW OXFORD STREET, LONDON WC1A 1DG. 01-497 2150

PLEASE SEND SAE FOR OUR LISTS OF COMICS, TITAN GRAPHIC
NOVELS, AND JUDGE DREDD, BATMAN, GERRY ANDERSON AND
STAR TREK PRODUCT LISTS.

ALSO AVAILABLE AT ALL GOOD BOOK SHOPS

Rat Graffiti (photo: Louis Benassi)

band Trouble Funk for stardom. It was a new dance market that other record companies were quick to jump on – London, Phonogram and Rhythm King all released compilation albums – but Island, with its near monopoly on quality Go Go, mysteriously released very little. It wasn't until '86 that they finally brought Trouble Funk over to Britain for two electrifying shows at THE FRIDGE and Town & Country Club, showing just how Go Go should be experienced – live, loud and for nearly three hours. In the end though, Go Go died an unceremonious death on club dancefloors, the two year hype not being sufficient to sustain the paucity of releases, and by the end of the decade Trouble Funk had ceased to exist.

The Gorbachevs Soviet superstars Mikhail and Raisa took the international stage in '85 and changed the way the West saw Russia. Gorbachev came across as a man totally averse to banging a furious shoe on the table and Raisa, the Joan Collins of the Kremlin, destroyed the view of Soviet women as 20 stone spanner wielding babooshkas. Frequently playing away, he shamed Western leaders with one peace deal after another and his commitment to the 'zero option' of a world free of nuclear weapons. Gorby, as he was affectionately referred to by even the British tabloid press, became an international Superman of the late '80s. Some even suggested that the Russian leader tucked his vest into his underpants. As unofficial fan clubs sprung up outside the USSR, his popularity at home decreased as he tackled Russia's problematic VODKA frenzy with restrictions on the purchase of ALCOHOL. In the West, where Smirnoff is still freely available, the man with the map on his head was seen less as a neo-prohibitionist and more as a symbol of pre-Aquarian optimism of the late '80s. *See CND and Glasnost*

Goths As the tail end of punk wilted it spawned its bad seed, Goth.

Goude, Jean Paul A global visionary, Jean Paul Goude was, until July 14 '89, probably best known as the man who 'created' – and subsequently married – GRACE JONES and who had (along with fellow Frenchman JEAN BAPTISTE MONDINO) helped define an idiosyncratic and instantly identifiable funky Eurostyle advertising. Celebrated on home territory the media hyphenate – illustrator, art director, stylist, visual engineer – found himself in charge of several million francs and told to stage an event to mark the bicentenial of the French Revolution. With his three hour parade complete with African rhymes, London fire engines, marching bands, the Red Army, replica steam engines, ballet dancers, nightclubbers, hordes of Chinese cyclists and more, Goude provided an extravagant exclamation mark at the end of a decade which may be chiefly rememberd for its stylistic excess, whilst simultaneously acknowledging the small 'p' political ideal of a united global family. *See Ciné Brats*

Rooted in Hammer House Of Horror re-runs, the Addams Family, THE OCCULT, black magic, vampires and 'The Rocky Horror Show', the look was appropriately enough, all black. Black crimped hair, leather jackets, fishnet stockings, leather jeans, pointed boots and heavy belts, bones, crucifixes, studs and lots of beads and cheap silver jewellery broke up this dark look with scarlet and red being the only acceptable complementary colours. Bands like The Cramps, Birthday Party, BAUHAUS and Virgin Prunes paved the way, with the Sisters Of Mercy emerging as the Hamlets of this last generation. Much misunderstood by the media because it was not suburban enough to be manipulated into

mainstream fashion in the same way that the soulboy/'50s preppy look has been watered down into the CHINO and striped shirt LAGER LOUT look, Goths were therefore the last standard bearers of punk. Pure Goths hardly exist now but have moved up via Zodiac Mindwarp, THE CULT, Danse Society bikers chic and GREBO, towards the LA metal, New York sleaze look.

Graffiti Fab Five Freddie, Futura 2000, Seen, Ali, TAKI 183 – these were some of the names that appeared literally overnight on the walls and subway train carriages of the Big Apple at the start of the decade. Not that you'd know it unless you were a part of hip hop subculture. For these 'tags' were illegible to the average commuter, spray-painted in a bubbled or jagged wild

STYLE which threatened to blur the distinction between typography and pictography. Interpretations varied. The Transit Authority called them vandals. The sociologists celebrated them as aerosol guerillas, recolonizing the alphabet and 'bombing' the city with their territorial markers. But they figured they were artists and were only too happy to change their comic-book pseudonyms into celebrity signatures. Hence Samo became Jean Michel Basquiat and got to work with WARHOL, and Kenny Scharf customised cars, household appliances and turned anything but the kitchen sink into ART. Meanwhile, Keith Haring gentrified the STYLE and cleaned up, moving to SCULPTURE when he realised that

the ART world had lost interest. By the end of the decade, graffiti had returned to the street, but with the renewed vigilance of the Transit Authority in New York and local councils in Britain, graffiti had become even more of an outlaw activity than before.

Grandmaster Flash With his rappers The Furious Five, Grandmaster Flash was responsible for two of the decade's most important records. '82's 'Adventures On The Wheels Of Steel' was an inspired cut-up megamix of Chic, Queen and various other records, which predated the DJ record boom by five years, and 'The Message' was one of the first social consciousness hip hop records. Flash elevated turntables to the status of instruments and became the first DJ star.

The Graphic Novel

In Europe the *Bande Dessinee* has been stacked in the serious book shops for years – only in Anglo/American cultural circles were comics considered fit for the sweetshop or the drugstore. In '87 the advent of the Graphic Novel changed all that. Art Spiegelman's *Maus*, an Aesop-style fable of the Holocaust, was picked up

by Penguin, while ALAN MOORE's superhero exposé *WATCHMEN* garnered favourable reviews in the quality press. It was all grist to the publishing mill and the end of the decade saw the release of Neil Gaiman and Dave McKean's poetic urban noir crime story *Black Orchid* along with translations of foreign material by genre legends like Moebius, Bilal and Liberatore. It's a long way from Smallville.

Gray, Muriel

Gallous Glasgow celeb who was one of the first of the untrained TRENDY TELLY presenters, making her name on early editions of 'THE TUBE' by calling horrendous videos horrendous. Has won a great deal of respect as a sharp, forthright female presenter who relies on her brains as well as her looks. *See Network 7, Night Network*

Greboes

The cult that wouldn't die, this hybrid of greaser and biker wouldn't wash either. You really had to live in the Black Country (ideally Stourbridge or Kidderminster) and spend your days tinkering with your Triumph for real authenticity, but bands like Pop Will Eat Itself and Gaye Bykers On Acid spread this strange, unhygienic LIFESTYLE around the land, leaving no green and pleasant pocket untouched by grubby trousers, long, lank hair and high decibel mock rock. Liable to react to soap like Dracula to a crucifix, approach with caution but never with detergent.

Graphic Design

MALCOLM MCLAREN always claimed that Britain's most original contribution to post-war design was youth culture. In the late '70s, punk certainly shook up the decade's rather conventional approach to graphics. Fine artists like Genesis P-Orridge started experimenting with type and Jamie Reid set the style with his inspirational work for the Sex Pistols, using fluorescent colours and blackmail cut-out letters. From these basic DIY methods photocopied fanzines like *Sniffin' Glue* were born. Of these, the most enduring was *i-D* magazine, the work of Terry Jones and his collaborators, their use of decorative borders, scribbles and cropped photographs widely copied. The other

important STYLE magazine was *THE FACE*, designed by Neville Brody, the creator of his own typeface and author of a best selling book of his own work. At the same time an original and distinctive feel to British graphics also came from work commissioned by the new INDEPENDENT RECORD LABELS. Peter Saville's sleeves for NEW ORDER, Malcolm Garrett's work for DURAN DURAN and Vaughn Oliver at 4AD Records proved to be inspirational. This group of graphic designers promoted an experimental STYLE, mixing typefaces, introducing images from ordinary life and playing with decorative elements and bright colour. In the late '80s their colourful exuberance may have given way to a more restrained mood, but for a while back there in the '80s, a small group of British graphic designers led the

Greenaway, Peter

British film director whose painterly cinema militates against the realist tradition of the 'Room With A View' school. Greenaway made his first feature, 'The Draughtsman's Contract', in '82, followed by 'A Zed And Two Noughts', 'The Belly Of An Architect' and 'Drowning By Numbers', increasingly complex exercises in the verbal and visual baroque. His last film of the '80s 'The Cook The Thief Was His Wife And Her Lover combined Jacobean drama, Dutch painting, *haute cuisine* and JEAN PAUL GAULTIER costumes. An indefatigable Renaissance man, Greenaway promises an unabated flow of films, painting, books, and operas.

L to R: The Watchmen. Goths '87 (photo: Monica Curtin). Goth girl '84 (photo: Steve Dixon). Gaye Bikers On Acid (photo: Derek Ridgers).

Green Awareness Before the '80s the word Green was merely an adjective denoting colour. As 1990 dawns there's no doubt that it's the buzzword of the minute. Suddenly everything's Green: Green politics, the Green economy, THE GREEN POUND, 'Greening' the city, going Green. Logically speaking the Green movement was an extension of the Conservation movement of the '60s and the Environmental movement of the '70s but it's telling that in the '79 General Election, Green issues barely surfaced. The '80s changed all that as people gradually realised the full global implications of pollution, toxic waste, intensity farming and the destruction of the rain forests. In '85 the SDP produced a document 'Conservation And Change' while '86 saw Labour respond with *their* thoughts on the environment issue. Both were little more than token gestures but, with the realisation that three million people in Britain belonged to Green organisations the media smelled a story and began the documenting of the Green Explosion. Soon the terms 'acid rain', 'ozone layer' and 'Greenhouse effect' became common parlance and what began as a pale Green trickle became, in '88, a dark Green tidal wave.

FRIENDS OF THE EARTH launched their ozone-friendly CFCs boycott, the Karin B ship carrying toxic waste was turned back, Prince Charles spoke out in favour of the Green Boom and, by the end of the year, even MRS THATCHER had realised the depth of public feeling and, rather belatedly and somewhat insincerely, pledged her concern (if nothing else). With the newly published *Green Consumer Guide* in their trolleys, shoppers began to realise their own power. In '89 newcomer ARK finally merged the two major concerns of the '80s into designer-environmentalism, and inevitably the record appeared – this time courtesy of GREENPEACE and entitled 'Rainbow Warriors'. And '89 also saw Britain for the first time taking THE GREEN PARTY seriously enough to vote for it – albeit only in the European elections. Yet despite all the hype the rain forests still tumble, the acid rain keeps falling, and Britain doesn't rank much higher than Brazil in the Save The Earth stakes. If the '80s saw the message finally hit home, the '90s will be the decade when good intentions will have to be translated into action.

The Green Party Set up in '73 as 'People' the name swiftly changed to 'The Ecology Party' and then again, in '85, to 'The Green Party'. Although its European conterparts swiftly became a firm part of politics, The Green Party in Britain was always considered a bit of a joke – what with its bearded candidates and ghastly hippy flower logo. Until '89. On May 4th 646 candidates in county council elections polled 8.6% of the vote while on June 15th 15% of the Euroelection vote went to the Greens. Post-election 'exposés' by the tabloids cheerily informed shocked ex-Tories that they'd voted for a "bunch of Communists". But while The Greens' more radical policies on tax and land ownership will certainly deter most voters in a General Election, their environmental message has really hit the spot, sending all the major parties scurrying to transform their own 'Green gloss' into something a little more tangible and enticing for the freshly Green public. A youth mock poll showed that if primary and secondary school pupils had the vote they'd have given the Green Party a solid 38 seats in a Euro Parliament.

The Green Pound The Green Pound has proved that even mere shoppers can exert pressure directly on manufacturers by what they either buy or, more importantly, don't buy. Boycotting of fur started the trend but the true force of the Green Pound was felt in '88 with the FRIENDS OF THE EARTH campaign against CFCs in aerosols. The ozone-friendly message spread fast with manufacturers falling over each other to create 'ozone friendly' sprays. Consumer demand for environment-friendly products grew and supermarkets suddenly sprouted a rash of bio-degradable detergents and recycled toilet paper. As the Green Pound gains more clout (one poll showed that 18 million in the UK are Green consumers – nearly half the adult population), the rumours of Green supermarkets may soon become fact. But environmentalists fear that '80s consumers won't learn the true lesson – that it isn't enough to merely consume the 'right' products, we must learn to consume far less. Sustainability will be a keyword of the '90s. *See Lynx*

Greenham Common What started as a simple march against the siting of nuclear weapons in this

country became a symbol of the '80s ambivalence towards the nuclear question. The march set out from Cardiff in '81 and arrived at Greenham, one of the proposed sites for NATO Cruise missiles. But, instead of returning home as planned, a camp was set up and women bivouaced outside the gates. Greenham became an archetype of peaceful protest and of the power of women. In '83 missiles finally moved in but, by the time the convoys (rehearsing for nuclear war) began in '84, the women had Greenham surrounded by a ring of camps. Cruisewatch was set up to clock the exact movement of each convoy proving that it was impossible to maintain military secrecy. In '87 the INF agreement was signed, aggreeing to destroy all ground-based INF weapons. On July 31 '89 the first Cruise missiles were moved

Greenpeace

Probably the best-known of the environmental groups as a result of almost 20 years of headline-grabbing campaigns. Its most emotive battle has been its valiant attempts to safeguard the world's whales, dolphins and seals. The ex-trawler Rainbow Warrior was launched in '78 and in its first year thwarted plans to kill grey seals in the Orkneys and exposed pirate whaling operations. 1980 saw the first actions against North Sea pollution with '83 achieving a halt to nuclear waste dumping at sea. In '85 Rainbow Warrior was bombed by the French secret service in New Zealand but the action backfired with membership doubling overnight. In '87 Greenpeace divers successfully blocked the Sellafield pipeline and by '88 they'd achieved a global ban on sea incineration. An active decade for an active movement – in '89 the new flagship Rainbow Warrior II was launched.

L to R: The Grey Organisation (photo: Andrew Catlin). The Guardian Angels.

Guardian Angels

The Angels were founded on 14 February '79 by Curtis Sliwa, who used to run litter and recycling projects from his home in Brooklyn. Sliwa had amassed a 400-strong litter patrol, and when local residents asked him to start a crime-fighting patrol, the core of his group formed the 'Magnificent 13', patrolling the No. 4 subway line to the South Bronx in winged T-SHIRTS and red berets. Ten years later, 5,000 Angels patrol a total of 60 US cities, they have a policy of only making citizens arrests if completely necessary, and the total Guardian Angels arrest count has still not reached 3,000. Sliwa came to Britain and started patrolling the London Underground with a small number of Guardian Angels in May '89; they have not, as yet, made a single arrest. *See Neighbourhood Watch Schemes*

out of Greenham Common, and although a major step in arms reduction, the INF agreement has merely re-directed the nuclear arms race – Cruise missiles launched from air or sea remained exempt. By 1991 all Cruise missiles will be gone, but warheads of an as yet undisclosed description will be moved in. The women will be there for some time yet. *See CND*

Grey Organisation In '85 four ex-public schoolboys with cropped hair and snappy suits declared themselves "ART anarchists" and proceeded to paint ART gallery windows grey, host multi-media events and generally attract the sort of sniggers normally reserved for Samantha Fox. Understandably peeved at the decidedly cold reception they received in their native land,

they moved to New York. They now art direct MTV programmes, have had three art shows, designed the DE LA SOUL album sleeve, and have achieved their goal. They are regarded as 'artists', so much so that they have a shave every morning, put the razor and whiskers in a jar, and sell it for $600. Now who's laughing?

Griffith Joyner, Florence The world's fastest woman and a marketing man's dream, Flo Jo turned three Olympic gold medals into her own cosmetics line, SPORTSWEAR clothing and ADVERTISING endorsements totalling £3.5 million. She is expected to earn £30 million by the year 2000, a world record that will probably never be beaten in her lifetime. *See Carl Lewis and Sponsorship*

Guns'N'Roses One of the most influential HEAVY METAL bands of the decade. Steaming in on a wave of Jack Daniels, drugs, psychological disorders and the odd rumour of AIDS in '87, Guns'N'Roses married punk's nihilism with metal and buried the old HEAVY METAL pantomime image under a wreckage of broken bottles, bleeding hands and self-mutilation. Lead singer Axl is so unpredictable that he travels in a separate tour bus, and the band often have to stop live shows to calm audiences down. It is far from certain that they will make it to the '90s.

Hair Extensions Although rudimentary hair extensions were widespread in the black community in the '70s, in '81 Simon Forbes, owner of Antenna Hair Salon, invented a new form of hair extension, securing synthetic fibres with a heated clamp. Droves of white youths immediately flocked to the premises to secure a head full of plaited 'bobtails' – they became known as WHITE RASTAS and paraded their pretend dreadlocks and borrowed credibility down the KING'S ROAD. In '82, Antenna developed many new styles, while salons copied the idea using untrained STYLISTS, and Evo-Stik, Superglue and even staples. Hair extensions were particularly

The Hacienda Manchester's best-known dancefloor and according to some the best club in the world. The Hacienda was opened for Factory Records by Bernard Manning on May 21 '82 and went through a period of poor attendance and financial crisis before its purpose-built industrial shell was 'rescued' by a financial intervention from

important amongst black women, offering new styles without the damage caused to sensitive Afro hair by perming and relaxing. By the end of the '80s, most black women had had hair extensions at one time or another, while famous white dreadlock wearers include PAM HOGG, BOY GEORGE, Kate Garner and Jeremy Healy from Haysi Fantayzee, Marilyn and DJ Jeffrey Hinton.

Hair Gel You could buy the Boots Country Born brand of hair gel back in the late '70s, its use pioneered by fashion STYLISTS before pop peformers like BANANARAMA ('82) and Wham! ('83) began to explore its possibilities. The film 'WALL STREET' ('87) presented gel as a vital adjunct to power dressing, and Gordon Gekko WANNABEES (un-

Factory pop stars NEW ORDER. From '86 onwards, DJ Mike Pickering's Nude Night was responsible for popularising HOUSE MUSIC in Britain and making it the most influential club outside London during '88's SUMMER OF LOVE.

L to R Hair Extensions from i-D no.10 '82 (photo: Jane England). Tony Wilson in The Hacienda (photo: Ged Murray). Katharine Hamnett (photo: N Rosen). Katharine Hamnett's Autumn/Winter '89 collection (photo: Claire Pollock).

aware that bum gel brands flake) crowded City wine bars, their pin-stripe shoulders afflicted by what looked like terminal dandruff.

Hamnett, Katharine The most successful example of bridging the gap between designer street fashion and designer shop fashion, Katharine Hamnett set up her own company in '79 on a reported £500 loan and, along with VIVIENNE WESTWOOD, proceeded to dominate British fashion in the '80s. In 1980 she was the first designer to utilise prewashed parachute silks, also producing cotton unisex utility clothing that was to become an important part of her early '80s STYLE. In '82 she was named

Designer Of The Year, and in '83 she launched the first of her range of slogan T-SHIRTS with the 'Choose Life' collection. Inspired by a Bhuddist exhibition it included slogans such as 'Worldwide Nuclear Ban Now', 'Save The World', and 'EDUCATION Not Missiles', and was a theme that she pursued in '84 when she confronted MARGARET THATCHER at a Downing Street reception wearing one of her own outsize T-SHIRTS bearing the legend, '58% Don't Want Pershing'. One of the greatest PR moves of all time, Hamnett's typographical ruse was one of her most successful – the idea of the MESS-AGE T-SHIRT has been copied by every high street store in Britain.

In '85 Hamnett launched the ill-fated *Tomorrow* magazine which folded after one issue, an over-

ambitious attempt to merge fashion and politics. For her post-feminist woman 'Power Dressing' collection in '86 she dispensed with the unisex STYLE of the past, dressing women in tight, secretarial styles that were unambiguously *sexy*, playing on the theme of sex as power. Three KATHARINE HAMNETT shops opened in the same year, including the enormous NORMAN FOSTER designed shop in Knightsbridge (now closed), and by '89 she had announced her intention to show in Paris instead of London, and the launch of her new DIFFUSION LINE 'Hamnett II'. Probably the world's foremost environmentalist designer, Hamnett is a campaigner, an idealist and a social maverick whose success hasn't

been attained at the expense of those around her. Her Autumn/Winter '89 collection chillingly stated her agenda for the '90s - 'Clean Up Or Die'. *See Fashion Designers*

Hatton, Derek In the mid-'80s, media stage management of an increasingly theatrical political game resulted in the identity of Liverpool deputy city Councillor Derek Hatton's tailor becoming more important than his political viewpoint. Hatton, a former fireman, became a breakfast table star after leading Liverpool's Labour council into overspending despite government demands to cutback. The former firebrand now courts media attention in a concerted effort to become a TV star.

Health Clubs The AEROBICS craze encouraged people to kill themselves to stay alive, spawning a

Hard Times

The Hard Times look was a club reaction to the flamboyance of the New Romantic STYLE and also a reflection of the general mood in Britain during the economic depression and social turbulence that marked the first few years of THATCHER's Tory government. A combination of punk, rockabilly, hillbilly and gay fashions, Hard Times was a return to the tough street image of punk. Instead of the flouncy shirts and effete smartness of the NEW ROMANTICS, clubbers switched to battered leather jackets, ripped LEVI'S, motorbike boots and sweat-stained BANDANAS. The image first developed at LE BEAT ROUTE, but soon percolated through most of London clubland. Its legacy, of RIPPED JEANS and biker jackets, has survived in clubland throughout the '80s.

L to R Katharine Hamnett's 'Classic' '86 collection (photo: Sean Cunningham). Heaven circa '82. Tasty Tim's Hair and more Hair. Main photo of Time coverboy '83 by Steve Johnston.

boom in health clubs and causing dance centres like London's Pineapple Studios to change tack. Dance became integrated with fitness and a new generation of gym-fitness centres cashed in. By the late '80s you could do degree courses in leisure management and sport science, and whole chains of clubs had sprung up, with US corporations like Bally muscling in on the market. As the AEROBICS fad faded, the emphasis shifted from people wanting to look like Jane Fonda to people wanting to live as long as Henry Fonda. Now, you work out for longevity and are given a body profile before you're allowed through the door. What started as a health fad has become a science, as people discover that

lifting weights doesn't only make you look better; it helps you live longer.

Health Farms Now called 'health hydros', the health farm has had a facelift. Once nursing homes for the frail and sickly, where fasting was the main weapon in the health armoury, they have become weekend rest homes for fast-living YUPPIES. A bewildering range of massages, manicures, seaweed baths, saunas and a carefully designed diet has transformed the dirty weekend into one of the healthiest activities available. *See Bodybuilding*

Health Food Springing out of the '60s 'peace and love' diet of back-to-nature food, the corner health food store struggled through the '70s and breathed a sigh of relief as the '80s body-consciousness saw a move back to true healthier living.

Sales slowly rose and supermarket brands suddenly became daubed with 'country fresh' and 'pure and healthy'. Wholefood restaurants saw their clientele change from hairy hippies to suit-clad businessmen and concern about additives saw a move in '88/'89 leading to demand for organic meat, organic veg and truly free-range eggs. As supermarkets realised the true extent of the Green Boom they began to stock a wider range of health foods while local entrepreneurs provided home delivery organics. Slowly the farmers have begun to move away from additive-intensive farming and, in the '90s, health food will no longer occupy the odd shelf - it will take over the whole store. *See Food Scares*

Heaven As the Global Village in the '70s, it was a mecca to jazz-funk dancers and progressive rock fans alike, but only when it re-opened as the gay club Heaven in November '79 did the huge venue under Charing Cross arches become central to London nightlife - the huge sound system, lazer lights and abundance of dark, private corners made it an ideal club, and the men-only New Years Eve parties became legendary. The Thursday night Asylum was supposedly mixed gay, but skins. punks, soulboys and transvestites of all persuasions mixed there amiably - it closed in '87, but is still a night remembered with affection. The venue saw the birth of ACID HOUSE/BALEARIC BEATS at Future, then nurtured it to full growth at the Monday night madness that was SPECTRUM, and has hosted a string of influential one-nighters.

Hair Getting your hair cut in the '80s was never so complicated. Hair categorisation became almost impossible with most defying description as the streets exploded with extravagant creations held together with soap, hairspray and glue. Styles became blurred with THE FLAT-TOP spawning a host of improvised variations and haircuts previously belonging to specific youth groups crossed all cultural and sex barriers, the cropped skinhead and baldhead became adopted by girls and boys, young and old alike. The demand for something *different* led to a proliferation of small hairdressers, often based in KENSINGTON MARKET or CAMDEN MARKET which became meeting places for their colourful clientele. Demop and CUTS in particular. Hair salon's like Toni & Guy and Vidal Sassoon took haircutting to new heights of creativity but by the end of the decade the barber regained popularity when hip hop culture spawned shaved insignia, patterns and a lexicon of haircut names *See Black And White Hair Grease, Hair Gel and Hair Extensions*

Main photo: Chris Clunn.

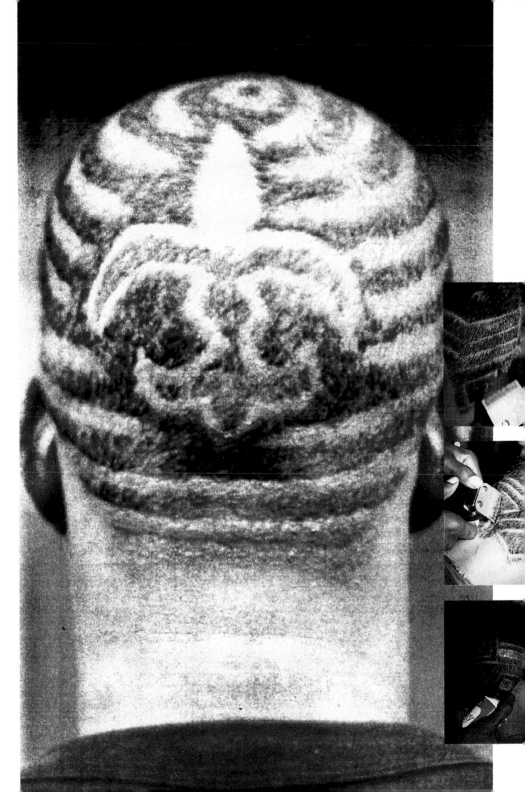

L to R Hattie i-D straight up '82. Pee Wee Herman.

Hauer, Rutger The dashing Dutchman became one of the first of a new breed of VIDEO stars when 'The Hitcher' survived a lacklustre movie release to become a home viewing chart-topper, giving his VIDEO stock of his other offerings ('Flesh And Blood', 'Ladyhawke', et al) an automatic boost. Catapulted into sex symbol status by Ridley Scott's

Heavy Metal In the '80s, heavy metal both fragmented and became more rigidly codified than ever. The classic metal ethos celebrated by *Kerrang!* magazine became fixed as a hedonistic amalgam of biker LIFESTYLE, New York Dolls glam and bondage borrowings. As the mystical pomp overtones of the '70s fell from favour, the speed-drunk frenzy of thrash bands like Anthrax and Metallica moved culturally closer to the more extreme legacy of neo-punk hardcore groups like DRI and Napalm Death. A more fashionable strain of nostalgic indie rock was developed by UK bands THE CULT and Zodiac Mindwarp, doomed to repeat the gestures of Led Zeppelin and Steppenwolf respect-

Henry, Lenny A Birmingham born comedian who began working on the traditional showbiz circuit, Lenny Henry eventually moved away from the Tarby School of comedy and became an honorary member of the alternative circle. His marriage to new wave humourist Dawn French is not entirely unconnected with a right on re-evaluation of his career in the mid-'80s. Having done his time on the hard chicken in a basket club circuit, Lenny is perhaps a sharper conventional comedian than

press, with images of wasted youth and cant phrases like 'chasing the dragon' prominent, and the government was forced to act. But rather than boost the funding available to rehabilitation clinics, it decided to spend its money instead on a national ADVERTISING campaign. The TV spots and posters were intended as graphic health warnings but some thought they risked glamorising what they aimed to condemn. If you're a junkie you lose your friends, your money, your looks, okay – but you also gain the romantic pallor of an Authentic Inner City Martyr. *See Crack and Ecstasy*

Herpes The forgotten virus of the early '80s, Herpes Simplex was of

'BLADERUNNER', Hauer's peroxide rebel robot created the mould for a series of cynically articulate Hauer villains. Time to check with the image consultants, however, as his series of Guiness ads are beginning to risk overexposure. Hauer was always a cult entity. He doesn't want to become a supermarket face.

ively. The crossover between HM and contemporary black music, supposedly initiated by Eddie Van Halen's appearance on MICHAEL JACKSON's 'Beat It' ('82), was most strongly felt in rap, with Run DMC making the *Kerrang!* front cover as a result of covering Aerosmith's 'Walk This Way' – although it took a white act, THE BEASTIE BOYS, to really make the hybrid bankable. But the only genuinely new statement in metal – musically and sartorially – has been from the black US band Living Colour, led by sometime avant-jazz guitarist Vernon Reid. *See Black Rock Alliance*

Heroin In '81 the number of recorded heroin addicts jumped 35% as cheap supplies flooded the country and smack replaced speed as the new down market drug. There was an immediate moral panic in the

any of his new university bred chums. His most important contribution to the '80s has been the introduction of a series of semi-credible non-stereotyped black characters in his TV series 'The Lenny Henry Show', and his annual involvement in Comic Relief. In a country where racism is still rife, Deakus and Delbert Wilkins are ultra effective weapons in the war against prejudice. *See Alternative Comedy*

two types, the common cold sores around the mouth, and the more severe genital ulcers. Not caught from lavatory seats, the genital variety was generally contracted through sexual intercourse with someone already suffering from it, or through having oral sex with someone with cold sores. After treatment, the virus remained in the body for the rest of the sufferer's life, leaving them prone to attack at any time. Until AIDS hysteria gripped the world, herpes was the big worry, but once CONDOMS, SAFE SEX and general avoidance of body fluids were on the agenda, interest waned. Perhaps this was also because, as DHSS figures imply, there actually was no simplex epidemic before, during or after the '81-'83 'boom time', merely a lot of sensationalist tabloid copy and huge numbers of

Nick Heyward, Perry Haines, 'Hellraiser', and Heavy Metal at The Hippodrome (photo: Adam Friedman)

L to R Speed Metal freak Alien (photo: Monica Curtain **See Heavy Metal**. Jeffrey Hinton **See Taboo**. Pam Hogg (photo: Kevin Davies)

people feeling unnecessarily guilty for having cold sores. Conspiracy theorists were quick to point out that the only ones to benefit from the panic were drug companies.

Hill Street Blues   First screened in Britain on CHANNEL 4 in November '84, 'Hill Street Blues' arrived with no less than 53 US awards for television and proceeded to show exactly why. Realism, sly humour, an inherent lunacy (a policeman who bites criminals' ankles?), and drama that treated social issues with an intelligence previously unknown for US series, it transformed police TV drama and opened the door to the talents of writer/producer Steven Bochco. By

the late '80s though, after countless 'Hill Street Blues' reruns, the backlash against sex and violence on US TV contributed to 71% of all new shows being dumped before the end of their first season, and caused Steven Bochco to comment: "Would I get 'Hill Street Blues' on the air now? Actually, I doubt it. I think the idea of it would frighten off the very grey people who run our industry these days." Expect 'Hill Street Blues' to be as relevant to the '90s as it was to the '80s.

Hi-NRG   Hi-NRG, the music of early '80s gay nightlife , was more about dancing and sweating than posing and pulling, it was flashing lights and jacking bodies, pounding bass bins and poppers. It flowered most nights of the week in its temple, HEAVEN, where DJ Ian Levine mixed

Hogg, Pam Her first collection was 'Psychedelic Jungle' in '81, and by '89's 'Warrior Queen', Pam Hogg had grasped the imagination of both the fashion press and the Sunday supplements with her mixture of loud, innovative fashion and pure Glaswegian mouth. Refusing to become a part of the *business* of fashion, the ex-printed textiles student sold her studded silver jackets and tasselled LYCRA numbers first in HYPER HYPER and later in her own shop in Newburgh Street. Inspired by punk, the BLITZ scene and later ACID HOUSE (she actually made a record in '88 with a group called The Garden Of Eden), Hogg has been described as a '100% party girl' and has designed clothes to match. She ended the decade as the most consistently inventive British fashion designer (alongside VIVIENNE WESTWOOD). *See Fashion Designers*

Hats The '80s was the decade when milliners became stars. Hat designers like STEPHEN JONES, Kirsten Woodward and BERNSTOCK/SPEIRS created collections that competed for attention with the work of fashion designers on the catwalks of Europe. This new-found status resulted in a growing market that became flooded with every imaginable hat. Classic hats reappeared in new guises, fresh ideas stemmed from both designers and the street, and specialist shops like BIG APPLE and The Hat Shop opened to cater for the new demand. Everything from the ten gallon BUFFALO stetson, Russian fur hats, prayer caps, BOWLER HATS, turbans and KANGOLS appeared alongside one-off creations and innovations from the designers, and every youth cult had it's own hat, from the ubiquitous hip hop BASEBALL CAP to the RARE GROOVE Hovis Boy flat cap.

a seamless, sensurround barrage of intense beats and soaring voices – like a hi-tech update of the NORTH-ERN SOUL records he collected. Levine also had his own label, Record Shack, for which he and Fiachra Tench wrote and produced most of hi-NRG's homegrown hits. The hi-NRG scene featured stars like Laura Pallas and Earlene Bentley – with cameo apearances by the likes of Sharon Redd, Eartha Kitt and Abba – but the biggest of all was Miquel Brown (Sinitta's mother), whose 'So Many Men, So Little Time' was the scene's anthem throughout most of '83. Hi-NRG's pumping, uptempo sounds were the only precedent for HOUSE MUSIC's popularity in Britain, its ethos – sweaty dance mania as a means to communal delirium – predating ACID HOUSE by many years.

Hip Hop Reggae *See Ragamuffin Rap*

Hip House
A logical dancefloor hybrid of HOUSE and rap, pioneered by Britain's Beatmasters on their '86 hit 'Rok Da House' but perfected by Chicago's Tyree and Fast Eddie, who injected new energy into HOUSE MUSIC in '89. When rappers saw the profit margins involved, they swiftly started cutting hip house tracks, fuelling a lasting collision between two previously separate scenes.

Homoeopathy
Although just one amongst many systems of complementary medicines which have flourished in the '80s, homoeo-pathy has proved the only serious threat to 'normal' allopathic medicine since the Middle Ages. Based on a similar premise to that of vaccination it does, however, treat the patient as an individual – two people with the same disease might well receive quite different remedies. When it emerged that the Queen had her own homoeopath, everyone raced to sign on with homoeopathic GPs. With demand far outstripping supply, the orthodox medical profession became nervous and have tried, on numerous

occasions, to formally 'disprove' homoeopathy and discredit it in public. However, the system con-tinues to notch up successes where the standard doctors fail and its popularity grows and grows.

Hopper, Dennis
The bad boy returns. After a self-imposed exile in Texas, Hopper, the jaded maverick whom no studio could control, returned to Hollywood true to radical form, choosing as his comeback vehicles two of the most contro-versial pictures in town. In 'River's Edge' he played a lame wino who gives refuge to an obese teenager who has quietly strangled his girl-friend for talking too much. In 'Blue Velvet', Hopper pulled out every stop for David Lynch's small town night-mare of drugs, murder and maso-chism. Stuffing his head full of pills and miming to Orbison's 'Candy Coloured Clown', he was a picture of dangerous depravity, who saved his real horrors for the frightened but willing Isabella Rossellini. His return to the director's seat was less auspicious, however – 'Colors' proved to be an action sequence in search of a story.

Hoskins, Bob
The busiest man in showbusiness, Hoskins got his initial break in (stereo)typically unpretentious style, standing at a theatre bar minding his own bus-iness, being asked to take part in an audition, never looking back, etc. 'The Long Good Friday' and 'Mona Lisa' sold him to a worldwide market and '89 saw him directing for the first

Human League A bloke with a silly haircut, two Sheffield Sharons and a synthesizer the formula was brilliant and the songs were even better. Later collaborations with Min-neapolis duo JAM & LEWIS may have paled in comparison, but The Hu-man League's 'Don't You Want Me' and 'Love Ac-tion' were two of the pop anthems of the '80s

time, in addition to starring in and writing the screenplay for 'The Raggedy Rawney'. Squat and balding, with a resonant London accent and an ability to nut people *and* win our sympathy, Hoskins looks to have the heart-of-gold reformed bad 'un market sewn up good and proper. After the universal success of 'WHO FRAMED ROGER RABBIT?' he re-mained loyal to the crew he's 'picked up along the way' rather than buying a one-way ticket to Hollywood. Arguably Britain's last truly British actor.

House Music
House music is the archetypal '80s music: upbeat, synthetic and hedonistic. Emerging out of the underground gay clubs of

L to R Dennis Hopper. Whitney Houston. The Housemartins. Bob Hoskins.

black Chicago, the house sound blended old disco with new tech-nology and matched rapid-transit dance beats with gospel vocals. Before it mutated into the 'acid sound', Chicago house was either dismissed as Hi-NRG hacked together under another name or championed as the dance sound of a new era. It produced a DJ with a great name called Frankie Knuckles and a group filled with religious lust called Ten City. It also spawned a series of sub-genres; DEEP HOUSE, HIP HOUSE, TECHNO and most impor-tantly ACID HOUSE, the music that soundtracked Britain's SUMMER OF LOVE in '88. House became one of the most influential musical forms of the late '80s, exploited by everyone from indie rockers to stadium soul stars. But the award for the panto-mime dame of the Chicago sound

Hyper Hyper
In September '83, London was crying out for a purpose-built venue where young designers could sell their clothes unhindered by unsympathetic retailers. When Lauren Gordon launched Hyper Hyper, it provided a launch pad for young designer business with financial guidance and business advice as well as a catwalk show during each fashion week. The dayglo pink Grecian statues and fluorescent logo initially caused the residents of Kensington some distress, and some designers resisted Hyper, preferring the cheaper rent of KENSINGTON MARKET, but after launching the retail careers of PAM HOGG and Ghost, this indoor designer 'supermarket' became world famous, offering 70 designers in one building and visited by 14,000 shoppers each week.

L to R Hyper Hyper circa '84.
Streatham Redskins **See Ice Hockey.**

must go to the corpulent soloist Darryl Pandy. At the height of his brief success, he breezed into a Bond Street shop demanding an expensive pair of 'house style shoes'. The hapless assistant tried to sell him slippers.

Houses Extended families of muscled boys and drag queens within New York's gay club scene, each presided over by their own (male) mother and father. At house balls, houses competed in dance, posing and VOGUEING contests for trophies awarded for 'realness' or 'face' in outrageous costumes that only a NY fashion gang member could carry off.

Hughes, John Chicago-based Hughes confused Hollywood by ignoring the clout of tinseltown echelons, safe in the knowledge that his string of interchangeable box office favourites kept him out of harm's/agents' reach. Films like 'The Breakfast Club', 'St Elmo's Fire', 'Sixteen Candles', 'Pretty In Pink' and 'About Last Night' reinvented the problem picture for the MTV generation and established a new mini galaxy of stars – Molly, Emilio, Demi, Judd and the rest of the Pack. Sporting a designer new wave look and humming with an English miserabilist sound, these prom-time rites of passage glossed the REAGAN Suburban Dream with a calculated splash of credit card angst. By the end of the decade Hughes had moved on with his audience – YUPPIE Nightmare comedies like 'She's Having A Baby' and 'Planes, Trains And Automobiles' – but his output was less prolific. His cast had grown out of its pimply stereotypes and failed to mature into a new set of caricatures.

Ibiza The rise of Ibiza from a cheap package holiday option to the birthplace of ACID HOUSE, is in hindsight not that surprising. Home to both nouveau hippies and holidaying FOOTBALL fans, it was inevitable that they would eventually meet. The north west town of San Antonio, with its British pubs and fish and chip shops, was a soul weekender nightmare. Ibiza town on the other hand, was the playground of the rich and famous, boasting fantasy discotheques and a haven from the animal antics eight miles away in San Antonio. In '85/'86 young UK clubbers, seeking refuge from San Antonio, started to join them, partying on a cocktail of sun, ECSTASY, and a mixture of records that only a

Mediterranean island could get away with. By '87 they had evolved a hippy idealism that they wanted to take back home with them, and at Paul Oakenfold's Project Club in Streatham, after the club had closed, the Ibiza reunion was let in through the back door. The rest, as they say, is history. Meanwhile, in Ibiza, the party still hasn't stopped.

Ice Hockey A sport that became one of the north's top sectator sports and potentially the perfect spectacle for the countdown to millenium, ice hockey combines elements of professional WRESTLING, the Harlem Globetrotters, kung fu movies, 'Rollerball' and *2000AD*. The UK's finest teams remain in the cold wastes of the north east (Durham Wasps and Whitley Warriors) and Scotland (Murrayfield

ISLAND

the music people

  ANTILLES

Racers, Ayr Bruins), but are still reliant on their quota of Canadian imports (a maximum of three allowed per team). Carlsberg, Heineken and Trophy Bitter have tentatively put forward SPONSORSHIP money and teams such as Streatham Redskins enter the arena to the sounds of 'Eye Of The Tiger' and 'Star Wars'. But with the world championships dominated by teams from frozen outposts (Canada, Russia, Scandinavia) and GLOBAL WARMING promising incrementally warmer winters for the UK, it's unlikely that a British team will crack the real big time.

i-D Started publishing in August '80 as a quarterly fashion fanzine, giving credit to the originators of ideas by

Inflatables

When Manchester City fans began waving inflatable bananas at home games, the rest of the FOOTBALL world copied them, introducing an ever-growing range of blow-up novelties to the Saturday game, which started to spill over into people's homes. By '89, no living room was complete without a six-foot wide inflatable fried egg.

the i-D World Tour, a package of DJs, dance acts and fashion that visited ten different countries in '89 alone. Incurably irreverent and persistently breaking new ground, i-D will continue to pioneer life beyond STYLE in the '90s.

The Independent In an era when most newspapers failed to get off the ground, *The Independent*, launched in '86 and aimed at young, educated well-off readers (ie. YUPPIES) managed to make it to the top of the fence, where it sits today, proving that papers don't need proprietors, that big pictures don't belong to the tabloids and that there is life after MURDOCH for a *Times*-style pseudo-objectivity.

Warriors Dance, all capitalised on a new market that put the likes of BOMB THE BASS, S'X'PRESS, YAZZ, and COLDCUT in the charts, and redefined the meaning of 'indie music'. Indie stalwarts like Rough Trade, and Mute even released dance records or set up their own dance labels, and indie champion JOHN PEEL riled many listeners with his insistence on playing club records and gripe about THE SMITHS always topping his Festive 50. By the end of the '80s, the word 'indie' had disappeared from the musical vernacular and the anoraks (if they ever really existed) had been swapped for hooded sweatshirts.

Insider Dealing It may have

L to R IDJ Dancers and Keith Williamson (photo: Nick White) **See Jazz**. Billy Idol. Blow-up Godzilla (photo: Eddie Monsoon) **See Inflatables**. Gino Latino, part of the new wave of Italian Disco. Back cover of i-D no. 1 August '80 (photo: Steve Johnston) **See i-D Straight Ups**

documenting people on the street. Often imitated, the head to toe i-D STRAIGHT UP became the basis of the magazine's identity and after 10 years is still the best catalogue of the times. A breeding ground for talent, the i-D mafia has spread into the establishment of media editorial while photographers like NICK KNIGHT, MARC LEBON, and Robert Erdmann now work regularly for the top glossy magazines of the world. Constantly evolving in design and content, its redesign in October '88 was a conscious decision to move away from the packaging of images and sheer consumerism that STYLE had become. With a slogan 'Life Beyond STYLE' and a return to matt instead of the ubiquitous glossy paper, i-D adopted a global view of trends in fashion, clubs, music and general culture, best represented by

Independent Record Labels

The tail end of punk brought a challenge to the major record labels with the popularity of the independent record labels. Lots of small labels putting out around a thousand seven inch singles of minor guitar bands established a fourth division of musical talent which the majors could cream off once they were established. To help their effectiveness these labels banded together with the independent distribution companies and by the mid-'80s the Cartel could get records out into major retail outlets. Suddenly it was possible for the indies to break acts into the top ten. In the late '80s though, the market shifted, as user-friendly technology and the rise of dance music encouraged a new generation of independent labels. Rhythm King, Big Life, Gee Street and

been old news in the Square Mile, but after THE BIG BANG insider dealing really went public, and playing with marked cards in the casino economy, they seemed to know their way round the terminals and the terminology, the chinese walls, the pac-man défence and greenmail – they actually understood how to work to their advantage the dematerialised system which fascinated and bemused the rest of us. But while Ivan Boesky and his multi-screen window on the world economy played up to this all-seeing image, the reality over here was more prosaic. Geoffrey Collier, first insider dealer to be publicly nabbed after THE BIG BANG was a bit of a nonentity – hardly the mythical smooth criminal, merely the necessary scapegoat the City needed to prove it could police itself.

Italian Disco

When Mark Moore (later of S'XPRESS) insisted that Rhythm King release a catchy Italian disco tune called 'I Love My Radio' by Taffy, he pre-dated the rise of Italian disco by two years. Moore had cultivated Eurodisco at his Pyramid night at HEAVEN, but as the suburban HOUSE scene warmed to Italian disco in '89, boosted by SHOOM DJ Danny

Rampling and *BOY'S OWN* DJs Terry Farley and Andrew Weatherall, British record companies started to pick up on the trend and the Italian sample-track 'Helyom Halib' by Capella hit the national charts. Proof that there is more to Italian music than a five foot female with a 48 inch chest.

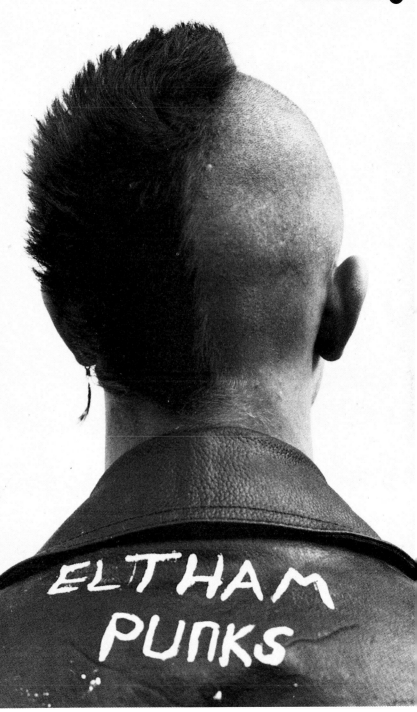

i-D Straight Ups The simplest and most effective record of the times is the i-D straight up. A head-to-toe photograph of people in the streets, clubs, and shops, over the decade nearly 1,000 people have appeared in i-D by simply being themselves. Some, like BOY GEORGE, have later gone on to be photographed by every magazine in the world. Others probably now wish they'd never had their picture taken at all. See i-D

Page 120 L to R (top to bottom): Martin Degville '81 (photo: James Palmer). Iona '83 (photo: James Palmer). Michael '89 (photo: Louise Ramsey). Dick, Maggie, Sid and Butch '82 (photo: Robin Ridley). Jill and Betty at Hammersmith Palais '83. Brian '87 (photo: Steve Johnston). Mark '82 (photo: James Palmer). Des, Rob and Brian '87 (photo: Steve Johnston). Donna and Keith '80.
Page 121 L to R: Dominique '83 (photo: James Palmer). Aitch '88 (photo: Johnny Rosza).

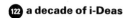

Jackson, Janet Janet Jackson didn't quite shoot to fame, she trundled. After a couple of inauspicious albums, Janet rejected her family's overweening advice, ditched her husband and recorded 'Control', the definitive feminine dance album, which briefly threatened to upstage her brother Michael.

Jackson, Michael He entered the decade barely in his 20s, with a near lifetime of public performing behind him. By the end of it he was perhaps the most famous man on earth and easily its most scrutinised performer. Michael Jackson was a near perfect mirror image of pop's growth and progress. He straddled and oversaw many of its develop-

ments – its growth as a multinational concern, the heavy SPONSORSHIP, and the advent of MUSIC VIDEOS, the public displays of pop charity, and the increased willingness to assimilate dance music into its mainstream. But his was also a story of contradictions. Here was a man who claimed that he only came alive when onstage and yet only undertook two major outings in the '80s, who retreated into a fantasy world, filled with Walt Disney animals and smiling children, and yet could outmanoeuvre his 'friend' Paul McCartney in the sharp thrust of the business world to acquire the rights to The Beatles catalogue.

'Thriller' was the key, eventually becoming the biggest selling album of all time. Helped along by the accompanying videos which were more like mini films, and a stunning

Jacuzzis Anyone can blow air into a bath of water, but it was a corporate American named Mr Jacuzzi who pioneered and marketed the technique of propelling air and water through specially designed jets to create a sort of underwater therapeutic MASSAGE. The phenomenon became very popular in London HEALTH CLUBS in the early part of the decade and has since caught on all over the country. Mr Jacuzzi, though, is purported to be very pissed off with all the whirlpool imitators. Jacuzzi, like Hoover, is the quality brand name, while all the rest are limp-farted pretenders. "Bit like comparing a Rolls Royce to a Mini," said one spokesperson.

L to R: Janet Jackson.
Michael Jackson.
Paul Johnson **See Gospel**.
Jon from Axiom circa '81.
Howard Jones.
Julian i-D straight up '82.
Yohji Yamamoto's
Autumn/Winter '86
collection (photo: Sandro Hyams).
Issey Miyake's
Autumn/Winter '89
collection (photos: Sean Cunningham) **See Japanese Designers**

performance of 'Billie Jean' at Motown's 25th anniversary, success did indeed breed success. Speculation over his relationships with stars such as Elizabeth Taylor, Brooke Shields and Diana Ross became a staple part of every newspaper as did stories of a specially constructed machine designed to keep him alive until 150 years old, and a top secret operation to lighten his skin. Jackson never publicly responded to these allegations until the publication of his biography *Moonwalker* which with its child-like simplicity threw very little light on his personal demons or outlook. By then he had finally released 'Bad' and attempted to bring some kind or terse sexuality into his work. Aligned with an incongruous

Janowitz, Tama An eventful decade for the literary bratette whose hairstyle earned as many column inches as her prose STYLE. She hung out with Andy, did the talk show circuit, endorsed Amaretto and Rose's Lime Juice, and made it into a *Spider-man* comic. She even found time to write a few books, the best being '86's *Slaves Of New York*, a

showed Michael in the company of people whose life experiences might just let them begin to understand one of the decade's most contradictory and confused figures.

Jam & Lewis Jimmy Jam and Terry Lewis were briefly the hippest producers in the mercurial world of modern soul. But since the halcyon days of the mid '80s when Minneapolis ruled the turntables, they have been displaced by LA and Babyface and New York's effervescent producer Teddy Riley. Hipness! How fickle is thy praise.

The JAMMS The Justified Ancients Of MuMu were the last white pop terrorists, grabbing tech-

ions for the first time on Parisian catwalks their sensationally 'new wave' designs made even the most embittered ladies of the press sit up and take notes. What they saw *was* new. The designers shared a new way of looking at women – no longer treating them as merely Barbie dolls to be dressed up. Their clothes were cerebral, and involved the abstraction of the body with volumes of cloth that featured new fabrics, new textures, and invariably the playing down of colour. Rei Kawakubo, designer for Comme des Garcons once said, "I use shades of black", until she changed her mind in the late '80s with a 'Red Is Black' collection which shocked the fashion press still further. Kawakubo ripped holes in flat

image of Jackson as a street tough, 'Bad' was a failure by Jackson's standards and a huge triumph for his record company. He became the first American artist to gain four number one singles off one album.

Jackson toured in '88 and presented a show which proved his superior skills as a mass entertainer, but less successful was his 'Moonwalker' film which broke no new ice in terms of fantasy cinema and merely reiterated the man's innocent concerns. In '89, he released 'Liberian Girl' as a single and sacked his manager Frank Dileo, a former CBS executive who had taken charge prior to 'Thriller'. The VIDEO for 'Liberian Girl' revolved around famous LA entertainers gathering for a party in Michael's honour, unaware of the camera pointing at them. It was contrived and hackeneyed and

biting, bitty satire on the Lower East Side ART crowd. Like the other literary brats, Jay McInerney and Bret Easton Ellis, Janowitz is currently trying to live down her LIFESTYLE and grow up to greater things.

niques from hip hop, HOUSE and Dada and ultimately reaching number one in '88 with their Doctor Who/ Gary Glitter pastiche 'Doctorin' The Tardis', then writing the definitive situationist pop book, *The Manual (How To Have A Number One The Easy Way)*.

Japanese Designers In '81 one line in *The Sunday Times* written by fashion editor Ann Boyd heralded the appearance of a new school emerging in Paris. The comment concerned Comme des Garcons and the new school, the Japanese – what *Figaro* newspaper rather rudely referred to as 'The Yellow Peril'. Previously Kenzo Takada, Issey Miyake and Kansai Yamamoto had made their presence felt, but when Comme des Garcons, Yohji Yamamoto and later Matsuda presented their collect-

fabric, and stitched it so it twisted and turned every which way. "I give the fabric history," was her only comment.

Yohji Yamamoto stitched a label in the collar of some of his designs which announced, "There is nothing so boring as a neat and tidy look". The shows of both created headlines: 'Shock Chic', 'Feminism Vs Sexist', and 'Paris – East And West'. Androgynous models tramped in single file wearing oblique make-up which earned them descriptions such as 'Bag Lady Chic' and 'Post Holocaust Look'. All the Japanese were tremendously concerned with presentation. Matsuda used photographers to create lavish booklets, Kawakubo created her own 'magazine', and Yamamoto utilised photographer NICK KNIGHT and Paris art director Marc Ascoli to produce unbelievably

national jøwelgraphic

Jewellery

Jewellery became far more than just an afterthought in the '80s with the anything-goes ethic coming into its own. Certain phases accompanied various fashion trends including salvage jewellery from the likes of JUDY BLAME, variations on costume pieces from, amongst others Andrew Logan, Eric Beamon and Monty Don, and the sculptural designer side was catered for by people like SLIM BARRETT, Atelier and Tom Binns. Many designers found their profile heightened after collaborating on CATWALK SHOWS with fashion designers. Street trends encompassed all things religious, military, ethnic or trash inspired and certain high street shops became corner-stones for this burgeoning interest in the accessory market such as Butler & Wilson, Detail and Pink Soda. Strangest of all though, must have been Simon Costin's dead animal heads or sperm necklace.

Judy Blame (photo: Marc Lebon. Styling: Judy Blame) See Blame, Judy.

luxurious catalogues which have become collector's items. Puffball pierrots, Edwardian school matrons, and metres of iridescent tulle later, the clothes of the Japanese still look strange.

Japanese Restaurants

Sushi is an artform – one which the Japanese have long enjoyed but which Britain discovered *en masse* circa '82. Eating Japanese, realised the men who lunch, was the perfect way to impress business colleagues: the food is madly esoteric, alcohol is *de rigeur* and strong, plus the whole experience can be impressively expensive. By '84 Japanese was fashionable, by '87 it was essential. The common mistake, however, is to

drink saki – the Japanese, of course, prefer malt scotch and any Japanese executive worth his miso has his own labelled bottle behind the bar.

Jarmusch, Jim

'Strangers In Paradise', 'Down By Law', 'Mystery Train' – three cult hits this decade isn't bad going by anyone's standards and in the field of independent film-making Jarmusch has no peers. Favouring long takes, a monchrome look and a deconstructed JAZZ feel Jarmusch is the man who took apart the cool aesthetic and put it back together as a sublime form of nonsense poetry.

Jazz

At the opening of the decade, the spirit of The Goldmine (and the influential Chris Hill) was all that stood between jazz and the peril of being confined to strange Polish cartoons on CHANNEL 4. But from '82

Japan The defunct group led by David Sylvian got the name first and the free trips later. Rising to prominence on the back of the NEW ROMANTICS Japan were a mass of cultural conflicts. Bassist and classical musician Mick Karn wanted to pursue his sculpting, David Sylvian wanted to visit their namesake, and their copious use of make-up was not initially appreci-

ated by their fans. Splitting in '82, Sylvian managed to make it to Japan (working with Ryuichi Sakamoto), Karn ended up working with ex-BAUHAUS Pete Murphy and they both still wear make-up. Probably too ahead of their time – the first ever NEW AGE Romantics.

L to R: Jim Jarmusch. Japan. Derek Jarman. Foot Patrol Jazz dancers at i-D night in Hacienda '88 (photo: Ian Tilton). The Jesus & Mary Chain.

onwards, the music thrived on the oxygen of young clubbers' interest. DJ Paul Murphy's dingy record basement on Berwick Street and his club at The Electric Ballroom were focal points for the interest created by the likes of Gilles Peterson, Kev Beadle, Russ Dewbury and the Midlands-based Bongo Go and Baz Fe Jazz, who discovered real soul in unearthed and reissued jazz and Latin cuts from the '50s, '60s and '70s. The PIRATE RADIO station K-Jazz run by DJ Gilles Peterson was an early response to the resurgence of interest, but it wasn't until Gilles got his own show on Radio London that legal radio acknowledged there was life in jazz beyond Ronnie Scott's.

Some of those who heard Lee Morgan's 'Sidewinder' first time around were scornful of this vinyl-centric activity, but found it harder to dismiss maturing musical talents like Courtney Pine, Steve Williamson, Andy Sheppard and, above all, the Jazz Warriors and Loose Tubes - the most influential jazz bands for two decades in Britain. The magazines *WIRE*, a centre of jazz purism, and *STRAIGHT NO CHASER*, its street-sussed opposite, catered for jazz's newly expanded audience. 1988's ACID JAZZ captured the move towards jazz for the '90s, blending jazz traditions with world beat influences and a spirit of adventure, in artists like The Jazz Renegades, Working Week and Cleveland Watkiss. In keeping with an '80s doctrine, every jazz DJ secretly wanted to make a compilation LP, and most did, but in '89 the success of London Radio in being awarded a legal license took everyone by surprise. A success for the old guard rather than the new, it nevertheless recruited Gilles Peterson as a director. Quite how it will interpret jazz's agenda will only be apparent when it starts broadcasting in 1990.

Job Clubs

A truly Thatcherite solution to the unemployment problem. They give you stamps and a phone and miraculously one in three get jobs. Typical of the downgrading

Jarman, Derek The voluble hero of the UK cinema's avant garde, Jarman is secretly admired as the film genius of his generation while publicly he is neglected by both financiers and audiences, who find his weird brew of polemic, homosexuality and art debilitatingly pessimistic. Between pictures (including 'The Tempest', 'Jubilee', and 'War Requiem') Jar-

man pays the rent by directing promos, introducing a gritty STYLE to the typically gloss-drenched world of record hype in work for THE SMITHS, Marianne Faithfull, and, most ambitiously, THE PET SHOP BOYS, for whose July '89 Wembley spectacle he created a cinematic backdrop.

See YTS

Jesus & Mary Chain The '80s' Sound Of Scotland emerged, dripping in terminal ennui and stretched out over sustained guitar feedback, from the Velveteen minds of brothers, James and William Reid. Snapped up and tailored to offend by Creation Records' supremo, Alan McGhee, their early London shows conformed to 15 minutes of white noise followed by the sound of disaffected audiences rioting. By '87, the monumental 'April Skies' purged the excessive feedback and, via the 'Darklands' LP, The JAMC headed chartwise via a deal with Warner Brothers. Once the holders of the thin-white-punks-on-dope mantle, their druggy ambience and output have tapered off, leaving a Bolanesque change of direction which has yet to bear fruit.

in the quality of statistics, this fact conveniently skirts around the truth. Discount those in temporary jobs, those who quickly return to the dole, those who go onto training schemes or the Community programme and those who fail to get a job in their area of skill, and the statistics look distinctly less rosy. One in three may get jobs, but two out of three of those jobs are complete crap. *See YTS*

Jones, Grace Grace Jones was originally perceived to be one of the Great Offenders, a refuge from the Studio 54 battlefield of the '70s who had usurped tradition and entered the performance field with few credentials apart from a reputation for being a party animal. Grace made no concession to the whingeing, she stood aloof and haughty, an androgynous figure who once remarked: "People complain that my live shows are all visual and nothing else. Well that's what they're meant to be." Grace was assisted in her crusade at the time by JEAN PAUL GOUDE, her then husband, who built a book, *Jungle Fever*, around her and complemented her ice cool image with brilliant visual flourishes. What people often forgot or failed to come to terms with was the quality of her music. Aligned with Jamaican kingpins, Sly Dunbar and Robbie Shakespeare, tracks such as 'Slave To The Rhythm', 'Nightclubbing' and 'Pull Up To The Bumper' were exotic, fiery and slightly intimidating dance records that have held fast against the test of time. But as with all pioneers, the innovations become commonplace. Her televised row with Russell Harty smelt a little of calculation and she soon switched her attention to Bond films, *Playboy* spreads with then boyfriend Dolph Lundgren and an erratic recording career. Whether she will have the STYLE to weather the '90s remains to be seen.

Jones, Tom Tom Jones is an enigma. When the rerelease of 'It's Not Unusual' soared into the charts 22 years after it originally launched Tom's cartoon cabaret career, there was still a welcome in the hillside. Tom came home from Las Vegas to pick off where he left off, his 'Last Resort' appearance when he performed a version of PRINCE's 'Kiss', launching him into the arms of a new generation and the discovery that 22 years later, women still threw bras and knickers to him on stage.

Joy Division If THATCHER played the largest part in making the '80s a pretty damn depressing decade, the contribution of glum

Johnsons

Opened in Kensington Market in the late '60s by Lloyd Johnson, Johnsons developed from being a mod hang-out to become *the* classic, fashion-conscious rock'n'roll haven in the '80s. They sold tailored drape suits, pegs and Tex Mex western cowboy gear, but it was their series of 'La Rocka' leather biker jackets, boots and skull-and-crossbones waistcoats that grasped the public imagination in the wake of The Clash's 'Combat Rock'. See Biker Boots

Jones, Stephen

An inhabitant of the same Warren Street squats as Boy George, Marilyn and Stephen Linard, Stephen Jones left St Martins in '79 and opened a small hat boutique in the basement of PX in Covent Garden. It was styled like a refined salon, and Stephen's hats evoked a mood of nostalgic, glamorous sophistication. Now one of the world's most innovative milliners, in part responsible for putting the hat back on ladies' heads, his one-off creations are worn by the club crowd and

rockers Joy Division should not be overlooked. Lead singer Ian Curtis barely made it into the '80s, committing suicide in May '80, but the legacy of adolescent, existential angst fuelled a generation of pale, pensive types with shaved necks and grey perspectives. NEW ORDER's forced jollity is some kind of atonement for their earlier incarnation.

Joyriding Joyriding in stolen cars became the logical progression from smashing up phone boxes for bored teenage youths who got their kicks from danger and destruction. In every major city, joyriders raced police, motorists and each other, risking life, limb and liberty in a search for the ultimate adrenalin rush. In Dublin

alone, 670 youths were arrested for joyriding within a three month period in '85, each of them spurred on by the illegal thrill of accelerating an unknown, high-powered motor out on to the open road, not giving a damn about anything.

The Jungle Brothers South Bronx social consciousness rap trio with a sense of humour, responsible for starting the trend towards Zulu medallions and African chic in hip hop, whilst prancing around in pith helmets and rapping nursery rhymes about wicked willies. They released a stark but funky debut LP 'Straight Out The Jungle' at the end of '88, which put them at the forefront of rap's intelligent 'new school', alongside DE LA SOUL and Queen Latifah. See African Colours and The Daisy Age

Conservative Party members alike. See Fashion Designers

Joseph The fashion entrepreneur, buyer and promoter of new talent, Joseph Ettedgui had an important influence on the careers of early '80s UK designers. His mini retail empire stretching from London, Tokyo to New York, not only provided showcases for the likes of KATHARINE HAM-

NETT, YOHJI YAMAMOTO, Kenzo, BODYMAP and RICHMOND/CORNEJO, but gave them a seal of approval that opened previously closed doors. His shops became design environments, most designed by Eva Jircna (who also designed the revamped Way In), and home for his own Joseph Tricot label.

L to R: Johnsons' jacket '86 (photo: Paul Gobel, styling: Sheree). Stephen Jones (photo: Nick Knight). Joseph Tricot Autumn/ Winter '85 collection (photo: Eamonn J McCabe, styling: Caroline Baker). Grace Jones (photo: Nick Knight).

K

Kangols Stuck between the golfing sweaters and the sta-press, Kangols have been sold in dodgy department stores since time immemorial, but it took rap to make them hip (briefly), bringing balding middle aged businessmen together with homeboys in a fundamentalist rejection of white fashion. There's the red round ones, there's the pink fluffy ones, the ones

L to R: **Kangols.**
'West One Searchers'
from i-D no. 37 '86
photographed by Nick
Knight (styling: Simon
Foxton).
Nick Knight portraits from
5th Anniversary issue of i-
D Oct '85.

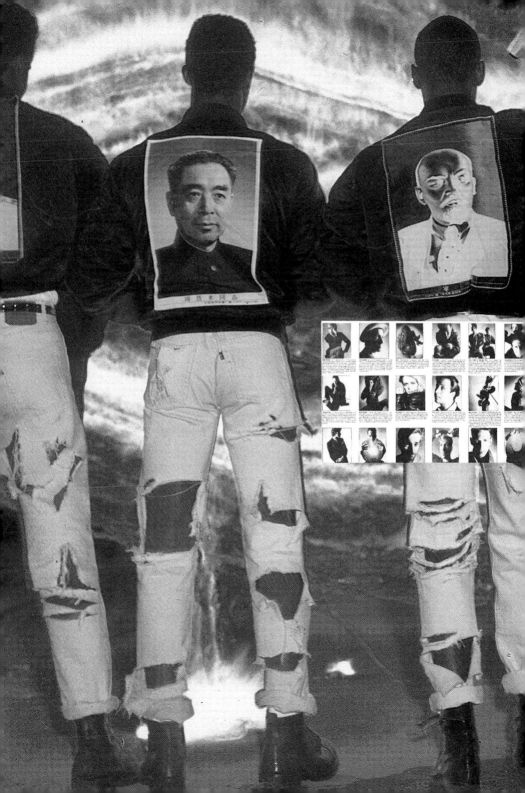

Karaoke Karaoke is the ART of impersonating your favourite singer to the backing track of your choice. Originating in Japan in the early '70s, it evolved with the eight track cartridge and by the '80s was a regular feature of every Tokyo bar. As JAPANESE RESTAURANTS in London introduced their own karaoke machines, pubs started experimenting with this curious Japanese pastime and discovered that the British were ideally suited. While Haoui Montaug and Anita Sarko's club I Lovee Karaoke Very Muchee was popularising karaoke in more esoteric club circles in New York, the UK had discovered that there was nothing the Great British Public liked better than making complete fools of

themselves on TV. 'The Karaoke Klub' hosted by The Frank Chickens started on CHANNEL 4 in '89 and proved, if ever there was any doubt, that the British have no pride.

Kelman, James The uncompromising Glaswegian writer who demonstrated with the sparkling grit of his three novels (*The Bus Conductor Hines, A Chancer, A Disaffection*) and one collection of short stories (*Greyhound For Breakfast*) that there was linguistic life beyond the Hampstead blinds of English Lit. With astonishing invention he welded Kafka to Hemingway and forged a tough forensic prose capable of registering the eloquent silences of pub companionship, the excrutiating absurdities of middle-aged unemployment, the quicksilver thrills of

gambling and, above all, the grinding resentment of life under Thatcherism. Destined to go down as one of the greats.

Kennedy, Nigel The *enfant terrible* of classical music, Nigel Kennedy has consistently diversified his musical activites. He has played with virtually every major orchestra in the world, recorded jazz albums, worked with Kate Bush, Talk Talk and Paul McCartney, and affronted musical propriety like nobody's business. The fact that he now commands in excess of $5,000 a "gig", as he calls it, indicates exactly how much of a business it has become. Undoubtedly Britain's most enterprising (and exciting) young violinist.

Kickers The happy shoes of the '70s, invariably worn by college students and their lecturers in a range of primary colours, this most inane and optimistic of footwear shuffled back into view in '88 as clubbers sought an alternative to their CONVERSE baseball boots and SNEAKERS, switching to Kickers to complement their dungarees and lilac sweatshirts. In June '89, Shelly's Shoes on Oxford Street reported selling 175 pairs of Kickers in three hours.

Kilts The images of punks in kilts outside Beaufort Market and Willie Brown's kilt-inspired designs for men in '81, inspired a hard core of kilt wearers including SPANDAU BALLET in the early LE BEAT ROUTE days, to later designer versions of men's skirts courtesy of GAULTIER and

Kensington Market In '81, when LE BEAT ROUTE and CHA CHA'S were at their height, so was Kensington Market. With '50s rockabilly fashion at ROCK-A-CHA, rocker gear at JOHNSONS and American Retro, and psychedelia at Sweet Charity, Kensington Market was not only at the forefront of street fashion but also the best place to get the latest club news and haircut. Young designers like RACHEL AUBURN, John Crancher, and Judy Littman found it the best and cheapest place to sell their wares, but by '86 cut-rate jean companies had started moving in, and although excellent stalls still existed

amongst the rag trade seconds, it wasn't until the end of '88 that the Market reasserted itself as a force in street fashion. Already housing Big Jesus Trashcan, Offbeat, Thunderpussy and Red Balls On Fire, in June '89 it opened up Pure in the basement, a new home for unknown designers. Despite the filthy surroundings and lingering dodgy stalls, Kensington Market is still an important feature of London street fashion.

VIVIENNE WESTWOOD, and even Ray Petri's BUFFALO boys.

King's Rd After a decade spent mostly in the doldrums, by the early '80s the King's Rd was hip again. Post-punks, POSTCARD PUNKS and neo-dandies used Saturdays as an open-air catwalk and found their spiritual home at VIVIENNE WESTWOOD's World's End, whilst BOY, ROBOT, JOHNSON'S, 20th Century Box, The Great Gear Market and more were regular haunts for both tourists and trendies alike. But as the majority of pubs succumbed to the call of THEME PARK Americana or cod-sophisto Parisian Brasserie decor, and despite the second generation of shop fronts (Jones,

FIORUCCI, AMERICAN CLASSICS), by the mid '80s there were signs of a move Westwards. Now the King's Rd, with its Next For All multiple fashion choices and glitzy arcades, is just another high street. The fall in fortune of The Road coincided with the regeneration of that other bastion of '60s style – Carnaby St and environs, or West SOHO as the PRs would have us call it. And in the '90s? Who knows...but Camden Lock is currently undergoing redevelopment. *See Camden Market and Kensington Market*

Kissograms A derivative of the American singing telegram service, a nation brought up on Page Three and Jim Davidson inevitably perverted the idea. Hapless victims whose only crime was a birthday found themselves crushed by the weight of a 20

stone suspended woman or kissed and crushed by a balloon-dancer. From harmless Tarzans and GEORGE MICHAEL lookalikes to Boobagrams, this spurious service became seedier and seedier. A bottomless pit of sexism, the kissogram was applauded as an example of successful free enterprise. *See Enterprise Culture*

Kit Kat Club The punk-inspired sibling rival to THE BATCAVE, the KK has been dancing to the sound of indie-Goth-trash faves ever since it first opened in '82. The regular crowd of androgynous spikey-tops in skimpy LYCRA or leather costumes have never grown tired of 'alternative' dance classics – even though the

club's host and DJ, Simon Hobart, yearned to enlarge the playlist from Cure/CULT/Sisters domination way back in '87. It's the archetypal one-nighter, pursuing a peripatetic journey around London's seedier venues – and still going strong at The Sanctuary after seven years – despite an 18 month gap following the POLICE raid on the all-nighter sessions at Westbourne Grove in '85. Themed on the 'Rocky Horror Picture Show' in its early years, it was fuelled by a drug diet of speed and dope and endless stories of outrage. Its survival is certainly a tribute to Simon Hobart's staying power.

Knight, Nick Photographer Nick Knight is the non-specialist in a profession of specialists, combining editorial portraiture, leading edge fashion and the demands of ADVER-

Kiss FM From Friday to Sunday for three years until December '88, PIRATE RADIO station Kiss FM provided London with some of the best dance music in the world, played by some of the best club DJs in the world (including Jazzie B of SOUL II SOUL, Judge Jules and Norman Jay), as well as running its own clubs and publishing its own magazine *Written Word* with comment from Kiss DJs like Jay Strongman and Matt Black and Jonathan More of COLDCUT. Kiss went off air to apply for a government licence to broadcast legally, but despite huge public support, in July '89, the London-wide licence was awarded to non-pirate London Jazz Radio instead. Kiss FM are to continue campaigning for a legal London dance station, however long it takes to achieve.

L to R: First four pictures – i-D straight ups Kensington High St '83. i-D straight up King's Rd '81. The Kit Kat Club circa '83. Nick Knight self-portrait. i-D straight up Kazuko '82. Paul King.

TISING, whilst keeping his integrity, credibility and strength of vision intact. He made his name initially with a series of portraits commissioned for *i-D*'s fifth birthday issue, which promptly landed him one of the most coveted and creative jobs in the business, shooting seasonal catalogues for designer Yohji Yamamoto. With art director and STYLIST Marc Ascoli and designer Peter Saville, Nick produced some of the most stunning fashion imagery of the decade. Widely imitated but always managing to keep at least one step ahead of the pack, Nick celebrated his creative coming of age with a highly successful exhibition in '89, in conjunction with Cindy Palmano at London's Photographer's Gallery.

Kraftwerk From DEPECHE MODE, Afrika Bambaataa to Detroit TECHNO musicians like Kevin Saunderson and Derrick May, everyone was claiming Kraftwerk as an influence. The group managed to release two albums of minimalist electronic rhythms, 'Computer World' and 'Atomic Cafe', before pulling their phone out of the wall so their record company would quit pestering them for further product.

KRS-One KRS-One emerged from the urban wasteland of the South Bronx to become a respected rap preacher. From the age of 13 he was homeless on the streets of New York, but after meeting DJ Scott La Rock in a men's shelter, formed the rap crew Boogie Down Productions. BDP recorded one LP, 'Criminal Minded', full of conscious street imagery and

resonant beats, with a strong reggae flavour, before La Rock was shot in a street altercation in the Bronx. KRS-One went on to find a more focused political voice on the albums 'By All Means Necessary' and 'Ghetto Music: The Blueprint Of Hip Hop'. After founding the 'STOP THE VIOLENCE' movement with a 'LIVE AID' STYLE all-star rap record and starting work on a book about hip hop, KRS-One ended the '80s as one of black America's most coherent rap philosophers.

Krueger, Freddy The ritual repetitions and box-office killings of the five 'Nightmare On Elm Street' serial thrillers have established Robert Englund as a new and unlikely middle American folk hero – Freddy Krueger, the razor-gloved bogey man with a cutting line in sarcasm and heir to the longrunning slasher tradition of 'Friday The 13th''s Jason and 'Halloween''s Michael Myers. Victim of a collective burning who returns as a flame-singed redskin to revenge himself on the children of his killers, Freddy would appear when least expected like a grotesque trickster from the burial mound of the suburban American Dream. In '89 the payback included $20 million in merchandising.

Kureishi, Hanif The angry young man of Barons Court, Kureishi switched from theatre to film in an auspicious feature debut with 'My Beautiful Launderette'. An elusive tale of racism, business nous, political disillusion and ambiguous sexuality, 'Launderette' broke out of its made-for-TV format to become the low budget hit of the year. Kureishi teamed up with the same collaborators (producer Tim Bevan, director Steven Frears) on 'Sammy & Rosie Get Laid', a harder, ruder view of THATCHER's Britain collapsing in a ruinous state of perpetual riot, self-indulgent adulteries and political disarray. An intellectual with a neat line in savage one-liners, Kureishi is attempting to lure a wary Frears back from the costumed excesses of 'Dangerous Liaisons' to add a final apocalyptic panel to his London triptych.

Lager Getting pissed was never so complicated as in the '80s. Brands and ADVERTISING campaigns proliferated, each offering different LIFE-STYLE images and ALCOHOL levels. This was also the decade in which lager finally vanquished bitter and became *the* national intoxicant, overcoming its original perceived image as 'weak, piss beer' and making Britain the third largest world

Latin   Hip Hop The music of Hispanic American youth, as popular and representative of its community as rap is of American blacks. Latin hip hop, a mixture of passionate, often kitschy female vocals and a throbbing electronic melody, went overground in '86 with acts like Sa-Fire, The Cover Girls and Exposé, produced by New York or Miami club DJs like Little Louie Vega or the Clivilles & Cole duo. Championed by radio stations like New York's Hot 103 FM and clubs like 10-18 and Hearthrob, Latin hip hop hit the British charts in '86 with Shannon's definitive 'Let The Music Play'. Later drawing in HOUSE influences and acquiring the alternative tag 'freestyle' as well as influencing pop artists like MADONNA and BOMB THE BASS, Latin hip hop largely failed to extend its base beyond America's Hispanic communities.

L to R: Patsy Kensit on i-D cover no. 25 (photo: Marc Lebon). Nick Kamen wearing clothes by Takeo Kikuchi '86 (photo: Marc Lebon, styling: Ray Petri). Latino fashion from Brazil '88 (photo: Willy Biondani). Puerto Rican rappers Latin Empire '88 (photo: Dave Edmonds). Marc Lebon fashion photograph in i-D no. 29 (styling: Carolin Baker). Marc Lebon self-portrait '84.

Lebon, Marc

A photographer, nurturer of talent and filmmaker, Marc Lebon captured the mood of the '80s in his photographs for *i-D*, creating the art of meshing photography with VIDEO techniques. Initially part of the BUFFALO gang of STYLE terrorists, he has made a string of pop promos and always harbours an energetic irreverence for his subject. He set up his own company Crunch Productions as a base for, not just his talents, but a group of like-minded cohorts. One of the true spirits of the '80s.

Lee, Spike Lee became flavour of the arthouse month with 'She's Gotta Have It', a standing room only hit at the '87 Cannes festival, but rapidly fell from grace when his first studio picture for Columbia, 'School Daze', received a universal critical drubbing. Lee's career got back in the fast track with 'Do The Right Thing' ('89), a personal view of race riots in Brooklyn. Based on actual events the film is typical of Lee's style, outlining and underlining key moments, giving the film the feel of a personal message to the audience while presenting an uncompromising view of the indignities and abuse suffered by NY blacks in Brooklyn. In the '90s Lee could become the serious voice in Hollywood a long suffering minority has never had.

L to R: Spike Lee. Early Lager Lout circa '82. Loose Ends. i-D straight up Lisza '83. i-D straight up Louise '82. Fashion designer Stephen Linard '81. Stephen Linard's Spring/Summer '87 collection. Annie Lennox. Emily Lloyd **See Wish You Were Here.**

lager market (after the US and Germany), with 200-plus brand names on offer. Approximately three-quarters of lager consumers are male, and they net the brewers over £20 billion a year, drinking millions of pints of pale yellow liquid, all of which is ultimately emptied down the toilet. *See Lager Louts and Low Alcohol Beer*

Lager Louts A term coined to describe the most violent hooligan of the decade and a creation of the increasingly strong lagers manufactured by breweries. Throughout the '70s Carlsberg Special Brew stood alone with its high alcohol gravity of 1086, but in the '80s more breweries got in on the strong lager

act with Super Tennants and Crucial Brew leading the market. Taken in large quantites it makes you aggressive, confused and mindless. Lager Louts dress like low-rent YUPPIES in large T-SHIRTS, CHINOS and Pepe jeans that are too long, striped shirts and off-the-shoulder cardigans. They have taken the '50s preppy look to its illogical conclusion and have short back and sides, slapper haircuts. Easily spotted they wander down the street slurring FOOTBALL chants, shouting sexist abuse at girls, vomiting and fighting. *See Lager and Low Alcohol Beer*

The Language Lab Run by TOM DIXON and Nick Jones, The Language Lab was the first West End club to feature live rappers and scratchers. During its two year lifespan from '81, the club became a

focal point for the capital's nascent hip hop scene and launched the careers of early British rappers like Dizzi Heights. Tom and Nick went on to run The Titanic in Berkeley Sq, using slide projectors and Super 8 movies with live rapping and sound system contests, and then carried their vision of nightclub hedonism to a spectacular conclusion with the DRIVE-IN DEMOLITION DISCO DERBY. *See Funkapolitan*

Laswell, Bill The most schizophrenic producer of the '80s, who first made his mark as bassist with protean New York band Material. As house producer to the Celluloid label, he brought together JOHN LYDON and Afrika Bambaataa for the 'World Destruction' single, and pioneered African-ELECTRO fusion incurring purists' undying wrath in the process. His policy of 'collision' brings together collaborators from wildly different spheres – teaming Sly and Robbie with Bob Dylan, Gambian kora player Foday Musa Suso with Herbie Hancock, and Ginger Baker with PiL. Although megalomania is reportedly alienating prospective collaborators, expect Laswell to contiue blurring genres well into the '90s.

Laurence Corner Along with Badges & Equipment in The Strand, Laurence Corner has always been the best place in London to buy ex-army shorts, battle-dress jackets, naval blazers, trousers, workmen's dungarees and every item of utilitarian clothing (since 1948 actually). They also sell a bizarre collection of battle

paraphernalia including gasmasks, medical equipment and bags, artillery waistcoats, military uniforms and diving helmets. The prices have virtually never increased and the Corner is still a valuable source for fashion editors, foreign STYLISTS and bargain hunters.

Le Beat Route Started in '81 by Ollie O'Donnell and Steve Mahoney, Friday nights at Le Beat Route quickly became compulsory for London's early clubbers. Originally appealing to the NEW ROMANTICS, Le Beat Route quickly toughened its image through the DJing skills of Steve Lewis. Mixing old funk classics, '60s soul gems and '40s big band cuts with the latest New York rap and ELECTRO, Lewis created an exciting alternative to the dominant jazz-funk sounds of the soul clubs and the soul-less ELECTRO-pop of the New Romantic scene. Friday nights soon became a barometer for what was happening on the capital's underground music and fashion circuits. From the flamboyance of the New Romantic STYLE to the RIPPED JEANS of the HARD TIMES ethic via bebop berets and ZOOT SUITS, what Le Beat Route regulars wore one week would surface weeks later in clubs across southern England. A cultural melting pot which was the spawning ground of bands like SADE, Animal Nightlife and BLUE RONDO A LA TURK the club was also immortalised on vinyl by SPANDAU BALLET ('Chant No. 1') who were some of its earliest regulars. More a way of life than just a club, regulars sang along with the

'Red Flag', the last record of every night. Although the club finished in '83 and its crowd moved on to the WAG CLUB and THE MUD, Le Beat Route earned its reputation as a watershed between the different youth movements of the '70s and the musically united underground clubs of the '80s. One of the most culturally important nightclubs of the decade.

Levine, Sherrie In an age where everything in ART that could be done had been done, it seemed the only thing left to do was to do it again – but with a twist. Something which American conceptual artist Sherrie Levine took quite literally. She photographed celebrated moments from the history of ART – most

notoriously Egon Schiele's expressionist self-portraits – and reclaimed the reproductions as her own originals. The theory was that this kind of art diffused the mystique of the original ART object and opened it up to other interpretations. And the ART? It was duly sold, framed and hung. A neat trick. But you can only do it once. *See The New Dealers*

Levi's Levi Strauss' original workwear became the only jeans to wear in the '80s. They crossed all fashion and age barriers, becoming a universal uniform for everybody from ROCKABILLIES, Hell's Angels, SKINHEADS, to RONALD REAGAN. It was the Levi's red tag 501 jeans that spearheaded the company's fortunes – after classic clothing shops like FLIP began selling original 501s at vastly inflated prices, the company re-

Linard, Stephen An original inhabitant of the infamous Warren Street squat that spawned BOY GEORGE, Stephen Linard graduated from ST MARTIN'S in '81 with a collection, 'Reluctant Emigrés', which brought the show to a halt and had the audience screaming for more. Rugged men with stubble, sideburns and tattoos, modelled see-through organza shirts, flamboyant astrakan coats and smug grins. Spearheading the NEW ROMANTIC designers, Stephen was always first to model his own new designs and always there when the photographs were being taken. Stephen is widely held responsible for the quasi-religious fad which had ghost-faced young hipsters dressing up like priests and popes (*See Ecclesiastic Fashion*). He was also the frontman of two of London's seminal fashion-based clubs, St Moritz and Total Fashion Victim. His contribution to fashion in the '80s? "I think I made people look at menswear in a different light." *See Fashion Designers*

marketed the button fly jean with a series of TV ads utilising images of a '50s mid-western America and timeless Atlantic soul. Probably some of the most influential ads of the decade (*See Boxer Shorts*), they ensured Levi's place in '80s mythology. Up until the early '80s, new Levi's were only available in workwear shops and many US lines are still not sold in the UK, but Levi's now have 17.5% of the denim market, the biggest in Britain. It's said that every generation makes an excuse for wearing jeans, and in the early '80s it was the somewhat spurious HARD TIMES reasoning, which stated that since times were hard, distressed clothes were all that could be afforded. BOY GEORGE was closer to

the mark when he asserted that people ripped their Levi's so as to show off their bollocks. *See Denim*

Lewis, Carl The first of the new breed of professional athlete, trained in accountancy as well as sport. Encouraged by his father (ex-sprinter) and mother (ex-hurdler), and inspired by meeting Jessie Owens at the age of 10, Lewis' career was planned from an early stage – even before he won gold medals at five events in the '84 Olympic Games he had his product endorsements and business deals worked out. In fact, so acutely aware of the benefits of sport is Lewis that after fingering Ben Johnson in the '88 Olympics he is now campaigning to get him reinstated. The money-spinning pay-off of a 'grudge rematch' being too hard to resist.

Lifestyle 1989's advertisement for the herbal fruit beverage 'Aqua Libra' said it all. A photo of a suave young blade with an accompanying CV that collated everything he did, saw, listened to and drank. The 'Aqua Libra' reference just sat there, calmly, alongside 'Fellini' and 'Tracy Chapman' or whoever. The inference would appear to be 'Product X can help you, but only as part of a carefully balanced lifestyle'. 'Targetting' is a result of ad agencies' obsessive will to minutely categorise via age, socio-economic grouping, EDUCATION etc, and the '80s has seen a proliferation of increasingly rarefied 'types'. And of course the media, as obsessed with the ADVERTISING industry as the ADVERTISING

industry is with targetting, help matters with articles on the lifestyles of the top ad man and on the semiotics of curry. Everyone laughs, no-one gets fooled, and sales soar. *See Style*

The Lift The Lift was important as a club simply because there had been little like it before in London. Organiser Steve Swindells has gone on to run a series of popular one-nighters for "gay people and their friends", from the much-missed Monday nighter The Jungle to the sophisticated sleaze of his piano bar Downbeat, but The Lift was his real innovation. It was a gay club that played hard, upfront rap, funk and soul all night; that welcomed women and discouraged misogynists; that mixed gay and straight, black and

*L to R: Loafers summer '87 (photo: Steve Johnston). James Lebon '88 **See Cuts** (photo: Dave Swindells). i-D straight ups Lucy and George at Elephant Fair '84. Lonsdale fashion (photo: Johnny Rozsa). Christopher Lambert. The Limelight Club London '87. Living Colour **See Heavy Metal**.*

Loadsamoney

Loadsamoney was the buzz-word coined by comedian Harry Enfield who brilliantly captured the values of Thatcherism in one vile persona. Dressed in trainers and disgusting T-SHIRTS, Loadsamoney succinctly captured two irrefutable realities: the vulgar greed of the THATCHER era and the rank stupidity of cockneys.

Loafers

When people talk about loafers they don't mean the European Gucci-style loafer much beloved of oil-rich Arabs, they mean the penny loafer worn at pavement level by generations of Ivy and given global popularity by the Preppy look popularised in the early '80s by Ralph Lauren. Sabago (overpriced), and Timberland (ditto) export loafers to the UK but the name that has become syonymous with quality is Bass Weejun – with or without beef roles at around £65. Dr Marten do a loafer which can be worn in the wet (which Weejuns can't), but the chunky sole sacrifices the basic minimalism of loafer design,

white; and that existed, in the end, solely for the music. The Lift was a place where you danced all night, or fell down drunk in the knowledge that someone would pick you up and put you into a cab. It opened in '82 at The Gargoyle and eventually closed in '86 at The Embassy. In between, it graced The Subway, Stallions and Fouberts, and held 12 Lift warehouse parties at a time when warehouses were just beginning. Mere mention of The Lift still brings a nostalgic smile to the regulars who went there.

Ligging

The age-old exercise of getting something for nothing, in the '80s, became a a way of life. The sprawling West Wonderland metropolis of clubs, launch parties and press previews, was a circuit that thrived on liggers, relying on them to pay for their free drinks with their personalities and livening up otherwise dull events. In March '85 BBC's 'Arena' programme presented 'Ligmalion', a dubious guide to this peculiarly '80s subculture, which revealed exactly how easy it was. By the end of the decade though, getting into clubs for free became a dying art. Not only did the new generation of clubbers all dress the same, but London's doormen were already wise to the following top ten tips:

1. *The 'empty record sleeve ruse'.* Now that DJs are pop stars they never turn up anyway.

2. *The fake press card trick.* After the tabloid hysteria over ACID HOUSE press have been banned.

3. *Pretend you want to 'check out' the*

club for a VIDEO shoot. After the tabloid hysteria over ACID HOUSE VIDEO crews have been banned.

4. *Act as if you own the place.* The bouncers now own the clubs.

5. *"Do you really not know who I am?"* Most clubs now have membership schemes.

6. *Wait 'til a group of famous people turn up and tag along.* Famous people don't go to clubs anymore.

7. *The 'I'm in the band ruse'.* Bands no longer play at clubs.

8. *Pretend your best friend's inside and their Porsche has been stolen.* Security men now have vodaphones.

9. *The classic "I'm on the guest list".* Most clubs give VIP cards to guests.

10. *The only one guaranteed to work:* "Do you want to audition to present

this youth TV programme I'm working on."

Linx

In the spring of 1980 Sketch and David Grant pressed up 1,000 copies of 'You're Lying' and immediately became the great Britsoul hopes of the decade. The duo declared their intention to be the Nile Rodgers and Bernard Edwards of British soul and spent the next two years being egged on by the media and music business alike. Their finest moment remains 'Intuition', which reached number 7 in March '81, and inspired a host of British soul acts from Loose Ends to Hot House. Unfortunately, they never fulfilled their early promise and David Grant left to pursue a solo career singing mediocre pop and wearing dodgy suits. One of the soul disappointments of the decade.

Little, Alastair

The most famous of the young generation of chefs who helped redefine British cooking in the '80s, Alastair Little had no formal training as a chef. When he opened his own eponymously-named restaurant in Soho's Frith Street in '86, his approach seemed revolutionary. He served food of the highest quality yet broke all the rules of traditional gourmet eating. His premises are deliberately designed to look like a cafe, you can see right into the kitchen, the waitresses wear jeans and diners are provided with paper (!) napkins. The menu changes twice daily and shows a similar disregard for culinary convention; typically, it might include sushi, risotto and salad Nicoise on the same day. Forced price rises mean that his clientele now largely consists of middle-aged business people, but, with the recent opening of a cheaper basement bar, he hopes to attract a younger crowd. *See Japanese Restaurants and Thai Restaurants*

Live Aid

In '85 when BOB GELDOF asked one billion viewers in 150 countries to feed the world, the world promptly sat back and gorged itself on a panglobal TV spectacular. For pop radicals Live Aid was an example of the benevolent exercise of Western technology, for insider sceptics a marketing exercise on behalf of DINOSAUR ROCK stars, and for conspiracy theorists a mass media exercise in 'consensus terrorism' ("Give us your fooking money"). But more than anything else it was a

Lonsdale In 1909, Lord Lonsdale gave his name to British boxing's most famous trophy, the Lonsdale Belt. 51 years later, in 1960, his great nephew allowed an ex-pro boxer called Bernard Hart to set up a boxing equipment company using the family name, and began to build a reputation for classic, reasonably-priced SPORTSWEAR. In the '80s, the Lonsdale shop on Beak Street attracted everyone from TOM JONES to Page Three girl Maria Whittaker to Wham! – not to mention the boxers. The Lonsdale logo was bootlegged in Japan and acquired a cult name in America, and as SPORTSWEAR began to make increasing inroads into the fashion world in the late '80s, its classic design became an integral part of street fashion.

sadistic exercise in hardcore entertainment – eg. starving African bodies used as the manipulative visuals for a Cars' song. It set a precedent. Ever since, no disaster from Zeebrugge to Hillsborough has been complete without its new liturgy of rememberance – a mercy dash from the Prime Minister, a benefit record produced by STOCK, AITKEN & WATERMAN ('Ferry Aid', 'Scouse Aid') and a spate of sick jokes.

Liverpool FC Liverpool FC have suddenly replaced Manchester United as the tragedy club. After more than a decade as a virtually invincible force in English FOOTBALL, Liverpool were successfully visited by

river to Westminster and a Labour backbench seat, where he continues to bring the colour to Tory cheeks and to occasionally embarrass the leadership of his own party.

Locusts Brooding in North Africa is the largest swarm of locusts the world has ever seen. Each year they follow the same path, destroying more and going further each time. Aided by the consistently hot weather, the natural cycle of the rising and falling of the swarm has been bent out of shape and there is no precedent to tell us how far they can continue growing. The insect of the decade without a doubt and possibly the first real disaster caused by GLOBAL WARMING.

out of male-dominated ego tripping and brought women centre stage. Jaime specialises in an off-beat subcultural soap, Gilbert in magic realist routines in a mythical Mexican village. Both continue to go from strength to strength – if you missed them in the '80s, don't miss out in the '90s.

Lover's Rock From its pre-eminence under the tutelage of the Hackney posse, who led the genre in the early '80s, Lover's Rock was the first UK based reggae form to have an impact. Carroll Thompson, Alan Weekes and Cleveland Watkiss emerged from the scene '80-'83, but the sweeter side of the reggae dancehall equation eventually slipped

disasters at Heysel, Hillsborough and their own home turf when Arsenal robbed them of their rightful hold on the league championship. With a monosyllabic Scottish manager, a Zimbabwean goalkeeper and a fanatical support who take their name from a famous battle in the Boer War, Liverpool FC are the stuff of legend. Only the whining memory of Emlyn Hughes stands between the Reds and immortality.

Livingstone, Ken A politician with radical cheek. Ken Livingstone made Tories and tabloids see red when he mixed media-smart STYLE with left-wing populist policies at the GLC. Unable to beat him at the ballot box, the government resorted to abolition. Red Ken didn't go down with the flagship of municipal socialism, but instead crossed the

London Marathon The mass rally of a generation born to jog, the city marathon came to London in '81 and by '89 around 31,000 entered (with 22,664 actually staying the course). Despite the post-Sport Aid incorporation of the marathon into the New Philanthropy, marathon runners remain the self-flagellants of body culture, anti-social ascetics prepared to sacrifice family, friends, even health in the manic pursuit of self-annihilating exhaustion and the heaven on earth of crossing the finishing line. *See Running*

Love And Rockets Drawn by Los Bros Hernandez, Jaime and Gilbert, *Love And Rockets* was the first really adult comic of the decade. It stuck a sharp pen into comic culture's inflated physique, let the air

into a poorly written and hastily arranged formula. The typically tuff rhythm tracks which made Thompson's 'Hopelessly In Love' a seminal work lost out to the funkier, lighter backing and weedy satchel-swinging vocals. In '85 Maxi Priest began turning Lover's into pop, joined later by veteran Freddie MacGregor and Trevor Hartley, though recent years have witnessed a return to traditional strengths, and the dominance of women – Ann and Sonia, Sandra Cross, Kofi, Winsome – in the genre and in reggae's turn of the decade charts. It remains however, for the true ragga, music to grope a woman to as the dance session closes.

Low Alcohol Beers Alcohol-free beers had one fundamental problem – they tasted awful. And when Barbican was launched in '80

L to R: Lycra cycling shorts '85 (photo: Eamonn J McCabe, styling: Wade Tolera). John Lydon (photo: Nick Knight).

LAGER – LYNX **141**

Lycra

The fashion fabric of the '80s. As the fitness ethic infiltrated fashion the baggy hide-it-all shrank to a blatant show-it-all courtesy of the stretchy fabric that hugs every inch of flab and lovingly embraces every well-honed muscle. GAULTIER, RICHMOND/ CORNEJO and BODYMAP started the love affair, and a combination of AEROBICS and OLYMPIC FEVER sent Britain into Lycramania. The ubiquitous '80s BLACK LEGGINGS went baggy without it, CYCLING SHORTS fell down without it and, by '88, it seemed as though you'd never lived without it. *See Catsuits*

with an ad campaign that featured FOOTBALL manager Laurie McMenemy its fate was sealed – nobody wanted to buy anything from a man in a sheepskin coat. But as ALCOHOL became a cause for concern (*See Lager Louts*) and the market shifted, the breweries realised that they had to do something. Tennants LA, Kaliber, Swan Light, Whitbread White Label; by the end of the decade there were 30 different brands of low alcohol beer and the breweries breathed a sigh of relief. The public drank it, profit margins were maintained and Billy Connolly managed to get back on TV. *See Lager and Lager Louts*

Lynx

Of all the single-issue campaigns of the '80s Lynx stands out as the most emotive and possibly the most effective. Taking a designer stance to the anti-fur lobby reaped dividends as audiences stood up in cinemas and cheered at David Bailey's famous 'catwalk' ad. Stylish T-SHIRTS were introduced in '86 and 100,000 people put their concerns on their chests and vilified the last of the fur-wearers. The fashion world caught on fast, making fake fur chic while Lynx went on to open their first

shop in January '89. And the net result? Thirty large fur retailers have closed in the last two years, huge retailers like Edelson and Conrad Furs have gone bankrupt, and Hudson Bay (established in 1670) is finally pulling out of Britain because of the massive public backlash. *See Animal Liberation Front and Beauty Without Cruelty*

Lydon, John

Nine, yes, nine albums since the demise of the Sex Pistols, Lydon's reputation wains with each waxing. Sickeningly photogenic in resplendently pasty skin, his relocation to California rather put the lid on any remaining credibility. He may remain to stick out like a sore thumb, but who needs a sore thumb? The Quentin Crisp of the Blank Generation, file under wrong decade.

MA-1 Flight Jacket The MA-1 flight jacket was developed during the 2nd World War as a cheap alternative to leather. Manufactured to army specifications, it came in three colours (sage green, black and blue) and had an orange lining, to be worn on the outside in the event of emergencies. Its combination of utilitarian fashion and belligerent chic found favour with SKINHEADS in the '70s and mods/scooterists in the early '80s, but it wasn't until Ray Petri incorporated the jacket into the BUFFALO look in the pages of *THE FACE* and *i-D* that the MA-1 entered the burgeoning lexicon of street fashion. Unisex, light and possessing a universal appeal, the jacket soon became an open canvas for London's

clubbers. Initially available only from Millet's, LAWRENCE CORNER and select army surplus stores, it spawned a thousand designer imitations (GAULTIER's being the most prominent) and soon every other shop and stall in KENSINGTON and CAMDEN MARKET were stocking it.

By '86 the MA-1 had become part of a club uniform that included black DMs, black LEVI'S, white T-SHIRTS, and eventually, black RUCKSACKS. Ensuring that the jackets became more than a five minute fad, clubbers started CUSTOMISING them with badges, patches, soviet emblems, cartoon characters, car emblems, photographs, safety pins and slogans. The customised MA-1 flight jacket peaked on the dancefloor of DELIRIUM, where b-boys, retro-trendies and ex-soulboys met in sartorial solidarity and

L to R: Original MA-1 Flight Jacket (photo: Roger Charity, styling: Ray Petri). Madonna in i-D ad. '87.

everybody refused, no matter how hot it was, to take off their N2B heavy weather MA-1 jackets with coyote fur-lined hoods and button-wind flaps. The jacket evolved in ever more dazzling shades and imitations, each copy adding different fabrics and colours, and by the time Brother Beyond had appropriated the jackets, they were the only ones still wearing them.

Macrobiotics The esoteric edge of the diet world, macrobiotics divides foodstuffs into 'yin' and 'yang' and structures a diet around what foods you need to balance your essential personality. Unlike VEG-ETARIANISM and VEGANISM, it's based purely on health motives. Highly fashionable Stateside, watch out for a boom in macrobiotic eateries in the '90s. *See Food Scares*

Mad Max George Miller's trilogy of mean machine science fiction movies made Mel Gibson the first credible movie star from Australia since Errol Flynn and defined a post-apocalyptic survivalist look for the '80s: dyed Mohicans and pumped-up muscles, distressed leathers, buckles and chains. The movies cannibalized imagery from STYLE subcultures (bikers, punks, clones) and movie sub-genres (west-ern, exploitation, demolition derby) to create an immediately recognizable industrial baroque aesthetic which influenced everything from Ron Arad's recycled furniture to JPG's mutant clubland fashions. *See Mutoid Waste Company*

Madonna Madonna Louise Cicc-one is the Queen of the '80s. Born August 16 '59 into a large Italian immigrant family in Rochester, Detroit, she decamped to New York, where she studied dance and theatre. She soon took up with Dan Gilroy, first in a long line of influential boyfriends. The pair formed a band, The Breakfast Club, with Madonna on drums, but she quit that to get up front and sing. Next step, her own band, Emmenon, shortened to Emmy;

L to R: i-D straight up Meka '82 (photo: James Palmer). i-D straight up Mandy '83 (photo: James Palmer). Mantronix. Marilyn at Blitz '80. Steve Martin. Massage by Rough Cuts Body Care circa '85. Malcolm McLaren (photo: Sandro Hyams).

an old Detroit boyfriend Steve Bray joined and they started working on demo tapes in earnest. About this time (1980), Madonna got a part in Stephen Jon Lewicki's low budget, soft porn romp 'A Certain Sacrifice', in which she was to appear in a nude love scene which would come back to haunt her in a later stage of her career. But the big break came when Madonna got a tape she'd made with Bray to DANCETERIA DJ Mark Kamins. This resulted in a signing with Sire, and in '83 'Holiday', written by flame of the time 'Jelly-bean' Benitez, started to do business.

These days, the woman's singles scoot up the charts. Her cinematic appearances are variable, but always a draw. Interest in her private life,

Mail Order Before '84, mail order clothes meant Freemans catalogues, maternity wear and crimplene slacks. But when Jeff Banks made well-designed Warehouse clothes available by post through his Bymail catalogues, it changed the face of mail order fashion. Bymail catalogues were put together by some of the top names in the fashion industry – photo-

TECHNO and swapping samples with Brian Eno.

Marks & Spencer In the '80s M&S switched from High Street worthy to essential snob stop, turning food into a status symbol. With ridiculously high prices and ludicrous convenience foods M&S took YUPPIE consumption to its ultimate limit and made a killing. Introducing new lines virtually every week and convincing consumers that they really need the latest variety of breaded seafood has proved highly profitable – '88 turned in food sales of £2,134,000,000. See Retail Revolution

Marley, Bob Reggae's first international supa, whose name is

dent celebrations for Zimbabwe in 1980, still fondly recalled by locals to this day. Today, Marley's teenage offspring attempt to carry their father's beacon. Though Steven Marley is most respected in Jamaica, where he regularly MCs at dancehall events, Ziggy is Bob's most famous progeny, signed to Virgin Records internationally, and carrying a contemporary version of the same roots and culture message. Ziggy & The Melody Makers (including Steven) released 'Tomorrow People' in '88, scoring limited success in Britain, but becoming the first reggae act to top charts in the United States. Food for thought: Ziggy's 'Tomorrow People' sold more in its first six months in the US than Bob Marley sold in his entire career there.

particularly the marriage to and subsequent split from bad boy Sean Penn, doesn't wane. Madonna has her detractors (Bette Midler claimed La Ciccone to be "a woman who pulled herself up by her bra-straps", something Midler herself knows something about), but that's just jealousy. Ciccone is a self-made phenomenon with nous and presence, who used what she had (her body, her music) to make herself a success. The '80s belong to her, and she deserves it.

Mantronix are basically a man and his machines. Touted by many as the future of rap in '86, the poor rapper who fronted the dynamic duo disappeared into insignificance as Curtis Mantronik left hip hop behind and graduated into mainstream production. Last seen talking

grapher Robert Erdmann and *The Times'* fashion editor Caroline Baker used well-known models and created images similar to magazine pages. But it still couldn't overcome the fundamental problem of mail order – the clothes still took around two weeks to arrive. This all changed when the Next Directory was launched in '86 and clothes were delivered from an exquisitely designed catalogue in under 5 days.

still a byword throughout the Third World for cultural consciousness and the spirit of social unity, died on May 11 '81 in Miami of lung cancer and a brain tumour. Increasingly regarded in his native Jamaica as having deserted his roots for financial and other rewards available in 'Babylon', Marley's death still elicited a seemingly endless string of tribute recordings from the island's DJs and singers. Marley's will became a *cause célèbre*, a reputed multimillion pound inheritance, overseen until May 19 '87 by Marley's wife Rita, when members of his backing band The Wailers went to court to claim a slice of it as payment for the album royalties he had never paid them.

A happier Marley legacy was the worldwide spread of reggae, and his internationalism. One of Marley's last big engagements was at the indepen-

M/A/R/R/S It may have been COLDCUT who made the first British DJ record, but it was M/A/R/R/S' 'Pump Up The Volume' that made the rest of the world sit up and listen. Originally a single by Colourbox it was transformed by DJs CJ Mackintosh and Dave Dorrell into a compulsive collage of samples, scratches and breakbeats that became the biggest selling 12" of '87 and inspired a host of imitations. Initially released as an anonymous white label (a device soon adopted by almost everyone), it became the subject of a High Court injunction obtained by STOCK, AITKEN & WATERMAN, who alleged that their 'Roadblock' single had been sampled. Arguments about the legitimacy of sampling ensued in the MUSIC PRESS, and the injunction was dropped after four days. Apart from the fact that SAMPLING was a major part of SAW's productions, counter-allegations suggested that SAW themselves sampled from 'Pump Up The Volume'. Although Dave Dorrell and CJ Mackintosh did not repeat the success with Nasty Rox Inc or numerous remixes, they have earned a place in dancefloor history. Unfortunately, they never received the full amount of money for their historical number one – the labyrinth of litigation was such that it took two years before they received the first royalties, and even then most of it had been eaten up in costs.

Martin, Steve Congenial American comic with a deft, left-field approach who has worked from his originally cult following to become a national hero – in the States, at least. Martin still has trouble with the British funny-bone, although 'Roxanne' and 'Dirty Rotten Scoundrels' have seen the British warm to his brand of acrobatic lunacy. But from 'The Jerk', 'The Man With Two Brains', to 'Dead Men Don't Wear Plaid' his louche mix of the surreal and the slapstick, has given '80s humour a much needed kick in the pants. Long may his subtle and subversive madness fester.

Massage It used to lurk in the small ads as a euphemism for a swift hand-job or a straight screw, but over the last few years, spurred on by the upsurge of interest in alternative therapy, the 'real' massage has returned. Hottest contender for 'massage of the moment' is probably aromatherapy which employs essential oils for therapeutic effect.

Max Headroom Hailed as the future of TV hosting in '86, the computer generated Max Headroom went the way of all flesh – dropped when the ratings dropped. It even turned out that it was an actor in a RUBBER mask and not a computer at all. What a swizz.

McLaren, Malcolm Punk guru, media manipulator and mentor of the era, McLaren spent the most part of the '80s repackaging cultures massively removed from the Dickensian Englishness of the Pistols, and one has to credit him, ironically, given the Pistols' '76 declaration, "We're not into music... we're into chaos", with having an ear for a good, marketable sound. 1982's 'Buffalo Gals' was for many an introduction to scratching, '83's 'Duck Rock' presaged the late '80s WORLD

The Manipulator Started by disaffected members of the photography magazine *Select*, *The Manipulator* is the 'ART' magazine that defies description. Big enough to sleep on, its pot pourri of photography, ARCHITECTURE, design and ART-related features are addressed to no-one in particular, and precisely for that reason, the magazine is essential. Refusing to conform to anybody's rules (hence the name) and much to the surprise of everyone concerned, it has proved a commercial success. Have *you* ever tried reading it on the tube?

Mapplethorpe Robert who died of an AIDS related illness in '88 aged 42, brought homoerotic photography out of the darkroom and onto the gallery wall combining a timeless classic approach with a contemporary edge that succeeded in both shocking, provoking and ultimately seducing the viewer. Mapplethorpe's legacy lives on in the work of a generation of photographers who perceive an integrity and truth beneath the clinically technical exterior.

MUSIC boom and set fellow producer Trevor Horn on the road to success with the ZTT label. He also gave BOY GEORGE his first career break, as Lieutenant Lush, backing singer with Bow Wow Wow in 1980. Bow Wow Wow – Adam & The Ants, plus Anabella Lwin – was McLaren's final real attempt at music industry subversion, using child sexuality and situationist lyrics, inciting kids to make illegal home tapes and 'WORK NO!'. But EMI, the label that fired the Sex Pistols and signed Bow Wow Wow, stymied him at every turn. The big boys wouldn't get fooled by the street urchin again.

Despite rather desperate musical plagiarisms and juxtaposition ('84's 'Fans' married opera and R&B, '89's

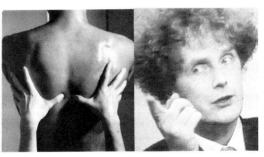

Waltz Darling' classical and funk), McLaren gave good interviews throughout the decade, particularly on TV, and he appeared to have a mischievous time swanning around the states as CBS films advisor. Hardly the stuff of media terrorism. Perhaps he's still awaiting a new Johnny Rotten figure to worry the industry for a few minutes. Whatever, he's been the role model for every two-bit 'entrepreneur' of the last ten years. And he was, along with former business partner VIVIENNE WESTWOOD, the first to import the New York trend of wearing one's baseball boots unlaced.

ME Dubbed 'YUPPIE Flu', probably because myalgic encephalomyelitis is as easy to wrap your tongue round as a curried egg sandwich, this

post-viral fatigue syndrome almost brought the stock exchange to a standstill and was responsible for interrupting the career of at least one pop star (Craig from BROS). Crudely put it is lethargy as a disease, and even if nobody quite knew what it was or how to cure it, it gave new lease to medical authors (at the last count there were two dozen ME books on the shelves), and an irreproachable excuse for not turning up for work.

Medialand Medialand is the square mile south of CHANNEL 4's Charlotte Street headquarters and the wine bars dotted around the BBC in Shepherd's Bush. The key-words are 'project' and 'commission', but no one has dared to create a movie script called the 'Monster Of Medialand' in which a gang of well dressed parasites swarm around looking for stories, angles, good interviews and real people. They eventually suck the blood out of society, lie back and talk about themselves.

Memphis Italian design group ('81-'86) founded by Ettore Sottsass to market his own work and that of others, including Michele de Lucchi, Nathalie du Pasquier, Peter Shire and George Sowden; although work by other designers, including architect Michael Graves and fashion designer Issey Miyake came under its umbrella from time to time. Reacting to Functional MATT BLACK designer objects The Memphis STYLE declared an intention to bring colour back into design, featuring patterned laminated

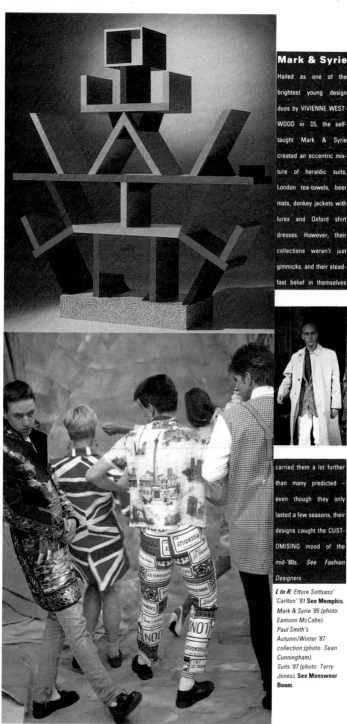

Mark & Syrie

Hailed as one of the brightest young design duos by VIVIENNE WEST-WOOD in 85, the self-taught Mark & Syrie created an eccentric mix-ture of heraldic suits, London tea-towels, beer mats, donkey jackets with lurex and Oxford shirt dresses. However, their collections weren't just gimmicks, and their stead-fast belief in themselves carried them a lot further than many predicted – even though they only lasted a few seasons, their designs caught the CUST-OMISING mood of the mid-'80s. *See Fashion Designers*

L to R: Ettore Sottsass' 'Carlton' '81 **See Memphis.** *Mark & Syrie '85 (photo: Eamonn McCabe). Paul Smith's Autumn/Winter '87 collection (photo: Sean Cunningham). Suits '87 (photo: Terry Jones).* **See Menswear Boom.**

surfaces, angular shapes and surreal-istic objects reminiscent of the cartoons of Tex Avery and George Herriman. The use of patterns and a shared philosophy brought together a unified look to Memphis products, though each designer's individual STYLE remained visible. Memphis brought what had been an elite, avant-garde STYLE to the public arena; its use of pattern and abhorrence of right angles was taken up in a thousand high street window displays for a while, and items from the '84 collection, thanks to a sharp stylist, found their way into a Dorma quilts catalogue.

Menswear Boom In '84 a seminar at the ICA hosted by journalist Thom O'Dwyer, PETER YORK and designer PAUL SMITH heralded the advent of the NEW MAN, a male who cared about his hair, body and clothes, and was willing to spend money on them. The NEW ROMANTICS had already turned the concept of male fashion on its head, putting men in make-up and skirts, but it wasn't until shops like PAUL SMITH identified the man as *consumer* and targeted their products accordingly, with designer suits and gentleman's accessories, that male fashion started to thrive, eventually crossing over into the High Street. Menswear fashion designers got their own exhibition (*See English Menswear Designer Collections*), advertisers identified men as poten-tial big fashion spenders, and retail chains like Next For Men, Wood-house, Reiss and Blazer spearheaded the RETAIL REVOLUTION. Young designers also brought out men's collections - Dean Bright, BODYMAP, RICHARD TORRY, NICK COLEMAN, JOE CASELY HAYFORD, John Flett, and STEPHEN LINARD, all encour-aged men to explore a fashion world they had previously ignored. As STEPHEN LINARD once remarked: "The taboo about men worrying about image and looks that were, until recently, the domain of homo-sexuals, has disappeared." *See Arena*

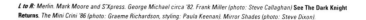

Menumasters Freedom for the way you live today. The idea of airline food at home, steaming fresh from microwaved plastic packets was a masterpiece of packaging over content. In the time it takes to toss a salad or cook an omlette, microwave meals bring the freedom to eat a very small piece of cod instead. Small portions are no problem though, it just means they can be sold as weight watching as well.

Message T-Shirts In '84 KATHARINE HAMNETT launched a collection of T-SHIRTS which carried a sentiment she hoped would be copied. Using banner headlines on plain silk shapes, she shouted her pro-environmental ideologies:

Matt Black Any colour as long as it's matt black was the order for accessories throughout the '80s. The colour that didn't come in shades, that symbolised an all-or-nothing power attitude, the colour that marked the end of colour, had been used for years by companies like Braun, who valued it for its utilitarian qualities and 'neutral and universal integratability'. London in

KRAFTWERK samples and pure misogynism, ripped out the back seats of their cars and installed giant speakers, generating a mobile bass culture that the local rappers reflected in records like Chill-C's 'My Trunk Is Boomin''. Bass music exploded in early '85, but was slow in catching on outside its hometown, and didn't reach Britain until '89.

Miami Vice Or how Michael Mann retooled 'Starsky & Hutch' for the designer decade, with the same maverick cop routines and buddy-buddy team talks from Don Johnson and Philip Michael Thomas but with the added Armani sheen of NEW MAN narcissism and with the action flipped from the East Coast to

than even he could have imagined. Most of all, he escaped the teenybop fix, escaping from Wham! – the most successful pop phenomenon of the decade – at their peak, and constructed his credibility from the ground up. Hardly the most prolific of writers, with only three non-compilation albums in an eight year recording history, his legacy remains the classic Brit-pop concoctions of his salad days with Andrew Ridgley; 'Wham! Rap', 'Young Guns (Go For It)', and his first solo outing 'Careless Whisper'. How many married mortgagees squirm when they hear the titles today but still pull out their dusty copies of 'Make It Big' come party time? Solo, George has fared less well in England, but why should

'Choose Life', 'Education, Not Missilies' and 'Save The Whale'. But it was when she visited 10 Downing St wearing the famous slogan '58% Don't Want Pershing' that her idea was imitated en masse, and during the summer of '85/'86 pop groups offered their own versions: 'Frankie Say Arm Yourself' and 'Choose Wham!'. While the fashion world hurried to state that 'Fashion Cares' in '87, the use of T-SHIRTS as walking placards was also picked up by condom companies Jiffy and Durex in order to promote themselves and SAFE SEX. By the end of the decade everybody from fashion designers to pressure groups were producing them.

Miami Bass In Miami, Florida, fans of the local rap strain, a mixture of raw, early '80s-style ELECTRO,

the late '80s though, saw a glut of matt black trinket shops, full of FILOFAXES and penknives with black blades, and the world waited to see what would replace this un-colour. As Green politics took over, a vote was heard for the natural, non-hardwood wood, but the odds are on that matt black will still dominate design in the '90s. *See Black Uniformity and Memphis*

America's porous Southern border. Johnson's Sonny Crockett is the symbolic inheritor of his namesake's Alamo heroism, a last frontiersman besieged by an urban vortex of cocaine drops, cash flows and Contra gun runs. And just as he's fighting a losing battle, so the show's narrative dissolves into a scrambled choreography of effects – pastel framed interior design shoots, swooning rock VIDEO inserts, homoerotic gestural tableaux and pause-button cameos (from JAMES BROWN to Phil Collins). The only TV series it's essential to watch with the sound off.

Michael, George Can this really be the Georgios Panayiotou who in 1980 was a 17 year old uncharismatic cog in ailing SKA band The Executive? George Michael has reinvented himself more successfully

he worry? In America 'Faith' notched up over five million sales and five successive number one singles, and while the British tabloids still have their knives out for him, America has clutched George to their expensive collective bosom and made him theirs. Whether the soul boy can stay the distance as a soul man in the fashion of his idol Stevie Wonder, the jury is still out. It's a tough job, but someone's gotta do it.

Millar, Martin Martin Millar is the dole card sharp from north of the border who since '87 has put the post-punk drifters and the dole-ites of Brixton squat culture into three self-consciously cultish novels, *Milk, Sulphate & Alby Starvation, Lux The Poet* and *Ruby & The Stone Age Diet*. Spikily surreal, sentimental yet sharp, Millar specialises in a distinctive brand of whimsy on the rocks, deliberately designed to leave a bitter after taste.

Millwall FC Millwall started off as the hooligans of British FOOTBALL and ended up as its saints. Many clubs realised the value of family stands, free tickets for parties of schoolkids, cheap entry for OAPs and UB40s etc, but Millwall also introduced a matchday creche, modern drama as pre-match entertainment, a weekly over 50s club and a WOMEN'S FOOTBALL team. When Millwall players visited local schools they talked not only of tactics but of the trappings of racism and hooliganism, and they even appointed former Northern Ireland troubleshooter John

Stalker as 'hooligan consultant' in an attempt to change their image. The club admit they have a long way to go (not least in updating the facilities on their own shabby terraces), but the Millwall anthem of "No one likes us, we don't care" doesn't ring quite so true as it used to.

The Miners' Strike With coal stocks at record levels and without a ballot, Arthur Scargill led Britain's miners into what was supposed to be the last great industrial battle. They faced MARGARET THATCHER who dubbed the miners "the enemy within", her American axeman Ian McGregor, who proposed to close nearly half the country's pits, and a POLICE force which displayed incredible savagery in a series of set piece picket line battles, most notably at Orgreave in May '84. With their

Mini Crini VIVIENNE WESTWOOD's Mini Crini, a miniature version of the 19th Century hooped crinoline skirt, made its debut appearance on the Paris catwalk in the Autumn of '85. Intended as a reaction against the body-conscious streamlined silhouettes that had gone before, it was badly received by buyers and press. It wasn't until October '86 that a deluge of exciting skirt shapes directly inspired by the Mini Crini hit the British catwalks (including the Blair Mini Pani) and what had started out as an idea without followers ended up changing the shape of the female silhouette. The Mini Crini drew attention away from the upper torso and shoulders, and refocused it onto the hips. The puffball skirt was the High Street version of the Mini Crini, without the essential boning, making the wearer look like a pregnant grub. Every woman bought a puffball in the summer of '87, and it was eventually mass-produced to death.

union's assets frozen, the miners depended on massive fundraising efforts; Wham!, the STYLE COUNCIL and Working Week are among those who played gigs, heralding the start of the benefit era. The year long strike ended in defeat in March '85. It created new legends and folk heroes, but ultimately divided families, communities and the National Union Of Mineworkers itself.

Minimalism Not the '70s ART movement but the '80s design fad. The minimalist look mixed MATT BLACK stylings, white space and hand-me-down Zen aesthetics to turn your bedroom into a buddhist monastery and give your living room that special unlived-in look – no books, no

mags, no records, no papers, no clutter, no sign of normal human life at all. Prettily vacant, the minimalist look expressed a fantasy of control ('If only my life could be that organised, that *pure*'), and was a vision of a dream home which never really existed outside magazine spreads and TV ads.

Mirror Shades If RAY-BAN Wayfarers became the suburban soulboy sunglasses of the '80s then teardrop shaped mirror shades did much the same for rock'n'roll outlaw chic. First populated by the US military in Vietnam particularly by helicopter pilots, they could be spotted on the likes of 'Easy Rider' Peter Fonda and Rolling Stone Keith Richard in the '70s. It was not however, until the return of the heavy duty Hells Angel biker look in the

mid-'80s that mirror shades resurfaced as the most credible way to attain the sort of instant mystique that made Andrew Eldritch, Zodiac Mindwarp and a host of GREBO stars. Mirror shades reflect the world back at itself and give no clue to the onlooker as to what the wearer's eyes look like – useful for hiding bloodshot eyes or contracted pupils brought about by ALCOHOL or drug abuse. This of course also adds to the charm.

Miyake, Issey See Japanese Designers

Mo, Timothy Hong Kong born of Cantonese-English mixed blood, Mo followed the same route as contemporary MARTIN AMIS, of St John's College Oxford to best selling quality novelist. There were a few differences: Mo wrote throughout the '80s for BOXING News, providing odds for bookmakers and making predictions. He was taken up by the British lit-crit establishment as a serious spokesperson for the Chinese underclass, with his tales of TRIADS, takeaways, opium wars and rites of passage. But he has remained detached from the world of the Groucho Club, preferring instead to watch BOXING and go skindiving, a hobby which his massive advances (he was offered £70,000 on the open market for his third novel) allow.

Modern Soul The midtempo and obscure soul sounds of the '70s, as adopted by soulboy purists who had outgrown '60s NORTHERN SOUL but weren't yet ready to enter the computer-friendly '80s. The scene started in the Modern Room at Northern Soul all-dayers in Blackpool in the early '80s, and continued growing slowly until '89, when Modern Soul DJ gurus like Richard Searling on Lancashire's Red Rose Radio and London's Bob Jones started to bring their Northern and Southern soul factions together at a series of highly successful Blackpool weekenders.

Modzart Responsible for some of the best T-SHIRTS of the punk era, John Dove moved his shop 'Kitsch' and wholesale label Modzart from the West End to World's End in '84, eventually ending up at HYPER HYPER in '89 (now known simply as Modzart). His screen printed jeans with fluorescent stripes, hearts, baked beans and Jackson Pollock splash effects were sold and imitated worldwide.

Mondino, Jean Baptiste The man responsible for the finest TV title sequence ever ('Rapido'), who put MADONNA in a peepshow ('Open Your Heart' video), shot PRINCE in the raw for an LP cover ('Lovesexy'), and who regularly produces both

ground-breaking ADVERTISING and fashion photography. An uncompromising iconoclast and prime mover in defining the images of '80s fashion and pop consumption.

Monitor Not so much a fanzine as a grad-zine, *Monitor* started in Oxford in '84 and used French theory from Foucault to Kristeva to champion wigging out and an idea of rock as a blissful, immobilising noise. It folded in '86 when *Melody Maker* offered its born again rockists – Simon Reynolds, David Stubbs and Paul Oldfield – a weekly platform for their influential brand of overeducated rock crit. The *Monitor* crew may sometimes seem rather humourless, but reading what they say about their favourite record is usually more entertaining than listening to them. *See Music Press*

Money Belts An essential '80s accessory. Although popular with European tourists, the street fashion for wearing the money belt (or bum bag, or fanny pack) stems from New York, where leather pouches with bootleg MCM or Louis Vuitton patterns are in most demand. Also popular amongst surfers and skateboarders, who prefer them in fluorescent colours.

Moonlighting Although 'Moonlighting' was launched on the back of Cybil Shepherd's career woman shoulder pads and goofy-eyed grin, the previously unknown Bruce Willis stole the show with his tongue-in-chic wit and the ubiquitous perma-smirk. Simultaneously come-on, put-down and put-on, it guaranteed iconic status for Willis' mix of NEW MAN and Nouveau Yob, and set the tone as 'Moonlighting' changed from a detective show into a full-scale, postmodern genre bender. Everything went into the mix – musicals, film noir, cartoons, old soul, outtakes – all held together by the regular in-car battle of the sexes backchat (some of the sharpest dialogue on TV) and the simplest, most cynical of hooks – just when would Bruce and Cybil make it into bed? When they did, the show shot its bolt, leaving Willis to head for Hollywood and Shepherd to carve out a career ADVERTISING hair dye. On form, one of the best TV shows of the decade.

Moore, Jonathan Moore smacked the early '80s theatre scene in the mouth with the double punch of 'Treatment' and 'Street Captives'. Written and directed for New London Actors, the company he formed with a group of similarly unemployed talents, they were angry tales of violence and abuse. A declared enemy of slice-of-life human tape recorders, Moore spouts a theatrical theory that demands something dangerous and larger than life. Since then his momentum has slowed and plentiful commissions notwithstanding, Moore has rarely reached the same level of grit or attention.

The Moral Majority Founded in '79 by Jerry Falwell, America's top TV preacher, it was an umbrella organisation for the religious right, a pressure group that sought to impose the evangelical churches' stance on issues – ABORTION, school prayers, divorce, pornography, teenage pregnancy – on a national level. The Moral Majority was politically involved with the Republican Party, and

has been credited with rallying the Christian support that got RONALD REAGAN elected the first time round. In 1980 the organisation also claimed responsibility for unseating enough left-leaning liberal senators to put the senate in Republican hands, but its backing of Pat Robertson's fundamental candidacy at the last election was ineffective, suggesting its power had waned. In June '89, at the Seven Baptist Convention in Las Vegas, Jerry Falwell announced the disbanding of the Moral Majority, saying that it had run its course. "The religious right is solidly in place," he told the audience, "and religious conservatives in America are now in for the duration." The most bizarre action the movement ever achieved

was the insertion of a sex scene between BATMAN and a woman in the '89 blockbuster film 'BATMAN' (they felt that BATMAN's four decades of sex-free crimefighting, with only young Robin by his side, condoned homosexuality). Autonomous state chapters of the Moral Majority still continue to function. *See Evangelism and Religion*

Mountain Bikes The mountain bike is best described as the bike for riders who don't want to be seen as 'cyclists'. That's why you see these tractor-tread monsters being ridden through the city streets instead of through the Rockies or along the Grand Canyon, where their extravagant features have at least some practical application. What we call the mountain bike evolved from the multi-terrain cycle developed in the

Moore, Alan

Credited with single-handedly transforming comics from playground pulp to graphic literature, Alan Moore is the Hippy Missionary of this previously unexplored new artistic territory and has staked his social conscience to all the big issues – feminism (*Halo Jones*), ecology (*Swamp Thing*), AIDS (*AARGH!*), the CIA (*Brought To Light*). Fair enough, but Moore's at his best when he stops telling the kids What's Going On and starts producing a less heavy-handed fiction of moral sentiment – as in the celebrated *WATCHMEN* or the futurist Britain folk tale *V For Vendetta*. All of which doesn't stop him from having the wildest hair this side of ZZ Top.

L to R: Mozdart circa '82. Troop Money Belt '89 (photo: John Dawson). Mountain Bikes circa '85 (photo: Ronnie Randall). Alan Moore (photo: Dick Jude). MTV graphics (photo: Tony Mottram).

States, and they made their British debut back in '81, when the first Ridgebacks – still the premiere name although Muddy Fox are the most popular – were imported. Prices vary from between £200 to £800 and one of London's funniest sights remains the rear view of a CYCLE COURIER turning the pedals of his mountain bike furiously as he fails to find the right gear. A triumph of image over need.

Movida The term 'movida' was first coined at the beginning of the '80s to describe the boom of artistic creativity in Madrid in the years following the death of Franco as Spain became a democracy. The pioneers of the avant-garde scene in

the first half of the '80s became firmly established as leading figures in their individual fields by the end of the decade. The most well-known movida figures are film director Pedro Almodovar; artist and film maker Ceesepe; designers Sybilla, Antonio Alvarado and Chus Bures; photographers Ouka Lele and Alberto Garcia Alix; and bands like Alaska and Dinarama, Gabinete Caligari and Radio Futura. The word really just means 'movement', in the sense of activity or liveliness, and from the mid-'80s it was used to describe Madrid nightlife in general.

Mr Dog Small tins of dog food for small dogs, Mr Dog was a stroke of marketing genius whose only stumbling block was the profound change in the nature of small dogs. In a decade in which Trixibelle became a

"more attitude...
less hang-ups"

KENSINGTON
MARKET

49-53 Kensington High Street London W8
Press Office 01 938 4343 Kensington High Street tube

girl's name, thwarted by the inexorable rise of the terrier, the poodle parlour was probably the only service industry not to prosper. The pampered pet had turned into a miniature guard dog and Mr Dog, too cute by far, was forced to change its name to Caesar.

The Mud Club Opened in January '83 by the flamboyant Phillip Salon, The Mud Club went on to become one of the most successful West End one-nighters of the '80s. The first Friday night of The Mud at the Subway Club in Leicester Square featured MALCOLM MCLAREN and his BUFFALO Girls leading 500 clubbers, models and former ROCKABILLIES in an orgy of square dancing and hip hip bebopping. With DJs Jay Strongman, Mark Moore and Tasty Tim (who later left) supplying a unique musical culture clash of hardcore funk, rap, rockabilly and glam rock classics The Mud had a crazed atmosphere that attracted clubbers from all over the country. Moving from the Subway to Fouberts in Carnaby Street its crowd grew bigger until it attracted over 1,000 people a week. In the summer of '84 The Mud moved to its final home, Busby's in Charing Cross Road, and its reputation as *the* London club grew even more, attracting a potent combination of young Sloane girls, b-boys and West End clubbers. The Mud was at the forefront of every fashion, STYLE and musical change during the second half of the '80s, and was also the first place to recreate a warehouse party atmosphere in the West End. Although The Mud was busier than ever before during the summer of '88 it gradually lost its more fashionable regulars and in the spring of '89 Busby's owners gave Salon notice to quit.

The Mudd Club While the old, rich and famous wiled away their hours at Studio 54 in New York, the young, poor and ambitious set up their counter 'downtown' headquarters at Dr Mudd (owner Steve Maas)'s loft space in the uncharted

territory of Tribeca (Triangle Below Canal). Officially opening on New Year's Eve '78/'79 it acted as a night school for the growing community of artists, performers, filmmakers, poets and posers who were occupying the southern part of Manhattan island, spawning seminal New York names from John Lurie, JIM JARMUSCH, Ann Magnuson to the B-52s. The seminal downtown Manhattan club.

Murdoch, Rupert An Australian newspaper tycoon who courted notoriety via his increasing hold on the British media through his ownership of *The Sun* (affectionately known as 'The Currant Bun' to its readership) and *The Times*. He used both these inky vehicles to demonstrate a slavish support for MARGARET THATCHER who he once described as "the only British politician who's any bloody good". Murdoch is said to be the tenth richest man in the world and also has shares in TV, radio and film industry across the globe. He made the headlines himself in '86 with the transfer of his British empire from Fleet Street to 'Fortress Wapping', introducing new technology based printing and production methods at a cost of 3,000 jobs. Conflict with the printing unions was inevitable. The sight of Page Three star Samantha Fox crossing the picket line in a tank seemed to indicate that Murdoch was enjoying the publicity the conflict brought about. Rupert Murdoch is currently attempting to ensure an equal amount of control of our TV sets with the introduction of SKY TV, a satellite channel which promises to be a visual equivalent of The Currant Bun.

Murphy, Eddie Heir to the foul-but-funny tradition of Richard Pryor, Murphy walked away with his mentor's crown and straight into huge Hollywood hits, landing him a furlined production deal with Paramount. Neutering his best imitator – Arsenio Hall – by roping him into the Murphy empire, may have postponed criticism, but Murphy's over-reliance

Moore, John

John Moore redefined footwear in the '80s. After graduating from Cordwainer's College in '84, he went on to inspire droves of imitators with his elegantly idiosyncratic ideas. Creating everything from a gold, tractor-soled training shoe to a high-heeled, commando-soled stiletto (for men *and* women), at the end of '87 he set up The House Of

Beauty & Culture in East London as a showcase for his work and that of fellow designers like RICHARD TORRY, CHRISTOPHER NEMETH and JUDY BLAME. John Moore died at the beginning of '89, but his former assistant Ian Reid continued to produce limited editions of his shoe designs at The House Of Beauty & Culture. *See Fashion Designers*

L to R: John Moore (photo: Simon Fleury). i-D straight up Moira '83 (photo: Steve Johnston).

on sexism and obscenity in his live act points up a dangerous lack of new material. He took his concert film 'Raw' very seriously – Pryor had had some of biggest successes with movies of his live act – but the film was upstaged by the violence surrounding the screenings, and Murphy's catchphrase, "motherfucker, moi?", began to sound less funny and more apposite.

Music Press The NME, Melody Maker and Sounds entered the '80s still riding on the coat-tails of punk although not knowing quite where they were going. The story since has been one of confusion, as a succession of new magazines chipped at their readership and stole the initiative. *SMASH HITS* cornered the pop market displaying the sort of irreverence that had been buried under mind-numbing pretension in the NME, and the STYLE magazines i-D, The Face and Blitz, who proved that music was but one facet (and an increasingly marginal one) of youth culture. Sounds made an early attempt to redefine itself by latching on to the dubious Oi movement, dumping it for heavy metal when it realised its mistake. Melody Maker recruited the writing talents of the Oxford University gradzine MONITOR, quickly replacing the NME as the thinking-dudes journal, while the NME languished in no-mans land. An attempt to revive the NME's sinking fortunes came when the paper realised that dance music was the only music not wallowing in the past, and made a spectacular but brief

Morrissey

When all looked lost for British pop, in '83 Morrissey appeared out of nowhere, well, Manchester actually, to call back the jury. Mordent pseudo music hall lyricism combined with Johnny Marr's trademark jangle enabled THE SMITHS to chart without compromising their indie credentials. Their split in '87 coincidentally coincided with their signing to EMI, whose marketing plan was to make them as big, globally as Queen. It hasn't quite worked. Solo, Morrissey has continued to send out bedsit bulletins which chart due to his undyingly loyal hardcore fans, but even his best solo work, 'Suedehead' and Every Day Is Like Sunday', has failed to find the guru of glum a larger following.

L to R: Morrissey (photo: Richard Croft). Moschino (photo: Roberto Carra). Moschino Spring/summer '87 collection

lunge at the sort of coverage the black music press should do but never have done. But its new direction, combined with a return to its political commentary of the late '70s, incurred the wrath of owners IPC who appointed a new editor and turned the *NME* into what it is today; a music paper writing for nobody but itself. With circulation figures falling further and heads continuing to roll, the major music newspapers are still primarily owned by IPC, the creaking corporation that turned down *SMASH HITS, THE FACE* and *Q*. On a good week they still compete for exclusive interviews with Nick Cave and print live reviews of THE FALL.

Music Videos When MTV first started rocking around the clock in '81 it revitalised a singles market which had been declining throughout the '70s and pinned down that most elusive and sought after consumer; the Distracted Rich Kid. Soon what had been marketed by the record companies as the latest promotional tool was being touted as a postmodern ART form. Celebrated by trendy academics as a moveable feast of images and slagged off by diehard rockists as moving wallpaper, the technology nevertheless became a valuable new asset to the culture industry, allowing VIDEO directors like Julien Temple, Bernard Rose and Russell Mulcahy to make (bad) movies and film directors like KEN RUSSELL, Martin Scorsese and John Landis to make (even worse) pop videos. Top five of the decade: 1. David Byrne's 'Road To Nowhere', 2. Phillipe DeCouffle's 'True Faith', 3. Julien Temple's 'Poison Arrow', 4. Tim Pope's 'Close To You', 5. Steve Barron's 'Don't You Want Me'. *See*

Moschino, Franco Franco Moschino is the Bad Boy of Milanese fashion. He makes the naff chic, and the chic naff, stressing that he is not so much a fashion designer as an artist, but he is also an exceptional stylist. Aiming to demystify fashion, his visual jokes include crazy catwalk shows with glamorous models scrambling on all fours like animals, wearing a kettle as a handbag, and replacing a hat with an aeroplane. From drawing Madonnas at the age of 15, his first shows in '82, to his present day £45 million empire, Moschino has always put himself centrestage – he styles all his own ADVERTISING and publicity, and even featured himself in all manner of poses for his '89 campaign. His theme tune is 'I Am What I Am'. *See Fashion Designers*

Jean Baptiste Mondino and Derek Jarman

Mutoid Waste Company

Although they look like 'MAD MAX' extras, the Mutoid Waste Company are authentic urban gypsies – they live on the road and live off the left-overs of modern life, surviving by selling their mutated junk to ART galleries or by staging post-industrial parties in London's derelict warehouses. Turning the mid-'80s recycling aesthetic of CREATIVE SALVAGE into an alternative LIFESTYLE, they have become refusniks from the refuse dump, the most visible example of the new mutant hippy culture of the late '80s.

Name Belts A

hip hop fashion accessory popularised by RUN DMC and THE BEASTIE BOYS in '86, the bold brass buckles stamped with the name of your choice were initially only available from the States. But as UK b-boy outlets such as Spe and World started to import them, and VIVIENNE WESTWOOD and Pink Soda started manu-

Name Of The Rose Best

sellers usually deal in shopping and fucking, cold war scare stories, or trouble at t'Mill. So trouble at t'Monastery, semiotics, 14th Century theology and a missing text by Aristotle might not be expected to do the business. But the decade's most unlikely bestseller, *The Name Of The Rose*, had all this as well as a critique of the destructive certainties of fundamentalism and a Sherlock Holmes-style plot. Published here in '83, Umberto Eco's brilliant medieval thriller has so far sold around 10 million copies worldwide, in the process starting a great annual publishing ritual, the search for the next *Name of the Rose*.

Nell's The natural

reaction to the big New York clubs of the mid-'80s was a small, more intimate supper club venue. So when Little Nell of Rocky Horror Picture Show fame landed in New York in '86 to host her *boite du nuit*, the chic were ready to join and reinstate elitism in the scene. Still going strong years later with its basement dancefloor and an

Calcutta', in which Barlow and Julian Hough confused Edinburgh fringe audiences by playing several hundred roles each. Quietly spoken, modest and bespectacled Barlow is fast becoming a contendor for Funniest Man in the country.

Neighbourhood Watch Schemes

Middle class vigilanteism swept through London's leafy suburbs faster than a wife swapper in a West End farce. Bands of decent citizens banded together to protect their videos, CD players and Molinex Masterchefs. In Barnes, only POLICE intervention stopped foot patrols harrassing bypassers who were considered 'shifty looking'. Apparently stabilised by the distraction of GUARDIAN ANGELS, Neighbourhood Watchers have gone back to peaking from behind the net curtains. The current phone call to arrest rate ratio is around 99.7% unsuccessful.

The Nelson Mandela Concert

See Artists Against Apartheid

Neo-Public Art

With the built environment of the '80s increasingly transformed into a semiotic riot of shop signs, ADVERTISING slogans and corporate logos, a group of north American artists decided it was time to fight back. Adopting a situationist tactic of ground level counter insurgency, the public realm became not only their target but also their chief weapon. Barbara Kruger pasted her feminist photo-collage texts over billboards ('You molest from afar'), while Jenny Holzer's provocative 'Truisms' and 'Survival' slogans appeared on a Piccadilly Circus electronic notice board in '88 ('Abuse of power should come as no surprise'). Meanwhile, Kryztstof Wodcizko projected a US missile on to Nelson's Column as part of an attempt to expose the repressed significance of public monuments. But how many punters thought these were all just clever clever ad campaigns? *See Art*

facturing their own, what originally started as street fashion ended up round the waists of BROS.

Naples Funk

Enzo Avitabile, Tony Esposito, Tullio De Piscopo... however unbelievable their names might sound, their Neapolitan funk grooves drew influences from GEORGE CLINTON and Miles Davis and developed a strain of fluid jazz-funk which was, in '86, totally divorced from the rest of the European dance scene. While everyone else was worshipping the computer, in true jazz-funk STYLE, these Naples guys could *really play*, man.

The National Theatre Of Brent

The undersung stage hero of the '80s, Desmond Olivier Dingle (aka Patrick Barlow) led his two-man company to cult status with renderings of 'Zulu', 'The Charge Of The Light Brigade' and 'The Black Hole Of

electric mix of JAZZ and blues performances, Nells has managed to keep its image intact.

L to R: Mutoid Waste Company (photo: Dave Swindells).
Name Belt (photo: Simon Fleury).
Nell Campbell (photo: Kevin Davies) See Nell's

L to R: Lyle Lovett (photo: Derek Ridgers) **See New Country***. Christopher Nemeth's collection '87 (photo: Moira Bogue). Christopher Nemeth (photo: Marc Lebon). Early New Romantics (photo: Peter Ashworth). Neo Geo artist Jeff Koons' stainless steel Rabbit '86* **See Art***.*

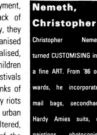

Network 21 Britain's first, and as yet only attempt at pirate TV. In '86, Network 21 broadcasted for 30 minutes per fortnight over a six month period; but due to the huge cost of equipment and the fact that any pirate TV signal can be pinpointed within seconds by the Department Of Trade And Industry and the perpetrators imprisoned, there have been no further attempts at pirate TV broadcasting – yet. *See Pirate Radio*

New Age Music New age music, also called 'ambient music' by Brian Eno, was hi-tech muzak for CD owners, aural valium that turned into a multi-million dollar business as new age entrepreneurs made an ART

form out of background sound. The leading new age record label, Wyndham Hill, was founded in '76, built up its sales in alternative bookshops and HEALTH FOODS stores rather than record outlets, and by '84 had sales of $20 million, proving that music didn't have to be exciting to sell.

New Age Travellers Branded "Medieval Brigands" by Home Secretary Douglas Hurd, the UK's new age travelling community featured heavily in the newspapers during the summer months of the '80s, and were ignored the rest of the time. The media marginalised them as people whose *raison d'etre* was dodging police roadblocks in order to hold a wild and crazy pop festival at Stonehenge on the summer solstice. Comprising of ex-hippies, punks and

others who'd tired of unemployment, inner city decay and the lack of natural 'reality' in urban society, they were actually far better organised than the powers-that-be realised, with 'The Skool Bus' for their children and a huge circuit of free festivals throughout the year. If the punks of the '70s presaged the inner city riots with their demands for the urban landscape to be radically altered, then the disaffected hippies of the '80s broke right out and called for, in the name of one of their bands, Another Green World. *See Green Awareness*

New Beat The electronic dance sound of Belgium, originally conceived in '87 by Antwerp DJs who slowed down Euro-beat records from 45 to 33 to attain a monotonous, pounding rhythm. Progressing out of clubs like Ghent's Boccaccio and Antwerp's Prestige, New Beat hit Britain at the tail end of the SUMMER OF LOVE, and enjoyed a brief domination of BALEARIC BEAT dancefloors. It became identified with leading Belgian fashion designer Walter Van Beirendonck (who used a purpose-built New Beat track for his '89 'Hard Beat' collection), and even spawned a Belgian 'New Beat Fashion' label. Belgium's major contribution to club culture, New Beat still rules the Benelux dancefloor.

New Country While old country's Nashville schmaltz was always good for kitsch value, Reaganomics and a little feminist

Nemeth, Christopher Christopher Nemeth turned CUSTOMISING into a fine ART. From '86 onwards, he incorporated mail bags, secondhand Hardy Amies suits, oil paintings, photocopies, sellotape and rope into his eclectic clothes, and followed no rule of dressmaking or tailoring, largely due to his untrained background. Even though his designs have spawned many imitators, their originality has never been equalled. The Japanese were the only ones to understand Nemeth, and in late '87 he moved himself and his whole operation to Tokyo. *See Fashion Designers*

Network 7 On CHANNEL 4 for three hours plus each week, Network 7 introduced trendy talking heads, info blips, image bombardment and, rather than fight the tyranny of the short attention span, catered to it. Initially reviled by critics of every hue, it is now seen as a watershed in Youth TV and the precursor to every teen-prog since. *See Janet Street Porter and Trendy Telly*

ideology helped to galvanise America's Country fraternity into accepting that the '80s had arrived. At the vanguard were Dwight Yoakam, Steve Earle and Randy Travis, and soon even the older lags leapt on the bandwagon. But there was a healthy broadening out of the category. Lyle Lovett had a big band and more than a hint of blues and KD Lang thought she was the reincarnation of Patsy Cline, sounded like the reincarnation of Patsy Cline and dressed like an Islington dyke. New Country at its worst, opened up the ears of record companies to life beyond rhinestones and at its best, Lang's 'Torch And Twang' LP, it compressed more emotion into a three minute track than could be found in the entire Billboard 100.

The New Dealers The unwritten law of ART dealing has always been: deal with artists of your own generation. But in the '80s the new breed of young artists broke all the rules, opened up shop and went directly to the serious collectors with their wares. Not unlike the growth in INDEPENDENT RECORD LABELS, artists ran their own collective galleries in dockside warehouses (The Young Unknowns, Crucial, Slaughterhouse, Submarine, Monolith). The New York phenomenon of the dealer becoming more important than the artist in the market place (I've got a Mary Boone, a Castelli, a piece from Arnold Glimcher, etc), wasn't repeated in Britain, but the galleries did exert a certain cudos. People flocked to the Crucial for its informal atmosphere and credibility – it certainly made a change from dealer galleries like Waddington, where it often felt like you were seeing a banker. Despite stock market jitters and high interest credit, London still hosts an increasing number of young independent galleries striving for international credentials – Pomeroy/Purdy, Runkel/Hue-Williams, Anthony Reynolds, Karsten Schubert, Raab, Nicoal Jacobs, Victoria Miro, Salama-Caro – but as

collectors become ever more conservative (the SAATCHIs are already
selling a lot of their contemporary
ART) the future does not bode well.

New Man The New Man-ia
began mid-decade as a seductive
male icon simpered through ads,
fashion shoots and magazine think-
pieces, and cultural arbiters tried to
figure whose side this homme fatale
was on. Did his softened body
language reveal the rise of real life
anti-sexist heroes, or was this sex
object designed for men only –
borrowed from gay iconography and
STYLE mags to educate male consumers into narcissistic vanity
shopping? Far from being a feminist
Mr Right, to left-wing conspiracy

theorists, he was Mr NEW RIGHT,
selling building societies and STYLE
consumption, promoting Tory efforts
to yuppify the working class. But a
New Man-icure on old hands doesn't
change much. Usually beneath the
moisturising cream lurks the Nouveau
Yob. A New Man can be hard to find,
despite his media visibility (the
Halifax Man, the Spa Man, the Man
in Grey), but there's no problem with
the Nouveau Yob – getting pissed on
Grolsch with the lads in a BRASSERIE
near you this weekend.

New Music Seminar
Originally a discussion and showcase
event for exploring new music held
in a half-built Manhattan hotel in '79,
the New Music Seminar has grown
into just another date on the
international music calendar held in
one of the plushest hotels in New

York. The actual seminars still exist, and occasionally issues do get discussed, but the important business is done at the revolving bar. An excuse for the music biz to get pissed together at their companies' expense.

New Order Alongside fellow Mancunians THE SMITHS, New Order were the independent heroes of the '80s. Formed from the remnants of JOY DIVISION they rapidly perfected a hybrid of catchy guitar pop and electronic dance beats which led to numerous global chart hits including '83's influential 'Blue Monday'. Keeping their respect by remaining aloof from the machinations of the London music business

and staying in synch with the dance pulse through their part-ownership of THE HACIENDA, work with ARTHUR BAKER and MICHAEL JACKSON's producer Quincy Jones, New Order ended the decade with as much credibility on the dancefloor as in the indie bedsit. See G-Mex

New Pop Lasting from around '81 to '83, New Pop's moment came when post-punk experimentalists swapped the margins for the mainstream. Abandoning secondhand chic and squat culture, the New Popsters became seriously hung up on gold lamé and nightlife, on showbiz artifice and soul manners, on pop's engineering of the psyche and the looks and languages of 'love'. Suddenly the charts, not the Peel Show sessions, were hip. Borrowing heavily from MALCOLM MCLAREN

and with a game plan constructed by journalists like Paul Morley; ABC, SCRITTI POLLITTI , Heaven 17, THE HUMAN LEAGUE (and later ZTT) pursued a pop entry-ism, suggesting that their Brechtian manipulations exposed and outplayed the corporate scheming. But as they paved the way for the Second British Invasion of the US charts, critics argued that they unwittingly colluded with the industry they sought to undermine. They did, however make the odd good record, and opened a few more ears to the pleasures of black dance music.

New Psychedelia The summer of '81 was almost a dress rehearsal for the SUMMER OF LOVE in '88. Mods who swapped their Jam shoes for suede Chelsea boots, GOTHS who exchanged their black uniform for ruffled paisley shirts, and 15 year old kids too young to remember psychedelia first time round, suddenly found they were buying the same records (Electric Prunes, The Byrds), seeing the same bands (Mood Six, The Times, The Marble Index, John's Children), and shopping at the same stores (The Regal and Sweet Charity in KENSINGTON MARKET). The London Dungeon one off in June inaugurated New Psychedelia as a media-approved youth cult, and with The Groovy Cellar in Piccadilly, The Bumpers 'experience' nights at The Bridge House, and psychedelic boat trips on the Thames, for a few months, Swinging London almost came alive. Inevitably the scene didn't last long – the GOTHS

New Ecologists From post-punk TRASH culture came the New Ecology – a casual fusion of ART, fashion, even film – which used waste as its raw material and the inner city cesspit as its playground. Groups like the MUTOID WASTE COMPANY and Primitive Urban Living paved the way, galleries like Crucial showed the work and hundreds of ART students who couldn't afford to use new materials followed their example. Most worked in isolation until late '88 when Reactivart was inaugurated – a network of artists and designers who not only employed recycling as a tool but consciously promoted it in an effort to educate the public into awareness of environmental issues and the need to re-use basic materials to create a sustainable society. Initially ignored by the mainstream ART world the group is now over 50 strong and attracting interest both nationally and internationally. See Recycled Salvage

L to R: DJs Pete Tong and Nicky Holloway **See Nightclubbing.** *New Model Army. Leigh Bowery, earliest exponent of New Glam, at Taboo.*

eventually ended up at ALICE IN WONDERLAND's and its spin-off shop Planet Alice, the mods rediscovered SCOOTERS, and the 15 year old kids evolved as BEATNIKS. But the seeds were sown and nobody was prepared for what was to come in '88.

The New Right The hooligan back room boys of the Adam Smith Institute had been polishing their steel-capped theories for years before a government arrived that was willing to try them out. Now the divisive effects of privatization, tax cuts and deregulation have been stamped across the country and you still can't go shopping on Sundays.

New Romantics In the late '70s and early '80s clubs like Billy's, BLITZ, Hell, Le Kilt and St Moritz spawned the first fully-fledged post-punk youth cult. With a penchant for Bowie (circa 'Young Americans') Roxy Music (circa 'For Your Pleasure') and KRAFTWERK as a soundtrack to many an evening of sybaritic cod-sophistication, the Movement – dubbed New Romantics, The Blitz Kids and The Cult With No Name – spawned a generation of bright young things, fresh out of their ART SCHOOL foundation year, whose idea of heaven was Hell. In retrospect what was seen as an aggressively peacock display of individualism now looks more like a Christmas party at Berman And Nathan's, but while the tabloids were still trying to find something to get worked up about with the vestiges of punk, a couple of hundred committed hedonists were intent on making their mark. It was easy to be a big fish in this most tiny and elitist of ponds; all it took was a winning way with the mascara wand and enough chutzpah to wear KILTS with conviction. There was no shortage of willing volunteers either. Before too long the phenomenon had spread the length and breadth of the land and created a fallout of designers, musicians, club runners and DJs who – for better or worse –

The New Glam
In '84 and '85 tacky '70s glam clothes dominated clubs like TABOO. Led by a coterie of fashion mavericks including LEIGH BOWERY, Trojan, DJ Tasty Tim and RACHEL AUBURN, a glam aesthetic developed that had nothing to do with glam rock but everything to do with kitsch *glamour*. PLATFORMS, fake fur, gaudy synthetics, copious use of make-up, bell-bottoms and sequins defined a look that was as varied as it was strong. BODYMAP and New York designer Stephen Sprouse echoed the new glam, but by '86 the clubs had succumbed to the more regimented rule of the MA1 FLIGHT JACKET. It wasn't until '88 that sequins, lurex and figure-hugging spandex appeared once more, but this time it was on the catwalks courtesy of KATHARINE HAMNETT, PAM HOGG, MARTINE SITBON and VIVIENNE WESTWOOD, who put men in sequined CATSUITS, girls in silver tasselled knickers and chaps, sequined, flared hipsters and christmas tree decorations.

helped to define the good-time guidelines for much of the decade that followed.

New Sounds New Styles
This Malcolm Garrett-designed 'STYLE' magazine folded in '84 after publishing 13 issues. Began life as a poor copy of THE FACE but discovered that the market wasn't yet downmarket enough for full colour pull-out posters. *See Sky*

News On Sunday
A financially viable, left-wing tabloid? They said it couldn't be done. And in '87 it took the disaster-prone, much criticized *News On Sunday*, the paper with 'no tits but a lot of knockers', around seven months and £6.5 million of its

shareholders' money to prove them right.

Next
See The Retail Revolution

Night Network
Britain's first "purpose-produced night time TV show" started in the London area in August '87. An ambitious attempt to provide night time TV for the first time in the UK, it was an immediate critical success with its formula of videos, chat shows, general features, reruns of BATMAN, The Monkees and lost Beatles cartoons. A year later all the ITV companies had their own diet of night time programming, prompting the BBC to extend their broadcasts past midnight. But the cost of producing original programmes eventually lost out to the cheaper re-runs and old movies, and in March '89, Night Network was

axed just as Emma Freud was starting to get by without the autocue.

Nine And A Half Weeks
Supposedly a crash course in hot sex for YUPPIES; in reality, of course, little of the sort. Nevertheless, the movie was fulsome with its designer accessories, and it has been said that the way the CD automatically eased into the CD player was the most erotic thing about it. The film featured MICKEY ROURKE as the 'WALL STREET' exec embarking upon a 'Last Tango In Paris'-style affair – that is, no names, no pack drill – with Kim Basinger's ART gallery guide. If the film was supposed to convince the rest of us that bankers are really

closet sex machines, it failed in a dismal fashion. But you can't deny the way Rourke looks in a suit.

Ninjas
Somehow ninjas, the masters of ninjitsu the ART of assassination, have become primary school entertainment. The VIDEO boom in the early '80s completely destroyed ninjitsu's credibility as a martial ART, featuring pseudo-magic and second rate scripts that led to a corporate emasculation to get it on TV. The comic *Teenage Ninja Mutant Turtles* now has its own TV series, is being made into a film, has grossed millions in merchandise and its three videos are constantly in the particularly lucrative market of the Children's Top Ten.

Nightclubbing
Probably more than anything else, the '80s was the decade of nightclubbing. What started in Billy's, a seedy Soho club run by Rusty Egan and STEVE STRANGE in '78, became a massive business that attracted up to 10,000 people in '89. The instigation of the one-nighter by Egan and Strange, through all their early clubs from BLITZ, Hell, Le Kilt, Club For Heroes, The People's Palace, THE CAMDEN PALACE to The Playground, was the blueprint for clubbing in the '80s. In tandem with Chris Sullivan's early Mayhem warehouse parties in '78/'79 and early '80s warehouse parties such as THE DIRTBOX and THE CIRCUS, the one-nighter took over nightclubs for one night a week and created the playgrounds for London's burgeoning deviant club scene. Warehouse parties were simply a response to the lack of nightclubs that would allow London's misfits through their doors, and were often little more than a sound system and a few cans of lager, but in the early '80s anything was better than nothing at all. The club scene became the unofficial catwalk and showcase of London's new talent, fostering the NEW ROMANTICS and allowing fashion to run riot, and producing pop talent from SADE, SPANDAU BALLET to S'XPRESS and BOMB THE BASS. The relationship between clubs, fashion and music, the triumvirate of the '80s, is such that you can rarely speak of one without the others, and from the HARD TIMES era of LE BEAT ROUTE, the fancy dress of TABOO, to the b-boy chic of the late '80s, they have defined an '80s youth culture that has been richer and more varied than any other decade.

LE BEAT ROUTE and THE LANGUAGE LAB in '82 were the first clubs to open their doors to black dance music and by '84 the suburban soul scene had started to converge on the West End. Nicky Holloway's Special Branch and SOUL II SOUL brought with them a new generation of clubbers whose roots lay in the SOUL WEEKENDERS and East End blues parties rather than the fashion ostentation of The BLITZ Kids, and by '85 London was a melting pot of club vagrants from different scenes. It was also turning into a lucrative business. Clubs had their own PRs, warehouse parties had become so highly organised that they went legal (WESTWORLD), and some even devised their own PRODUCT PLACEMENT (RAW and Sapporo lager). And then ACID HOUSE happened.

The impact of the SUMMER OF LOVE is still being felt. Apart from embracing an even wider club crowd than before, and its nurture of a club uniform that crossed CASUAL fashion with SKATE/SURFWEAR, its most

Niche Marketing

Niche marketing was the term coined for the practise of plugging a gap in the market with a single product. It all began in April '83 with the opening of the first Sock Shop by Sophie Mirman, and has since snowballed with the emergence of Tie Rack and Knickerbox. As well as aiding and abetting Mac-Donalds and THE BODY SHOP in the homogenisation of the UK's high streets, they also transformed London's major railway stations into identical SHOPPING MALLS.

Nostalgia Of Mud

VIVIENNE WESTWOOD's shop in St Christopher's Place became renowned as the home of her '82 'Buffalo Gal' collection. With hobos in muddy petticoats, crumpled hats and leather frock coats, all decorated with mud-caked oil cloth, it resembled an archaeological excavation rather than a shop. Nostalgia Of Mud closed down in '83 when Westwood's European commitments became too demanding.

spectacular effect was the transformation of the warehouse party into the warehouse *event*. New warehouse crews like SUNRISE, Biology, Energy and Back To The Future have made the warehouse a spectacle, with thousands of pounds worth of lights and special effects and attracted numbers that could fill football stadiums. Talk of Woodstock revisited is not just idle chatter but isn't entirely accurate either. Beyond 'togetherness', drugs, HOUSE MUSIC and the occasional cry of 'mental!', the warehouse event has no desire to change the world. They are large-scale businesses, run by serious, money-minded entrepreneurs, who have turned nightclubbing into an extravaganza nobody could have predicted. The question is, how much bigger can it get?

Northern Soul Northern Soul is the ultimate secret subculture. Sticking close to the roots of mod, it hung on to '60s soul music, digging deeper into the rare music of Detroit, Philadelphia and Chicago. Now nearly 25 years old, the scene has fragmented into so many sub-sets it resists description more than ever before and you still need a mortgage to buy a copy of The Del Larks' 'Job Opening' on the original Queen City label. *See Modern Soul*

Notting Hill Carnival

West London's annual August bank holiday weekend bacchanal, the only time police ever put down their warrants and dance with black people in the area, had become the largest street arts festival in Europe by '85, when some 1.5 million visitors enjoyed the feast of Caribbean pageantry and SOCA, live bands and wall-to-wall competing sound systems. Despite the massive attendance, Carnival never made the locality any money. Two years later, as after-dark battles between local youths and the ever-

increasing POLICE presence increased, moves to wrest control of the organisation of Carnival from the black community were publicly mooted. Costume band organisers became unhappy with the structure of the 'Mas', screaming about committee incompetence. The murder of a coke dealer in '88 was followed by funding body pressure and a coup in May '89 which led to represent-ation of the POLICE on a new steering committee. As Carnival stalwarts left disillusioned, the rallying cry 'Don't Stop The Carnival' took on a more plaintive air.

Nouvelle Cuisine

Small portions big prices. Art on the plate, easy on the stomach. Who was it that said you can never be too thin? Surely the massed ranks of nouvelle cuisine restauranteurs?

Numan, Gary

The point at which the BAUHAUS met the English suburbs. Numan came to prominence in '79 after a Top Of The Pops peform-ance of 'Are Friends Electric?' during which he remained immobile. Quite willing to discuss his hair transplants and desire to make heaps of money, he appealed to a hardcore following (Numanoids) who tatooed their skins with his image and en-sured that his records reached the lower regions of the charts despite the curious total lack of Radio One airplay. His image changes every year, from Chicago gangster to MAD MAX, his parents manage him, he earns £12,000 per annum flying in the North Weald Airport Aerobatic team, and the Numanoids continue to flock to north London pub/shrine The Flag for their regular Numan Discos (with raffle).

L to R: New Romantics. Northern Soul dancer (photo: Kevin Cummins). Raw's bar '87 (photo: Dave Swindells); Boy George and friend out and about '88 (photo: Dave Swindells) **See Nightclubbing.**

1992 1992, the by now familiar shorthand for the completion of the single European market, promises to become the most important date in European history since 1945. Despite the apparent contradiction, it will almost certainly turn out to be the greatest invention of the '80s. No-one was very interested when Bruce Oldfield, the celebrated dress-maker, first appeared on our TV screens to herald the abolition of barriers to trade in Europe. That was way back in '87; now the Department Of Trade And Industry claim that 90% of business people understand its implications. It seems that we've finally got the message, though it took a public brawl between the Prime Minister and one of her

predecessors to make some people sit up and listen. The single market is the logical conclusion of a process which began, in '57, with the formation of the Common Market. What its critics fear is that the process won't end there, that the single market is just another step towards the homogenization of Europe. What is certain is that the dismantling of restrictions will create a free-trade area of 12 countries and over 320 million people, and com-panies will be able to sell their wares as easily in BARCELONA or Brussels as in Brighton or Birmingham.

The implications for the British fashion industry are already being spelt out – Maria Cornejo has already moved to Paris, KATHARINE HAMNETT caused a minor furore when she declared her intention to show in Paris, and everybody from

John Richmond to PATRICK COX now produce from Italy. Unless UK manufacturers, the government – who provide no financial assistance to one of the UK's biggest exports, and worse, are cutting funding to ART SCHOOLS – and The British Fashion Council sort their priorities out, London's claim to being a centre of fashion will become severely threatened.

However, to some, 1992 has already started. Ever since the early '80s, one of Britain's most colourful exports has been its club culture, but by the late '80s the cultural exchange had become mutual. British DJs, clubs and clubbers had begun travelling to Amsterdam, Dublin, Berlin, Paris and Stockholm, forging links with Continental scenes that have become increasingly stronger. Belgian NEW BEAT, ELECTRONIC BODYMUSIC, BALEARIC BEATS and ITALIAN DISCO have been the most obvious result of their excursions, and with trips being organised from Amsterdam to THE HACIENDA, Europe is quickly turning into a global dancefloor. How long London can remain the capital of club culture as well as fashion, remains to be seen.

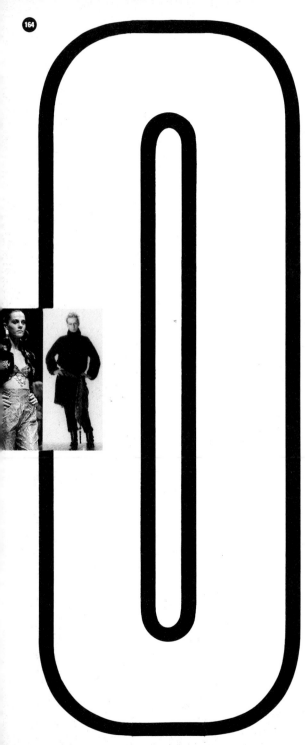

The Occult Magic and witchcraft have, of course, been around for centuries, but the '80s witnessed a phenomenal growth in occult interest, as people sought alternatives to the rampant consumerism of the '80s. Publishing houses spotted a potential boom area and jumped on their broomsticks to provide endless reprints of old favourites and snap up new chroniclers of esoteric wisdoms. The 'soft' edge saw a proliferation of fortune-tellers, Arthurian magic circles and purveyors of charms and spells. The 'harder' edge saw Magic blend with the tail end of punk, drugs and squats to provide offshoots such as 'Chaos' and 'Ma'at' magic – mixing anarchy and feminism with older traditions. MPs like Geoffrey Dickens have attempted to outlaw the Occult in a repeat of the Witchcraft laws and '88 saw the tabloid press hysterically trying to link 'Black' Magic with child abuse to the fury of pagans everywhere. The '90s are bound to see the barricades drawn up. *See Religion*

Oldman, Gary Britain's finest young actor has carved out a niche playing doomed anti-heroes. A disturbing but convincingly dumb Sid Vicious in 'Sid And Nancy', his most oustanding performance was as Joe Orton in Stephen Frears' classic biopic 'Prick Up Your Ears'. Quiet and publicity shy, Oldman has a bizarre ability to transform himself, and in 'Prick Up Your Ears', actually grew to look like Orton. Human chameleon or accomplished technician?

Olympic Mania In '84, the fashion world discovered the Los Angeles Olympics. VIVIENNE WEST-WOOD's 'Witches' collection featured tracksuits and her now famous three-tongue platform trainers, and heralded a flood of brightly-coloured SPORTSWEAR and cycle chic. Even PAUL SMITH brought out a range of tasteful Olympic-inspired limited edition T-SHIRTS and Keanan, a ST MARTIN'S fashion student, introduced glam rock to SPORTSWEAR with a dayglo plastic sweat suit worn

O'Connor, Sinead This bald-headed shrimp of a girl was *the* new female face of '88. She started out with unfashionably long hair in the Dublin outfit Ton Ton Macoute, graduated to soundtracking the film 'Captive' with U2's the Edge in '86, and there collected together the confidence, the thoughts and the voice for her stunning debut LP 'The Lion And The Cobra'. Signed to Chrysalis, she was encouraged to think up a promotional image, and struck on a punk/skinhead hybrid that ensured many column inches of editorial and striking front covers. Her wayward female rock has found many fans in America, and she has proved herself versatile, collaborating with performance artist KAREN FINLEY and rap artist MC Lyte. As the decade drew to a close she became well-known for two things: slagging off U2 and wanting to sleep with MICKEY ROURKE.

L to R: Rifat Ozbek's Autumn/Winter '89 collections (photos: Claire Pollock). Fashion Designer Richard Ostell. Sinead O'Connor (photo: Kate Garner).

with high heel SNEAKERS. A test run for the UK designers before the big SPORTSWEAR race in the late '80s.

One Pound Coins If inflation has had an immediate impact on our everyday life it has been the relegation of the mighty one pound note to loose change. Now the £2 coin is with us, how long before the five pound note goes metal?

O'Rourke, PJ The original Republican Party Reptile, PJ O'Rourke is *the* American humourist of the REAGAN years, the Fred Flintstone of the '80s. His appointment, in '78, as editor of the traditionally liberal *National Lampoon* magazine prefigured a decade when INSIDER TRADING became fashionable, conspicuous consumption became chic and tabloid TV became the norm. His seminal essay, 'How To Drive Fast On Drugs While Getting Your Wing-Wang Squeezed And Not Spill Your Drink', liberated an entire generation of young, repressed conservatives.

Ozbek, Rifat Born in Turkey, Rifat Ozbek's exotic background is essential to his design. His collections are eclectic mixes of travelogue tourist souvenirs and urban city scavenger hunts, and his dresses are worn by pop stars (MADONNA, Whitney Houston, BANANARAMA) and princesses (Diana). Ozbek's aim is to make women feel sexy wearing his clothes. Women will tell you they do. Voted Designer Of The Year in '88 his collections have been inspired by the palazzas of Italy with cropped jackets, ruffled blouses and high waisted leggings, and Arabian harems with swirling coats and slinky cut dresses. His wit is uppermost when he designs, his cut and sense of colour unbeatable. *See Fashion Designers*

The Ozone Layer *See Global Warming*

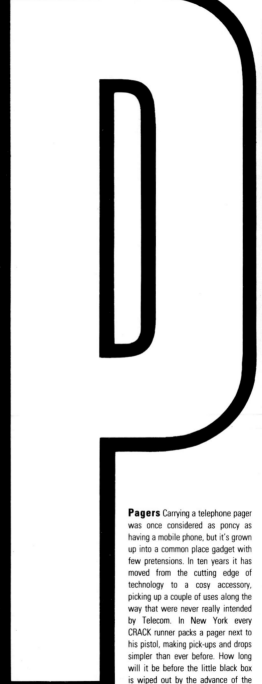

Pagers Carrying a telephone pager was once considered as poncy as having a mobile phone, but it's grown up into a common place gadget with few pretensions. In ten years it has moved from the cutting edge of technology to a cosy accessory, picking up a couple of uses along the way that were never really intended by Telecom. In New York every CRACK runner packs a pager next to his pistol, making pick-ups and drops simpler than ever before. How long will it be before the little black box is wiped out by the advance of the cellphone?

Paninari In '86 Italian streets from Milan to Rome were full of teenagers wearing rolled up 501 jeans, bright padded ski jackets, Timberland shoes, checked shirts, preppy blazers, white trousers, backpacks, RAY-BANS, Charro belts, and beige driving gloves for their loud trial bikes. They called themselves 'Paninari', literally translated from the word 'sandwich', although they gathered outside burger bars and lived on a diet of fast food. So strong was the trend that it even had its own magazines: comic book A5 manuals like *Preppy*, *Paninaro* and *Wild Boys* depicted violent RAMBO-like escapades as well as ads for quilted ski jackets and massive buckle belts. Paninari music included DURAN DURAN, Patsy Kensit, MADONNA, SPANDAU BALLET and THE PET SHOP BOYS (who adopted the look and made a record called *Paninaro*), and its fashion spread throughout Europe. *See Casuals, Dressing Down and Eurostyle*

L to R: Paninari (photos: Phil Ward). Pee Wee Herman.

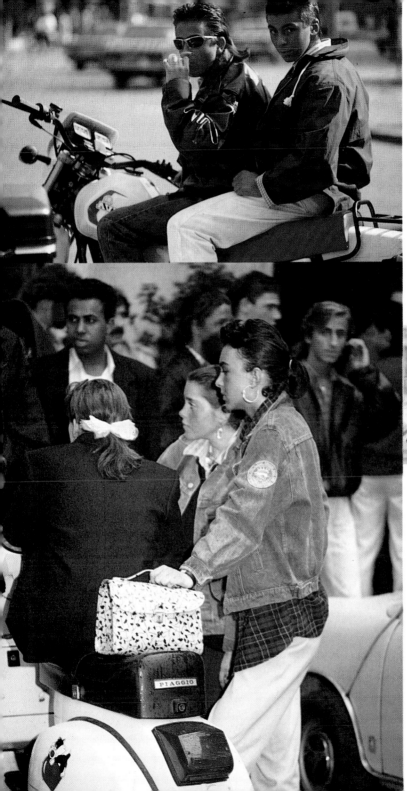

Pee Wee Herman A manic human pipe cleaner created by 'new wave' American comedian Paul Reubens at the beginning of the decade for the college comedy circuit, Pee Wee eventually ended up with his own TV show, 'Pee Wee's Playhouse', which quickly became the most popular American children's programme of '86. Despite the fact that

this squeaky clean stick insect seemed too bizarre a concoction for American kids used to 'The A Team' the pallid Pee Wee, a toy come to life, attacked an adult audience attracted by the camp nostalgia of his '60s retro world. A comic misfit whose greatest contribution to comedy was to create a show "where anything can happen" and invariably did, Pee Wee's greatest cultural debt was to 'The Banana Splits'.

The Palladium The late Steve Rubell and Ian Schrager, the comeback kids of Studio 54 fame, opened this mega club in May '85 and showed exactly how far New York was prepared to go with interior design. The Japanese architect Arata Isozaki transformed the space into a magical palace where the rich and famous met the young WANNABEES, and artists like Francesco Clemente, Keith Haring, Kenny Scharf and Jean Michel Basquiat had permanent displays. It was the place everybody wanted to be seen in, bringing together the old Studio 54 and MUDD CLUB crowds, as well as models, photographers, investment bankers, and the flamboyant youth of NY. Possibly one of the most important

were once blinded by flashbulbs on leaving a nightclub about three years ago, something clearly had to give... and we know for a fact that Sinitta had stayed in to wash her hair that night.
PAPARAZZI MEAL TICKETS
PRINCESS DI
Koo Stark (miraculously, she and Andrew were never actually photographed together)
Fergie – pre-engagement, or, subsequently, in a bikini/latest hideous frock
MADONNA's wedding/divorce/jog round the park/leg wax
MICHAEL JACKSON in disguise/flotation tank
BOY GEORGE in anything
Joan Collins looking rough

Personal Stereos When Sony brought out the first personal stereo, The Walkman, in '79 they didn't realise just what they had unleashed on an unsuspecting public. Listened to on the tiny headphones music becomes so intimate it feels like it is running up the inside of your skull. Check the intro of THE PET SHOP BOYS' 'Paninaro' on side two of their 'Disco'

heady with a soulful house blend that became known simply as GARAGE. Some say it was the best club in the world; certainly, almost two years after the building was handed back to the phone company that owned the lease, New York still mourns its passing.

Parliamentary TV When CHANNEL 4 started broadcasting live from the House Of Lords in the mid-'80s, they didn't quite realise how uninteresting the spectacle of sleepy old men lecturing each other could be. The televised House Of Lords was soon reduced to edited VIDEO highlights, while the televising of House Of Commons debates in '89 posed even more problems. The

nightclubs in the world when it opened, it now hosts concerts for MTV.

Paparazzi Triggered by the public's seemingly insatiable demand for the ROYAL SOAP OPERA, the paparazzi thrived in the '80s as never before. Some paparazzi like Richard Young became almost as well-known as their victims. Mid-decade saw boomtime; packs of paps were apparently quite happy, in the absence of royalty, to turn up for the opening of a toilet seat in the hope of catching Chris Quentin, Su Pollard and other third division stars at their friskiest. The colour supps, in turn, were starting to devote pages and pages to the stuff. Saturation point was inevitably reached – the tide has since turned and editors are now a little more demanding. When we

George Michael and lover *Mandy Smith* and/or topless wild child of your choice

Paradise Garage At the two-day closing party for the Paradise Garage in '87, Gwen Guthrie was carried onstage wearing a handful of diamonds. "You know why I'm here?" she said, gesturing to the audience. "Because you bought these for me!" Guthrie is not the only singer who owes her initial success to the Garage: with one of the world's finest sound systems to play with, DJ Larry Levan could afford to take risks, and the crowd – an amiable, multiracial mix of all sexual persuasions – would dance 'til way after dawn. A warren of small rooms with a roof garden and large main dancefloor, the club served no ALCOHOL but kept the atmosphere

album for a great example of these internal sound games. Now accepted as part of street static noise they can make the world feel like one large VIDEO. Try Eric Satie for walking in the park, 808 State's 'New Build' for riding tubes and THE PET SHOP BOYS for supermarkets and SHOPPING MALLS.

L to R: UK P-funkers The Phunklawds (photo: Dave Swindells). Andy Polaris '80. Print and tie-dye collection from Boy '83 (photo: James Palmer) See Textile Designers. Iggy Pop (photo: Fran Vogel). John Peel '82. The Pet Shop Boys.

restrictions on coverage ruled out creative camera-work, leaving head-and-shoulders shots only and no views of the public gallery (ruling out abseiling lesbians and dung-throwing protesters). However, in the face of widespread absenteeism amongst MPs, televising of Parliament could give democracy a real boost – if your MP isn't there on the screen, he's not doing his job properly.

Peel, John Radio One DJ with brains, Peel, with his support of all kinds of unfashionable '80s music, built up the hopes of guitar wielding youths across the land. In the early '80s he had a complete stranglehold on the musical preferences of British teenagers looking for something more 'significant' than *SMASH HITS* controlled chart pop. In the late '80s, though, his influence waned. Even though he played HOUSE and hip hop, encurring the wrath of JOY DIVISION obsessives in the process, the total dominance of dance music forced him to take a back seat.

Perrier Perrier was the mass-marketed mineral water that opened the floodgates for countless other brands from Evian to Apollinaris. In the '80s, mineral water consumption increased by 30% every year, *The Good Water Guide* was written to make sense of it all, and by the end of the decade Britons were spending more than £200 million a year on bottled water. In fact, sales of bottled water had increased so much that by '89 it was being delivered to your door.

Petri, Ray *See Buffalo*

Phonecards Everything else was plastic in the '80s so why not phonecards? One of the few wise moves on the part of the ailing privatised and much-hated British Telecom, the cards were welcomed by all but phone-thieves, and helped to cut vandalism at a stroke. *See Smart Cards*

The Photon The wargaming equivalent of ACID HOUSE, The Photon is a team game with lasers, lightshows and pumping music. By '86, million dollar Photon game centres were being erected all over the USA, giving every red-blooded American the chance to shoot their best mate with a laser phaser, but it wasn't until the Quasar centre opened in London in June '89 that space-age gunslinging hit Britain.

The Pink Pound An early '80s marketing term coined to take account of gay spending power. However, the colour of gay men's money really began to matter to the straight business world when it realised that what the Pink Pound bought one day, the NEW MAN's cashpoint-fresh blue fivers might buy the next.

Pirate Radio One of the outstanding UK musical phenomena of the age, a grassroots reaction, spearheaded by the black music industry and club DJs, to their disenfranchised position in broadcasting and growing impatience with mainstream programming. Early pioneers were DBC (Dread Beat Broadcasting), who championed the concept of legal black community radio until their closure in '85. But it wasn't until London pirates Horizon and JFM came on air in '83 that the pirate scene as we know it evolved. By '84 they could claim peak audiences equal to all the legal stations in the capital put together, building their base through the now traditional pirate method of hosting club nights. By '85, lucrative local ADVERTISING and cheap technology had made the ways of the wireless accessible to almost all; as fast as the Department Of Trade And Industry could track and raid, new stations would spring up, rostered by enthusiastic club-based DJs (and increasingly more women), who contrary to popular belief, most often paid to do their shows.

The pirates, according to unofficial surveys, were now more tuned in to what the public wanted than their mainstream rivals, and the popular less chat, more music format even prompted Radio 1 to respond with a day blissfully free of the usual inane self-indulgences in early '88. Pirate DJs like Tim Westwood (Starpoint) and Ranking Miss P (DBC) made the leap over to the legal mainstream, and stations like KISS FM were largely responsible for breaking club records in the charts. The number of pirates peaked in the summer of '87, before the government invited tenders for new community radio licences – but only to those not operating illegally, troubling "emergency frequencies". Some pirates were successful, notably WNK, who won a share of the north London franchise in June '89, but KISS FM lost out in the London wide stakes to London Jazz Radio and Spectrum in July of the same year. Whether the pirates who 'go straight' can shake off the old images of late arriving DJs, starting records at the wrong speed, and amateur advertisements remains to be seen. But with The Broadcasting Bill scheduled to come in 1990 with severe penalties for illegal transmitting, the future of pirate radio looks decidedly shaky.

Pit Bull Terriers An economy sized dog with family sized teeth, pit bulls are an American import with the temperament of Morton Downey Jr on angel dust. Manipulating the genes of this little dog has given it a jaw which clamps shut and just won't let go – an American POLICE sergeant attacked by a pit bull shot the dog eight times, but the dead dog had to be prised off his leg, which was later amputated. Pit bulls are fighting dogs and the 'sport' of pit bull fighting has blossomed into big business. So dangerous that they are not recognised by the British Kennel Club, after the ROTTWEILER scare of the late '80s, the pit bull terrier is a dog waiting to terrorise the '90s.

Platforms You were positively underdressed without your platforms at TABOO in '85, but it wasn't until '87, when the SEVENTIES FASHION revival was in full swing, that clubs became full of people who couldn't

dance (or even walk steadily) but looked great. Red Or Dead discovered a load of bankrupt stock somewhere in the East End and proliferated the trend, and in '88, Christine Ahrens came up with the ultimate girl's platform shoe in real snakeskin. Platform shoes are proof that fashion can defy gravity.

The Poetry Olympics An annual 'happening', inaugurated at Poet's Corner, Westminster in 1980 as an immediate response to the political problems surrounding the Moscow Olympics. Its stated aim ("the pursuit of poetic excellence in an international and non-competitive environment"), and its cry ("poets of the world unite") fit more easily into the unreal idealism of the '60s. Names such as William Burroughs and KATHY ACKER have appeared over the years, while the 'younger' poets, from Linton Kwesi Johnson, John Cooper Clarke to Attila the

The Pet Shop Boys Much maligned champions of mature, thoughtful synthi-pop, Neil Tennant and Chris Lowe have too much brains to be written off as fly-by-night scream-fodder; besides they are too old and too knowing. Both in their 30s Neil's apprenticeship was not slogging around the pubs and clubs but slogging around the features section of *SMASH HITS* as a journalist. Interviewing the fledgling Wham! amongst others before launching his own career, if he can't see the pratfalls who can? Camp, coy, miserable as sin and as English as murder at the vicarage, they are indeed, as they were once wryly described, THE SMITHS You Can Dance To.

Pierre et Gilles

French high priests of pop kitsch, Pierre et Gilles specialise in lurid retouched photographs in which exaggeratedly pretty boys and girls portray assorted cultural and religious icons. They take their stylistic inspiration from '50s and '60s kitsch, and their iconography from homoerotica, Catholicism, and the sort of imagery that usually

adorns snowstorm paperweights.

Planet Alice

Originally called Sweet Charity (which began life in Kensington Market and later moved to Portobello Road), Christian Paris changed his shop's name to Planet Alice in '86 after the success of his ALICE IN WONDERLAND club. This haven for psychedelic GOTHS became the only place in Britain to buy patchwork loons or crushed velvet frock coats.

Stockbroker have often found it their biggest platform. Dissident Attila has also staged an Alternative Games, and other ranters claim that the PO is the establishment, a poetry 'mafia'. Originally the idea of Michael Horovitz, the PO has been, despite the bitching, the principle British forum for new poets.

The Pogues

An emphatically post-punk Anglo-Celtic collision emerging out of the chaotic vision of lead singer-songwriter, Shane MacGowen. Since their '81 debut single 'Dark Streets Of London' as Pogue Mahone (Gaelic for 'Kiss My Ass'), their sound has grown from a Celtic punkabilly hybrid into a multifaceted, though still recognisably Irish, cross cultural signature. Consequently, they have progressed from their pub roots to the theatres and stadiums of the globe, trailing boisterous and inebriated audiences in their sway. Their most recent album, 'Peace And Love' hints at internal confusion and an overall loss of direction but, as a bacchanalian night out, The Pogues provided the '80s' most abandoned entertainment for an audience completely in tune

with their dark undertow.

The Police

The decade that finally bid a fond 'evening all' to the bobby on the beat and replaced him with helicopters over council estates. The swamping of 'troublespots' effectively said goodbye to the softly softly approach in '81 when RIOTS erupted in Toxteth, Brixton and inner cities all over Great Britain and tactics were decidedly heavy-handed (although it wasn't until the mid-'80s 'disturbances' at Broadwater Farm that CS gas was used on the mainland for the first time). The police reputation was further tarnished by Manchester chief James Alderton advocating castration for rapists and informing the populace that he was the mouthpiece of God. THE MINERS' STRIKE was another watershed in community relations – you could always spot bobbies from the Met notching up overtime on the picket duty – they removed their identifying numbers from their shoulders. Smashing the Stonehenge Peace Convoy has become as much of an annual ritual for the British police force as heading for Salisbury is for the harmless hippies. If you want to know the time... buy a watch.

Poll Tax

If someone told you in 1980 that in ten years time you would be taxed for walking down the street, you would have laughed it off. But the Poll Tax (now euphemistically called the 'Community Charge') introduced in Scotland in '89 and due in England and Wales in 1990, is no joke. The culmination of years of tax breaks for the rich and cuts in public spending, it replaces domestic rates with a new system in which the poor subsidise services which mainly benefit the rich. But it doesn't just involve the redistribution of wealth. There's more. Setting up a national database (the first step towards I-D cards), it will disenfranchise a sector of the population, swelling the ranks of the invisible poor, the Fourth World who have fallen off the social map.

L to R: Shane McGowan from The Pogues (photo: Gabor JF Scott). Self-portrait by Pierre et Gilles. Samantha Fox (photo: Nick Knight) **See Personal Stereos.** Postcard Punks '87 (photo: Simon Fleury).

Postcard Punks

You must have seen them, the postcard punks who used to populate KING'S RD and who now hang out at Piccadilly Circus and Trafalgar Sq, strutting round London charging tourists a fiver to photograph their peacocks. Postcard punks are youth culture's answer to Beefeaters and probably, still, it's greatest export. But it took Matt Belgrano to turn it into more than just a pocket money industry, when in '85 he revealed his 15 inch scarlet mohican, started being written about in the gossip columns, appeared in adverts and made a record. Matt Belgrano was eight years old in '76. Proof that punk was British youth's biggest ENTERPRISE CULTURE.

Positive Punk A damning reminder that right time is as important as right look. All those students who had missed out first time round couldn't wait to kick-start the still-born revival in '83. Leading pseudo-Pistolians Brigandage ended up turning into BOYS WONDER. And they were the successful ones. Everybody else slunk even more quickly back into obscurity.

Postmodernism The trickiest term of the decade. For Marxist theorist Fredric Jameson in '64 it described the termination of 20th Century modernization and the re-trenchment of an aggressive post-industrial capitalism. For ART critic Hal Foster in '86 it meant the end of Heroic Modernism and the return of free collective bargaining between commerce and culture, ART and trash. For West Wonderland copy-writers by '88 it spelled anything novel, exciting or trendy. The back-lash set in the same year with the emergence of a new mutant strain of pop modernism and mandarin hip-sterdom, christened Fogey Modern-ism by indefatigable STYLE hacks Steve Beard and Jim McClellan. The key postmodern events? ABC, *In Search Of The Crack*, Jeff Koons, 'MOONLIGHTING', BAUDRILLARD, 'BATMAN', *SMASH HITS*, NIGEL COATES, GAULTIER, *THE FACE* and Los Angeles. Compare with key Fogey Modernism items THE PET SHOP BOYS, *The Colour Of Memory*, Stephen Conroy, 'HILL STREET BLUES', Wittgenstein, 'BLUE VEL-VET', *NME*, RICHARD ROGERS, VIV-IENNE WESTWOOD, *ARENA*, Paris.

Poststructuralism The most obscure term of the decade. The '80s saw the literal deaths of all the Roaring Boys of '60s structuralism – Roland Barthes, Jacques Lacan, Michel Foucault. And where they went, their intellectual systems followed. For a New Age of surface not depth, STYLE not content,

structuralism's devotion to binary opposition was simply an Old Time Religion. Nature/culture, real/imagin-ary, legal/normal – it's all the same thing to the poststructuralists. Who cares about meaning anymore? Their cultic aesthetic is one of pleasure, play and drift – Fogey Modernism without the sweat. The key post-structuralist texts? SCRITTI POLITTI, *THE CRYPTO AMNESIA CLUB*, Keith Haring, 'MIAMI VICE', Derrida, 'One From The Heart', *Melody Maker*, Frank Gehry, Yoshiki Hishinuma, *i-D*, Tokyo.

Prince As a musical decade, the '80s was rich in ideas, sounds and movements, but poor in terms of individual musicians or groups of any noticeable stature. Prince was the main exception, dominating the decade wth his insufferable ego, his

whimsical musical experimentation and his downright un-'80s sense of personal STYLE. Signing to Warner Brothers in the late '70s, the Minneapolis maestro had from day one the kind of autonomous deal his predecessors like Stevie Wonder and Marvin Gaye had fought for years to get. After reaching the last levels of international stardom with his rockish 'Purple Rain' album (and film), Prince shied violently away from any success formulae, his racially/sex-ually mixed band reflecting his music's openness. Prince seemed to relish meeting the challenge of every new hyperbole heaped upon him, but when he got RELIGION his ever-present ego overwhelmed any re-maining shreds of judgement, and he began signing his name 'God'. In a decade obsessed to the point of sterility with taste, Prince displayed

Princess Di

Mystery cover girl of *i-D* no. 5, Princess Di went on to grace more covers than any other celebrity in the history of publishing and sell more British fashion abroad than anybody else. From Caroline Walker to Bruce Oldfield (whom Di is particularly fond of, frequently appearing at his Barnado dinners), Di has been a walking mannequin for UK high fashion, selling more frocks by smiling for the cameras than any advert could ever achieve. But Di was far from being the first fashion conscious royal, despite what the tabloids insisted. Edward VII was pretty dapper and the Duke Of Windsor pop-ularised Prince Of Wales check and had a tie knot named after him. Di was, however, definitely the first royal to be seconded from Sloane stock and the first woman to marry an heir to the throne in a NEW ROMANTIC dress.

L to R: Prince.
Princess Di on cover of i-D no. 5.
Early Psychobillies.
PX (photo: Martin Brading).

all the right influences – Little Richard, Hendrix, JB, Sly Stone, CLINTON – but never let them confine him. And whilst other name acts peddled stagnant music with elaborate scams and attitudes, Prince was undeniably and massively blessed with the rarest of qualities, talent. Without him the decade's musical landscape would have been a lot flatter.

Private Health

After ten years of Tory rule, the NHS finally looked like being dismantled when, in '89 a white paper was published entitled 'Working For Patients'. It contained a prescription for a 'competitive health market' to be implemented in 1992 with the UK's health districts

receiving grants according to the size of their resident population rather than their socio-economic needs. The instantly predicted result was that many inner city hospitals would be forced to close, unable to compete with leaner, fitter and stronger rivals. It was hardly surprising, given the government's cutting policy, that the interest in private health insurance had increased massively, doubling in the '80s to 5.4 million people covered, with a market value of £1 billion. As BUPA, the traditional provident association, began canvassing people with a free magazine stylishly titled *Upbeat*, new operators entered the market, from building societies to commercial life insurance companies with a confusing array of schemes. With the most basic standard cover amounting to around £1,000 per year at the end of the

Product Placement

In a New Age Hollywood where the biggest billing is reserved for anonymous personalities like William Hurt and Meryl Streep, it's unsurprising that the names which excite the most devotion are brand names. From Adidas in Sly Stallone's 'Rocky 4' to COCA COLA in Bill Cosby's 'Leonard Part 6', commodity fetishism is a

bigger money spinner for the studios than the fading aura of stardom and is regularly worth over $50 million a year.

decade, the government offered tax relief for the elderly, but the central problem for that generation, unused to everything being marketed as a consumer product, was to know who to believe. Perhaps the one body to not believe in was the government who kept declaring, "The NHS is safe in our hands".

Psychic TV

The visual and sonic wing of the Temple of Psychic Youth, Psychic TV formed in '81 after the demise of proto-industrialist band Throbbing Gristle. Led by veteran squatter, performance artist and correspondent of Manson and Burroughs, Genesis P-Orridge, they were signed up by WEA, kicked off for unseemly behaviour, signed by CBS and released the LP 'Dreams Less Sweet', using holophonic recording techniques. They set up their own label, Temple Records, and entered their 'hyperdelic' phase, which revolved around the concept of 'Angry Love', a kind of militant hippy ethic. It was little wonder, given their agenda that PTV were among the first to work with an aesthetic that became known as ACID HOUSE. Operating under the name of Jack The Tab, P-Orridge released several singles in '88. For PTV, the process of creation has always been as important as the 'product', and P-Orridge tends to have several projects on the go at any one time, so it's perhaps unsurprising that no single artefact has been particularly successful.

Psychobillies

An accurate moniker for the lost tribe of '80s youth culture. A marriage of the sheer nihilism of punk and raw basics of rock'n'roll, psychobillies fed from a variety of disparate scenes. GOTHS, ROCKABILLIES, retro-trendies and stray punks found themselves 'chicken' dancing to the same beat. Inspired by bands like Theatre Of Hate and The Meteors in '81, they cultivated gravity defying quiffs thus contributing to the destruction of the ozone layer, and threw themselves

about at gigs with complete disregard for injury. Peaking with the arrival of the clowns of psychobilly, King Kurt in '84, who showered the audience with flour, psychobillies subsequently went into decline. Klub Foot at the Clarendon in Hammersmith perpetuated the scene, releasing a string of compilations and putting on ever obscurer bands. When Klub Foot finally closed in '86, the only psychobillies left were French tourists who'd read about it in the *NME*.

Pulp Crime

The literary GBH of American pulp crime muscled back into book shops in the '80s. But with RETRO-NUEVO stylings all important, pulp had to look the part to sell. The

hefty text-book style Black Box collections of Jim Thompson, David Goodis and Cornell Woolrich bombed, while Black Lizard Press hit the spot by publishing the same authors in pocket-sized paperbacks with 'authentic' covers. Old and new, literary crime paid. Bored by the Literary Brats' vision of the city as a YUPPIE playground, hip readers turned to modern crime's metropolitan inferno. Hard-boiled heroes like George V Higgins, Elmore Leonard and Charles Willeford received highbrow acclaim, the new princes of the city, Andrew Vachss and James Ellroy made the STYLE mags and the New Noir became *the* guidebook to the American urban jungle.

Punk Celluloid

Too loose a collection spread over too wide a range of cities and years to become

Public Enemy

America's most radical rappers, Public Enemy preached black power over music so harsh that people were forced to sit up and listen. Their first LP 'Yo! Bum Rush The Show' in '87 was the strongest political statement rap music had witnessed, and when PE toured with onstage para-military guards (from their bodyguard-cum-black study group the Security Of The First World) toting Uzi sub-machine guns, the image was complete. Adored by the rap hard-core, after a second brill-iant LP 'It Takes A Nation Of Millions To Hold Us Back', they ran into trouble over the pro-Nation Of Islam (and suspected anti-Semitic) views of their 'Minister Of Information' Professor Griff, views which were to cause charismatic lyricist Chuck D to sack him from the group in '89 after many US record chains refused to stock their albums. *See Spike Lee*

*L to R: Public Enemy (photo: James Griffin). Raw club (photo: Dave Swindells). Sylvester Stallone **See Rambo**.*

a self-contained genre, Punk movies range from the mystic-cynics of ALEX COX's 'Repo Man' to the vagabond mohicans of PENELOPE SPHEERIS' 'Suburbia'. Viable entries for the genre are films where 50% of the audience walks out and the rest think they're experiencing the work of a genius. Certainly 'Liquid Sky' fulfilled the first function, but struggled to get through its outraged walkouts to become one of the hardier inter-national ART hits of its time. Its sci-fi meets sex (the alien invades and eliminates you at the point of orgasm) and its gender ambiguities with one actress playing brother and sister made it an often infuriating, sometimes beautiful curiosity. Other contenders for punk permits: 'Boys

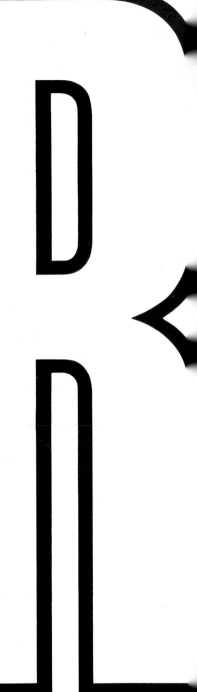

Next Door', 'Videodrome', 'Dogs In Space', 'Ghosts Of The Civil Dead', 'Out Of The Blue', 'River's Edge', 'Sid And Nancy', 'The Last Of England', 'Smithereens' and Kenneth Anger's entire oeuvre.

PX Opened in '78 by Helen Robinson and Steph Rayner, it became, along with World's End, the place for all NEW ROMANTICS to purchase their frilly shirts. At its height, PX offered velvet suits, pigskin Robin Hood laced jackets, then the ragged and frilly hippy look. With STEVE STRANGE as mannequin and shop assistant and STEPHEN JONES' millinery delights in the basement from 1980 onwards, it became a daytime haunt for all the BLITZ Kids. The Endell Street shop closed in '86, but Helen Robinson continued to design, selling her clothes from HYPER HYPER.

Rambo The least appealing success story of the decade, Stallone stole Schwarzenegger's thunder as the self-made man of Hollywood, creating a body that now racks him with pain. Monosyllabic and nasal, his jingoist maverick 'Rambo' proved the independent success of the '80s, 'Rambo II' reaped over $150 million worldwide, while the 'Rocky' series gathered

equal booty for producers Chartoff and Winkler. The right-wing laughing stock nobody dared take the piss out of (in public), when Stallone got creative control it was as if the moron had taken over the asylum. Now he charges over $12 million an appearance, but efforts to expand outside the 'Rambo'/'Rocky' stereotypes have left the public cold. Where next? Back to the gym for a steroid refill?

Ragamuffin Rap Product of the convergence of two of the most potent new forces in dance music: dancehall reggae and hip hop. As rap developed in the States, its debt to Jamaican-style chat became increasingly clear. By '88, rappers KRS-ONE, Don Baron and MC Shinehead were established as part of a lineage stretching back to U-Roy and Big Youth. Helped by a substantial influx of migrants from the islands, ragamuffin rap became the generic name for a vocal style which borrowed from the Jamaican dancehall style, even if,

as with KRS-ONE's work, the result remained within the confines of hip hop. In the UK, the traditionally strong presence of reggae led to rootsier hybrids with more tangible Caribbean associations. Longsy D produced the '87 club classic 'Hip Hop Reggae', a tough merging of the two styles which topped reggae and funk charts for several weeks, and became a term used to describe the UK's version of ragamuffin rap. In the summer of '88, Rebel MC, a baby-dreadlocked rapper, began mixing JA-style chat with HOUSE and

sampled rocksteady rhythms. A year later, this had developed into acid SKA, fusing early reggae anthems like 'The Liquidator' with acidic, uptempo dance beats and gurgling synths. Both Longsy D ('This Is Ska') and Double Trouble and Rebel MC ('Just Keep Rockin') scored substantial club, then chart success. Like cricket, the Henley Regatta and 'It Ain't Half Hot Mum', hip hop reggae and acid SKA could only happen here.

Rainbow Warrior See *Greenpeace*

Rare Groove For eight months during '83 and '84, a DJ called Norman Jay was running a club called The Bridge in Southall, Middlesex, drawing 700 dancers every Monday night with a strict diet of old funk and soul. A similar STYLE of funk oldies was spinning at THE WAG's Black Market night in '84, a genre which was given a name when Norman Jay began his 'Original Rare Groove Show' on the pirate KISS FM in '85. An underground scene based around '70s funk beats started growing rapidly, and was given a boost when Barrie Sharpe started his Cat In The Hat club in '86 with its heavy emphasis on JAMES BROWN records. In response to the '70s music, dancers started adopting

underground jams in its surrounding boroughs. The ravers scene kept soul alive, nurtured the inner city 'street soul' movement which would later propel SOUL II SOUL into the charts, and were the first clubbers to adopt the SWINGBEAT of BOBBY BROWN and Teddy Riley when it crossed the Atlantic in '88.

Raw In September '85 Oliver Peyton opened Raw under the YMCA on Tottenham Court Rd. With giant sculptures created by ex-MUTOID WASTE COMPANY members, an inventive series of FLYERS, and the DJ talents of Dave Dorrell, it didn't change the face of London clubland overnight. What it did do was discover the best West End venue yet

Ray-Bans Ray-Bans Wayfarers were the fashion story of spring '83 and that summer – the hottest since '76 – they were worn by Wham! at the 'Club Tropicana'. Ray Ban Aviators were developed for the American military by Bausch and Lomb back in the '30s, but retro-fever and the broiling English summers of '83 and '84 established the '50s designed Wayfarer as

unforced charisma, idiot grin and consensual one-liners allowed him to call the shots in the photo-opportunity media politics of '80s America, and he became not so much a president as an Everyman emperor who embodied and resolved the contradictions which gripped an empire in terminal decline. Most Americans seemed too busy checking Ron's nationally syndicated cancer scans or reading about Nancy's endlessly expanding wardrobe to bother with the budget deficit, political corruption, welfare cuts and Contragate. Unsurprisingly, the American Daydream and the 'don't worry, be happy' post-politics continued with the Bush administration, but with the heir to the throne short

 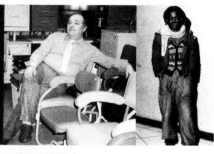

SEVENTIES FASHION, and inspiring not only a slew of press articles on rare groove and flared fashion, but also new groups like Diana Brown & The Brothers, Push and the Brand New Heavies. However, when Norman Jay returned from a trip to Amsterdam at Easter '88, the first warehouse party he went to wasn't playing rare groove, but a frenetic mixture of rhythms that would soon be known as ACID HOUSE.

Ravers A term first used in the Jamaican idiom and immortalised in Triston Palma's dancehall tribute 'Raving' of '82, it came to mean predominantly black clubbers who preferred soft soul over rap or HOUSE MUSIC, wore designer casual labels like Chipie and Avirex, and found their raves not in the West End of London but at house parties and

and cultivate the dancefloor melting pot that London was becoming – suburban soulboys, b-boys and fashion victims filled the day-time gym until the spring of '88, when Oliver decided to have a holiday, the YMCA decided that enough beer had been spilt and clubbers had decided they'd had enough. Raw's queue was probably the slowest in the capital's history.

Reagan, Ronald America's long night of post-Vietnam, post-Watergate angst ended in 1980. Suddenly it was 'Morning in America' again, as ex-actor Ronald Reagan became the USA's Acting President. Never much of an actor, when he had to act like a real politician, Reagan usually fluffed his lines. The Great Communicator's real skills lay in just being himself and acting natural. His

a modern classic. GEORGE MICHAEL these days favours the classic Aviator glasses and Orion were worn by Grace Kelly – but Wayfarer (in black or tortoiseshell) are the bestseller. So much so, that in '89, to control the influx of fakes, all pairs carried an individually numbered seal.

L to R: Ravers (photos: Dave Swindells. Tommy Roberts of Practical Styling. i-D straight up Rauf '84. Jamie Reid and Margie Clarke (photo: Kevin Davies) See Frank Clarke. The Residents.

on charisma and long on boredom, it was now time for 'Yawning in America'. A nationwide wake-up call is overdue.

The Red Triangle The Red Triangle was CHANNEL 4's semiotic response to Mary Whitehouse. When sex and violence were due to rear their ugly heads the trusty triangle would warn the innocent viewer. Inevitably, it became more interesting than the films themselves.

Red Wedge Led by vociferous and articulate young Londoner Anna-Joy David, Red Wedge is a broad left alliance of musicians, artists and writers that supports but is not affiliated to the Labour Party. Set up in '86 in an unprecedented effort to garner the youth vote, Red Wedge soon became high profile with its music and comedy tours and headlining stars such as BILLY BRAGG and Paul Weller. Neil Kinnock was quite happy to endorse the group on his path to the '87 General Election, and although Labour lost and for a while Red Wedge was in the doldrums, it has kept its momentum, in '88 alone starting 30 new youth projects throughout the country. From something that started on a wing, a prayer and a set of ideals, Red Wedge gave new meaning and effectiveness to the term 'pressure group'. *See Artists Against Apartheid and Club Sandino*

The Redskins Ostensibly a skinhead band, The Redskins were members of the Socialist Workers Party, played left-wing benefit con-

certs and raw soul music, and spouted anti-Nazi slogans at every opportunity. They built up a fanatical following of anti-Nazi skins who sometimes clashed with NF SKINHEADS, the worst violence erupting at a GLC-sponsored concert on the South Bank in '83. Although some 'real' SKINHEADS regarded them as a pale imitation of the real thing, they were probably the most influential 'skinhead' band of the decade, even if their red Harrington jackets never did catch on.

Religion Against a background of global disasters, ecological instability and world conflict it's hardly surprising that religion, swept aside in the '60s and '70s, should rear its head in the turbulent '80s: It's happened two ways. Firstly the 'alternative' religions have gained in

popularity: there's been an upsurge of interest in 'fringe' faiths such as Wicca (or Witchcraft), Voodoo, Shamanism plus a scouring of world religions from Buddhism, Sufism to Taoism. But alongside the search for alternative truths there has been a return to the basic tenets of childhood catechism as Christianity shook itself and turned evangelical. Suddenly fundamentalism was under scrutiny and, far from dismissing it as cranky stupidity, many people found comfort in religions that told you exactly what to think, what to do and when and how. 1988 saw a replay of the '79 indignation over Monty Python's 'Life Of Brian' – this time Christians picketed 'The Last Temptation' – but it wasn't until '89 that Britain saw religious intolerance reach a zenith with fundamental Muslims calling for the death of SALMAN RUSHDIE. *See Evangelism and Spiritualism*

Remixes An indication of the rising status of the DJ and the growing power of the dancefloor to create chart hits. In 1980, producers completed their final mix of a song, the record company released it, and that was that. By '88, record companies were commissioning second, third and even fourth mixes of songs intended to increase their dancefloor potential, keep DJs happy by offering them different versions to play with, and cash in on hardcore fans who would buy every available version of their heroes' record. Star mixers like Shep Pettibone, the Cole & Clivilles team and ARTHUR BAKER

made a career out of remixing other people's songs, and every DJ from New York's Tony Humphries to Nottingham's Graeme Park wanted to augment their income by remodelling tracks for the dancefloor. The latest development is the remix album, where artists' whole back catalogues are revamped for the contemporary dancefloor – often without their consent. Faced with her '89 remix LP 'Life Is A Dance', Chaka Khan commented: "I don't want this to ever happen again. This is not cool."

Re-Search Magazine Seminal American magazine specialising in the unconventional and featuring exhaustively-researched articles and interviews with total weirdos (including William Burroughs, Charles Manson and various avant-garde film-makers), and used as a source manual by everyone from Genesis P Orridge to JONATHAN ROSS, who based his entire 'Incredibly Strange Films' TV series on an issue of *Re-Search.*

The Residents They came from California, they wore eyeballs on their heads and made indefinably strange pop music. Their '83 'Mark Of The Mole' stage revue was the weirdest live experience Britain had ever witnessed, and their surrealistic videos changed the face of the standard rock promo forever.

Retro-Nuevo Term invented by American R&B critic Nelson George to characterize the devotion to passionless pastiche in everything from the Lite Classic soul of Anita Baker to the Clean-Machine Metal of THE CULT. In the '80s, nostalgia ruled. Half the time it seemed that the only pop passion left was in the dehumanized electronic burblings of ACID HOUSE. But that's hardly surprising. In an exhausted culture which has given up trying to represent its own micro-chip modernity, the aesthetic styles of the past provide a safely renewable resource for the nostalgia industries of the present. Blurred and reworked, they

Religious Iconography

By '84, GOTHS were wearing enough crucifixes to ward off legions of vampires, but it was 'Like A Virgin' period MADONNA who turned the simple cross into the essential fashion accessory for the mid-'80s. In '88 God-fever hit a fresh high: James Hamilton linked religion with politics in his jewellery, while Big Jesus Trashcan hurled the Virgin Mary and Jesus Christ onto T-SHIRTS in larger-than-life dayglo prints. Hitting ACID HOUSE's spiritual high head on, God showed up in various guises on badges, sweatshirts, jackets and even shoe buckles. In '89 the focus shifted towards the Eastern religions. Half of the Big Jesus Trashcan outfit became Paradise and launched the Hindu goddess Kali as the year's T-shirt pin up, while the yin and yang symbol of Taoism cropped up on everything from car stickers to watch faces. The recurring popularity of religious iconography is conclusive proof that fashion moves in mysterious ways.

get used to manufacture a timeless historical hybrid of Postwar American Cool evident in everything from SOHO's reconstructed diners, Hipster Dream Machine movies like Coppola's 'RUMBLEFISH' and Walter Hill's 'Streets of Fire' to the simulated teen myths of the LEVI'S 501 ads. Don't know much about history? We can all buy that.

Riots When the Chinese authorities smashed the student protest in Tianamen Square, Beijing in June '89, the state described the upheaval as a 'riot'. In Britain too, in the '80s, the blanket term 'riot' was applied to violent events which had many underlying social and political causes. In '81 the streets of Northern

The Retail Revolution

From '80 to '87 retail sales rose by 76% as shopping became a favourite national recreation and the chain stores bought into the design decade, after discovering the selling power of a big name paint job from Fitch or Conran. The big entrepreneurial hero on the high street frontline was George Davies, the man behind Next. Starting

Ireland witnessed their worst crowd violence since the early '70s, as protest raged against the deaths, on hunger strike, of ten Republican prisoners. Ireland was used to it, but England was surprised when more than 30 towns and inner city areas experienced rioting. The year's disturbances began during April in Brixton and peaked with four days of fierce rioting in July in Liverpool's Toxteth. Both were inner city areas with large black populations and high unemployment. Brixton had erupted on April 9th, three days after the POLICE had launched the heavy-handed Operation Swamp. A subsequent inquiry by Lord Scarman attacked policing methods, called for a new inner city social policy and declared "racial disadvantage is a fact of current British life".
   The lessons of '81 appeared not

in women's fashion and following up with menswear, accessories, jewellery, interiors and home and garden, bit by bit he reinvented the department store for STYLE culture and built a new Harrods for penny-pinching YUPPIES. See Fashion Designers

Richmond/ Cornejo

Richmond/Cornejo were the punk rockers who managed to make an impact on the fashion establishment. They advocated 3-D design – Destroy Disorientate Disorder (the slogan from their first show in October '84), creating thoroughly modern outfits for streetwise women and men. Modern fastenings were a favourite – safety pins, press studs, zippers – while figure-hugging contours gave their work an undeniably sexy edge, although an equally androgynous one. Bright pink, lime green and citrus yellow exploded from their catwalks, and their models looked like Star Trek extras, part sci-fi, part gangland. John Richmond and Maria Cornejo parted company in '87 and are now designing independent collections in London and Paris respectively. *See Fashion Designers*

L to R: Religious Iconography in New York '88 (photo: Simon Fleury). Religious Iconography in London '88 (photo: Adrian Peacock). Richmond/Cornejo '86 (photo: Martin Brading). Richmond/Cornejo's Spring/Summer '88 collection (photo: Tim Green). Richmond/Cornejo's Spring/Summer collection '86 (photo: Mark Lewis).

to have been heeded when, four years later, rioting broke out again in Brixton after police shot and wounded a black woman, Cherry Groce, during a dawn raid on her home. The violence of '85 had begun in September when Birmingham's Handsworth district, where over 50% of black youths were unemployed, was engulfed in battles between locals and the POLICE. It culminated in October on the Broadwater farm estate in Tottenham. PC Keith Blakelock was killed in rioting sparked off by the death of Cynthia Jarrett who suffered a heart attack when POLICE raided her house. By the end of the '80s, Britain was equipped with a POLICE force ready to spring into paramilitary action at

an instant's notice, as a London student demonstration discovered to its horror in November '88. Plastic bullets, which have killed 16 people including seven children in Northern Ireland, were deployed, but not used at Broadwater Farm. In '87, British POLICE forces held more than 20,000 plastic bullets in stock.

Rip, Rig & Panic The sound of young Ladbroke Grove via Bristol, the wilfully obscure boho beatsters took their name from an old Roland Kirk number. Their mission in the early '80s to popularise jazz certainly helped to make it hip but hardly shifted units; their greatest achievement, apart from pioneering the non-wearing of socks, was to boast NENEH CHERRY in the ranks. Other alumni have moved out of the commercial arena; pianist Mark

Springer is more classically based these days, Steve Noble percusses in avant-garde groups but Sean Oliver helped to engineer the rise of TERENCE TRENT D'ARBY, Bruce Smith now drums with PiL and Gareth Sager is still plugging away at pop in the rumbustious rockers Head. Even if they didn't know it then, a seminal band of the '80s.

Rock Dinosaurs The earliest indication of the longevity of rock dinosaurs came when RUN DMC collaborated with Aerosmith on 'Walk This Way' in '86, a stroke of marketing genius that got RUN DMC their crossover hit and discovered another market for Aerosmith – teenagers. By '87 the inexplicable attraction of teenagers to '60s/'70s dinosaurs was confirmed by the Grateful Dead revival. Known as 'little kids' by the long-standing Deadheads (committed Grateful Dead fans who followed the band from city to city), they bought enough of the new LP 'In The Dark' to make it Grateful Dead's first ever platinum album. THE BEASTIE BOYS' plagiarisms of Led Zeppelin introduced a new generation to the 40 year old heavy rockers, allowing lead singer Jimmy Page to pursue a solo career in '88. Meanwhile, Pink Floyd reformed in '87, launched a mammoth 'The Momentary Lapse Of Reason' world tour, visiting the UK for sell-out dates at Wembley Stadium and Manchester's Maine Road to find that nearly half their audience were teenagers. By '89 The Who were conducting their second 'farewell tour', The Rolling Stones were beginning a tour that was expected to net them £60 million, there were two versions of Yes touring and Aerosmith were playing bigger stadiums than at any other time in their career. If ADULT ORIENTED ROCK started off addressing the CD-touting baby boom generation, by the end of the decade it had recruited their children.

Rockabillies Perhaps the most important and influential youth move-

Ripped Jeans Part of the essential club uniform of the '80s, ripped jeans started out in clubs and warehouse parties as part of '82's HARD TIMES look, hit the catwalk in '84 with KATHARINE HAMNETT's designer-distressed denims, and ended the decade covering the bums of BROS.

Robot When Robot opened in Beaufort Market in KING'S ROAD in '77, it became the place to buy designer ROCKABILLY gear. Apart from their Gibson shoes, creepers and brogues, they were also the first people to sell designer DMs, later followed by Red Or Dead, JEAN PAUL GAULTIER and Helen Storey. At their height in the early '80s, they offered classic box jackets, drapes and pegs and inspired a host of shops selling similar items. With shops still trading in Covent Garden and the King's Road, Robot's biggest exports are still size two creepers to Japan.

L to R: Rockabillies from Milan '83.
Robot suit '84.
Ripped Jeans '87 (photo: Steve Johnston).
Jonathan Ross (photo: Kevin Davies).

ment of the '80s, the rockabilly scene grew from humble English working class origins in the mid-'70s to become the trend setter for almost an entire generation of fashion-conscious youths across the Western hemisphere. Started in '75/'76 by working class teenagers who loved the American rockabilly sound of the '50s but who hated the stereotyped British Teddy Boy look, the first wave of rockabillies sported FLAT-TOP haircuts as opposed to the greasy quiffs of the Teds, wore workmen's Donkey Jackets, LEVI'S and big boots, and preferred the music of rockabilly legends like Gene Vincent and Johnny Burnette to the Teddy Boy idols of Jerry Lee Lewis and Buddy Holly. Growing steadily

Rock-A-Cha

Rock-A-Cha opened in KENSINGTON MARKET in the summer of '79 and became the first shop in Britain catering strictly for ROCKABILLIES. Avoiding the usual '50s clothing mixture of Teddy Boy drape jackets and boot-lace ties, the shop's owners, Bob Lewis and Jay Strongman, aimed at recreating the original American '50s look as

worn by the likes of Eddie Cochran, Johnny Burnette and Fats Domino. Pink peg trousers, flecked box-jackets, Hawaiian shirts and Gene Vincent T-SHIRTS were all best sellers, and the usual confederate flags and Elvis pictures found in other '50s retro shops were replaced by photos of the '56 Hungarian Revolution and southern freedom marches.

jackets and bowling shirts. In fact the whole range of US '50s teen looks, from Hillbilly to College Boy were revived during '79 to '83 and the rocking STYLE spread to the underground club scene, where a uniquely British mixture of '50s fashions and '80s dance rhythms created an image that was to dominate UK club (and eventually mainstream) culture for most of the decade. The more extreme of the rockabilly crowd split off to become PSYCHOBILLIES while others developed a passion for '40s R&B and '50s JAZZ. By '84 the rockabilly scene became so commercialized that the hardcore enthusiasts went back underground to a club scene that is still going strong today. *See Flip, Levi's and Robot*

Rogers, Richard Billed as one of the last great architectural modernists, Rogers is responsible for the controversial Lloyds Building. Finished in '86, its high-tech gothic of pipes, ducts and vents became a symbol of the New City, a new tourist landmark, an eye-popping backdrop for TV ads and brought Lloyds lots of free publicity. It also brought Rogers commissions from businessmen in Japan, Italy and France, all after a name building to put their company on the map. In the '80s ARCHITECTURE began to resemble ADVERTISING and, despite his modernist ethic, Rogers now finds himself in the very postmodern business of corporate image building.

Roosterfish A tiny unassuming Greek restaurant under Centrepoint on Tottenham Court Rd, Roosterfish never started before 4am and always served warm beer. The only after-hours club for two years up 'til '88 simply because there was nowhere else to go to, the police raided it regularly until host Phil DIRTBOX had had enough. Remembered mainly because of the chronic overcrowding and inexplicable name.

throughout the last years of the '70s the rockabilly scene attracted youths disenchanted with punk, power pop, jazz-funk and the NEW ROMANTICS. By 1980 rockabilly was the largest single youth movement in the country with former soulboys, ex-punks and young Sloane girls from Chelsea and Hampstead all flocking to rocking clubs like the Bobby Sox in Neasden and the Manor House in Finsbury Park.

On the strength of the rockabilly scene, retro '50s groups like The Stray Cats, The Pole Cats and Matchbox all reached the top 30 of the national pop charts while the speed with which new styles and looks were adopted by rockabillies recalled the heady days of early '60s mods. FLAT-TOPS were bleached at the front or dyed blue or red, jeans were swapped for peg pants, box

Ross, Jonathan Ross began his TV career in '83, working as a researcher on the 'Loose Talk' chat

FREELANCE PARIS ALEXANDER ROMA TOOTSIE NEW YORK STUDIO D'ARTISAN OSAKA PARISOTTO FIRENZE VOGUE DUSSELDORF & HAMBURG

show. With colleague Allan Marke he strived to make 'Loose Talk' funny, lobbying to get Tommy Cooper as a guest, but to no avail. Marke then introduced Ross to the US 'David Letterman Show', and the two of them suggested to CHANNEL 4 commissioner Mike Bolland that an English version would be a viable concern. On January 9 '87, he was on screen, hosting 'The Last Resort', the first UK show to acknowledge the fact that a late evening audience is not the same as any other evening audience. Ross was the sharp geezer down the pub whose nervous energy (and endearing slight speech defect) seemed to stem from his delighted surprise at finding himself with his own TV show. In '88, with his own production company Channel X, he made a series 'The Incredibly Strange Film Show' which profiled the subcult greats of sleazy cinema. What was apparent with that and the best moments of 'The Last Resort', was that here was a fan who was always delighted to be in his heroes' presence but was never overawed.

Roth, Tim The angry young man of the Brit pack, Roth's roles always seem to involve a threatening snarl and a jabbing finger. A man with a Method, in preparation for his role as the psychopathic skinhead in Trevor Griffiths' 'Made In Britain', he could be seen surly and shaven, lurking in the corners of Camberwell's posher pubs. The best spot in patchy film work was his nervy soulboy in Steven Frear's 'The Hit'. As hitman John Hurt's sidekick, he was all mouth and no muscle, a blunderer without the crucial cool. Roth went on to prove his stage credentials as Beatlemaniac Josef K in Berkoff's muscular adaption of 'Metamorphosis', which had him dropping ten feet on to the stage every night at the Mermaid.

Rottweilers As the ENTERPRISE CULTURE seeped down through every layer, even the criminal classes and villains got more professional. Heavy duty street dudes and dealers ensured their own safety and power

Royal Soap Opera When King Charles lost his head, the ancient regal fiction of divine right bit the dust. When Prince Charles got married, a glitzy new fiction was found to replace it – The Royal Soap Opera – a headlining hybrid of Dynasty and 'Carry On At The Palace' in which the reverence granted earthly divinity has been replaced by the gossip provoked by soapy celebrity. Randy Andy and Porn Queen Koo, Di-Nasty, Prince Wimp, Charles 'A Loon Again', Anne and the Hunky Flunky, Fergie's Bum – as long as it sells papers, it'll run and run, and whilst it's hardly the pop republicanism it's cracked up to be, the Palace Dallas syndrome is still an amusing alternative to the standard media arselicking by appointment. There's just one problem. At least in the SOAPS they axe the odd character. It looks like we'll be stuck with the same old Windsor Bunch for a while yet. Carry On At The Palace just about says it. *See Princess Di*

L to R: Salman Rushdie (photo: Matthew Smith). RAW comic. Mickey Rourke.

to intimidate without recourse to guns. Aggressive dogs trained to guard and protect became a fashion accessory for those who wanted to walk on the wild side with impunity. Top of the canine carnage cruisers was the Rottweiler, a beast by design and nature. An old breed from northern Europe, they were originally used by German tribesmen and cattlemen and the Romans used them as war dogs. In '89 they made the news when five people were mauled within a week, and the British Rottweiler Association received 200 panic stricken phone calls from frightened owners. By the end of the week MPs were demanding an end to the breed through sterilisation, and for a brief moment the public's fear

about dogs surpassed any other social issue. *See Pit Bull Terriers and Mr Dog*

Rourke, Mickey There's madness in his method, lots of it. Rourke is America's last great composite character; the smirk of Jack Nicholson, the pout of James Dean and the brains of Bugs Bunny, he has made a career out of his many moods. A fridge puncher of considerable calibre, his first major role was in the classy ensemble piece by Barry Levinson, 'Diner', but as the Motorcycle Boy in 'RUMBLEFISH' he discovered his mumbling metier. Rourke has made some of the most memorable films of the '80s, not necessarily brilliant but memorable – the YUPPIE sado-sex of 'NINE AND A HALF WEEKS', the conscience stricken IRA hitman in 'A Prayer For

The Dying', the brain-shattered coulda bin a contender of 'Homeboy'. Looks great, acts convincingly in the right roles, just needs to be kept out of trouble night and day.

The Roxy The early '80s saw the importation of the hip hop scene from the Bronx to downtown Manhattan with Edit deAK nights at THE MUDD CLUB, and the Kool Lady Blue's nights at Club Negril. In '82 Blue teamed up with promoter extraordinaire Vito Bruno to popularise the scene with Friday nights at The Roxy on 18th Street and 10th Avenue. These legendary events regularly drew thousands of people and the press coverage that followed probably did more for the initial success of hip hop and BREAKDANCING than any other single factor. *See British Rap*

Rubber Rubber was always the big bad sister of leather – whereas leather connoted merely 'mad, bad and dangerous to know', rubber shouted sex, sex and more sex. But when She-An-Me garbed Hot Gossip in it in '74 the material that sticks to your skin and won't let go went public. Punk did a fair bit to debunk the fetish connotations of rubber but they never really went away until designers like Daniel James applied rubber to fashion, particularly with a series of fashion photos by Bob Carlos Clarke for the book *Dark Summer* in '86, featuring Laurie Vanian and Diane Brill as models. Krystina Kytsis and Kim West also started producing rubber fashion and

by the late '80s KENSINGTON MARKET positively oozed with the stuff. By '88 even the likes of *Vogue* and *Elle* had allowed it on their pristine spreads but it was left to Aquagirl to finally move rubber into the good clean fun market – with bright jolly colours and lace trimmings. *See Catsuits and Skin Two*

Rucksacks The most popular accessory ever? In '85, Wright & Teague marketed a black rubber rucksack, which rapidly became the accessory to MATT BLACK DOCTOR MARTENS, LEVI'S and the MA-1 FLIGHT JACKET. Its legacy can be seen in every high street copy be it leather, fluorescent, small, massive, bootlegged or just plain ridiculous.

Run DMC Run DMC were one of the '80s most important rap groups, forging the genre's progression from craze to mainstream cultural language. Just as the world was closing the file on the turn-of-the-decade's Sugarhill explosion, word spread of an odd-looking duo from Hollis, Queens who were rocking every block party in town with their

fusion of aggressive rhymes and slow, minimal beats. Run DMC took rap from the disco to the street, exchanging the jovial display of vocal dexterity it had been for a drawling sneer of anger. Even the many critics who loved them expected the radical rudeness to Run DMC's sound to preclude any mass success, but their following spread like wildfire until in '86, their single 'Walk This Way' bust into America's national top ten, with its parent album 'Raising Hell' selling over six million copies. 'Walk This Way', a rap cover of the Aerosmith classic (with cameos from Aerosmith's mainmen), was the culmination of Run DMC's pioneering rap-HM fusion and a formula that was later to bear fruit for other rappers like Tone Loc. Another single off 'Raising Hell', 'My Adidas', was Run's first shot in their battle to become the first non-athletes to get a sports company SPONSORSHIP deal. The decision whether or not to sponsor Run DMC almost split the Adidas company, but after the deal went ahead, Adidas attributed $35 million of their annual profit gain directly to Run DMC. Suddenly other

rappers found themselves being courted by every sportswear company in town. By '87 they'd got a reputation as the world's most uncooperative interview partners, which people put down to the fact that they didn't need to do interviews to sell records, but by '89 this was less of an issue – they'd already been overtaken by newer hip hop trends. *See Def Jam and Rock Dinosaurs*

Running The early '80s was the age of the Marathon Boom, the motivation for most being to complete a 26 mile 385 yard course once in their lifetime. Since its inception in '81, however, The Great North Run half marathon has become Europe's most heavily subscribed road race, leading to similar shorter events throughout the UK, and prolonging the life of a sport that was threatening to produce more than its fair share of coronary cases. Now, each spring sees the appearance of numerous wonder-soled shoes claiming to prevent energy dissipation, and straining from pounding pavements. For many, though, the spiritual side of running persists. At the end of the '80s, London's top equipment shop, was 'Run & Become' owned and managed by followers of eastern guru Sri Chinmoy. *See London Marathon*

Russell, Ken From the year of his birth, 1927, the film director has been an agitator and iconoclast. Every Russell movie is marked by twin components; a quirky attitude to sex, often fetishistic, sometimes unintentionally ridiculous; and some element of shock, even if it's only achieved by camera angles. Much of Russell's best work has been accomplished during the '80s, the latter part of the decade seeing him returning to Lawrence for 'The Rainbow'. With his straggly white hair and interesting clothes sense, Russell often looks like someone's hippified granny, and he is often derided for overdoing his effects. Nevertheless, he takes risks and, though these don't always pay off, he's brave enough to try.

Rumblefish A timeless teen pic shot in neo-expressionist black and white and Coppola's most achieved film of the decade. In '83 'Rumblefish' mixed the fat man's directorial madness with BRAT PACK pretensions to method, and gave MICKEY ROURKE one of his best roles as the Motorcycle Boy, a brother-father figure to Matt Dillon's pouting fool, and a ruined monument to the glories of Wasted Youth.

Rubber dress at The Circus '85 (photo: Dave Swindells).

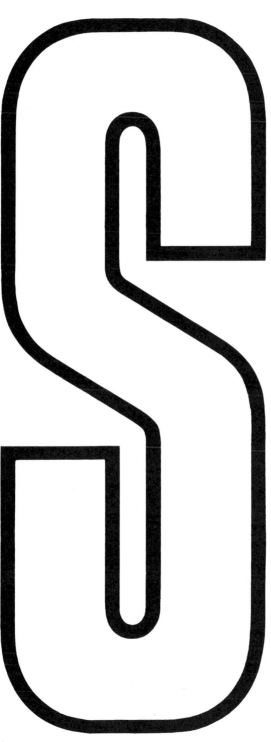

Rushdie, Salman

Salman Rushdie had a talent for controversy if for nothing else. In '81 his epic novel of Indian national independence *Midnight's Children* won the BOOKER but lost him credibility points with the Delhi government. He caused similar annoyance to Pakistan soon after with *Shame* and then had a go at the REAGAN administration in '87 with his pro-Sandanista Nicaraguan travelogue *The Jaguar Smile*. A year later he took on the Muslim fundamentalists with his comic baroque fantasy *The Satanic Verses* but this time got more than his fingers burned as the Ayatollah Khomeini sentenced him to death and copies of the book fuelled bonfires throughout Bradford. An attack against free speech undoubtedly. But it was ironic that the West had become so immune to the media promiscuities of the Image that it took a determinedly backward country like Iran to remind it of the inconoclastic power of the Word.

Saatchi And Saatchi

The ad men who ate the world. Starting from scratch in '67, by the end of the '80s, the Saatchis had become the world's biggest ad agency, Charles (and wife Doris) had bought up the New York ART world, and Saatchi And Saatchi PLC had tried (in '87) to buy Midland Bank. With ex-Saatchi man Tim Bell being one of Mrs Thatcher's closest advisors, this wasn't something Tory politicians needed telling. In fact Saatchi And Saatchi does seem like a permanent sub-department of Tory Central Office. Or is it the other way round? The Saatchis are now bigger than most of their clients, and since, for better or worse, marketing speak has become the new language of power, and politicians worldwide have 'presentational difficulties' (one Saatchi commission was airbrushing the Turkish government's dodgy human rights record), the brothers can only get bigger in the '90s. *See Advertising*

Safe Sex

Emotionally and spiritually sex has never been safe, but once AIDS hit the streets in the mid-'80s everyone got coy and started to talk about the New Puritanism, celibacy and abstinence as a solution. Being human however and having a built-in need for the warm physical contact of other humans, 'Just Say No' was not a sane, logical or compassionate way to deal with AIDS. So safe sex meant contraception, CONDOMS, and more commitment to one partner; and mutual masturbation became a way of staying happy, involved and alive. *See Condoms*

Sampling

Theft as ART. Sampling offered non-musicians the chance to copy any recorded sound to use in their own work, and after M/A/R/R/S' 'Pump Up The Volume' went to number one in the charts in '87, everyone was doing it. Although rap, HOUSE and many commercial artists seized on the sampler as a creative new instrument, others suggested that it was destroying musicianship and, in some cases, breaking the law. ►

Sade Helen Folasade Adu, half Nigerian, half British, combined stunning good looks with a light soul cocktail that caught and massively popularised early '80s cult trends in sophisticated nightclub JAZZ. Evolving from the Latin-funk group Pride, Sade (the band and the singer) sold 12 million worldwide with the LPs 'Diamond Life' ('84) and 'Promise' ('85), moving from the cover of i-D in '83 to the cover of *Time* magazine three years later. After suffering a near nervous breakdown, Sade retired to BARCEL-ONA where she penned most of the '88 LP 'Stronger Than Pride'. Slow, assured and always stylish, Sade's cosmo-politan sound will run well into the '90s.

L to R: Sade '83 (photo: Nick Knight).
Salvage Fashion – dress by Christopher Nemeth, string and earrings by Judy Blame (photo: Marc Lebon).

See Customising

Salvage Fashion

Salvage fashion was clothes and jewellery created from found objects, like CHRISTOPHER NEMETH's postal-sack suits and JUDY BLAME's Marlboro cigarette-packet hat. Salvage styling started during punk with safety pins and crisp packets as jewellery. Stylist Amanda Grieve used salvage ideas in her work for *i-D* and *THE FACE*, then took the concept to the catwalks for JOHN GALLIANO. Designers like JUDY BLAME, CHRISTOPHER NEMETH and MARK & SYRIE turned it into an ART, and with the advent of the TRASH AESTHETIC in the latter half of the decade, the number of salvage fashion designers started to grow. Anne Delaney turned the PHONECARD into a skirt with her graduation collection in June '88 and Fiona Cartiledge incorporated remnants of curtains and carpet bags into her RELIGIOUS ICONOGRAPHY jackets. In late '88, the NEW ECOLOGISTS introduced an ecological awareness to creative salvage with their use of wholly recycled materials.

See Customising

Seventies Fashion

During the '70s funk revival of '87, the logical conclusion to a dancefloor full of James Brown and RARE GROOVE was the return of Seventies Fashion. A flared groove mix of Blaxploitation imagery from 'Shaft' and 'Cleopatra Jones' – loon pants, floppy hats, tank tops and platform boots all topped with an afro wig – Seventies

SCRATC

Fashion was acquired first from jumble sales and Oxfam shops and later from fashion entrepreneurs like The Duffer Of St George. SMILEY was a Seventies Fashion motif that eventually became the universal symbol of ACID HOUSE, but the real legacy of Seventies Fashion is the continued acceptance of flares. *See Baldricks*

When it was discovered that producer Trevor Horn had used sampled instrument sounds instead of 'real musicians' on FRANKIE GOES TO HOLLYWOOD's LP 'Welcome To The Pleasuredome' in '85, the rock press was outraged. Three years later, this was standard practice, as a boom of records composed almost entirely of samples (and often created by DJs, as in the case of BOMB THE BASS' number one hit 'Beat Dis') went into full swing. Everyone who makes records now uses samplers in some way; their possibilities are endless, and the exploration has only just begun.

Sapeurs Members of *La Societe des Personnes Elegantes*, sapeurs

IDEO

were Zaire's best dressed exports. Young Zaireans packed their Armani suits and went to Paris, determined to show the French that they were not the only ones populated with 24 karat fashion queens. Their unofficial leader was the musician Papa Wemba, the Johnny Rotten of AFRICAN MUSIC, who strangled tradition with wild manic guitars and a Christian Dior tie, and dedicated songs to GEORGIO ARMANI. By '88 the *sapeurs* had launched their own fashion labels in Paris, the capital of their former French colonial masters.

Satellite TV 'This time the revolution will be televised' declared the techno-prophets, announcing the advent of satellite TV. In America, satellites did change viewing options bringing on screen whole new worlds of TV trash – televangelists, TELE-

SHOPPING and the rock-around-the-clock POSTMODERNISM of MTV. Over here, satellite TV was something you read about rather than saw – unless you were prepared to go on a waiting list for the chance to catch Sky's has-beens in space. As British Satellite Broadcasting struggle to turn a marketing concept (the Squariel) into a working piece of media pie in the sky, the word is that the satellite revolution is already over. Techno-prophets now say that the future of telecommunications is interactive fibre-optic cable, and that satellites are orbiting follies, a Third World technology. Perfect for Britain in the '90s.

Sauna Parties By the mid-'80s club-runners were falling over each other to be the first with a new idea. Just off the Kentish Town Rd, Lawrence Malice came up with a plan to create the ultimate in water sports. He hired a series of saunas starting with the Camden Tiger and hey presto, the sauna party was launched. He stuck a DJ at the front door, piped the sounds throughout, you brought a bottle, bikini, trunks and got wet. People came armed with enough bubble bath to leave the Thames frothing at the mouth and the JACUZZI japes meant you left at the end of the night with a lot more friends than when you'd arrived. Certainly the inspiration behind Wetworld later on, where the emphasis was on fun *and* games (dinghy dodgems, wavemakers, chutes) and where swimwear became fashionwear for probably the

Schnabel, Julian Of all the young artists to emerge in the last decade, Julian Schnabel has come to typify 'success' '80s STYLE. A belligerent, stocky American who, encased in his flapping designer suits, toured the ART world being feted by dealers keen to interact with the newly rising artniks. Schnabel's career grew along with the myths; hated by influential critic Bob Hughes of *Time* magazine, offered one million dollars (reputedly) to move from the Mary Boone Gallery to Pace Gallery, Mary Boone being the dealer most NY artists would die to be represented by; punched out by fellow artist Brice Marden, writing his memoirs at 35, and so on. Schnabel's painting first came to the British public's notice at the Tate Gallery show in '82 with his paintings on tarpaulin with broken crockery attached. American collectors still take advantage of Schnabel's travelling repair service, whereby a minion goes around the country sticking fallen ingredients back onto his works. *See The New Dealers*

first time. *See Westworld*

Saville, Peter *See Graphic Design*

Scandal 'Scandal' the movie closed the decade of Cecil Parkinson and Sarah Keays, Oliver North and Fawn Hall, Rock Hudson and AIDS, Gary Hart and Donna Rice, Jeffrey Archer and 'Monica', Jim Bakker and Jessica Hahn, Harvey Proctor and rent boys, Ken Dodd and the tax man, Mr Papaendreou and the dancing girl, and Pamella Bordes. The appearance of Ms Bordes, a former Miss Universe contestant, at precisely the beginning of the 'Scandal' promotional blitz, didn't worry the UK tabloids one jot, and why should it? In a decade of 'RAMBO killings' it

was all just more grist to the mill, as Pamella was shot by the PAPARAZZI with various Tory backbenchers. And then, as the movie ended its provincial runs, Pamella disappeared. Unlike the Keeler/Rice-Davies case of the movie, the Bordes affair(s) came nowhere near toppling the Conservative government.

Schwarzenegger, Arnold Big Arnie's career flared like a real stellar body in a series of fast, hip, ultraviolent action movies after 'Conan The Barbarian' first gave him the chance to flex his pecs. 'The Terminator', 'Commando', 'Predator' and 'The Running Man' were all star vehicles designed not so much to showcase the Schwarzenegger physique as to record the technical performance of his Nautilus-tested body parts against those of other ▶

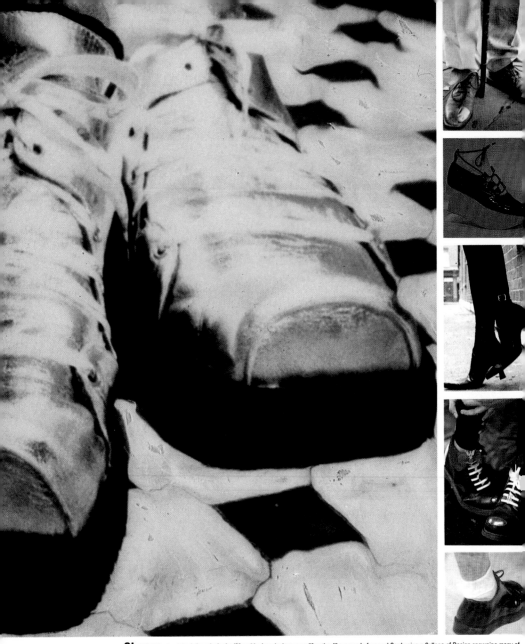

Shoes Feet got the full works in the '80s with shoe designers proliferating like never before and Cordwainers College of Design spawning many of the best, including JOHN MOORE, Trevor Hill, Christine Ahrens, PATRICK COX, Elizabeth Stuart Smith and Emma Hope. Their multitude of barrier-breaking ideas for this long ignored fashion item forced many FASHION DESIGNERS to look to their feet with a new found inventiveness, and the benefits were twofold as shoe designers designed for the entire silhouette. Despite the domination of DOCTOR MARTENS, it didn't seem to stop many street styles re-emerging like the wedge heel, PLATFORMS, cowboy and BIKERS BOOTS, six inch spike stilettos as well as classic variations on the brogue, with the more accessible end of the designer market being catered for by teams like Freelance and Red Or Dead. At the close of the decade though, SNEAKERS seemed to be coming out top as the universal footwear of the '80s. *See Converse and Kickers*

◄ technologies – missiles, computers, trucks, planes. Such films demanded a new kind of post-Brechtian acting to succeed and this was something duly supplied by the misfiring Austrian accent and the graceless steroid frame.

Scooters Scooters never really went away. Although scootering went into decline after the '60s mod era, it had established a firm power base in the North, Midlands and Scotland, and started to gain a higher profile as more scooterists (a union of stray mods, skins and northern soulboys) started customizing their bikes, adding extra mirrors, spotlights, racing seats and even murals to the standard model. Bank holiday rallies attracted numbers in excess of 5,000, *Scooter Scene* magazine catered for the thriving scooter gangs, and even though talk was of liquid-cooled four-stroke scooters with automatic transmissions, the Vespa or Lambretta was still the only machine to own.

Scratch Videos Scratch video was born in the early '80s when people realised you could use a VCR for more than keeping abreast of the SOAPS. Inspired by William Burroughs and Bronx DJs, propagandist scratchers like the Duvet Brothers set out to get under the government's skin by cutting up ads, old films and TV news. Others, like George Barber, aimed to provoke a more pleasurable itch with their seductive small screen collages. The theory behind scratch said that anyone could do it. Unfortunately that included admen and TRENDY TELLY TV producers. By mid-decade, after MAX HEADROOM, scratch had become simply irritating.

Scratching After hip hop DJs discovered they could control the strange sounds made by twitching a record back and forth under the needle, dance music never sounded the same again. No rap record was complete without a display of wacky scratching effects and GRAND-MASTER FLASH marketed the 'Flash-

Sigue Sigue Sputnik Ex-lynchpin of Generation X, Tony James made use of all the times he had seen 'The Great Rock & Roll Swindle' and attempted a MCLARENesque master-plan of his own. If only he'd realised that the swindle was a load of post-priori bollocks he may have modified his own *Weltanschaung*. SSS made a few space age

meets Bo Diddley singles and earned a lot less from EMI than the £4 millions they boasted about before the public lost interest. At press time the 21st Century rockers still existed.

L to R: Martin Degville from Sigue Sigue Sputnik. Green from Scritti Politti. Martine Sitbon's Summer '89 collection (photo: Javier Vallhonrat; art director: Marc Ascoli).

former', a device for automatic 'transformer' scratching. Eventually the DMC World Mixing Championships made stars out of scratchers like DJ Cash Money and CUT-MASTER SWIFT, who confirmed scratching's status as the hip hop equivalent to hyper-technical rock guitar solos.

Scritti Politti The single 'Sweetest Girl' ('81) was a moment of cathartic pop perfection that severed Scritti Politti leader Green's obsession with punk's DIY ethic and embraced the emerging hip hop aesthetic from New York. Presaging the dominance of black dance music on the pop agenda by some two years, it was a vision of synthetic white soul that Green has never managed to repeat since. Worth keeping an eye on just in case he finds what he's looking for.

Sculpture In the '80s British sculpture came from nowhere, emerging out of '70s obscurity and the shadow of MINIMALISM, to virtually rewrite the parameters of traditional three dimensional study. The post-'50s sculptors had tried to renege on tradition with different materials, kinetics and conceptual pieces, but the '80s artists diversified into a myriad of directions that defied description. Richard Wentworth, Anish Kapoor, Stephen Cox, Anthony Gormley, Richard Deacon, Bill Woodrow, Tony Cragg and David Mach – whose 'Polaris Submarine' made from old car tyres on the South Bank was destroyed by an arsonist in '83

– formed a power base along with the Lisson Gallery to re-educate the ART public. A spin off from this successful strategy was demonstrated in the new interest in ARCHITECTURE and architects (ROGERS, Stirling, FOSTER: buildings as sculpture/artworks). Artists like Andy Goldsworthy made 'works' which could never be exhibited or sold in the traditional sense (ice sculptures at the North Pole), while Richard Long exhibited photographs of experiences such as: 'A Line Of Stones In Iceland' and 'Walking A Line In Peru'. An energy which still hasn't burnt itself out.

SDP At the beginning of the decade, four MPs – David Owen,

Shirley Williams, Roy Jenkins and William Rodgers – made a dramatic exit from the Labour Party. They were, they said, forming a new political party to replace the outdated dinosaur that Labour had become. The world, said the SDP, had changed, and Labour couldn't cope with the changes. The era of workers wanting to be represented by unions was over. Now workers wanted to be individuals, and the Labour Party, largely funded by the unions, was an anachronism. The idea worked for a short time but soon ran into trouble. Owen, Williams and Jenkins had trouble deciding on any policies, Rodgers looked particularly bumbling and inefficient, and the only Conservative they could attract was the colourless Christopher Brocklebank-Fowler. After a poor '83 General Election showing, the SDP decided to

Sitbon, Martine

Martine Sitbon has been described as "France's best-kept fashion secret", and even though her first show was held in Paris in March '86, her designs were slow to gain global recognition. She pioneered the revival of the Mexican flare and the Elvis '60s collar, which she put onto beautifully-tailored jackets. A Velvet Underground fan, shy of media attention, she remained in the shadow of JEAN PAUL GAULTIER despite her wealth of ideas. But with Marc Ascoli, the man responsible for the Yohji Yamamoto catalogues, as her right hand man, her work with couture label Chloe and the fashion world at her feet, Sitbon is due for mass recognition in the '90s *See Fashion Designers*

merge with the Liberals. But to what extent? Nobody seemed to know. In the '87 General Election the new Liberal/SDP Alliance took a hammering. Then most of their members left and formed the SLD, a new version of the Liberal Party. The SDP, headed by David Owen, still exists in depleted form, as does speculation about the party's future.

Semiotexte The little black books which did for the '80s what Mao's little red book did for the '60s – ie. establish an OCCULT philosphy which only the intellectually hip could pretend to understand. Buzz-words were traded like status symbols – 'ECSTASY of communication', 'pure war', 'nomadology'. French names were paraded like designer labels – BAUDRILLARD, Virilio, Deleuze and Guattari. And that's just from reading the spines. Mind you, that's about as far as most self-styled intellectuals actually got.

Sequels Summer seasons in the film business began to read like football scores as sequel mania gripped the studios – 'Star Trek V', 'Indiana Jones III', 'Ghostbusters II' – now every hit means a repeat. But there's no guarantee that the same talents will work the same magic. Take 'Jaws', which from the classiest suspenser of its year was turned in successive incarnations into just another made-for-TV disaster movie, before opting for 3D gimmickry. The missing ingredient each time – STEVEN SPIELBERG. With some titles the sequel sequence has become a big in-joke – like 'Friday The 13th Part VIII', 'Nightmare On Elm St V' – each one guaranteeing a quick net return on an economy budget, delivering formula fodder to primed audiences. Some sequels have improved on their originals either in revenue ('RAMBO III' far outstripped 'First Blood') or quality (Leonard Nimoy's 'Star Trek IV' was widely praised as the best of the series). Genuine interest surrounds repeats with all the talent intact, but actors shouldn't let it fool them into thinking that they're bigger

than the concept. When Crispin Glover shilly-shallied over contractual niceties Spielberg and Zemeckis sacked him from 'Back To The Future 2' and 3, replacing him with a lookalike newcomer.

SFX Short lived cassette magazine launched in December '81 after extensive market research by one Hugh Salmon. With the emergence of the Walkman it was assumed by Salmon that the future would be taped. The industry got miffed and claimed that SFX was encouraging home taping and began turning the screw, allowing only the briefest of musical snippets to be used, thus bringing about the swift demise of the enterprise.

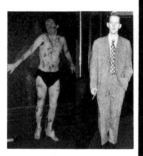

Shambling Bands Post-POS-ITIVE PUNK, the duffle-coated class of '84 revisited their brother's Undertones and Buzzcocks albums to come up with a composite of rambling and shuffling (c. John Peel). But too many bands thought small, got lost behind their fringes and indie-ethic ideological non-compromise. A few bands made the gentle scramble for major contracts, but success-wise no-one got much further than the *NME*'s C-86 compilation album, except for the JESUS AND MARY CHAIN and the spiritual heirs of the movement, The House Of Love.

Shepard, Sam A kind of mystical, down-home, myth-generating guru, Shepard is *the* playwright for the '80s and, without doubt, the '90s too. He's been a waiter, guitar-picker in a band, a poet, and

Ska 2-TONE's grey demise in '82, and a suitable 'cooling-off' period of a few years, may have convinced you that it was acceptable once more to play Trojan's 'Tighten Up' series without fear of ridicule. No chance. A grassroots re-emergence of the R&B-derived boom-ska-boom rhythm, albeit with a contemporary yet authentic approach and legions of SKINHEAD followers, was first sighted on the horizon as far back as '86. Like the Armada, however, rumours of its imminent arrival were exaggerated. Finally, in '88 and '89, the invasion was on, with all-dayers attracting massive crowds spearheaded by the Glasgow based fanzine *Zoot* and the bands The Potato 5, Maroon Town, The Deltones, and veterans of previous campaigns, Bad Manners, plus a myriad of young ska bands around the country and throughout the world. A sure sign of its enduring relevance though, came with the advent of acid ska, a peculiarly '80s phenomenon that affronted purists as much as it attracted new fans. *See* Ragamuffin

Rap

of late, a movie star. The first money Shepard made from writing was $68 for a monologue about orgasm, and his first real taste of fame was playing astronaut Chuck Yaeger in 'The Right Stuff'. His later plays and scripts ('Paris, Texas'; 'True West') drew on more lasting emotion. "In order to do something worthwhile, you have to suffer," he has said and, although this is a shade melodramatic, it's a sentiment that has informed all of his works which, experimental and otherwise, make the breath catch in the throat. He's the sort of person Lou Reed dedicates songs to.

Sherman, Cindy The post-feminist American photographer whose

genre was always the self-portrait but whose subject was never herself. For although she was in front of as well as behind the camera in her 'Film Stills' and 'Untitled' photos, she nevertheless called the shots from both sides, putting herself through a kaleidoscope routine of clichéd expressions and compositions. The point? That there is no 'real' Cindy Sherman just as there is no 'artificial' Cindy Sherman. Identity is always an image away and the image is always a stereotype. *See Directive Photography*

The Shoom The club most associated with ACID HOUSE, not just because of its adopted SMILEY logo. Starting at the end of '87, Danny and Jenny Rampling's underground Saturday nights in Southwark St became legendary as '88 pro-

L to R: Phillip Salon. i-D straight up Steve '83. Shinehead **See Ragamuffin Rap.** i-D straight ups Sharon and Sheila '82.
Alexei Sayle **See Alternative Comedy.** Siouxsie & The Banshees. Sue early i-D straight up '80 **See Ska.**

195

gressed. West End club-runners, club faces (LEIGH BOWERY) and pop stars (BOY GEORGE) literally rubbed shoulders with south London crowds dressed in little more than shorts and BANDANAS. With a punishingly low ceiling, you could feel the sweat while queueing outside, but you could also feel the atmosphere. Inside, regulars gave each other presents, wandered round mumbling poetry or thrust their hands in the air transfixed to one spot. In fact, so communal was the feeling that The Shoom produced a mini-fanzine propagating the Shoom philosophy on life. After many breaks, a brief sojourn at the YMCA in Bedford Ave and frequent one-offs, The Shoom moved to The Park in Kensington,

traditionally the home of teenage models and slumming Sloanes, and perhaps its biggest triumph. From Southwark to Kensington, The Shoom's manifesto of love, peace and good music converted everybody it encountered.

Shopping Malls As design buff Stephen Bayley argued that shopping was "one of the great cultural experiences of the late 20th Century", shopping malls turned into fantasy palaces, baroque temples to THE CREDIT ECONOMY, make-believe worlds built on make-believe money. The days of the utilitarian multi-story public conveniences, like Manchester's Arndale Centre, were over. Now themed design, simulated natural landscapes, galleries and funfairs (as in Newcastle's Metro Centre) combine to encourage a

carnival of dreamlike consumption. With their sanitised environments, crowd control systems, air-conditioning and surveillance cameras keeping an eye on disorderly mall rats – they have become a vision of a free market future, where there's nowhere to go but the shops, and all you have to do is spend.

Short Films For a while it seemed all our debut directors were graduates from the flashy inanities of the pop promo, making movies that looked like jeans ads. All hail then the return of the Short, a three way initiative between CHANNEL 4, British Screen and the BFI, and the only real training ground for future feature talents. Yet to hit the wide screens, the first fruits are still manically inconsistent, but the medium has already thrown up writer-director Philip Ridley, and watch out for Glaswegian Bernard Rudden whose 'The Chalk Mark' is far and away the best of the BFI crop to date.

Simple Minds Began the '80s as a European modern dance outfit trailing KRAFTWERK influences, but by '85 their cross channel ambience had been forsaken for an emphatically Transatlantic sound that had grown out of their dedication to live touring. After 'Don't You Forget About Me' took the American number one slot, their big music made them stadium regulars. Since that transformation, Jim Kerr's muse has moved ever more towards the messianic, their once pristine and suggestive sound now approximating a Scottish

U2. A perfect example of '80s redefinition, Simple Minds managed to remain implausibly naive *and* utterly contrived.

The Sinclair C5 Sir Clive Sinclair – the Tony James of British science? Calculators, mini-TVs and home computers were among his brainchilds, which he invented but failed to market as well as others. But the apotheosis of boffinry was this feeble little unsexy car that he was convinced would revolutionize traffic and travel. The only reason no-one was splattered under a juggernaut was that so few were sold and the death race go carts were swiftly discontinued. Not even the Japanese could have marketed these atrocities successfully.

Siouxsie And The Banshees After the risible Damned knocked it on the head once and for all in '89, Siouxsie & The Banshees stood as the only survivors of the class of '76. Siouxsie Sue became the icon for the massive female GOTH contingent, and played the role of the ice maiden to the full. Her look became so archetypal that few could differentiate between the fans and performer. The early '80s witnessed much activity from the Banshees with their ever changing guitarists (only Siouxsie and Steve Severin have gone the distance) and from offshoot combination The Creatures, comprising of Siouxsie and percussionist Budgie. Vocal chord nodes threatened to end her career, but the band continued to quietly plug away, with their songs about exotic but barren landscapes, carving themselves a super-cult niche among black clad types.

Situationism What had started out as a street-level guerilla game-show directed against the 'society of the spectacle' in May '68 became a MALCOLM MCLAREN media event in '77 and an ICA museum event by '89. Quite appropriate really, given that by the semiotic-smart '80s the Situationist Internationale's brand of cultural

Skate fashion '85 (photos: Nick Knight, styling: Simon Foxton)

Skate/ Surfwear

Throughout the greenhouse effect summers of the late '80s, surf and skatewear became de rigeur street STYLE. It was an extension of the DRESSING DOWN phenomenon, as people moved away from the strict T-SHIRTS and shorts uniform of ACID HOUSE and started exploring the dazzling array of prints and colours. The established overseas companies – Quicksilver, Life's A Beach, Vision and Gotcha – muscled in with their loose fitting padded shorts, and several UK skaters set up their own clothing companies, such as Kowabunga, Poizone and Pig City. California's Stussy, with his use of rap and reggae imagery, became one of the crossover successes, his range of surfwear even extending to jackets. Footwear was strictly US, with Airwalk, Etnies and CONVERSE usurping the '70s domination of the Vans company. By the end of the decade skate/surfwear had become so popular that the only people who didn't seem to be wearing the clothes were the skateboarders themselves.

See Skateboarding

revolution was already a living fossil. A new kind of resistance was called for in a demystified decade which saw the SI's patent on the manufacture of subversive spectacle trademarked as the standard Factory-tested new marketing tool. SCANDAL, shock and disruption were no longer used to wake the slumbering masses but to stimulate the jaded consumer – eg. ZTT's Frankie scam, KATHARINE HAMNETT's Pershing T-shirt stunt. After all that, plain dumbness begins to look almost radical.

Skateboarding Skateboarding never went away, it just moved from the Californian coastline and became an urban phenomenon. After the polypropylene craze of the late '70s where every UK council provided unskateable concrete transitions for the kids, only the diehards remained, constructing a LIFESTYLE around their boards. Those boards became wider,

the kids became older, the soundtracks hard(core)er, and an underground information network evolved. The sport gained overground popularity when Michael J Fox rode a skateboard in 'Back To The Future' and by May '89 skatezine *Skate Muties From The 5th Dimension* had announced that it was ceasing publication because skating was no longer an outlaw activity. The UK now boasts three nationally distributed skateboard magazines, *RAD*, *Skateboard!* and *Skate Action*, all of which thankfully refrain from attempting to emulate the punk OD American bible *Thrasher*. The streets and secret location homemade wooden ramps are the preferred sites for skating and one suspects, with the advent of 'STRAIGHT EDGErs' who neither smoke, ingest drugs, drink ALCOHOL or eat meat, that the activity will remain at least partially underground.

Skating The sounds of wheels on

wood, ELECTRO music and jazz funk, and the sight of hundreds of kids circling, weaving and spinning on their roller-skates; skating hit Britain with a vengeance in the late 70s and reached its peak in '82. The parks and streets were full of skaters, causing havoc with the traffic and heartache with the police, and clubs like the Starlight in Hammersmith (which was open from 1980 with Tim Westwood as DJ) and the Electric Ballroom in Camden Town (with DJ Paul Anderson and his Jazzi-Funk club) catered for the craze. By '84, club skating was underground again, with venues like the Ace in Brixton full of mainly black kids, while Andrew Lloyd-Webber's roller musical 'Starlight Express' ensured that wheels on heels would never be fashionable again. *See Street Hockey*

Skinheads The skinhead was the bogeyman of '80s youth culture. Originally a working class culture that

Skin Two In the early '80s, fetish images were part of a grubby sex industry, but in '82 David Claridge and Daniel James launched the club Skin Two, providing a meeting place for serious RUBBER and leather fetishists and inspiring others such as Der Putsch later in the decade. By '84 Skin Two had become a magazine as well, reclaiming the medium from pornog-

raphers (the 30 year old *Atomage* being the only exception), and in '88, it opened a shop stocking the best in the new RUBBER designers such as Krystina Kitsis, Angela Murray, Julian Latorre and Kim West. Probably the most important factor in the rehabilitation of the fetish scene this decade.

L to R: Sly & Robbie (photo: Kevin Davies). Frank Sidebottom. Young Sloanes outside The Dome '88. The Smiths '83. Air Jordan Sneakers (photo: Eddie Monsoon and Richard Ellis).

evolved in the late '60s, its mix of SKA and aggressive STYLE became increasingly polarised as the '70s turned into the '80s. The image of repressed violence and intimidation was given rein as the Oi movement gained ground in the early '80s, and old punks shaved their heads and joined the British Movement. Wearing combat gear, knee high boots, completely bald and mouthing Nazi slogans, they were a perversion of the original skinhead spirit of '69 (called 'boneheads' by real skinheads). Media hysteria, although not unwarranted, didn't help matters. Skinheads quickly became synonymous with Nazi violence and the National Front eagerly embraced their new recruits. A fanzine called *Hard As Nails* was the first visible sign that 'real' skinheads were starting to make themselves heard. Started in the mid-'80s it aimed specifically to reclaim the initiative from the boneheads and inspired a host of skinhead fanzines to do the same.

When THE REDSKINS arrived in '82, they gave many skins an alternative focal point and were the first 'skin' band to come out with such a strong anti-Nazi stance. However, it took the resurgence of SKA bands like The Potato 5, The Deltones, Maroon Town and Capone & The Bullets, together with flourishing skin fanzines like *Zoot*, *Spy Kids* and *Bovver Boot*, to give the 'real' skinhead an impetus and identity. Although by the end of the '80s, the spectre of Nazi skinheads became topical once more, it was more a

European phenomenon – in Britain the formation of SHARP (Skinheads Against Racial Prejudice) was more representative of the scene. The rehabilitation of the skinhead image and reassertion of the Spirit of '69 has only just begun. Whether or not the public will ever believe it though, is another question.

Sky Magazine Originally a fortnightly magazine, the self-proclaimed '*Next* of STYLE magazines', was never expected to be a success. After a shaky start it went monthly, proprietor Rupert Murdoch's money eventually making sure that its populist ethic had the sales figures to match.

Sloane Rangers PETER YORK first sighted a generation of Carolines in the vicinity of Kensington Gardens in the late '70s and with Ann Barr, dubbed them the Sloane Rangers in *Harpers & Queen*. Living proof that cults are neither exclusive to the lower classes or youth, the proliferation of pearls, flatties and giggling exploded exponentially when the most successful Sloane, Lady Diana Spencer, married her Prince Charming. Later on Fergie even out-Sloaned her in-law, giggling louder and wearing copious swathes of navy blue and getting well stuck into wellies, Barbour jackets and weekends in the country. Sloanes can be of any age; however, the more mature variety sport Hermés scarves over their bunched up ponytails. Infinitely preferable to their male counterpart, the Hooray Henry, who is equally brainless but is often in rather dangerous proximity to a shotgun when out of London and distantly related to their arriviste cousins in America, the Preppies.

Smart Cards Cash cards, Football ID cards, PHONECARDS, parking cards in Westminster, cards which translate languages – in the '80s plastic got more intelligent by the minute. Even the humble tube ticket went smart, and Digital EVANGELISM arrived in the form of a card

version of The Bible. Smart Card Address Books though, had all the charm of calculator watches, but in the '90s technology will bring us computer cards which will make the Psion Organiser look as outdated as a stereogram.

Smash Hits IPC Magazines are wary of new ideas. In '79 their whizzkid editor of the (then) top-selling *NME*, Nick Logan, offered them the idea for a new pop glossy that would seize the teen market and blow out its rivals. IPC looked at *Smash Hits* and sniffed. "No, too risky," was the reply. *Smash Hits* was then launched by thrusting new publishers EMAP, and IPC have been kicking themselves ever since. It was

immediately successful, devoting itself to chart pop in a colourful, witty and accessible way. Now the largest selling UK music publication, it attracts a curious mix of readers, the largest group (58%) of course being teenagers, but the second largest being the over-35s. Like the rumbustious Saturday morning TV show 'Tiswas', adult fans like *SH*'s capacity to take the piss. It'll be going for a while yet. *See Music Press*

Smith, Paul Paul Smith took the classic English STYLE, gave it a twist with innovations in the cut, fabric and colour and found himself in the middle of the MENSWEAR BOOM. Moving from Nottingham to Covent Garden in the late '70s, his retail empire and wholesale business has expanded to include five shops in the UK, one in New York, 17 in Japan,

Jo Marsh – London Skinhead '88 (photo: Dave Swindells).

and his wholesale label now exports to 22 countries. Initially making his name from his high quality shirts, Smith extended to trousers, jackets, ties and then a host of men's accessories that now include Japanese toys.

The Smiths An ultra successful independent mid-'80s pop group. Fronted by witty pseudo depressive Steven MORRISSEY they appealed mainly to angst ridden students via a formula of chiming '60s flavoured melodies courtesy of guitarist Johnny Marr and Morrissey's self-centered northern tales. The Smiths cleverly targetted a previously untapped market – an audience of late teens unimpressed by the glamour

wear. The first fashion designer to create her own trainer was VIVIENNE WESTWOOD, with the three-tongue square-toed shoe featured in her Autumn/Winter '84 collection 'The Witch'; JOHN MOORE followed this with his own gold and silver sneaker, but it was hip hop fashion that elevated the training shoe to the level of status symbol. Rappers owned a pair of 'box-fresh' shoes for every day of the week, RUN DMC did a song called 'My Adidas' and were sponsored by the company in return, and the TROOP sportswear company derived almost their entire income from the hip hop scene. As sportswear crossed over into fashion in '88 and '89, by the end of the decade the range of sneakers became ever

and simplicity of *SMASH HITS* pop. After seven albums (the most successful being 'Meat Is Murder' in '85, which displaced BRUCE SPRINGSTEEN as number one) the group split up and MORRISSEY went on to pursue a solo career. The Smiths remain, however, Britain's most British pop group.

Sneakers Training shoes, trainers, or *sneakers*, as the Americans called them. A German athlete called Adi Dassler started making gym shoes in 1920; in 1948 he formed a manufacturing company called Adidas and began developing the designs that would become today's training shoe. Comfortable, casually cool and available in a seemingly endless range of colour combinations, it wasn't long before they became the universal leisure foot-

daunting and bizarre. Nike now produce a new design every month and the launch of 'rear-entry' trainers, the two-tone detachable hi-top and the chameleon trainer has made it obvious, if ever there was any doubt, that the sneaker has become more than just SPORTSWEAR.

Snooker Snooker, traditionally a game played in working men's clubs or special snooker halls, became the most popular spectator sport on TV after it appeared on 'Pot Black' in the early '80s. As the competition got fiercer so too did the skill involved in winning the marathon tournaments which ran for days, and so too did the money – in '77 the total prize money was £22,000, by '87 it had reached £3 million plus. While Alex Higgins burnt out on booze some

Smiley An image spawned by the '60s hippy underground culture, it became associated in the '70s with the pimp soul of stars such as Isaac Hayes, and was consistently res-urrected in the '80s on club FLYERS. DODOs was probably the first club to use the symbol, but it wasn't until the '70s RARE GROOVE revival that Smiley became common currency. By the end of '87

GET UP! GET HAPPY!

ALAN MOORE had put it on the cover of *THE WATCHMEN*, THE SHOOM club had adopted the image as its own, *i-D* magazine had put it on its cover, DISCOTEQUE had utlised it on its invites, and in '88 BOMB THE BASS' appropriation of Smiley popularised the image even more. As the ACID HOUSE exploded, Smiley became the most plagiar-ised image of the decade – High Street stores sold garish T-SHIRTS, badges

*L to R: Smiley i-D cover no. 54 '87. Moa and Mats at i-D night in Sweden **See Smiley** (photo: Peter Strid). Sue Ellen from 'Dallas'; Harry Cross from 'Brookside' **See Soaps**. Mandy Smith modelling at London Fashion Week '87.*

young players were linked to coke and speed, and some old-timers needed to resort to tranquilising beta blocker drugs to cope with the long hours of stress and tension. Steve Davis however, became a symbol of the British sportsman of the '80s. With neat hair, immaculate shirt and waistcoat he did not apear to sweat even after hours of on the edge concentration. But will Steve Davis reign supreme throughout the next decade or will young rising star Steve Hendry stay the pace and eventually take over? Watch the ubiquitous snooker TV and find out (400 hours a year of it).

Soap Ads Those annoying ad 'mini-series' featuring lovable stereo-

types like the Oxo Family and the Gold Blend couple have been working on blurring the boundaries between 30 second SOAPS and 30 minute ones. Enthralling viewers with their vacuous suavity, the Gold Blend YUPPIES' micro-lifestyles rang as hollow as a *Playboy* editorial. The Oxo mum confused things further by escaping to 'All Creatures Great And Small', but she never really managed to get out of the kitchen. How long before we get Omnibus editions? *See Advertising*

Soaps In the '60s soap operas were daytime fodder (eg *Crossroads*) churned out for schoolkids and housewives – trivial, routine and reassuring. It wasn't until the early '80s that soaps became big, glitzy, American and prime-time. Super-soaps like 'Dallas' and 'Dynasty' not

only pulled in a mass audience, they also earned a hip credibility and suddenly found themselves pegged as structuralist strip-downs of the American nuclear family. Meanwhile, the home-grown soaps hit back. The capsule political allegories of 'Brookside' developed a cult following, while 'EastEnders' took its brand of music hall grotesque into living rooms across the nation. But at the end of the decade the soap bubble burst. 'Dynasty' was axed and with the triumphant suburban nothingness of 'Neighbours' ('Crossroads' with Aussie accents) soap returned to its origins as mini-pop saccharine.

Soca The nearly man of WORLD MUSIC, soca is the modern offspring of Trinidad's calypso, and has inherited its parent's virtues of razor wit, political astuteness and a passion for dancing. Arrow first broke the news of the birth to the world with the anthemic 'Hot Hot Hot' ('84), but he doesn't count as far as Trinidadians are concerned, because he's from Montserrat. Trini's champion is David Rudder, a quiet, middle-class intellectual whose allegorical and innovative socas found a wider outlet through London Records. But soca stars like Gypsy, Baron, Scrunter and even the feted Rudder failed to reap the success their quality deserved, and by the end of the decade were looking increasingly to the huge market in Brooklyn for success beyond their island confines.

Soho Soho's always had that frisson of sleaze-chic running through

and whole ranges of paraphernalia. But when the tabloids discovered ACID HOUSE, media hysteria resulted in Smiley T-SHIRTS being withdrawn from Top Shop and KENSINGTON MARKET stalls, and by the end of '88, Smiley had fallen from grace – it was even barred from clubs that had previously championed it.

Smoking During a period when smoking was banned from the London Underground, theatres, offices, restaurants, aeroplanes and even some pubs, for the first time this century, smokers became the social pariahs that ASH (Action on Smoking and Health) had been working towards for 19 years. By '88 opinion polls showed that 85% of the public agreed that smoking was a health hazard for everyone, and 81% of smokers thought non-smokers had the right to work in smoke-free air. However, in '88 the number of smokers rose for the first time this decade. The reason? The price of cigarettes fell in real terms for the first time. Proof, if any were needed, that the power of money is supreme.

its narrow alleys. The sex shops and peep shows sat for years happily alongside the media sideshow – after all, is there that much difference between selling your body and selling your soul? The old Soho-ites sat in Bar Italia and The French House since the beginning of the '80s and well before; St MARTINS' students ate in the Pollo because it was cheap rather than chic and clubbers hung around the Spice Of Life simply because it was there. But, in the early '80s, Soho was a place you passed through – about the only shop worth perusing was the excellent DEMOB on Beak St. 1983 saw the Helvetia pub throw out the last of its disreputable regulars to reopen as the Soho Brasserie, and ever since Soho has been the place to be. Fred's and Moscow followed the Groucho as exclusive watering holes, Old Compton St watched the sex parlours move out in '87 and the likes of American Retro moved in. Meanwhile, the other end of Soho was enjoying a little revival of its own. 1987 saw a flurry of openings in unheard of Newburgh St: Helen Storey and Karen Boyd flung open their doors, as did Academy. The next two years saw them joined by John Richmond, PAM HOGG and finally, in '89 GAULTIER Junior. Rents soared, cobbled paving went down and London's newest 'fashion centre' was born. Too good an opportunity to miss, the PRs muscled in and '89 saw 'West Soho' launched with an open-air catwalk show presided over by not one, but three PR companies. West Soho is the changing face of designer retailing and could only have happened at the end of the '80s – you can now obtain a 'West Soho' membership card entitling you to discounts and a newsletter. *See Kensington Market and King's Road*

Soul Underground Started in October '88 with an initial print run of 600, *Soul Underground* aimed to fill the void which the black music press chose to ignore. Concentrating on club-based dance music (mainly rap and HOUSE) it became in instant success, quickly evolving from a fanzine into an essential magazine for any serious club-goer. Now into its 17th issue its 12,000 copies sell in Sweden, New York and Japan and it has reached the first major watershed for any music publication – record companies now take it seriously enough to fly its journalists abroad.'

Soul Weekenders A uniquely British phenomenon, soul weekenders almost became mini Club 18-30 holidays for the suburban soulboy. A product of the burgeoning late '70s suburban soul scene, the first one was the Caister weekender in Great Yarmouth in '79, which by

the early '80s was attracting 3,000 people who had adopted a uniform of shorts, whistles and T-SHIRTS declaring their membership of 'Paddington Soul Partners' or 'Magnum Force', living on a diet of cheap lager and hot dogs. Ostensibly a gathering of soul music lovers, weekenders were invariably an excuse for sex, booze and letting off fire extinguishers; in other words, the traditional activities of British youths abroad. In April '86, the Livewire soul weekenders started, intent on attracting a new audience and using younger DJs such as Nicky Holloway, Gilles Peterson and Pete Tong. Their Bognor Soul Weekender drew 3,500 clubbers, drawing on the 'alternative' West End club scene that had sprung up in the wake of LE BEAT ROUTE and THE DIRTBOX for the first time. In fact, so successful was it that six months

later they held another one. But it took club entrepreneur Nicky Holloway to adapt the soul weekender to the new soul audience. His Rockley Soul Weekender in '87, which included a performance of JOHN GODBER's play 'Bouncers', banned shorts and whistles and catered exclusively to a new generation of clubbers who wanted to dispense with the hooligan antics of the past. Now a British youth culture institution, the weekender serves as a bizarre initiation ceremony for many first time clubbers and completely bewilders visiting American performers. "I've never seen anything like it," Joyce Sims once said. As surreal as soul ever gets.

Spectrum: Theatre Of Madness When Spectrum opened in March '88 ACID HOUSE was still a phrase held in contempt by most southerners (*See The Hacienda*), and it never took off in the instantaneous way that THE TRIP did. For the first month or so, SHOOM regulars monopolised the club, waving sparklers and grateful that they had another club to themselves. But by June Spectrum was drawing more clubbers than it could handle. With DJ Paul Oakenfold championing BALEARIC BEATS and the club often closing the doors an hour after it had opened, Spectrum became a victim of the first wave of tabloid hysteria in the autumn. Changing its name to Phantasia after ending up on the front page of *The Sun*, then dropping it after alleged drug associations, Spectrum ended up as Land Of Oz in '89.

Spheeris, Penelope US film director and chronicler of American youth subculture. In the '70s, Spheeris directed MUSIC VIDEOS and segments of 'Saturday Night Live' before making her name in 1980 with 'The Decline Of Western Civilisation', a documentary on the West Coast punk scene. Her films since, from 'Suburbia' to 'Decline Part II', have featured Preppy serial killers, cowboy punks and heavy metal. If, as she

Spandau Ballet *'She used to be a diplomat/but now she's down the laundromat'* ('Highly Strung'). With lyrics like those was it any wonder that Gary Kemp, brother Martin and their Islington chums put so much emphasis on their appearance? Distracting the public long enough with a succession of KILTS, quilts and tablecloths Spandau Ballet took New Romanticism onto 'Top Of The Pops' and were briefly brand leaders of pretty boy pop until DURAN DURAN came along. Still going briefly after a debilitating contractual dispute which lost the momentum that peaked with the grannies' favourite, 'True' in '83, The Kemps still intend to one day play their beloved Kray Twins on celluloid.

L to R: Rockley Sands Soul Weekender (photo: Dave Swindells). Spandau Ballet '84. Stephen Sprouse. Troop tracksuit '88 (photo: Simon Fleury), Soul II Soul Sportswear '89 (photo: Johnny Rozsa) **See Sportswear.** *Stetsasonic.*

intends, she manages to hit Hollywood in the '90s, the decade could prove interesting.

Spielberg, Stephen The world's richest filmmaker, with more than half the all-time top ten films to his name, has yet to gain a critical kudos to match his commercial popularity. With the belated exception of the third 'Indiana Jones', Spielberg attempted to clear his name of the cartoon slur it had garnered with a series of space-kid and disaster movies by moving into serious drama and talking earnestly about writers saving Hollywood. His efforts at adult drama have fallen badly short of the mark, however, and the Academy's ruthless Oscar time

snobbery has left Spielberg looking a dignified but injured party. *See ET*

Spitting Image Telly satire at its sharpest since 'That Was The Week That Was', Fluck and Law's vicious puppets, writers of the calibre of *Private Eye*'s Ian Hislop and impressionists that included Harry Enfield, kept the latex lampooning going through most of the THATCHER years, managing to annoy most Rotarians with its no holds barred irreverence. Beneath the bottom and fart jokes lay the seeds of true anarchy.

Sponsorship is nothing new, but as public funding of the arts shrank, sport professionals and amateurs realised their true worth, and companies sought cheaper alternatives for TV exposure, everything was for sale. The '84 Olympic Games, watched by 2.5 billion viewers, had 150 official sponsors – from the official breakfast cereal Kellog's corn flakes to Head And Shoulders, the offical shampoo. Harp lager launched a series of concerts in '85, Crunchie sponsored a Five Star tour, Reebok underwrote the $10 million deficit for the AMNESTY INTERNATIONAL 'Human Rights Now!' concert in '88, and BORIS BECKER played the '89 Wimbledon Final without the Puma logo on his racquet because the company refused to pay the astronomical fee he demanded (he still netted £7 million for his Fila clothes contract). FOOTBALL, however, was sold lock, stock and jockstrap. The Football League became the Barclay's

course of the fashion world. Although, in the last two years of the decade, designers have come up with their own variations on basic sports themes, like VIVIENNE WESTWOOD's rugby suits and Walter Van Beirendonck's cycling wear, it is the actual sports companies – Nike, Reebok, Adidas etc – who have led the way. Hip hop culture's sportswear elitism and brand-name devotion has profoundly affected the development of sportswear, particularly SNEAKERS and tracksuits, with companies like Troop existing purely to cater for the rap market. ACID HOUSE and BALEARIC BEAT culture popularized the beach bum look in '88 and led to a surge of interest in the brightly-coloured creations of SKATE/

Spiritualism

Along with witchcraft and the OCCULT in general, over the past decade there has been a resurgence of interest in Spiritualism – a recognised religion which believes in reincarnation and the possibility of contact with spirits who have 'passed on'. Keen to lose its image of elderly women presiding over dimly-lit seances, there are over 700 Spiritualist churches in

press but the cold shoulder from his fans. The irony of 'Born In The USA' ('84), with Springsteen posing in front of the American flag on the cover and its themes of economic insecurity and Vietnam, was lost on some (REAGAN took it as an emblem of patriotism), and sold 11 million copies worldwide. During his '84 tour though, Springsteen made sure that there was no misunderstanding – he urged fans to contribute to food banks to feed the victims of "the economic policies of the current administration". Playing a key role in '85's 'We Are The World' record, singing lead vocals in the 'Sun City' single and performing at AMNESTY INTERNATIONAL's Wembley concert in September '88, Springsteen has consistently put his

League, the amateur Southern League became the Beazer Homes League and the League Of Ireland, at one time, was sponsored by Pat Grace's Fried Chicken. Shirt sponsorship began with Liverpool's Hitachi advert in 1980 and led to the bizarre sight of Nobo (Brighton), Wang (Oxford) and Durex (Cardiff) gracing football fields and confusing the opposition. How low can it go? One football team's half-time pies were sponsored by a company called Thomas Crapper.

Sportswear In the '80s, sportswear was the street fashion that wouldn't stop growing. From the OLYMPIC MANIA of '84 onwards, it had an ever-increasing influence on fashion, demonstrating perhaps more than anything else in the '80s, the power of street trends to alter the

SURFWEAR companies like Quicksilver, Life's A Beach and Gotcha as well as inspiring the phenomenon of DRESSING DOWN. By the end of the decade, the bouncer's excuse of 'no trainers, no tracksuits' (often used to exclude black people from clubs) had become almost useless, as *everyone* was wearing sportswear. *See Cultural Cross-Dressing* and *The Daisy Age*

Springsteen, Bruce The all American rock'n'roll hero of the '70s, Bruce Springsteen decided to show us that he was more than just RAMBO with a Telecaster guitar in the '80s. The album 'Nebraska', released in '82, presaged what was to come. A rough-cut acoustic set recorded on Springsteen's home four track, its socio-political leanings received critical acclaim from the

Britain and membership of the two main organisations (the Spiritualist National Union and the Greater World Association) has soared in the last five years.

social conscience on public display.

Spritzers What kind of person dilutes their wine with soda water? Someone taking a business lunch, maybe; someone, in any event who wants to keep a clear head. The spritzer is the 'in' drink for those not uncool enough to say they're teetotal but who want to keep their wits about them when all around people are falling off their chairs. For power lunches rather than piss-ups.

St Martin's School Of Art
A prime source of artistic creativity in the '60s/'70s (GILBERT AND GEORGE, Duggie Fields et al), St Martin's virtually invented the '80s. From fashion designers KATHARINE HAMNETT, Bruce Oldfield, STEPHEN LINARD, STEPHEN JONES, Fiona Dealy, Richard Ostell, Dexter Wong,

JOHN GALLIANO, John Flett, RIFAT OZBEK, JOE CASELY HAYFORD, to pop stars SADE and Swing Out Sister and even the staff of *i-D* magazine; its students were a prime influence on the decade. By the late '80s though, the school had partially become a victim of its own success. Like all ART SCHOOLS it fell victim to EDUCATION cuts and courses became geared to the market place – whereas once it took equal pride in SCULPTURE, painting, photography, and filmmaking; now it increasingly promoted just fashion and graphics, the two growth STYLE industries of the '80s. Furthermore, the SPONSOR-SHIPs and bursaries of companies like Courtelle and LEVI'S, where money was awarded to students who

designed commercial clothes, en-couraged conformity rather than creativity. The perfect student now, is not someone with a broad know-ledge but someone who has some-thing to sell, and by the late '80s they even had their own PRs before they graduated. If you ever got stuck in a lift with an '80s St Martin's student, you'd probably think they were in ADVERTISING. But then, in a way, every '80s student is. *See Fashion Designers*

Stanley Knives The theory went something like this: if you got caught holding one you could always claim you were on your way to fit a bit of shag pile. Liverpool never had so many carpet fitters. 5" long, 1" wide with a 2" retractable blade (the record is over 300 slashes), the Stanley took violence out of hurting

and into maiming. The change in Offensive Weapons Law, however, seems to have placed them back in the tool box. *See Casuals*

Steroids 1988 was the year of the steroid – the year when time, medical technology and the sporting public finally caught up with the fact that cheating was an institution in top class athletics. The event was the 100 metres blue riband race at the greatest stage for amateur achieve-ment, the Olympic Games. Ben Johnson – black, musclebound, barely able to talk through his childhood stutter, provided the per-fect villain. Banned in '75, steroids are said to be what built the physique of footballer Diego Maradona. Their use is rife in AMERICAN FOOTBALL even in college teams – and in weight rooms of gyms up and down Britain. But the *Olympic Games*? Johnson came under intense scrutiny after 'clean' competitor and rival CARL LEWIS pointed the finger. But as long as the money involved makes the cheating worth spent livers and kidney failure, athletes will continue to piss blood and play hush.

Stock, Aitken & Waterman The most successful British pop production team · ever, SAW have soundtracked the teen mainstream for the best part of the '80s. Depending on youth pop cultural overview, they're the purveyors of soulless production line pop or this decade's answer to the Mickie Most, Chinnichap tradition. Their output varied from the sublime – Mel &

Kim's mid-'80s 'Respectable' – to a deluge of disposable, retro disco dross as personified by Sinnita and Sam Fox. They turned the ever more vaccuous BANANARAMA into the biggest girl group of all time, made 'I'd rather jack than Fleetwood Mac' a suburban statement of intent and, in their one perfect moment of radical cheek, pulled the wool over the ears of the West End's RARE GROOVE importers with the superb 'Road-block', a pseudo-soul classic served up as pastiche. By '89 though, they had nurtured the inexorable rise of soap sud pop à la Jason Donovan and Kylie Minogue.

Stop The Violence Founded by rapper KRS-ONE to highlight black-on-black violence in New York, the Stop The Violence Movement made an all-star hip hop record 'Self Destruction' and contributed to the trend towards 'consciousness rap' in '89.

Straight Edge A strand of hardcore punks who emerged in '88, rejecting the boozy violence that punk had become. They gave up drinking, smoking, drugs and casual sex and instead spent their time writing fanzines propagating the Straight Edge attitude, playing hardcore thrash music and generally being nice to each other.

Straight No Chaser *See Wire*

Strange, Steve From shop assistant at PX and general London ligger during punk, leading BLITZ kid and NEW ROMANTIC, star host of '81's Club For Heroes and THE CAM-DEN PALACE, to creator of Visage, who sold two million copies of FUTURIST pop singles like 'Fade To Grey' in '81, Steve Strange has been described as 'the perfect social anim-al' and made his career out of marketing that very quality. Though largely forgotten during the mid-'80s, Strange resurfaced in Scotland in '89, organising club nights and giving interviews to the local press about how he conquered his HEROIN addic-tion.

Staller, 'Cicciolina' Ilona

In '87 Ilona 'Cicciolina' Staller was elected to the Italian Parliament. A porn star of movies such as 'Hot Lips' and 'Boiling Meat', La Cicciolina (roughly translated as 'sweetie-pie') conducted a campaign for The Radical Party on the basis of her nipples and with slogans like 'Grope Your Local MP'. Attracting

the protest vote and the attention of males everywhere, she proceeded to campaign for prison reform (sex facilities for prisoners), give political speechos at her striptease shows, and make a record. Italy is still in a state of shock.

L to R: Sting. i-D straight up Sarah '84. Steve Strange. Jazzie B from Soul II Soul. Ilona 'Cicciolina' Staller (photo: Phil Inkelberghe).

Starck, Philippe French furniture and interiors designer whose 'trademark' was the three-legged chair and who announced his intention of becoming as famous as a rock star. This hasn't happened as yet, but Starck broke through the Italian dominance of the field in which critics saw a marriage of high-tech and art

deco, aided by the French government's determination to retrieve the nation's reputation for high STYLE in time for the '89 bicentenary. One of the foremost furniture designers of the '80s.

Style Originally, style denoted individual flair – the man who dared to wear make-up to a rugby club dinner, or the woman who made heads turn without taking her clothes off; the person who dared to be that little bit *different*. At the beginning of the decade, in the wake of The BLITZ Kids, Britain's youth started dressing up and experimenting with style like never before. Style was something that you wore on your sleeve, and everybody's was different. When the style magazines were launched (*i-D, THE FACE, BLITZ*), each one responded to the phenomenon in a different way. *i-D* documented it as a street phenomenon, *THE FACE* concentrated initially on the music and evolving cultural codes, and *BLITZ* examined its wider impact. Their success reflected the shifting codes of youth culture and identified a creative energy that was to surface in fashion, music and eventually ADVERTISING. The influence of the style magazines cannot be underestimated – as much a product of the era as a document, the people involved were, at times, almost writing about themselves. Design students, journalists, photographers or just people with good ideas, all contributed to producing a visual guide to the times, and the photography and graphic styles were copied and assimilated by the ADVERTISING industry, record companies and a host of other magazines.

The consumer industries cottoned on, waking up to a new market and a new approach to packaging, and elevated design from its previously subordinate status to become the maxim of '80s consumerism. Pretty soon, style had become a commodity, a new word for selling old products, as THE RETAIL REVOLUTION reinvented high street shopping and wrapping things up became the preoccupation of the decade. That wasn't a new pen you were buying – that was a new *style*, and anybody could buy it. In a hot phase of consumerism, the function of products became replaced, as a selling point, by the *form* – in other words, you buy things not because of what they do, but because of what they say about you.

Some people, of course, went right over the top. They hired psychologists and went in for the whole LIFESTYLE bit – which LAGER would the fashion-conscious, one foreign holiday a year boy or girl buy, and so on. But style has made its mark throughout the whole of society – even pensioners are more likely to buy colour-coded packets of tea bags these days – as the design of products has become all-important. What started as a desire to dress up has become an industry that has dressed up every conceivable shop window, so much so that it now all looks the same. The question is, has the design fetish turned us into a nation of passive consumers or have the aesthetics of design increased our expectations? Do we really care what we buy anymore so long as it looks *stylish*?

Street Hockey The early '80s saw roller disco – ICE HOCKEY boots plus skateboard wheels and polished wooden rinks – mutate into Street Hockey, a physically charged game that until late '82 had no rules or leagues, but was strictly street. The British Street Hockey Association was formed and by '89 organised national competitions for some 350 teams in four different age groups. Tennents Super began sponsoring the annual national championships in '87 and CHANNEL 4 covered them in their minority sports slot. Though the games are now played indoors, the top two teams' roots lie firmly in the great urban outdoors: Battersea Street Warriors and Street Force Titans of Camden. Is the Camden success due in any way to the heavily subscribed roller disco nights at the Electric Ballroom in the early '80s? And is the emergence of the Warrington team perhaps because roller disco is still popular in that town? *See Skating*

Street Soul The sound of the inner city bedroom as distilled through the various musical influences of American, VANDROSS-style soft soul, LOVER'S ROCK and low-tech hip hop. Although the first genuine street soul was produced by Loose Ends and 52nd Street, it was groups like Deluxe in East London, Smith & Mighty in Bristol and Chapter & The Verse in Manchester who developed this truly British soul sound on low budgets and home recording equipment throughout '87 and '88. Street soul triumphed in '89 as SOUL II SOUL reached number one in the charts with 'Back To Life', and the Americans started to copy British soul for the first time ever.

The Style Council Just as The Jam had become the Slade of the '80s, so Paul Weller stumbled upon the Isley Brothers back catalogue and had a similar identity crisis. The Jam had always been R&B/Motown

driven, but with The Style Council, this was a backwards step to authenticity rather than a headstart to happiness. Stubbornly refusing to write the classic pop that he could once pen over a quick capuccino, The Style Council gradually lost momentum, losing their status as the voice of political pop to the likes of BRAGG and The Blow Monkeys. Bad points about The Style Council? Their dubious affectation for Inter-nationalism in general and their rampant Francophilia in particular. Good points about The Style Council? They gave Weller a chance to show he had a sense of humour (if not a sense of STYLE) and early on they did make some hugely magnificent singles. In '89 though, The Style Council discovered HOUSE MUSIC. It proved a watershed for Paul Weller, letting his fascination for contemporary club trends and CYCLING SHORTS stretch the loyalty of his old mod fans. How many will still be there in the '90s remains to be seen.

Summer Of Love In '67 Bob Dylan had gone electric, The Beatles released 'Sgt Pepper', The Blarney Club in Tottenham Ct Rd was full of dopeheads listening to Pink Floyd, and San Francisco was the centre of the universe. That was the first Summer Of Love, a drug-induced haze of anti-Vietnam demos, love-ins and radicalism. The second Summer Of Love in '88, symptomatic of its age, was less complicated – it was pure hedonism. Undoubtedly fuelled by ECSTASY, thousands of perspiring bodies danced under one roof

screaming their heads off. Although paisley patterns, face-painting and peace symbols were worn with benign smiles, they were never more than the trappings of a past era – everybody was sure that it was the second Summer Of Love, but weren't quite sure why. By '89, with the growth of warehouse parties like SUNRISE, clubbers were even staging their own love-ins; flopping cross-legged in fields as dawn broke, asking each other how they were going to get home. Come 1990, they'll probably still be there. See New Age Travellers, The Shoom and Zippies

Sumo Wrestling The ancient Japanese art of two fat men pushing each other out of a circle, Sumo was first screened on British TV by CHANNEL 4 in '88 in an effort to give

Stockings In '84, socks were available in a previously unheard-of range of shapes, sizes and colours, and it was only a matter of time before the same happened to stockings. Early designer versions from BODYMAP and VIVIENNE WESTWOOD incorporated a range of bold prints, and in '86, the trend for rolled-down stockings started. The sock industry responded with over-the-knee socks and Liverpool designers Creative Stable made their name from hand-painting and printing on old original nylons. Garters were usually ineffective for securing the stocking just above the knee, so elastic was often tied tightly round the leg; fortunately however, rolled-down stockings gave way to LYCRA leggings nine months later, and a national epidemic of varicose veins was avoided.

L to R: i-D straight up Sarah '83. Jay Strongman. Sweet Charity circa '84 **See Kensington Market.** *Stockings (photo: Moira Bogue, styling: Caryn Franklin.) Suit '87 (photo: Terry Jones).*

exposure to minority sports from around the world, and became an instant hit. Commentator, Dr Lyall Watson, was successful in his efforts to contextualise the spectacle, which was probably just as well as bouts rarely lasted very long. For a season, advertisers picked up on the sport, using it in campaigns for *Soho News* (which lasted about as long as one of the bouts), Ferguson TVs, washing powder and, surprise, surprise, Japanese Airlines.

The Sunbed Kids The growing popularity of cheap Continental package holidays meant that the fashion for bright holiday outfits emerged as one of the main trends on all levels of clothes design in the

'80s. 18-30 sun-seekers bought lots of white dresses and shirts, beach shorts, surf BAGGIES and dayglo T-SHIRTS. Fine for two weeks in a Spanish resort but what do you do with these outfits when you get home? The answer is that the tan has cost money to acquire and is therefore a status symbol and must be displayed. So as a way to keep the tan was essential, sunbed parlours suddenly found a new lease of life. This had a big impact on nightlife dress codes. Even in cold northern towns when the skies were heavy with grey clouds and rain The Sunbed Kids ignored the elements and carried on living out their Bounty Bar ad fantasy. With temperatures adding goose pimples, girls started to expose more areas of flesh – flashing midriffs and letting a T-shirt top strap hang down over one shoulder. The

boys joined in the fun by wandering around in shorts. Even men's BOXER SHORTS became acceptable to wear without jeans, and golden, deep fried limbs made an exotic cocktail in an otherwise dreary landscape. Tacky essential beverages include CRAP DRINKS like Malibu and Lilt. *See Casuals, Eurostyle and Dressing Down*

Sunday Sport A telephone sex directory with a guaranteed double figure nipple count, the *Sunday Sport*, launched in '86, began to make the news when it started to make its news up. Taking British 'Carry On' culture into *National Enquirer* territory, it created a weekly carnival of gross bodies, SF camp ('Satellite Takes Picture Of Heaven!'), and lunatic revelations ('Adolf Hitler Was A Woman!'). Having nothing to do with the real world it caught the tone of the times, its circulation rising enough to allow it to bust out into two weekday editions, but unfortunately there didn't seem to be enough vampires in Putney to go round. Now it seems just like any other nudespaper.

Sunrise Parties If ACID HOUSE in '88 was synonymous (rightly or wrongly) with THE SHOOM club, the ongoing series of Sunrise warehouse parties, more than anything else, symbolised the state of the scene in '89. Although the first Sunrise parties in '88 amassed 4,000 people, it wasn't until '89 that Sunrise broke the 5,000 barrier and became the biggest party organisers in Britain. ▶

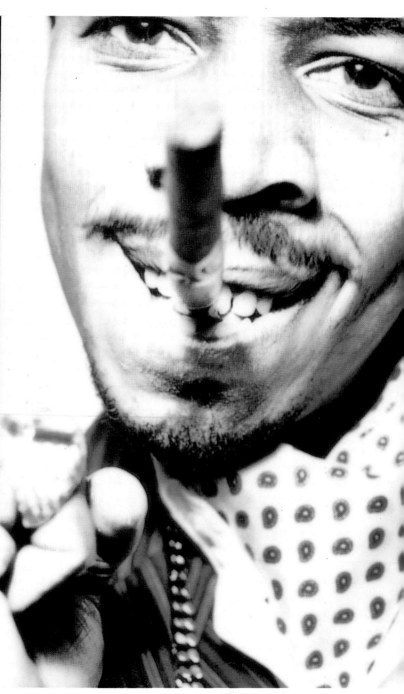

Stylists In the '70s, fashion images in magazines were created by fashion editors, there was no such thing as a stylist. Except for a handful of editors like Grace Coddington at *Vogue* there were very few who created 'images' – most worked on the basic matching of outfits – and the fact that MUSIC VIDEOS didn't exist and ADVERTISING was not yet an option, meant that there were no other mediums for creating fashion images. It was the STYLE magazines who created stylists, people like Caroline Baker, Ray Petri (BUFFALO), Simon Foxton, Mitzi Lorenz and Amanda Grieve, who created new looks and styles of dressing in the pages of *i-D*, *THE FACE* and *BLITZ*, and spawned a thousand imitators. Undoubtedly one of the professions of the '80s.

L to R: Styling by Simon Foxton in i-D no. 49 '87 (photo: Nick Knight). Styling by Caroline Baker in i-D no. 34 '86 (photo: Robert Erdmann).

◄ With their battalions of runners with Vodaphones, other warehouse outfits like Energy and Back To The Future competed to equal Sunrise's sheer numbers, and it became inevitable that the tabloid media would pick up on the trend. After Sunrise's 10,000-strong 'Midsummer Night's Dream' party in an aircraft hanger in Berkshire in June '89, they did. 'Spaced Out!' screamed *The Sun*, as the *Daily Mail* insisted that warehouses were mere fronts for drug dealing, and the London *Evening Standard* tried to recreate the anti-acid hysteria of autumn '88. The police responded in kind, busting every warehouse in sight, but the only result was that more people than ever wanted to attend these

events. *See Nightclubbing*

Superbikes In '69 Honda turned the motorbike industry on its head with the introduction of the CB750. With four cylinders, disc brakes, electric start and a top speed of 125 mph, it became the blueprint for other bikes throughout the decade. The acceleration game has now become a deadly one with bikes looking like they have just burnt out of Mega City One with Judge Dredd fighting hard to keep up. State of the art in '89 was the Yamaha FZR 1000 with a radical five valve per cylinder engine, a power valve in the exhaust and an incredible 165 mph top speed. Not a bike for Sunday drivers.

Swingbeat The uptempo, 'swinging' contemporary soul sound developed by producers Teddy Riley and

LA & Babyface in '88. It enlivened the traditional soul vocal with hip hop rhythms, was originally marketed by a hesitant MCA Records as the 'Sunset Sound', but gradually acquired the street name swingbeat. *See Ravers*

Swinton, Tilda Of the actresses and comediennes streaming out of Oxbridge onto television screens and film sets Tilda Swinton has proved the most radically unpredictable. Eluding the neat and tidy packaging of BBC light entertainment and the routine casting calls of the RSC and National, she has ducked the mainstream for a life with the avant-garde vanguard. Her work with DEREK JARMAN ('Caravaggio', 'The Last Of England', 'Aria' and 'The War Requiem') has proved an inspiring collaboration. The next Vanessa Redgrave? Probably better.

Sydney Sydney has the largest gay community in the world and from the end of '88 it also hosted the largest warehouse parties in the world. Growing out of an accelerating club scene ignited by ACID HOUSE, come New Year's Eve '88, 20,000 people had gathered for a 'Dance Party', and by the middle of '89 there was one virtually every week. Definitely a contender for the party capital of the '90s.

Synchronised Swimming The bizarre ritual of synchronised swimming was given the international seal of approval at the '84 Los Angeles Olympic Games when its debut as a medal event sent the hard-won credibility of women's sports momentarily right down the plug-hole. Performers executed watery choreography in a nose plug, rictus grin and make-up like the glaze on a fruit flan. Oh dear. Should, but won't, sink without trace.

L to R: Styling by Mitzi Lorenz in i-D no. 21 '84 (photo: Roger Charity).
Styling by Amanda Grieve in i-D no. 34 (photo: Robert Erdmann).
Corinne Drewery from Swing Out Sister.

ing strategy – Swatch seem to think the only way is up (market).

S'Xpress Mark Moore, DJ at THE MUD CLUB amongst others, always had an eclectic taste in records. Learning his skills from early Mud DJ Tasty Tim, he never thought twice about playing The Sweet or Sylvester next to hip hop and it was two years before he discovered a slip mat. So when he decided to make a record, it was always going to be different. 'Theme From S'Xpress' released on Rhythm King (the most prolific of the new independent UK dance labels) married '70s disco with house and went to number one. The album 'Original Soundtrack' (co-produced with Mark McGuire), explored the possibilities of blurring musical categories even further. After remixing for PRINCE and Philip Glass, the '90s should prove a veritable playground for the DJ with the most colourful wardrobe in London.

T

Taboo Taboo was both revolutionary and a throwback to the mixed gay hedonism of Billy's, BLITZ and CHA CHA'S. In place of ELECTRO-pop and the original club queens, it had DJ Jeffrey Hinton's wildly eclectic mix of trash disco and dancefloor faves (MADONNA meets Mozart) and the uninhibited energies of LEIGH BOWERY, who hosted the club with Tony Gordon. For two months only a handful of their fashionable friends came, then it suddenly became monstrously popular. Everyone who wasn't GEORGE MICHAEL claimed to be a designer, a photographer or a Japanese TV crew, while at least half the club looked to be totally off their collective face on ECSTASY (which partly explains the bizarre sex scenes in the toilets). Fashion victims flocked to join the daunting poser's parade and the dancefloor maelstrom, and its door policy was legendary: the story of the late Mark Golding holding a hand mirror up to a hapless face in the massive queue and asking, "Would you let yourself in?" wasn't apocryphal, it was pure Taboo. You loved or loathed it but you could never deny its energy. Like all the best clubs, it died in its prime and its loss led to a stream of like-minded one-nighters (Anarchy, Sacrosanct, Ascension. Daisy Chain).

Talking

Heads

Talking Heads, or rather David Byrne, symbolised the '80s drift away from skinny white boy problem pop to textures more exotic. 1980's 'Remain In Light' LP saw them assimilating African rhythms, and thereafter Byrne acquired a reputation as a scavenging traveller intent on picking up on anything worthwhile outside the FM waveband. A genuine auteur, whatever he picked up on was given his signature by way of an immense songwriting ability. The mid-'80s saw him involved with regional America (captured evocatively in the 'True Stories' movie) and the end of the decade found him in Paris, the capital of cultural crossroads, recording with various world musicians and producing genuine hybrids rather than cloying reverential WORLD MUSIC works. With his forays into film making and more avant garde projects, Byrne is Rock's Renaissance Man, a performer for both the ART house and the mainstream.

to R Trojan, early Taboo revellers. The Taboo Family including Leigh Bowery, Rachel Auburn, Trojan and Mark Golding (photo: Nick Knight). Talking Heads.

Tackhead Sonic terrorist group led by ace producer Adrian Sherwood who combined dub reggae techniques with hip hop beats and avant-garde cut-up and SAMPLING skills. Not just a mixing desk project, Tackhead incorporated ex-Sugarhill Gang musicians Keith LeBlanc, Doug Wimbish and Skip MacDonald into a live outfit capable of bone-crushing rhythmic assaults. Sherwood and LeBlanc were also responsible for two political music projects, the Malcolm X 'No Sell Out' single and 'Strike' by The Enemy Within, a fund-raising record for striking miners in '85, featuring a taped Arthur Scargill on lead vocals.

L to R Talking Heads. Tank Girl. Nicholas Parsons **See Trendy Telly**. Tartan i-D straight ups '82/'83. Theresa i-D straight up '82. Tim i-D straight up '81.

Tank Girl Created by Jamie Hewlett and serialised in *DEADLINE*, Tank Girl is the postmodern girl for the '90s. A comic character with an armoury of tanks, bazookas and foul language, she is a shero who has a solution for every eventuality. Modern mythology in the making.

Tapas Bars Tapas bars are basically places where self-obsessed travellers go to imagine they are Spanish peasants. Over priced, over rated and over here, they sell small plates of food to disguise the fact that the wine is ten times dearer than an off-licence and are very handy if you want to talk about the part you would have played in the siege of Guernica.

Tartan A fabric rich in cultural associations, loved by the fashion world and American tourists alike. VIVIENNE WESTWOOD was the first designer to create a tartan bondage suit in '79; the NEW ROMANTICS and Spandau Ballet adopted the KILT, and in '84, both CROLLA and PAUL SMITH designed tartan trousers for

Trendy Telly

Trendy telly was a cynical term coined by the tedious STYLE journalist Stuart Cosgrove when he ridiculed youth programming on Ludovic Kennedy's 'Did You See?' The term passed into everyday usage when programmes with drunken camera angles, overactive presenters and irritating graphics became the norm. Trendy telly programmes are virtually indistinguishable from the adverts that interrupt them, leading the programme makers to believe they are exponents of daring POSTMODERNISM and the viewers to switch off in ever increasing numbers. See *Network 7* and *The Tube*

Thatcher, Margaret

Margaret' to patrician Tory peers, 'Thatcher' to right-on radicals and 'Muggie' to the tabloid press, the longest serving PM since God knows when is almost a fact of nature to the rest of us Radical Conservative, elective dictator, populist sectarian, the Original Housewife Superstar embodied the contradictions of the decade and resolved them into something as unpredictable and unavoidable as the weather. For someone who's meant to have transformed us into a nation of go-getters, it's ironic that her longevity depends entirely on the traditional British qualities of fatalism, masochism and perverse humour. Her obsolescence would be her greatest success.

men. In autumn '87, VIVIENNE WESTWOOD, MARTINE SITBON and JEAN PAUL GAULTIER brought tartan back to the catwalk, but it was Glasgow-born PAM HOGG who most successfully mixed her own cultural heritage with stretch lurex and fake fur.

emblems. In '87 John Richmond designed a collection that included jackets and shirts with tattoo motifs, and VIVIENNE WESTWOOD used fake ones in her 'Britain Goes Pagan' collection. Transfer tattoos even enjoyed a brief popularity, with Tattoos To Go producing the most successful range. But "signing up for the long haul" as American artist Ed Hardy describes it, was definitely something more people were willing to do. NB. So far nobody has caught AIDS from a tatooist's needle, but choose one that has a Government Health Certificate.

Terry, Todd The producer of '88, a shy, Brooklyn-born 21 year old whose single-minded, abrasive dance

Tattoos

Became a chic accessory in the early '80s when Paula Yates had her upper arm coloured by respected UK tattoo artist Dennis Cockell. Punks and GOTHS continued to have spiders webs, bats and butterflies scratched over their faces throughout the decade, but more imaginative work that you wouldn't feel ashamed of when you sobered up was being undertaken by a growing number of UK practitioners, notably Mr Sebastian, Lal Hardy, Mickey Sharpez and George Bone. Sharpez gained a reputation as the finest Celtic armband artist and had his work featured in the UK magazine *Body Art*, which turned thousands of people onto the ART. FASHION DESIGNERS started appropriating tattoos in '85 when BERNSTOCK SPEIRS presented their first collection entitled 'Yobbos' using tattoo

statements like 'Can You Party?' by Royal House, 'A Day In The Life' by Black Riot and 'Bango' by the Todd Terry Project displayed a talent for creative SAMPLING and adrenalin-boosting rhythms which fired ACID HOUSE dancefloors throughout the SUMMER OF LOVE.

Test Department

Making music and political statements about the dignity of labour out of the detritus of industrial society, Test Department dragged their oil drums around London's subterranean dens to create an almighty din in the early '80s. During THE MINERS' STRIKE they struck up on apocalyptic unholy alliance, gigging with a Welsh Male Voice choir. Since then they've gone all arty on us, working on more theatrical pieces with writer JONATHON MOORE.

JAMIE HEWLETT

The The If you are ever feeling sorry for yourself, mortgage getting you down, spots on your chin, spare a thought for Matt Johnson As one man pop martyr of the '80s, The The, here was a man with the problems of the world on such young shoulders Since his debut album 'Burning Blue Soul' at the beginning of the decade Johnson has inflicted his tortured artistry on the world with mixed results The subsequent albums, 'Infected' and 'Mind Bomb', suggested that his source work was the *Guardian* front page - you name a global catastrophe, Matt'll write a song about it. Not the most prolific of writers, Armageddon is probably more imminent than his next album

Techno Detroit's experimentalist Techno sound claimed influence from European synthesizer outfits like KRAFTWERK, combining computer beats and raw electronics into a sub-genre of HOUSE MUSIC which, at its best on records like Rhythim Is Rhythim's 'Strings Of Life' and 'Nude Photo' of '87, exuded a mixture of adrenalin, introspection and raw sex.

Tent City The tent cities of '85 were a protest against government rules that seemed designed to create a new class of vagrants in Britain. Whitehall had decreed that unemployed under-25s living in bed and breakfast accomodation would have their benefits cut unless they moved every two, four or eight weeks. The stated intention was to "encourage" 180,000 people to find work.

Thousands of people threatened with eviction flocked to bedouin protest camps organised by HASSLL (Homeless Against Social Security Legal Limits) at venues such as Newcastle city centre or Clapham Common in London. By '88 the defiant tent cities had become defeated cardboard encampments. Cardboard cities were most common in London where, at night, the walkways of the South Bank and the arches beneath the Embankment's bridges took on the appearance of squalid refugee camps. A November '88 survey in a 1.75 square mile patch of London's West End counted 2,073 people 'skippering' (sleeping rough), in night hostels, in bed and breakfast hotels or involuntarily

spending the night in hospital beds and POLICE cells.

As '89, began the official number of homeless people in Britain was 370,000, practically double the figure when Mrs THATCHER came to power in '79. But official statistics excluded many of the 'hidden homeless', including single people, and local authorities had spent the late '80s redefining the concept of homelessness – in London, Irish and Bengali families found themselves under threat of deportation because they were judged to have made themselves homeless by leaving their native countries. The charity, Shelter, estimated the real number of homeless to be one million. New social security regulations, introduced in April '88, exarcerbated the problem – urgent needs payments were abolished and supplementary benefit was replaced by income support, a payment made two weeks in arrears. Homeless people simply did not have the money to book into lodgings or to buy food, and many swallowed their pride to beg on the streets.

In the first two months of the new benefit rules, Centrepoint in SOHO, recorded a 35% increase in the number of young people seeking admission to its night shelter. They had come to the capital from all over Britain; 99% had less than £10 in their pockets, and 18% had been approached to become involved in prostitution. The problem would be compounded by the end of the decade. In '89 no new council housing was built in Nottingham, Liverpool, Bradford, Plymouth, Portsmouth, Southampton and the London boroughs of Merton, Brent, Enfield, Wandsworth and Westminster, and the idea of public housing had become as redundant as the GLC.

Tech Noir Flipside to the almost mythical urban chic of film noir 'updates' like 'Body Heat' and 'The Postman Always Rings Twice', was the hard, slangy, contemporary urban look of the science fiction restyling of the genre Tech Noir. For movies like 'Escape From New York', 'The Terminator', and 'Trancers', '40s hardboiled romanticism became '80s survivalist nihilism as all the imagery of the contracted postmodern city burst thrillingly onto the screen. Brand names, computers, supermarket bag ladies, mutant punks, 9mm Uzis, GRAFFITI, serial killers, fast food joints, drugs, paramilitary cops – the degraded social refuse of everything from skid row to the shopping mall got thrown into the visual mix. The plots may have been all time travel and killer robots but the mean streets background was pressingly real.

L to R Ann Scott's Tattoos (photo: Nick Knight, styling: Simon Foxton). The The. Gary The Tattooist. Richard Torry (photo: Dan Leopard). Anne Smith.

Textile Designers Once the anonymous hands behind printed clothes, in the '80s textile designers almost achieved equal recognition to fashion designers. Tie-dye was one of the cheapest ways to create textured design on fabric and in the summer of '81, suddenly the market stalls of KENSINGTON MARKET were flooded, particularly after WESTWOOD endorsed the hippy revival with her 'Pirates' collection. An epidemic of tie-dye and African inspired fabric prints popularised textile design, and shops like New Masters, DEMOB and Salon Su Juris sold clothes made from heavily bleached, rough fabrics and encouraged young textile design talent. Throughout the following two seasons print designers like Anne Smith and English Eccentrics continued this trend on the catwalks with more sophisticated print techniques, and in '82 Elaine Oxford sold her African print collection to DEMOB.

VIVIENNE WESTWOOD designed her 'Savages' collection with a bold geometric print and SUE CLOWES sold her Hebrew inspired print to a shop called The Foundry where manager George O'Dowd was busy securing a deal with a man from Virgin Records. BOY GEORGE eventually had a hit with 'White Boy' wearing SUE CLOWES' textile designs, and textile design businesses flourished during '82/'83, including La Palette (Corinne Drewery of Swing Out Sister's former company along with partner Mo), Anne Smith for Additti and Steve Wright. Eventually, by '84 the textile designer had gained

L to R Trouble Funk **See Go Go**. Tigi and Sandra i-D straight ups '81. Tanita Tikaram (photo: Nigel Law).

equal recognition with fashion designers, as people like BodyMap used the prints of Hilde Smith as an intrinsically linked part of their collections.

Thai Restaurants An aromatic blend of Indian and Chinese food, Thai can blow your mind but beware that it doesn't blow your head off. The perennial satay is the pork ball of Thai but unavoidable are the curries with a combustible thermonuclear device lurking somewhere within the second mouthful. At the last count there were more than 50 eateries like this in London (a handful in 1980), which are now being challenged for exotic supremacy by Vietnamese cuisine for a nation's jaded palettes and jangling pockets.

Thailand Holiday and honeymoon hotspot, the Thai peninsula rivalled Turkey for trendy travellers' top vote throughout the decade, but what were they looking for – Spalding Gray's stoned reveries on a beach at Phuket or the bogus bargains of rip-off Rolex and Polo marques down the market? Many ventured no further than the steamy sideshows of Bangkok's thriving bar-room bordellos, bringing the grim spectre of AIDS into this nation of smiling people. Rival to Manila for its trade in underage services, now even the lustre of Bangkok is fading as intrepid backpackers take their Visa(card)s to the offshore islands of the Phillipines in search of that unspoiled scenery, spoiling it as they go.

Theme Parks Yet another American invention of the '50s that Britain bought into in the '80s – from the £170 million redevelopment of Battersea Power Station to the £200 million Wonderworld to be built in Corby on the site of an old steel plant. Each symbolises the way the service sector is replacing manufacturing, the way that, unable to come up with the real goods, we now trade in images instead. French theorist JEAN BAUDRILLARD has suggested that a theme park's

obvious hyperreality is there to disguise the hyperreality of its surrounding environment. With the theme-ing of Britain's cities, it's easy to agree. Add themed pubs, clubs, restaurants, malls, housing estates, and ARCHITECTURE to the new reconstruction of a vanishing industrial past, and you get a glimpse of one side of '80s Britain – Theme Park UK, a Fantasy Island which has forgotten the future in favour of an endless repackaging tour of the past.

Thirtysomething *See Yuppies*

Thompson, Daley British decathlete whose sense of humour has become almost as noteable as his athletic skill. Winner of two gold

TROUBLE FUNK

medals in consecutive Olympics, he has consistently offended establishment propriety and provided a source of amusement for sports commentators everywhere. In the '84 Olympics he wore a T-shirt emblazoned with 'Is The World's Second Greatest Athlete Gay?' (referring to CARL LEWIS), and whistled during the national anthem. However, in the '88 Finals in Seoul, Thompson failed to amuse anybody, ending up a long way behind the medals and finally severing his relationship with the British sporting public. One of the great sportsmen of the decade and the first UK sporting superstar since Henry Cooper to realise it. In years to come Thompson's face will probably be remembered more for his Lucozade ads than his achievements.

Tikaram, Tanita Musically

Telephone Chat Lines Telephone chat lines created anxiety in Britain's households when it became apparent that the nation's children were running up two grand phone-bills talking to prostitutes about their leather underwear. British Telecom tried to occupy the moral high ground by discontinuing some of the sleaziest chat-lines but they still let Russell Grant ramble on about the moon in uranus.

Teleshopping The SF dream of a high-tech housebound life came closer when American shopping channels turned TV screens into shop windows. If, as some claim, shopping is an ART form, then teleshopping is an avant-garde conceptual performance. See it, buy it, forget it, and when that must-have combined nail clipper and sellotape dispenser arrives two weeks later, quickly stash it in a back room with all the other unopened purchases and get back to the shopping channel to make sure you don't miss a bargain.

somewhere between Joni Mitchell and Leonard Cohen, Tanita Tikaram is everything a teenager shouldn't be. Versed in Shakespeare, morose and obsessed with the past, she is every YUPPIE's fantasy – an intelligent female who can quote Sylvia Plath and appreciate the finer aesthetics of CD sound. Never-smiling and now 20 years old, her debut album 'Ancient Heart' sold two million copies in Europe in '89, and she looks poised to become as big as her '60s mentors. Whether you like it or not, this is the new face of teenage Britain.

Time Out A child of the '60s, *Time Out*'s progress in the '80s is a reflection of the changing aspirations

of its staff. The strike in '81 over pay parity was a conflict between middle class hippies trying to come to terms with the '80s and produced two magazines: one which wanted to be a success (*Time Out*) and one which wanted to hold on to 15 year old principles (*CITY LIMITS*). Now a mini independent publishing empire, co-owning *i-D* and *Paris Passion*, and publishing *20/20*, filofax guides, student guides, visitors guides, sports, services, film and shopping guides; *Time Out* is a success story that is still growing up.

Tin-Tin Although Tintin has been one of the world's most popular cartoon characters since his creation by Georges Remi back in 1929, it's only really been in the '80s that the boy detective has made his mark on

Trevor and Marculus i-D straight ups '82. Troy i-D straight up '81. the Titanic crew. Tracy i-D straight up '81.

British 'youth culture'. His famous tufty haircut was adopted by ABC (briefly), trendy ROCKABILLIES and a clutch bag of male models, and Tintin T-SHIRTS and badges were worn by all age groups from six to 60. His growing appeal in this country is reflected by the success of the Tintin shop in Covent Garden which stocks nothing but Tintin-related products from books to duvet covers, and if The Thompson Twins are remembered for nothing else, it will be for their namesakes.

The Titanic *See The Language Lab*

Torry, Richard Most notable for his waxed Daliesque moustache,

Richard also created some of the most innovative menswear, incorporating origami techniques in the cut. He left Middlesex Poly in '81, started designing his own collections in '82, and by '85 he had become adopted by the Japanese who licensed a series of eight collections over the following two years. This collaboration continues to this day under the banner of Richard Torry at Studio V. *See Fashion Designers*

Tottenham Hotspur FC If MARGARET THATCHER was a FOOTBALL fan she'd surely support SPURS. A club with shares on the open market, plush sponsors lounges and a choice of 76 executive boxes from which to view the most expensively assembled team outside Glasgow, Tottenham are one of Europe's

Transvision Vamp The self-appointed saviour of rock-'n'roll, Wendy James is a sex kitten with a school-bag of secondhand ideas and a bottle of bleach. From 'Revolution Baby', 'Pop Art' to 'ANDY WARHOL's Dead' it was obvious that Wendy wished the decade had been the '70s she never had, and proceeded to make herself one of the

most unpopular women in pop. Critical of anybody who didn't like her, she concentrated on becoming the female Marc Bolan and waited for the '80s to end. In '89, the second LP 'Velveteen' went straight in at number one and little WANNABEE Wendys packed out every gig. A contender for the MADONNA of the '90s.

richest clubs. Whereas THFC did not have a very profitable '80s, THPLC showed how you could still win. A mere 30% of THPLC's income was derived from footballing activities. Lucrative subsidiaries included: Hummel sportswear, a lingerie factory, publishing company, travel and ticket agency, Synchro Systems Ltd, and the rights to market England souvenirs. By the end of the '80s Spurs had a sounder financial base than possibly LIVERPOOL. Kenneth Burkinshaw said it all when he resigned as manager in '84: "There used to be a football club over there."

The Trash Aesthetic When the objects which fall off the production line end up in the gallery

or the archive they get a new price tag – they're industry classics, they're even ART. When they end up in the skip or on the shelf then they become part of the collective unconsciousness – they're trash. The same object can be trash or it can be a cult item, but it can't be both at the same time. It flips from one status to another (eg. Russ Meyer's porn films). Which means that the 'trash aesthetic' is a contradiction in terms. As soon as trash is aestheticized rather than critically transformed then it's no longer trash. It's kitsch. What was a tacky relic becomes a precious souvenir. Watching Captain Scarlet first time round is trash: seeing it revived on 'NIGHT NETWORK' is kitsch. Trash is always spontaneous, superficial, disposable. Kitsch is nostalgic, ironic, laboured. Trash can yield treasure (eg. Anne Delaney's

PHONECARD skirts and crisp bag tops). Kitsch yields only the kiss of death (eg. Jeff Koon's porcelain figurines of cartoon characters). Trash: The Real Roxanne's 'Bang Zoom, Let's Go Go', Troma's 'The Toxic Avenger', Transformers. Kitsch: TRANSVISION VAMP's 'Revolution Baby', JOHN WATER's Polyester, PEE WEE HERMAN's 'Playhouse'.

The Triads At the end of '88 the British media discovered The Triads, the Honk Kong equivalent to The Mafia, and something that the British Chinese community had been living with for years. Even though a House Of Commons committee maintained that there was no such thing as The Triads in Britain in '85, the police knew different and have been trying to build up a rapport with the Chinese community for the last few years. However, the frightening hold that the secret societies have over the community is compounded by a distrust that the Chinese have for the UK POLICE and language barriers. The fact that The Triads' reach stretches to law enforcement agencies (a former Hong Kong POLICE officer was jailed for 11 years in Glasgow for his part in a Triad attack), the shortage of interpreters prepared to speak in court, and the seemingly impregnable wall of silence of Britain's Chinatowns (of which the fastest growing is Manchester's, not London's), adds to an unsavoury scenario that will undoubtedly escalate in the run up to 1997, when Hong Kong is handed back to China. The movie 'Sour Sweet' based on TIMOTHY MO's book provided some insight into what may happen next – The Triads have not dealt heavily in HEROIN since the '70s.

The Trip The club that introduced ACID HOUSE to the masses. Opening in May '88 at The Astoria, the phenomenal success of Nicky Holloway's club took everybody by surprise, including Nicky. The queues started at 7pm, the club often shut its doors by 11pm, and after 3am Charing Cross Rd was filled with clubbers screaming 'aceeed!' who would halt the traffic and continue partying in a car park across the road. The police looked on in bewildered amusement, car-drivers gave up and joined in, and 1,200 clubbers swore

The Tube The 'Tube' is traditionally touted as the last great pop programme. Somehow its blend of live music, filmed reports and professional amateurism managed to package pop in ways that were acceptable to both the artists and the audience. It ended in disarray soon after presenter Jools Holland made his "groovy fuckers" faux pas on national television.

York where he learned to box under the watchful eye of his surrogate father Cus Damato. Speaking with a painfully shy lisp and built like The Commodores' 'Brick House', he became the undisputed champion of the world and the major boxer of the hip hop era. Broken homes, broken marriages, broken promises and broken noses litter his life, but Tyson is the undisputed king.

2000 AD The science fiction weekly which, despite an occasional tendency to slip into HEAVY METAL bombast, raised the reputation of the British comics industry to new heights in the '80s with a series of fast, violent, trashy strips. John Wagner's *Judge Dredd* was the big

Trent D'Arby, Terence At the beginning of '87, British pop pundits became obsessed with one man Terence Trent D'Arby, a name that could have been fabricated for fame (in fact the only COSMETIC SURGERY was the addition of the apostrophe! and with a biography that could have been written by a scriptwriter. It mattered not that revelations later suggested that his past history was just that – because Terence had achieved what he set out to do; he'd become a star. First interviewed in *i-D* he was acclaimed by all and sundry, and held everybody's attention with a series of outrageous claims ("I'm a genius") and some brilliant live performances. Although his tendency to hyperbole produced the desired effect (constant media interest) he never had a number one. After recently relaunching his career after a year's sabbatical, one thing has become obvious – he has learned to keep his mouth shut. Perhaps the most bewitching performer (live or otherwise) this decade.

that it was the best club they'd ever been to. Along with SPECTRUM, The Trip was the club that generated the euphoria for the SUMMER OF LOVE, but as tabloid hysteria whipped itself into a frenzy at the end of '88 the club changed its name to Made On Earth, and finally Sin. Although traffic jams no longer occur, Sin still manages to live up to its name. The queues are murder.

Trivial Pursuits Trivial Pursuits was a board-game which enjoyed a brief wave of popularity in the mid-'80s. Nobody knew why but they all knew who invented penicillin.

Tyson, Mike Mike Tyson could have fallen from the script of 'On The Waterfront'. A juvenile delinquent obsessed with pigeons, he was sent to a remand home in up-state New

Announcing his suspension to a waiting press Jools said, "I've been carpeted, well and truly axministered." It was a fitting requiem for rock's Friday journey into the unknown, the well-known and the instantly forgettable. *See Trendy Telly, Night Network and Network 7*

selling point. A future city fantasy of slum crime and summary justice, it was the template for most of the other lonesome hero stories in the comic like *Rogue Trooper*, *Strontium Dog* and *Robohunter* But the best strips were those, like ALAN MOORE's feminist space opera *Halo Jones* or Grant Morrison's punk superhero pastich *Zenith*, which tempered the clanking machinery of the action serial with a spot of irony. *2000 AD* has nurtured the careers of numerous British writers and artists and in '88 created its most ambitious spin-off. The first UK popular comic to tackle politics head-on, *Crisis* could prove to be the most important British comic contribution to the '90s.

L to R Outside The Trip '88 (photo: Dave Swindells). The Specials ('Gangsters' video '81) **See 2 Tone**. *Terence Trent D'Arby (photo: Marc Lebon). Anne Delaney's graduation collection '88 (photo: Nigel Law)* **See The Trash Aesthetic.**

2-Tone In June '81, 'Ghost Town' by The Specials was released, a single which reached number one in the charts, confirming that the 2-Tone label was far more important than just a 'SKA revival' outfit. 2-Tone records were often political, sometimes bitter and almost always fun. Using a characteristic updated SKA rhythm, the first 2-Tone release was The Special AKA's 'Gangsters' in July '79, and although that was the label's peak year, with releases by Madness and The Selecter, 2-Tone went on to discover The Beat (two members of whom later founded the Fine Young Cannibals) and issue the political pop classic, the Special AKA's 'Free Nelson Mandela' in '84. Madness was the longest surviving 2-Tone group, taking their ironic melodies into the late '80s with consummate success, while 2-Tone figurehead and Specials organist, the toothless Jerry Dammers, went on to help found ARTISTS AGAINST APARTHEID.

T-Shirts

In the '80s, the T-shirt was finally exploited to its fullest potential and became the most universal fashion garment of the decade. Every product under the sun was sold on it, every joke or innuendo plastered on it, and everyone from MADONNA, Virgin Mary to SMILEY stared from it. By '88 the original fitted shape got larger and larger as the demands of ACID HOUSE and clubs in general made it the only practical shape (cooler and less restricting), and by the beginning of '89 the long-sleeved T-shirt had taken over, with artists like Rob Shepard and Wigan realising that if you could wear an ADVERTISING slogan on your chest you could certainly wear ART

See Dressing Down

L to R Katharine Hamnett's 'Worldwide Nuclear Ban Now' T-shirt '84 (photo: Nick Knight).
A selection of T-shirts from Safe Sex, Designer, Religion to Surf/Skatewear (photos: Claire Pollock, Richard Faulk and John Dawson).

Uninterrupted Test Match Cricket In August '89 the uninterrupted delivery of ball-by-ball cricket commentary from Brian Johnston, Henry Blofeld, Bill Frindall, Fred Trueman, et al on Radio 3, finally became a victim of BBC rationalisation. The commentary team, whose predilection for turning the sometimes soporific world of international cricket into free-wheeling, multi-hued, entertainment rivalled the West Indies teams of '78/'88 as ambassadors of the game. In fact, frequently, the finest broadcasts were performed on days when rain had destroyed any prospect of play. Like strawberries without cream, cricket will just never seem the same again. *See Ian Botham*

United Colours Of Benetton In the decade when politicians bought into ADVERTISING, it was perhaps no surprise that ADVERTISING agencies bought into politics, and attempted not just to push product but to promote world peace. Masterminded by the photographer Oliviero Toscani, the United Colours Of Benetton campaign mixed vivid colours, ethnic models and 'no frontiers' styling by Caroline Baker among others, to fashion the ADVERTISING equivalent of LIVE AID's global pop humanism. Whilst it's undoubtedly good for business, this designer detente glosses over a few issues. A utopian image of a world without frontiers, certainly, but it's also a vision of the multinationals' dream of a global market without trade barriers. Recognise the tune? They'd like to teach the world to spend, in perfect harmony.

Unleaded Petrol Originally added to petrol to improve fuel performance, lead is also a brain poison. It's a fact that we've known for some time but it wasn't until the Green Machine moved out of first gear that anybody started to do anything about it. In '88 one in ten petrol stations sold unleaded petrol – by '89 it was one in three. But as motorists congragulated themselves

Underwear As Overwear In '83 VIVIENNE WESTWOOD showed her 'Buffalo' collection, featuring satin bras over hooded tops, and in the following months underwear as overwear became the most logical solution to summer heat. LEIGH BOWERY designed a collection featuring a highly suspect pair of nylon Y-FRONTS and designers including

No? Yes!, Willie Brown and Swanky Modes highlighted satin bras and suspender skirts in their collections. MARKS & SPENCER sold lacy basques by the thousand and MADONNA, never slow to spot a good idea, displayed her own bra straps and never looked back

U C K E R

L to R *Oliviero Toscani self-portrait* **See United Colours Of Benetton.** *Lizzie Tear wearing Underwear As Overwear (photo: Robert Erdmann, styling: Caroline Baker from i-D no.22 Feb '85. Ultravox.*

on being newly enrolled FRIENDS OF THE EARTH, campaigners warned that lead was only one of the harmful elements in petrol. A pedal bike seems the only way to secure an easy conscience in the next decade. Perhaps Norman Tebbit, the CYCLING industry's unpaid spokesman, got it right first time.

U2 The best bands in the world have a habit of getting there when nobody is looking. One minute Bono, The Edge, Adam Clayton and Larry Mullen Jnr were Ireland's BUNNYMEN/JOY DIVISION copyists, the next Bono was taking tiffin with BRUCE SPRINGSTEEN and monopolising LIVE AID. Edge's guitar hero histrionics were always well-restrained but the

passionate powerhouse of Bono had a dubious tendency to drag the band over into rock'n'roll grand guignol. After the Year Zero post-punk thrash of the early albums, 'The Joshua Tree' (which in its first week of release one in four people bought) and 'Rattle And Hum' in particular, found them digging up their beat roots, going 'Graceland', playing with BB King and covering 'Helter Skelter' and 'All Along The Watchtower'. At their worst the apotheosis of pop pomposity, at their best, one of rock's last great apologists.

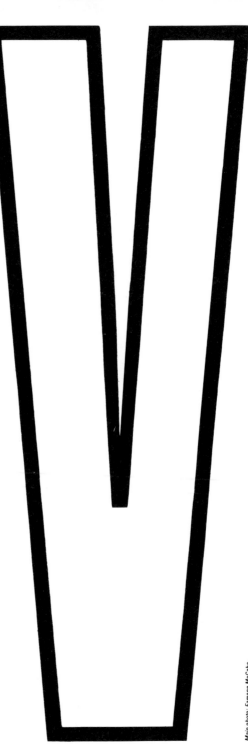

Vintage Leather Leather jackets were primarily cult uniforms for bikers and punks, usually heavily adorned with logos and badges; until '82, when companies like Avirex and Schott attempted to re-create their classic motor-bike and flying jackets. Avirex even used a special hand-distressing process to create a 'lived-in' look. However, interest in orig-inal vintage leathers still far outweighed the de-mand for the new ver-sions, and businesses like AMERICAN CLASSICS, FLIP and the many of the London markets took ad-vantage of that demand to sell originals for prices up £1,000 The demand for authentically-distressed leather was such that at one time it was even rumoured that U2 dem-anded that the new leathers bought for them to wear on tour were to be strapped to the back of motorbikes and driven around until suitably battered. Chevignon's fly-ing jacket proved popular, but ultimately it was only JOHNSONS pale blue dis-tressed leather bombers, which came out in '82, that gained a cult status equal to VINTAGE DENIM.

Main photo: Eamonn McCabe.

Veganism The fundamentalists of the diet world, vegans go one step beyond vegetarians and drop all animal by-products (eg. milk, eggs, honey, leather). Like vegetarianism it's on the increase – founded in 1944 the Vegan Society claims around 4,000 card-carrying members and reckons that, as the '80s closed, there were around half a million vegans in Britain.

Vegetarianism The 'rabbit food' of the '70s has become the 'safe' food of the '80s as more and more people realised that, not only is meat production often cruel and uneconomical, but that with increasing levels of hormones, antibiotics and disease, meat isn't just murder it's potential suicide. 1988 saw a significant 3% of the adult population going meat-free while 12% of 14-25 year olds stuck to the green and leafy stuff. Restaurants and cafes sprung up like alfalfa shoots and even institutions like the House of Commons now offer meat-free options.

The Vermorels Authentic pop ◄ subversives, Fred and Judy Vermorel have been ambiguously celebrated as "the most evil pair in pop". Their mission was to mess up the newly respectable profile of '80s chart pop, demystify its most celebrated icons and undermine its ecumenical pretensions. Their choice of weapon? The devotion of the fans themselves. Because, as they documented in their ground-breaking '85 exposé *Starlust*, pop stars are not the manipulators but the victims of their audience; props for mass hysteria and resentment, and are most threatened when most desired. That's why the Vermorels have been so interested in stretching the form of the pop biog, having wrapped one around GARY NUMAN and hung two round the neck of Kate Bush (she apparently had a nervous breakdown). And they call it puppy love.

Video Nasties During the recession of the early '80s one way to erase the dead time of unemployment was to reanimate your nerve endings via the VCR by hiring a horror VIDEO from one of the 16,000 outlets which had sprung up round the country by '83. That way you could thrill to the Steadicam rush of Sam Raimi's 'Evil Dead', cheer on the neo-boho avenger in Abel Ferrara's 'Driller Killer', laugh at the spastic uselessness of the living dead underclass in Lucio Fulci's 'Zombie Flesh Eaters'. Who said this stuff was escapist? It was aversion therapy for coping with the real world. Even so it was too much for some. Mary Whitehouse invented the term 'video nasty', the tabloid press worked itself up into a moral panic and the government banned anything it didn't

like the look of with its '84 VIDEO Recordings Act.

Vitamins You used to get enough from your cornflakes, but as the decade got progressively more health conscious the manufacturers caught on. In '88 the vitamins market was worth £120 million, a 30-35% increase on '87 and a business that the Health Education Council observes with concern. They think a balanced diet should suffice and think the general public are getting ripped off. At about £2 a bottle they might have a point.

Viz From 150 copies in late '79 to a print run of 800,000 in less than ten years has to be one of the most amazing feats in British publishing history. Imitators such as *Smut* and *Brain Damage* appeared in '88, but

Volkswagens

The VW Beetle was the cult car of the decade and a triumph of pre-war German technology. Buying a Beetle was a revolt against the box-like uniformity of contemporary car design, all the more hip because by the late '80s it was out of production. Labelled the 'people's car', the Beetle was worshipped at 'bug jams' (rallies) all over Britain, but when THE BEASTIE BOYS started wearing chrome VW radiator badges on chains round their necks, fans followed their example and began prising the emblem off every VW in sight. POLICE and TV reports followed, VW owners started pulling the badges off themselves and hiding them at home, and the VW company even went to the lengths of offering free ones to Beastie fans. As late as '89, half the VWs on the road were missing their radiator badge.

*Van Beirondonck, Walter **See Belgian Fashion**.*
Photo: Ronald Stoops, drawing: Jan Bosschaert.

Beetle pic: Nigel Law.

AGN 764W

Video

The crucial test of '80s consumer smarts: should you get a VHS or Betamax? At the start of the decade, when hardly anyone had a piece of the new technology, it was quite a poser. By '82 over 20% of homes owned a video and the market had decided in favour of VHS. Now part of the furniture, video was a revelation when it first arrived. The small-screen equivalent of the personal organiser, it allowed you to arrange your viewing habits around your LIFE-STYLE and watch what you wanted when you wanted. Even better, it meant you could watch a film on your own terms – fast-forward through a boring plot, rewind a special effect. Nowadays things have moved on and the video is almost like a kind of back-up memory – videoing it means having it handy and never having to watch it.

they remained pale imitations of the comic that has perfected toilet humour as an artform.

V-movies

'Graveyard Shift', 'Class Of Nuke 'Em High', 'Zone Troopers', 'From Beyond' – once you might have called them B-movies, but now that the long nights of the double feature are over and low budget celluloid goes straight out on video, they're V-movies. They can be big name flops, Italian spaghetti splatter, or BRAT PACK leftovers, but usually they're born again exploitation from outfits like Empire Films or Troma. They come in garish boxes, with sick strap lines and campy come-on titles ('Nice Girls Don't Explode') and usually look and sound

better in the VIDEO shop than at home. But with V-movies you never know. You may discover a pulp classic with a hotline into the collective unconscious, or you may find yourself staring into a superficial abyss. If it stares back there's always the fast forward button.

Vodka

Vodka was the drink of the decade, but while British Smirnoff sold itself as the drink of kings, the Soviet Stolichnaya became the drink of the people. Both Russian and Polish vodkas turned up in restaurants, bars, clubs and corner shops in the strangest flavours: lemon, lime, pepper, lemon grass, plum, cherry. But it's still best enjoyed mixed with tomato juice into a Bloody Mary, or straight out of the freezer in frozen glasses.

Vogueing

Growing out of the HOUSES of New Yorks' gay club scene, vogueing became one of the most hyped dances of the '80s. A mix of catwalk histrionics and balletic break-dancing, it was performed by Manhattan's gay fashion fraternity and nobody else. Used by MALCOLM MCLAREN to furnish his album 'Waltz Darling' with a focal point and marketing angle, it never became anything other than a curious New York phenomenon that became mythologised in the pages of Sunday supplements and in the lenses of foreign camera crews.

*L to R JVC Video (photo: Martin Brading, styling: Kim Hunt).
Video screens.
'Day Of The Dead'* **See V-Movies.**
*Voice Of The Beehive.
Luther Vandross.*

Vogueing photos: Janette Beckman.

The   Wag
Club Run by Chris
Sullivan and Ollie O'Don-
nell The Wag Club opened
in '83 on the site of the old
Whiskey-A-Go-Go and has
been at the centre of West
End nightlife ever since.
The first, and still one of
the only London clubs custom built for the under-
ground scene, The Wag
has become synonymous
with NIGHTCLUBBING in
the '80s. It's the first club

hat every tourist tries to
go to and its brightly coloured   Cubist   wall-
paintings and decor have
featured in almost every
single STYLE magazine in
the world. Open six nights
a week The Wag has nev-
er gone out of fashion and
almost every DJ on the
West End/warehouse cir-
cuit has worked there at
some time or other.

L to R Wigging out at the
i-D Party Dec '80 (photo:
Eamonn McCabe), Wayne
i-D straight up '83 (photo:
Steve Johnston), queuing
at The Wag Club

Waits, Tom Beatnik blues poet who discovered avant-garde jazz and classical sounds and used them to catalyse his inspired American street life album trilogy: 'Sword-fishtrombones', 'Rain Dogs' and 'Frank's Wild Years'. Waits also acted in a number of prestigious Hollywood films, usually playing a mumbling bum character – in other words, himself.

Wall St Filmed when the serious money fever of the New York stock market was at its peak, Oliver Stone's ARMANI morality tale gave Michael Douglas the role of the decade as kingpin dealer Gordon Gekko, charismatic ego monster and fallen angel of an over-the-top

CREDIT ECONOMY. Douglas grabbed the part with both hands. His ferocious performance not only won him an '88 Oscar it also demonstrated how much power itself today is phrased as a drama of the body – all sharp reflexes and snappy dressing. Key scenes: Gekko in trademark red braces, fielding a client on the phone and sizing up a proposition in the office while simultaneously measuring his blood pressure.

Was (Not Was) Drawing on the indigenous music of Detroit, from Motown, GEORGE CLINTON to Iggy, would-be disco producer Don Fagensen and JAZZ critic David Weiss pulled together the first truly eclectic group of the '80s. Arguably the first group to marry heavy rock to dance, their '81 debut LP, 'Was (Not Was)' also pioneered 'mutant dance'; in

The Watchmen Touted as the GRAPHIC NOVEL of the decade, this was the comic-book which literally transformed the image of the medium when it was released in '86/'87. A cape to cowl stripdown of the Pax Americana superhero myth, it was a brooding tale of conspiracy and salvation only slightly marred by writer ALAN MOORE's pious observance of old hippy grievances: Nixon, the Cold War, Vietnam. Dave Gibbon's artwork was fluent, atmospheric and subtle, intricate almost to the point of neurotic compulsion in its use of ironic cross-cuttings and rhyming images. Despite the critical applause, it all added up to a landmark achievement curiously uncertain of its effects – neither slick enough to be a trash masterpiece nor sustained enough to be a genuine literary success.

L to R Charlie Sheen in 'Wall St', Tom Waits, Vivienne Westwood's 'Buffalo' '82 collection in i-D no. 8, Westwood's 'Pirate' '81 collection, Vivienne Westwood

other words, anything goes when played over a dance beat. Bizarre permutations were taken to the limit when Ozzy Osbourne, Mitch Ryder and Mel Torme amongst others, guested on 'Born To Laugh At Tornadoes' ('83) which their record company deemed "a marketing nightmare" and promptly suspended them. But with 'What Up Dog?' ('88) this influential group found both a sympathetic home and surprisingly enough, hits.

Waters, John Baltimore's most famous son and America's king of movie kitsch, John Waters teamed with the late but great Divine to bring trashcan culture to the screen. Divine's antics with dogshit and sex

criminals confined 'Pink Flamingos' and 'Female Trouble' to the midnight screening until VIDEO liberated them and everyone screamed along in the safety of their sitting rooms. The deplorable duo struck it big with '50s extravaganza 'Hairspray' in '88, a classy fun-for-all tale of love, ozone-destroying aerosols and racial segragation in '60s America, featuring all of Waters' favourite film stars – Pia Zadora, Sonny Bono and Debbie Harry. But Divine died of heart failure before he/she could capitalise on this newfound mainstream appeal. Waters wiped away his (genuine) tears and went back to Baltimore to start another film.

Weber, Bruce The iconoclastic New York photographer turned filmmaker Bruce Weber set a standard by which much fashion photography in

the '80s has been judged. His series of portraits of 250 US Olympic hopefuls shot through most of '83, remain quintessential Weber images; pictures that summed up both the '80s obsession with the body beautiful whilst redefining a classical approach to both the nude and the portrait photograph.

Westwood, Vivienne Employing a mixture of subversion and innovation, Vivienne Westwood was the decade's most important designer. Based in her shop, World's End (formerly Let It Rock, then Sex, then Seditionaries), her consistent anticipation of trends was almost uncanny. Alongside MALCOLM MCLAREN, she was at the forefront of the punk movement in the late '70s; her '81 'Pirates' collection fuelled the NEW ROMANTIC movement; she was responsible for dressing ADAM ANT and Bow Wow Wow; New York graffiti artist Keith Haring was engaged to work on her '83 collection 'Witches', and she also pioneered the idea of UNDERWEAR AS OVERWEAR.

In '85, Westwood unveiled her MINI CRINI collection in Paris. The fashion world took one look at her truncated 19th Century skirts and decided that London's Queen Of Fashion had at last crossed the borders of eccentricity and completely lost her marbles. One year later crini copies filled Britain's shops. Since then, she has concentrated her eccentric, subversive sensibility on redefining classic 'English' looks using tweed, fake

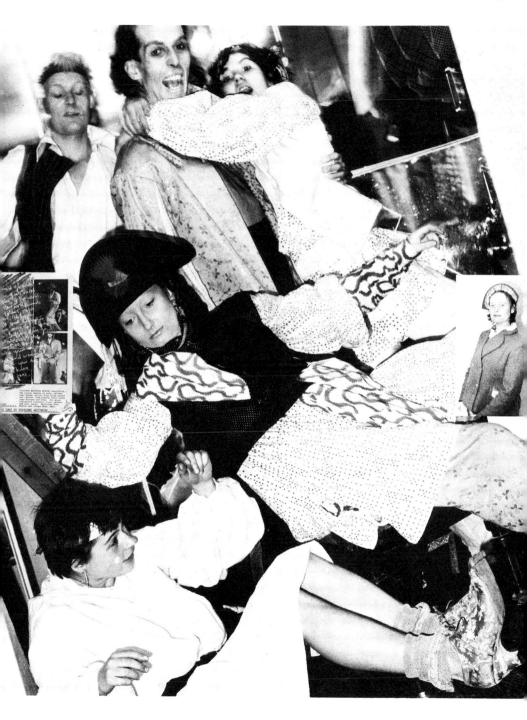

ermines and crowns. Consistently
ignoring the pressures of the fashion
marketplace, Vivienne Westwood has
described herself as "the most
modern designer there is", and
although true, this has also proved to
be one of her major problems.
Westwood designs are often *too*
modern, and usually find themselves
reinterpreted by other designers a
few seasons later, for far greater
financial rewards. A designer who
commands the respect of all her
peers (no mean feat) Vivienne
Westwood is an '80s fashion pioneer
and icon who will undoubtedly be
leading the way in the '90s. *See
Fashion Designers and Nostalgia Of
Mud*

Westworld The first Westworld
warehouse party in Battersea in '85

marked a watershed in '80s nightlife.
There had been warehouse parties
before, but nothing like this: massive
queues, dodgems, wild decor and
5,000 people dancing. Graham Ball
was among a posse of promoters of
this event and he later teamed up
with Joel Coleman, setting out to
show what warehouse parties could
be like with high production values
and real imagination. But after a
heavy POLICE clampdown on warehouse parties, they had to go
overground and legal. They launched
a series of huge parties at the
Academy in Brixton, which brought
fairground rides and the best of
clubland together under one roof and
one theme (Westworld 3-Disney,
Westworld 5: Gotham City, and so
on). Everybody went, from b-boys in
their customised MA-1s and artfully
shredded 501s to older clubbers and

Wannabees

Slightly more calculating
than a BIMBO, a Wan-
nabee wants to go further
than looking pretty. Wan-
nabees sprung up in their
thousands after MADON-
NA popularised her '80s
philosophy of 'find it, fuck
it, flaunt it'. The London
Wild Child cult was a good
example of this, with
(blonde) Emma Ridley
stripping off and leading
the pack of precocious,
middle class female Wan-
nabees through tacky Lon-
don nightclubs. Remem-
ber, being a Wannabee
you don't always get to Be

Warhol,
Andy The clown
prince of the celebrity un-
dead ceased to be in '87,
but that, of course, wasn't
the end of Andy. Warhol's
first law – in the future
everyone will be famous
for 15 minutes. Warhol's
second law – old pop
artists never die, they just
turn into media events.

◄ *L to R* World's End circa '81 **See Vivienne Westwood**, Westwood's Spring/Summer '89 collection (photo: Sean Cunningham), Spring/Summer '88
collection (photo: Tim Green), Autumn/Winter '88 (photos: Marc Lebon and Declan Ryan), Sarah Stockbridge modelling Westwood's Autumn/Winter '87
collection (photo: Declan Ryan, styling: Vivienne Westwood)

Sloanes still dressed in ballgowns. At Wetworld they put the same big ideas into a swimming pool in Fulham and at the Carwash party in January '88 they organised an event that was to be the high point of the SEVENTIES FASHION revival. In '87 they launched their first weekly club, Enter The Dragon, attracting a healthy mix of young Sloanes and hardcore ravers, followed by the ACID HOUSE beach party in '88, Myami Is Your Friend. Never short of ideas, expect Westworld to explore ever more varied corners of clubland in the '90s.

Wham! See George Michael

Wheelclamping A testament to the failure of London's public

transport system, as increasing numbers drove their cars into the West End and police had to resort to radical methods to dissuade them. Even after the introduction of wheelclamping, the traffic situation became worse than ever, public transport continued to deteriorate, and you *still* couldn't find a place to park.

Who Framed Roger Rabbit? After the disastrous 'Black Cauldron' and the defection of the talented Don Bluth and his team, Disney's animation was in tatters and its reputation rested on the classics, rereleased in six year cycles. Then along came SPIELBERG, Zemeckis and Universal, with a crazy idea of three dimensional interaction between cartoons and actors and Disney were back in the animation business. A technological leap in animation

The Warehouse Started in '83 by Dave, Frank and Harry, its original illegal home in Kentish Town featured the first purpose-built bar and lounge area in any outlaw rave and by the time of its forcible closure by a massive POLICE raid it was one of the most popular Saturday nights in London. Moving to the Electric Ballroom in Camden in '84, it became the first warehouse party to go legal and featured a funkabilly mix from DJ Jay Strongman which echoed his DIRTBOX days. The Warehouse's influence on North London's club fraternity was enormous and Saturday nights became a haven for a thriving Camden and Hampstead rockabilly scene. However, due to license difficulties The Warehouse shut in '87, briefly reopened at the Astoria in '88 and then disappeared into the mists of club memory.

*L to R DJ Wolf (photo: Steve Johnston), two regulars at Leed's Warehouse club circa '86, The Jazz Defektors **See The Wire** (photo: Kevin Cummins), Haysi Fantayzee '82 **See White Rastas** (photo: Steve Johnston)*

that created the box office sensation of the summer of '88, once again producer SPIELBERG was frozen out of Oscars, as Williams and his team picked up technical Oscars. Ironically, the animation was all done in Camden Town by the Canadian freelancer Williams and his team. So where does that leave Disney's ART department?

The Wire The jazz renaissance that took place in the '80s demanded and got its very own media. Too specialist for a mainly uncomprehending MUSIC PRESS, both *The Wire* and *Straight No Chaser* came to represent the tension between young and old JAZZ fans. Under the editorship of Richard Cook, *The Wire*

took an uncompromising academic approach to its writing which, for an emerging, young audience proved to be way off the mark. Into this vacuum Paul Bradshaw launched *Straight No Chaser* and established a looser attitude to the music. In this scene, JAZZ was not a lonely pursuit nor a precious commodity. It was as much about dancing to The ART Ensemble Of Chicago at one of Gilles Peterson's Sunday sessions at Dingwalls as it was digging Art Blakey at Ronnie's or encouraging new groups such as The JAZZ Renegades. *Straight No Chaser*, with the advent of ACID JAZZ, wanted to wrench jazz out of its musty confines and invite all into the party, to appeal to those who found no contradiction in listening to Eric Dolphy one minute and DE LA SOUL the next. *The Wire* held its ground with principles of tradition and a high

White Rastas Haysi Fantayzee have a lot to answer for, but probably not as much as BOY GEORGE. Dreadlocks were just one more weapon in an armoury of white middle class rebellion, wilfully perverse and more than slightly silly. *Kensington White Rastas running for cabs/This I have seen*, sang Mark E Smith, summing up the absurdity of the whole thing. But dreadlocks have never really been the essence of Rastafarianism and another totally separate development was the growth of the White Rasta, with or without locks. White-run sound systems like Armoury and Manasseh have broken down many of the barriers surrounding reggae by getting respect for the music they play and a breed of genuinely intentioned White Rastas has grown up around them. *See Hair Extensions*

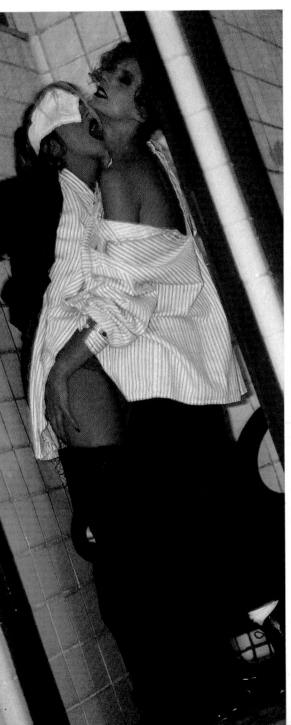

minded approach. Neither would give
ground but both were invaluable in
keeping the music alive. It is doubtful
that in the '90s, the two will ever find
common ground.

Wish You Were Here Emily
Lloyd kicked up her heels and walked
into a Hollywood embrace with this
zesty '87 debut as a seaside Lolita,
desperate for passion but oppressed
by a prudish father. A fine example
of the much-vaunted British renaissance (and one of the few Brit hits not
to feature Julie Walters), 'Wish You
Were Here' was an auspicious
directorial debut for screenwriter
David Leland, and a movie responsible for introducing the raucous war
cry "Up yer bum!" up and down the
country that summer.

*L to R Sometimes, girls
will be girls See Women's
Toilets (photo: Marc
Lebon), Kim Wilde, Tom
Wolfe See Bonfire Of The
Vanities (photo: Dorothy
Low)*

Women's Football When
Liverpool's Leasowe Pacific beat
Friends Of Fulham 3:2 in the '89
British Women's FA Cup Final, it was
a special occasion, not just for the
winners but for the game as a whole.
It was the first time the match was
televised, in recognition of the
growing status of women's FOOT-
BALL. By '88 there were over 235
women's clubs established in England alone, and star players like
Fulham's Sallie Jackson and Millwall's Shauna Williams had joined
professional teams on the Continent.
With the emphasis on skill rather
than brute strength, on stylish play
instead of aggression, Women's
Football in the '80s gained fresh
respect, attracted more and more
young players, bigger and bigger
transfer fees and looked forward to
that crucial professional future.

LASSIC JEANSWEAR EASY™

PHOTOGRAPHY CHRIS WEST

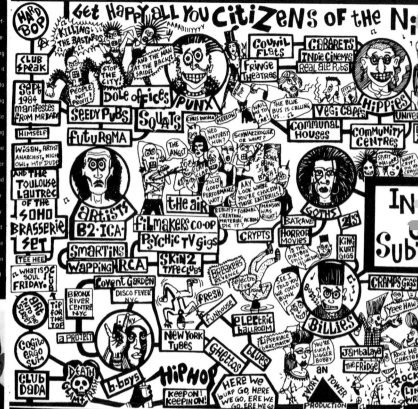

Windsurfing

A mariner's miracle, surfing without waves, the decade's fastest growing sport has at last made it possible for Europeans to hang ten, thus blighting every Continental lake with thousands of cruising human ants. Today the trend is towards smaller and smaller boards, and there are more windsurfers in France that anywhere else in the world. As wind, not waves, are the power source, Britain boasts the best windsurfing conditions around

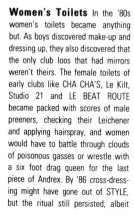

Women's Toilets In the '80s women's toilets became anything but. As boys discovered make-up and dressing up, they also discovered that the only club loos that had mirrors weren't theirs. The female toilets of early clubs like CHA CHA'S, Le Kilt, Studio 21 and LE BEAT ROUTE became packed with scores of male preeners, checking their Leichener and applying hairspray, and women would have to battle through clouds of poisonous gasses or wrestle with a six foot drag queen for the last piece of Andrex. By '86 cross-dressing might have gone out of STYLE, but the ritual still persisted, albeit with BLACK AND WHITE GREASE rather than Harmony hairspray. During the SUMMER OF LOVE though, the toilets were completely empty. ACID HOUSE male clubbers did not drink lager in large quantities and only wore make-up if left on their cheeks by females.

Word Processors The 'Electronic Cottage' of sophisticated technology predicted by American futurist author Alvin Toffler in 1980 in his revolutionary book *The Third Wave*, came sooner than we expected with the introduction of the personal computer and the word

processor. The word processor is like an electronic typewriter which enables you to store written information on disc, move it about and correct it. At £500 or less, even the most penniless hack could feel like a proper new age journalist. A bad back and rapidly deteriorating eyesight seem to be the only drawbacks. Is this the future?

World Music Possibly the vaguest music definition ever to receive media blessing, World Music was the term coined by 11 independent record companies in '87 to promote the music they dealt with.

Workers For Freedom In '85, Graham Fraser and Richard Nott chose the name Workers For Freedom as a statement of their intention to design clothes which circumnavigate the confines of fashion. They have since created an identity based on the use of self-embroidery, hand-painting and simple fastenings to evoke an age of craftsmanship. Suns, moons, birds and hearts are just some of the folksy motifs

L to R The late Steve Walsh, the late Willi Smith of Williwear, Nightclubbing graphic illustration by Wigan in i-D no. 19 '84, Western waistcoat '87 (photo: James Martin), Workers For Freedom's Spring/Summer '89 collection (photo: Claire Pollock)

The term embraced the increasingly popular music of the Third World as well as unlikely characters such as BILLY BRAGG, Suzanne Vega and, quite possibly, the Queen of England. In meaning anything to anyone, World Music meant something to everyone. The national folk circuit, buoyed by the emergence of WOMAD in '82, had already removed the finger from its ear to international 'roots' music. The adoption of World Music throughout '87 by *NME*, *Q* and the national newspapers reaped benefits for visiting artists like Ali Farka Toure, an unlikely media hero in other times, but far more for DJs,

record companies, the combative *Folk Roots* magazine and National Sound Archives. Criticised for "colonising traditional music" and treating areas of Africa as "their exclusive vineyard", the World Music bourgeoisie bristled with indignance through their mouthpiece *Folk Roots*. British artists (Peter Gabriel aside) were slow to adopt a 'world' stance in their music until May '89. Robert Palmer's 'Change His Ways', replete with yodelling and other fashions alien to the north of England, explained their reluctance. Quite what World Music will mean in the '90s, is anybody's guess.

Wrestling Professional wrestling disappeared from British TV screens in '88 because advertisers had deemed it irretrievably downmarket – watched only by the working class and elderly addicts of 'junk' sport without money to spend on what was plugged during the commercial breaks. Wrestling always lacked substance and the demise of such TV favourites as Mick McManus and Jackie Pallo meant it had also long lacked STYLE. How many times could *you* watch Big Daddy beat Giant Haystacks just by sitting on him? Darts looks set to follow the same path to small hall obscurity.

which the pair adore. Working out of their shop in Piccadilly, they have kept their business purposefully small to be able to remain in control of every aspect of their careers, and despite this small-scale operation, their beautiful clothes have gained worldwide acclaim. *See Fashion Designers*

Y

Yamamoto, Yohji *See Japanese Designers*

Yazoo A girl called Alf and a man called Vince. Alison 'Alf' Moyet sang moody ELECTRO-pop songs like 'Don't Go' and 'Only You' before progressing to her own hugely successful solo career. On the run from DEPECHE MODE, Vince Clarke twiddled the knobs and blueprinted the user-friendly STYLE that would make his subsequent camp pop group, Erasure, so popular from '87 onwards.

Yello Boris Blank (music) and Dieter Meier (words – especially interviews) are the Zurich based twosome who more than anyone this

Yazz Bright, breezy and extremely tall, former model Yazz rode in on the crest of the British clubland HOUSE wave with her hit version of 'The Only Way Is Up', which made the best-selling single of '88. Her light melodic voice and ebullient club-STYLE was efficiently showcased by the mixing techniques of COLDCUT, proving more versatile than many at first suspected. An avid cam-

L to R Yello and Yazz.

decade kept the ELECTRO-disco faith. A whole series of precision-engineered Eurotrash albums seemed to float leisurely out of Switzerland and into nowhere before 'La Habanera', a cut off '87's 'One Second', got caught up in the '88 BALEARIC BEAT vortex and gave that year's album, 'Flag', the push it needed to finally score them a hit. Not that they were too bothered. According to Meier, music for Yello isn't a career or a vocation so much as an epic folly of the idle rich, a kitsch extravaganza tinged with melancholy (which is why they worked on 'One Second' with slightly absurd operatic voices like Shirley Bassey and Billy Mackenzie). Of course, he's lying.

Y-fronts What designers like GIORGIO ARMANI and Calvin Klein had been doing since the '70s,

paigner of interracial pop, bringing British HOUSE and humanitarian ideas firmly into the mainstream, Yazz is British pop's wolf in sheep's clothing

namely producing high quality Y-fronts that didn't lose their shape and were worn with the branded elastic showing above your trousers, fell victim to the LEVI'S 501 ad. When Nick Kamen took his jeans off to reveal a pair of white BOXER SHORTS, the underwear of the British male changed overnight. It wasn't until another LEVI'S ad in '89, when a bronzed hunk revealed his white Y-fronts in order to aid a damsel in distress, that the Y-front reclaimed something of its former glory. Originally produced by Jockey 50 years ago, the figure-hugging underpant was led into the battle for Britain's bums by Nikos' Olympiad designer Y-fronts, which enabled men to avoid the dreaded visible pantie line.

York, Peter The UK's original answer to American pop anthropologist Tom Wolfe, York emerged in the early '80s with the two best-selling person-watching books, *Style Wars* and the *SLOANE RANGER Handbook*. In fact he'd been around, writing for *Harpers & Queen* and running a city firm of market research consultants since the mid-'70s, and was more than prepared for a new generation of spotty post-punks sneering at his posh voice and suits. His TV project, 'Teenage', with Jon Savage researching and Julien Temple directing, was shelved by Granada, but all three dined out on it for some time, explaining to all who'd listen that Punk Rock had marked the end of the teenager as prime target consumer. The late '80s concept of 'youth', meaning anyone who could remember 'Thunderbirds' and 'Noggin

The Nog' or who was slightly younger than JANET STREET PORTER, appeared to bear out their claims.

The Young Ones Alternative TV comedy series first shown in October '82 based on the anarchic exploits of four repulsive students living in a classically filthy house. 'The Young Ones' made names of a whole series of new wave comedians including Ben Elton who co-wrote the series, Rik Mayall and Alexi Sayle. 'The Young Ones' became *the* series to have on VIDEO and pointed to the total failure of comics like Little And Large to communicate with the under 30s. When asked why he thought the series had been so successful, Elton replied, "everyone hates students, even students hate students." *See Alternative Comedy*

Youth TV *See Trendy Telly*

YTS YTS (Youth Training Schemes) were designed to provide employment opportunites for school-leavers. In reality, although some did provide real training and subsequent 'proper' jobs, they were more effective in 'massaging' the unemployment figures of the past decade. YTS became notorious amongst teenagers as a source of cheap and plentiful labour, and often led to injury or worse. Some were injured in industrial situations where safety, training and supervision were less than adequate (if you worked on a YTS you were twice as likely to be killed or seriously injured at work than the average mechanical engineer). By the

Young Couture In winter '86, a group of young British designers – NICK COLEMAN, RICHMOND CORNEJO, JOHN GALLIANO, JOE CASELY-HAYFORD and others – acquired the collective label of 'young couture', a name that signified a move upmarket in British fashion generally. The young couture designers took their street themes and refined them, keeping one eye on the market.

JOHN GALLIANO turned his previously unwearable clothes into a spectacular collection which was one of the successes of that year's Olympia, while NICK COLEMAN updated classic wool and gaberdine menswear for the '80s. The fashion press raved, the buyers spent their budgets, and the more accessible direction taken by the young couture designers spelled instant recognition and success. *See Fashion Designers*

L to R Yohji Yamamoto's Autumn/Winter '86 collection (photo: Nick Knight, art direction Marc Ascoli). Peter York. Joe Casely Hayford's Autumn/Winter '86 collection (photo: Sean Cunningham). John Galliano's Autumn/Winter '86 collection (photo: SC) See Young Couture. A Yuppie (photo: Simon Fleury).

late '80s, 90% of all 16 year old school-leavers entered the YTS scheme (for those without a job there was little option) and its image had deteriorated so much that a series of TV advertisements had to be commissioned. *See Job Clubs*

Yuppies Like the model consumer of the guidebook tourist the Yuppie was always somebody else. No-one would ever admit to being one even as they read *THE INDEPENDENT* over their croissants, bought their shoulder-padded suits on a PAUL SMITH charge account or drove to the design consultancy office each morning in their Suzuki jeep. And that's because lurking behind the 16 hour days and the high-geared investments of the Yuppie work aesthetic was the whispered accusation of 'sell-out'. Yup was the '80s subcult that dared not speak its name. For it was a fair bet that if you prised apart the power wardrobes of most Yuppies you'd find an old mohair suit inside. The Yup was the mod 20 years on – the same devotion to conspicuous consumption and upward mobility, but now only a folk devil in the sense that he'd stopped being one. But when did it all start?

The Yuppie as all-purpose media handle for 'new middle class' was imported over here on the back of the '84 Presidential campaign of Baby Boomer candidate Gary Hart. The same year saw the publication of *The Yuppie Handbook* in the January issue of *People* magazine and as ever, they did things differently in the States. There the repressed '60s reference for the Yuppie was the hippie – with the same psychobabble narcissism and LIFESTYLE avant-gardism, but now plugged into the system rather than camped outside it. By mid-decade Hollywood had jumped on the latest media anti-hero with a vengeance and in a string of Yuppie Nightmare comedies like 'Lost In America', 'Desperately Seeking Susan', 'After Hours' and 'Something Wild' the lid was taken off the pressure-cooked careerism to reveal the fear and loathing (and desire) beneath.

Rather late on the scene was '87's TV serial 'Thirtysomething', the excruciatingly compulsive family drama whose obsession with kids and careers gave a new twist to the

old counter-cultural slogan 'the personal is political'. The media bubble didn't last long. The Yuppie and all his alphabetical cousins (Buppie, Muppie, Guppie) went the way of all STYLE tags and ended up in the obit pages after the October '87 stock market crash. Three years on, Yuppies were supposed to have made their pile and retired into doing something Green and caring – like market gardening. But don't you believe it.

L to R Dwight Yoakam **See New Country**.
ZZ Top.
Encyclopaedia Psychedelia **See Zippies**.

Zodiac Mindwarp (photo: Richard Croft)
See Heavy Metal.

Zanzibar The black club in New Jersey which became the adopted home of GARAGE MUSIC after PARADISE GARAGE closed in '87, largely due to the inspirational mixing skills of DJ Tony Humphries.

ZG The arts and mixed media mag which set the theoretical agenda for the decade with a series of themed issues called things like Image Culture, Future Dread, and Desire. Set up in '81 it proved a forum for the speculative analysis of fashion, music, philosophy and film – often all in the same article. Everything in the pop semiotic playpen was up for grabs, from Calvin Klein to country & western, but the major preoccupation was avant-garde ART. CINDY SHER-

MAN, SHERRIE LEVINE, Barbara Kruger, Jenny Holzer, Richard Prince, Jack Goldstein and Dara Birnbaum all featured prominently in early issues before going on to make it big. But that was just the magazine living up to its name ('zeitgeist').

Zippies Zen Inspired Professional Pagans, Zippies are dedicated to harmonising the two usually contradictory hemispheres of '60s hippy, with its spontaneity and open-mindedness, and late '80s technoperson with its rationality. The harmonic convergence results in the Techno '90s Hippy, whose organ, *Encyclopaedia Psychedelia International* commenced publication in '86 and, printed on recycled paper and looking not unlike early issues of *i-D*, addressed all New Age issues from 'Healing The Patriarchal Dis-ease' to

◄ **Zoot Suit** The

zoot suit as an '80s British phenomenon (rather than '40s American) appeared in '81 worn by that short lived but exquisitely fashion conscious band of retro musicians BLUE RONDO A LA TURK. Exaggeration is the key to the zoot voluminous pleated trousers anything up to chest height worn under a big shouldered, usually single-breasted jacket cut to hug the hips and reach anything down to knee length. Bands as disparate as Madness and SPANDAU BALLET sported the outfit more traditionally associated with post-war jazzmen, Harlem pimps and the New York prize fighter, Rocky Graziano. For a while the zoot was the male uniform for Lt BEAT ROUTE dancefloor but by '83 only Kid Creole was championing the cause and we all know what happened to him.

six months and the moral umbrage of Mike Read to top the charts. A string of hits for Frankie subsidized a lengthier string of misses for Andrew Poppy and Propaganda. In '87 the label found itself sued by its star attraction Holly Johnson who escaped from the strictures of his dubious contract to launch a solo career. Fondly remembered for Bernard Rose's outré video for 'Relax' and its attempt to foist upon the public, not just a seemingly infinite number of remixes, but also Walter Benjamin boxer shorts. A first in merchandising, the last word in intertextual outrage.

Zulu Nation In the '70s, during his high school years, Afrika Bambaataa won a trip to Africa. On his

ACID HOUSE. In '89, Andy Weatherall, a DJ at THE SHOOM club, began writing a column for the *EPI*, and the editors heralded ACID HOUSE as the beginning of a new, stronger wave of summer loving. A THATCHER cut-out doll was given away in early '89, with instructions to press particular meridian points and thereby transforming her into a kind and considerate person. Within days she was pressing for the release of Nelson Mandela.

Zippo Lighter The Zippo is, let's face it, irredeemably retro, an authentic piece of Americana that has survived the passage of time and technology only because in the '80s it benefited from our hankering for nostalgia and our obsession with artefacts. The Zippo was good news for the GI at Iwo Jima taking time out from fighting the Japanese to light up a Lucky Strike because even those Pacific storms wouldn't stop it from igniting. But now? It will put a hole in the hip pocket of your 501s and make your jacket smell like a filling station. There are cheaper, more

efficient, less messy alternatives. But as everyone who owns a Zippo knows, that isn't the point.

Zouk The Caribbean musical success story of the decade, gusting out of Martinique and Guadeloupe in the Creole-speaking French Antilles from '84 onwards, as the old-STYLE cadence was subsumed by a hi-tech, funky, horn sound. Kassav, the amoebic big band, were Zouk's leading lights, and unlike other components of the African hi-tech scene, had a considerable following amongst black Londoners. Zouk albums, it should be noted, are amongst the worst-dressed in the world.

ZTT Arguably the first postmodern record label, Paul Morley, Trevor Horn and wife Jill Sinclair set up the label in '83 taking the name from either a FUTURIST poem or the sound of a penny dropping onto a bass drum, depending on the many moods of Morley. From humble origins, FRANKIE GOES TO HOLLYWOOD's debut, 'Relax', took the best part of

L to R Kid Creole in a Zoot Suit.
Afrika Bambaataa See Zulu Nation.
Act See ZTT.
Zoff from Birkenhead i-D straight up '83 (photo: Steve Johnston).

return, the ex-gang leader decided to start the Zulu Nation, a loose collective based around a mixture of Islam and African culture, whose aim was to replace gang warfare and dependence on HEROIN with BREAKDANCING, rapping and a belief in black pride. Almost every American rapper had Zulu Nation connections, and Bambaataa's influence percolated through to Britain in the early '80s in records like 'Planet Rock', and was strengthened when he visited London in '86 to set up a chapter. Essentially a mercurial organisation, interest in the Zulu Nation increased with the rise of black consciousness rap in '88, and Afrika Bambaataa still holds yearly parties at the Zulu Nation's original home, the Bronx River Community Center. *See African Colours, Public Enemy and The Jungle Brothers*

Time Out
Weekly £1.10
The biggest - selling
weekly guide to
everything that
happens in London.

20/20 Magazine
Monthly £1.50
The entertainment
monthly featuring what's
new and exciting all
over the country and
around the world.

i-D
Monthly £1.80
The global guide
to fashion, i-deas,
clubs, music
and people.

The full range of Time Out

Publications are on sale

now at all good

Paris Passion
Monthly £2.00
The essential guide
to Paris, in English.

f =

newsagents and bookshops.

Time Out Filofax guides

are on sale at all main

Filofax stockists.

also

available

as a

Time Out/

Filofax

guide.

The Time Out Film Guide
£9.99 770 pages
Everything you need to
know about the films you
really want to know about.
Over 9,000 films from
the world over reviewed
and assessed.

latest

Eating Out in London
£5.75 220 pages
More restaurants than
ever before listed and
ed in easy to use format.

**Sport, Health and
Fitness in London**
£4.95 164 pages
A comprehensive guide
to the capital's sports
venues and health
and fitness centres.
Where to watch, play
and get fit.

Collection

Shopping in London
£4.95 228 pages
The best, the biggest,
the most interesting
and the most unusual
shops in London.

Services in London
£4.95 164 pages
A comprehensive and
informative directory
of the useful and
often intriguing services
available to Londoners.

Time Out Student Guide
£1.75 180 pages
This twelfth edition of
our London Student
Guide includes a 32
page National
Supplement and is
packed full of vital
and original information.

The London Guide
£6.95 292 pages
The insider's guide
to London for visitors
and residents. What
to see, where to stay,
what's happening and
how to survive.

**All these titles can
also be obtained by
sending a cheque for
the full amount
(postage is free) made
payable and mailed to:
Time Out Distribution Ltd,
Tower House, Southampton
Street, London WC2E 7HD.
Please state clearly
which titles you require
together with your
name and address.**

Contributors

INDEX